Trilogy

KATE THOMPSON

The Switchers Trilogy

RED FOX

THE SWITCHERS TRILOGY
A RED FOX BOOK 978 0 099 47283 4

Switchers first published in Great Britain by The Bodley Head
Children's Books 1997; Red Fox edition 2001
Midnight's Choice first published in Great Britain by The Bodley Head
Children's Books 1998; Red Fox edition 2001
Wild Blood first published in Great Britain by The Bodley Head
Children's Books 1999; Red Fox edition 2001;
imprints of Random House Children's Books

This edition published by Red Fox 2004

The Random House Group Limited makes every effort to ensure that
the papers used in its books are made from trees that have been legally
sourced from well-managed and credibly certified forests. Our paper
procurement policy can be found at: www.randomhouse.co.uk/paper.htm

 **Mixed Sources**
Product group from well-managed
forests and other controlled sources
www.fsc.org Cert no. TT-COC-2139
FSC © 1996 Forest Stewardship Council

Red Fox Books are published by Random House Children's Books,
61–63 Uxbridge Road, London W5 5SA,
a division of The Random House Group Ltd

Addresses for companies within The Random House Group Limited can be
found at: www.randomhouse.co.uk/offices.htm

THE RANDOM HOUSE GROUP Limited Reg. No. 954009
www.**kids**at**randomhouse**.co.uk

A CIP catalogue record for this book is available from the British Library.

Printed in the UK by CPI bookmarque, Croydon, CR0 4TD

For Clio and Dearbhla,

my two Switchers,

and

Oisin and Sara Jane

I would like to thank the Tyrone Guthrie Centre at Annaghmakerrig, the Ennistymon Library and Jane Tottenham, who have all made work space available to me at crucial times.

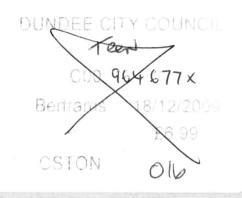

CONTENTS

PART ONE

SWITCHERS

CHAPTER ONE

The bus seemed to take hours to crawl through the Dublin traffic. Tess looked out of the window at the passing streets, but she wasn't really seeing them. She was hoping that the boy would not be waiting for her when she got off the bus. She didn't want to have to face him again.

He had been there for the first time on Wednesday, and then again yesterday, and both times he had done the same thing. He had started walking when she got down from the bus, keeping pace with her on the opposite side of the street until she turned into her own road at the edge of the park. She could feel his eyes on her almost constantly, but every time she had glanced across he had looked away. If she quickened her pace, he quickened his. If she stopped and pretended to examine something in the hedge, he stopped as well, always watching. It was almost as if he were teasing her and it unnerved her.

Tess sighed, pulled the band from the end of her french plait and teased it out, releasing her long dark hair from its confinement. It was Friday, and there were two whole days of freedom ahead. She wanted to enjoy the walk home in peace, so that she could make plans.

'Want a piece of chewing gum?' said the girl sitting beside her. Tess smiled and shook her head. In a sense it was dishonest. She would have liked a piece of chewing gum. What she did not want was the embarrassment of someone trying to make friends with her. It was easier to stay out of it from the beginning, rather than face the disappointment which inevitably followed. Because she had been through it too often now to believe that things could ever be different. All her life her family had been on the move. A year here, two years there, following her father's promotions wherever they took him.

Tess had found it difficult at first but she had come to accept it as the years went by. Her parents encouraged her to make new friends wherever they were, and had even gone as far as arranging parties for her, but they didn't understand. They couldn't. She went along with their parties and sometimes went as far as to invite someone home for a weekend, to please them. But it was the best she could do. She had long ago come to realise that she would never really be able to make close friends. She was different and that difference was something that she would never be able to share with anyone.

The girl beside her got up as her stop approached. 'Bye,' she said. 'See you Monday.'

'See you,' said Tess. There were still a few girls, like this one, who were making an effort, but it wouldn't last long. Soon she would be forgotten and ignored, dismissed as a swot or as too stuck up to bother with. That was painful sometimes, but it was easier than having to pretend to be like everyone else.

The bus stopped and the girl got off, pulling on her gloves. Students from the local vocational school were about on the streets. They didn't have to wear uniforms, and they looked relaxed and human compared to the girls in her school with their matching gaberdines and hats and shoes. Tess had wanted to go to the vocational school instead, but her parents said they wanted the best for her. She might have put up a stronger protest, knowing that they felt guilty about moving yet again, but she couldn't argue too hard. She had already used up all her influence insisting that they get a house beside the Phoenix Park. It had been vital. She could not have survived in any other part of Dublin.

The city traffic was always at its worst on a Friday evening, but at last the bus reached her stop and she got down, and walked a few yards along the main road. It was bitterly cold again and she cursed herself for forgetting her scarf. This freak weather had been going on for some time now, and there was no excuse for forgetting. She pulled up her collar and braced herself against the icy autumn breeze.

As she turned off the main road into the tree-lined avenue which led to her road, she groaned inwardly. He was there, leaning against the wall, waiting for her. There was no one else about. Tess walked quickly, looking firmly down at the ground. Today she would not be drawn. She would not look over and give him the satisfaction of catching her eye. She watched the paving stones intently and said to herself: 'He doesn't exist. If I don't look at him, he isn't there.'

But he was there, and today he was more there than ever. Out of the corner of her eye she saw him crossing over the street towards her, pushing his fair hair away from his eyes in a gesture that was already becoming familiar.

Her first instinct was to run, but she knew that it would be useless. She was strong, despite her small and wiry frame, and given the right circumstances she would be hard to beat over a short distance. But today she was wearing narrow shoes with heels, part of the ridiculous uniform, and her schoolbag was heavy. If he wanted to catch her she wouldn't have a chance and if he didn't, if he was just trying to unnerve her, then he would have succeeded, and she would look and feel a fool. So she carried on walking, but looked determinedly away from him, towards the houses.

He walked on the very edge of the footpath but even so, Tess moved in towards the walls and hedges they were passing, as far away from him as possible. The street seemed endless.

'Cigarette?' he said.

'No.'

'Ah. Don't smoke?'

'No.'

'Very wise.'

Tess glanced at him. He was holding a very crumpled pack from which he extracted an even more crumpled cigarette. She noticed that he had no gloves and wondered how he could bear to have his hands out in the cold. In the brief instant that she looked at him, he caught her eye with a sly, sideways glance. His eyes were slate grey and very hard. They gave her butterflies.

Tess raised a hand to her hair, aware that it was

6

still crinkly from the pressure of the plait. 'What do you want?' she said.

'Oh, nothing much,' he said. 'What's your name?'

'None of your business.'

He stopped, abruptly, to light his cigarette, and quite automatically, Tess stopped too. She caught herself and went on again immediately, but it was too late. He would take it as a sign of acceptance and encouragement, and that was the last thing she wanted.

The strange weather was bringing an early autumn to the country. Leaves swirled in the wind, many of them still green. Even with her fleece-lined gloves and thick tights, Tess was feeling the cold. The wind stung her cheeks, giving them a colour that they usually lacked. She stuffed her hands into her armpits as she walked.

The boy caught up with her in a few strides, light-footed in his worn trainers. For a while he said nothing, puffing at his cigarette, concentrating on getting it going. Tess sneaked a glance out of the corner of her eye. He wore an army parka, frayed around the cuffs, and a pair of dirty jeans with holes in the knees. He was older than she was, fourteen or fifeen perhaps, but he wasn't any taller. If he was going to give her any kind of trouble she thought she could probably hold him off until someone came out of one of the houses. Assuming they did. But what could he possibly want with her, anyway? Money? He certainly looked as if he was short of it.

'It might be, and it might not,' he said.

'What?'

'It might be my business and it might not.'

Tess glared at him and he looked nervously away.

'Your name,' he went on. 'Mine is Kevin. Or Kev. Take your pick.'

'No thanks.'

He laughed then, a high-pitched, musical laugh. Suddenly, Tess had had enough. She stopped in her tracks and turned on him, no longer uncomfortable, just furious.

'What do you want?' she shouted. 'Why don't you just leave me alone?'

He jumped and stopped dead. Tess took advantage and walked quickly away, but he caught her up. They were getting close to the edge of the park where Tess's road began.

'Don't be like that,' he said. 'I just want your help, that's all.'

'Well you can't have it,' she said, more confident now that she had turned the tables. 'I don't have any help to offer.'

The corner drew nearer. She would soon be home.

'Perhaps you do,' said Kevin, walking closer now, and Tess thought she detected a hint of urgency in his voice. She noticed that he seemed to be constantly glancing around him, as though he was afraid of being seen. She wondered if he was on drugs, or if the police were after him.

'If you want help so badly,' she said, 'you should ask my father.' As she spoke she heard herself using a tone she despised, the snooty little rich girl, the spoiled brat. But she couldn't stop herself. She turned towards him, her dark eyes taking on an expression of disdain, and said: 'Or shall I ask him for you?'

They were at the corner. On both previous days the boy had parted from her there and turned in the opposite direction. She knew he wouldn't follow her.

But as she made to swing around the corner, he caught hold of her arm. She shook herself free, but he darted round and stood in front of her, his hair flopping into his eyes again.

'Wait,' he said.

She stepped aside and went past him.

'And what if I told your father about you?' he said.

A cold chill ran up Tess's spine. She stopped and turned back. Kevin was standing still and his face showed the tension he was feeling, but for the first time he was looking her straight in the eye.

'What do you mean?' she said.

'I know about you,' he said. 'I know what you do.'

The chill spread, prickled through the base of her brain and up into her temples. She was trapped by the intensity of his gaze, and for a moment she was helpless and afraid. Leaves swirled around in the breeze.

'I won't tell,' he said, 'but you must help.'

Tess turned away. 'I haven't the faintest idea what you're talking about,' she said.

CHAPTER TWO

On Saturdays it was traditional for Tess to go shopping with her parents. It was supposed to be the high point of the week, to wander around whatever town they were in, buy what they needed and have a slap-up lunch at the best restaurant they could find.

Tess's parents often spoke about money being short, but Tess didn't really know what that meant. She knew only that from time to time she was embarrassed by the fact that she was one of the better-off girls in her school. Her father was hard-working and well paid. If there was something that Tess wanted, she generally got it.

On the whole, however, she didn't want all that much. Her parents saw her as a quiet child, perhaps too quiet, who was given to reading in her room after school and taking long walks in the countryside at weekends. During the holidays they saw little of her. She would set out on her walks after breakfast, whatever the weather, and return when she felt like it, often quite late, though seldom after dark. She didn't talk much about these walks, but her parents were proud of her knowledge of nature and in particular of wildlife. The last house they had lived in was on the edge of a small town in the south-east. It had faced out into the open countryside, but backed on to the built-up area. Tess had loved it there. The park was a poor substitute, but it was better than nothing.

For Christmas one year her parents had bought Tess a bicycle and often she set off cycling instead of walking. They had offered her riding lessons, too, with a view to buying her a pony of her own, but she had declined. 'Ponies are such fun,' she had said. 'I couldn't bear to sit up on top of one and boss it around.'

So they had dropped the idea and left Tess to her own devices. They saw no reason to do otherwise because she seemed, despite her lack of friends, to be quite content with life. When they learnt of the imminent transfer to Dublin, they both knew that it was going to be hard on Tess, but even so, they were unprepared for the strength of her reaction. She burst into tears when they told her, and locked herself away in her room. When she came out, she refused to speak to them at all for several days, and her mother came as close as she ever did to losing her temper about it. Instead, as usual, she became angry with Tess's father, and the house was full of slamming doors with bristling silences in between.

Eventually, Tess capitulated and agreed to move to Dublin on condition that they get a house either on the outskirts or beside the park. It wasn't easy, but they managed it. It was just as well, because Tess would have gone out of her mind if she had been made to live hemmed in by houses. Her 'walks' were the only thing that made the difference between happiness and misery in her life.

On that particular Saturday, her father had some work to do and told her that they would not be going into town before mid-day. Tess hid her delight. Now she would have the morning to herself. An unexpected bonus.

'All right if I go for a walk, then?' she said.

'Are you sure?' her mother asked. 'It's bitterly cold out.'

'I'll wrap up,' said Tess.

She put on jeans and her new puffa jacket, hat, scarf and gloves, and went outside. The wind wasn't strong, but it was colder, if anything, than the day before. Tiny particles of ice drifted in it, not quite snow yet, but a warning of it.

Tess looked up and down the road. During the summer holidays, there wasn't a parking space to be had for miles along the edge of the park, but today there were few cars. One or two stalwart owners were walking their dogs, and a few determined-looking families were playing soccer or frisbee, but mostly the park was deserted. In particular, to Tess's relief, there was no sign of Kevin. If he wasn't there today, the chances were that he hadn't been there on other Saturdays either. And if he hadn't, then he couldn't have followed her to the secret place she had found, and he couldn't have seen what she did there.

She began to relax a little as she walked across the bare fields of the park. She had always been careful, after all, very, very careful. It was vital that no one should see her and she had always made sure that they didn't. Kevin had just been bluffing. It was a clever bluff, too, because what teenager has not done something in their life that they would prefer their father not to know about? But a bluff was all it was, she was sure about that. If he tried again, she would invite him to come home with her and see what he had to say to her father. There was no way he would come.

She felt better, even light-hearted, as she came to the rough part of the park where her place was. Sometimes, when people were around, it was a little awkward getting in there without being seen, but today there was nobody within sight at all.

It was an area of small trees, ash and elder, with plenty of brambles and other scrubby undergrowth to provide cover. Tess looked around carefully. A woman had come into view, walking an Irish wolfhound which bounded with graceless pleasure across the open space of the park. Tess knew how it felt. She had tried a wolfhound once.

To be extra safe, Tess walked around her favourite copse and peered into one or two of the neighbouring ones as well. Well trodden paths ran between them all, and there was always a chance that somebody might be approaching, hidden by the trees. She stood still and listened for a long time. She knew the ways of the birds and small creatures well enough now to understand their voices and their movements. There was nothing to suggest that anyone apart from herself was making them uneasy.

She looked around one last time, then slipped into the copse. It was a place where she would not care to come alone at night. Even in broad daylight it was dark in there, and a little eerie. There were light paths through it that were clearly used quite often, and scattered here and there throughout the undergrowth were fast food wrappers and empty cans and bottles. Tess went on towards the middle, standing on brambles which crossed her path and ducking beneath low branches until she came to a place where the trees thinned a little. Here the undergrowth had grown up taller and thicker because of the extra light. A long time ago, a fairly large tree had fallen here, and the brambles had grown up around its remains. The smallest branches had rotted away, but the bigger ones were still intact and made a kind of frame.

Tess looked and listened one last time before she stooped and crawled into the narrow passage which led into the dark interior. Once inside, she was completely hidden from human eyes by the dense growth of brambles which covered the carcass of the tree. When she came out, she was a squirrel, full of squirrel quickness and squirrel nervousness, darting and stopping, listening, darting again, jumping.

Everything and anything in life was bearable as long as she had this. What did it matter if she had to wear that absurd uniform and go to that snooty school? At the weekends she could be squirrel, or cat, or rabbit, or lolloping wolfhound or busy, rat-hunting terrier. What did it matter if that vain and hungry boy was pestering her, trying to scare her? What did he know of the freedom of the swift or the swallow? What did he know of the neat precision of the city pigeon, or the tidiness of the robin or the wren? She would call his bluff and let him bully someone else. But just now, she would forget him as she forgot everything when she was squirrel, because squirrel hours are long and busy and full of forgetfulness.

The sun poked through the branches above, and if it wasn't the warm, autumn sun it might have been, it still didn't matter so much. Its bright beams added to the dizzying elation of scurrying about and jumping from branch to branch, and Tess was too busy to be cold.

Squirrels do as squirrels must. It didn't matter that she would not be there to hibernate during the winter. Autumn was collecting time, so collect is what she did. But because she wouldn't have to eat her store of foodstuffs in the winter, it didn't particularly matter what she collected. Some things, like rose hip seeds and hazel nuts, seemed urgent, and could not be resisted. She stuffed the pouches of her cheeks and brought them to her den. Other things, like sycamore wings and the mean, sour little blackberries that the cold, dry autumn had produced, were less urgent, but she brought them anyway because they looked nice, and there wasn't anything else in particular to be done. If the other squirrels found her habits strange, they were too busy with their own gathering to give her their attention. The only time they bothered about her was when she ventured too far into someone else's territory, and then a good scolding was enough to put her right.

She knew most of the other squirrels. Earlier in the year, before school started, she had often spent time playing with them, engaging in terrific races and tests of acrobatic skill. She always lost, through lack of co-ordination or lack of nerve, but it didn't matter. It was sheer exhilaration to move so fast, faster than her human mind could follow, and to make decisions in mid-air, using reflex instead of thought. She remembered some of those breathtaking moments as she encountered particular squirrels, but there was no time for that kind of thing now. Life was rich with

15

a different kind of urgency. Food was going to be scarce this year.

There was a clatter of wings in the treetops. For an instant the thicket froze like a photograph, and then its movement began again. Nothing more than a grey pigeon making a rather clumsy landing. Tess caught a brief glimpse of something shining on the ground and swooped down a tree trunk head first to investigate. At first she thought it was a ring pull from a drinks can, but as she got closer she saw that it was a real ring, a broad band of silver, scarcely tarnished at all. The metal grated unpleasantly against her little teeth, but she was determined to have it. She took a firm grip on it and pulled, but it would not come. A sharp blade of tough grass had grown up through it and become entwined with other grasses on the other side. She tugged again, and all at once was aware of another of those sudden woodland silences which always spell a warning.

She froze. She could see no enemy, but she smelt him, and he was close, very close. It was a smell she had never encountered before. She looked around carefully, and found herself face to face with the strangest squirrel she had ever seen. He was small and strong, his ears were sharp and pointed, and he was red, with black and white stripes running down his back. Every other squirrel in the copse was still, looking down at this oddity.

'He's not a squirrel at all,' thought Tess. 'He's a chipmunk. What on earth is a chipmunk doing in the Phoenix Park?'

As quick as any squirrel, the chipmunk darted forward and took hold of the ring in his teeth. As though reassured by this, the other squirrels relaxed and went back about their business. But Tess was infuriated. Whatever he was, wherever he came from, he was not going to have her ring.

She sprang forward and took a grip on the ring beside him. It may have seemed like a courageous thing for her to do, to take on this intruder, but she was supported by the knowledge that if she were in real danger all she had to do was to change back into Tess. Not only would she escape, but she would give her enemy the fright of his life.

Only once, so far, had she needed to do it, and that was when she had been a rabbit at dusk, not far from their last house. A fox had appeared from nowhere, and she had fled with the other rabbits towards their burrows. But the chap in front of her had been slow to get in, and the fox had been just about to close his teeth on her thigh. Instead, he was brought up short by a human leg, and he ran away home extremely frightened and bewildered.

She had been lucky. There had been no one around to see it happen. It was a last resort, but here in the darkness of the thicket she was prepared to use it if she had to.

But she didn't. As soon as she took hold of the ring, the chipmunk released it and used its teeth instead to cut through the tough grass. The ring came free, and Tess raced off along the thicket floor, holding her head high so that the ring would not get snagged on plants or fallen twigs. The chipmunk followed. At the door to her den, Tess dropped the ring and scolded him soundly. He backed off some distance and sat on the stump of the fallen tree, watching her with a sly gleam in his eye which was disturbingly familiar. Tess picked up the ring and marched in through the tunnel entrance, then went into the deepest corner of the bramble patch and dropped it there behind a big stone. But when she turned round, she found the chipmunk right behind her, watching every move she made. She sprang at him, chattering and scolding as loudly as she could, and he bolted away towards the light at the tunnel entrance.

Tess turned back to find another hiding place, but no sooner had she done so than he was there with her again, his tail high behind him, darting this way and that, always just out of reach of her teeth. For all the world he was behaving like a young puppy who wanted to play.

Tess stopped haranguing him and watched. Perhaps chipmunks weren't busy gathering at this time of year? Or perhaps he had escaped from a zoo or a private collector, and didn't know what he was supposed to be doing. Cautiously, she followed him. When she reached the end of the tunnel, he bounded off and leapt half way up the trunk of a tree, and then down again. He raced back to her, and then off again, into the branches this time, tempting her, teasing her. And why not, she thought, why shouldn't she play? There was no need for her to be gathering. She followed, slowly at first, so that he still went ahead and came back, until she gained confidence and ran up beside him. Now they were off, speeding along together through the trees and across the open spaces between them. They went from thicket to thicket, exploring them all at the highest possibly speed, and from time to time they raced out onto the open part of the park, running and jumping through the tangled grasses as far as they dared, then returning helter skelter to the safety of the trees.

Tess gave herself over completely to the game and the joy of companionship. It happened occasionally that she met a friend of a sort in the animal world, but as with human friends, it always seemed to be hard work. This was different. The chipmunk was as eager for company as she was. This time it was he who had found her and asked her to play. She couldn't remember when she had last felt so happy, and she didn't try. There was only now, the perfect moment, and it went on, and on, and on.

Until, suddenly, Tess caught sight of the sun. She had forgotten why, but she knew that it was much further across the sky than it ought to be. She stopped on a branch, her whiskers twitching, trying to quieten her flighty little squirrel brain so that she could think. All that came into her head were nuts, and a strong and compelling need to return to her den.

She raced pell mell back to the copse and the fallen tree. The chipmunk followed, still trying to play.

As soon as she was in the den, she remembered. The trip to town. She didn't know the time but she knew that it was late, very late. Her parents would be anxious. They'd be angry, too, and probably quarrelling. The chipmunk had followed her into the den. With all the squirrel fury she could muster, she turned on him and drove him out. He hovered at the door looking perplexed, but she sprang at him again, chasing him further away. Then she raced back into the darkness and, before he had time to follow her, she made the change. As she crawled on her hands and knees back out of the den, she expected to see him running away in terror, but there was no sign of him. None at all.

Halfway home across the park Tess realised that she had forgotten the ring. She sighed. It would be there again tomorrow. If she wanted something to worry about, she need only look ahead.

19

CHAPTER THREE

When Tess arrived home, breathless and contrite, her mother said: 'Never mind. If your father hadn't been working this morning, none of this would have happened.'

Her father stayed silent. He had become engrossed in an international football match on TV, so Tess and her mother took the bus to the centre of the city and had tea together in Bewley's. Afterwards they split up to do a bit of shopping. Tess spent some of her pocket money on a book about rodents which had a whole chapter on chipmunks, and the rest on a huge bag of sunflower seeds.

When they got back, Tess went upstairs and lay on her bed intending to read the rodent book, but she was so exhausted by her squirrel adventures that she fell asleep and didn't wake up until her father called her down for dinner. During the week the family ate formally around the dining room table, but quite often at weekends they relaxed in front of the living-room fire with trays on their knees. Tess sat down in an armchair and picked up her knife and fork. Her parents were watching a soap opera on the TV, but it was one that she found boring. Her mind wandered, back to the first time she had Switched and discovered that she did not always and evermore have to be just Tess.

She had been quite small, just seven or eight, and she had woken unusually early on a summer's morning because she was uncomfortably hot. There were images in her mind of a strange dream that she had been having, but they vanished before she could capture them. She sighed, and it seemed to her as she did so that time had slowed down. The sigh took for ever, both coming and going, as though there was room in her lungs for more air than she had thought.

Outside, the birds were singing unusually loudly, and the sun was streaming through a gap in the curtains and on to her bed. She realised that this was probably why she felt so hot, but when she lifted her hand to throw back the covers, something brown and furry jumped up on to her chest.

Tess was not a screamer, even at that age, which was probably just as well. If she had attempted to scream at that moment, the noise would have woken half the street, and everything might well have been ruined. Instead she stayed motionless for a long, long time, waiting for the creature to show itself again. When it did not, she began to relax a little. Whatever it was wasn't all that big, and surely she would be able to frighten it away. Slowly, carefully, Tess sat up. As she did so, she could see that the furry thing was still there on the top of her quilt. In slowly dawning horror, she realised that it was not a small creature, but the paw of a very, very large one. She swung round, expecting to see the rest of the beast crouching on the floor beside her bed, but there was nothing there. And as she turned back, she knew. She lifted her hand, and there was no hand, just the great, brown paw lifting to her face to feel the long snout and the round, furry ears. Tess had turned into a bear.

For a long time she stayed still. She had read about such things in fairy tales. They were usually caused by wicked spells or curses laid by witches or evil fairies. Tears of hopelessness rolled down her hairy cheeks and spilled on to the quilt, making a dark patch that widened and widened. She listened to the birds, wondering how they could seem so joyful when she felt so sad. She might have stayed there indefinitely, weeping a great stain into the quilt, were it not for the fact that bears find it uncomfortable to lie on their backs for so long.

Her fingers would not work properly. The quilt snagged in her claws as she tried to push it off, but she managed to get herself disentangled and scrambled down on to the floor. It was surprising to find how comfortable a bear can be, and for a while she just ambled here and there around the room, getting accustomed to her strange limbs.

After a time the sound of the birds and the fresh scent of the morning drew her to the window. On the third attempt, her clumsy paw caught the curtain and hoiked it to the side, and she stood on her hind legs and leant up against the windowsill, blinking in the bright light. The smell, the sound, the feeling of the fresh air in her nostrils was so delicious, it was almost magical. She was filled with delight at being a bear and she stretched her nose up towards the cool gap where the window was open. Just at that instant, however, she caught a scent, and then a glimpse, of the paper boy cycling down the road.

As quickly as she could, Tess dropped back to the floor and away from the window. The horror of the situation returned. What on earth was going to happen to her? From the room beside hers, she heard her parents' alarm clock ringing, and put her heavy paws up to her ears in dread. Any minute now she would hear her father padding along to the bathroom to wash and shave, and then he would pop his head around the door and say, 'Rise and shine,' or, 'Show a leg.' Sometimes he came in and drew the curtains. Sometimes he even sat down on her bed and chatted for a while before he went down and put on the kettle. But what was going to happen now? What would he do when he saw, instead of his girl, a brown bear?

He was humming now in the bathroom as he shaved. Would her mother be more likely to understand? If she looked her carefully in the eye, would she recognise her own Tess?

Tess shambled miserably around the room, feeling huge and heavy and clumsy. As she went by it, she knocked over the dolls' house. The crash it made as it landed scared her, and she jumped and knocked over the Lego. It scattered across the floor and as she walked the sharp edges hurt her paws.

The bathroom door clicked shut. Tess heard her father's footsteps in the hall. She sat down in the middle of the room and prayed with all her might to be a little girl again.

The door opened. 'What's all the noise about?' said her father.

Tess sat still and looked carefully up towards the door.

'What have you been doing?' her father said, as he came into the room.

Tess stared at him in astonishment. How could he not have noticed?

'Are you all right, sweetheart?' he said, squatting on his heels beside her.

She stared wide-eyed into his face, then looked down at her hands. She was Tess again, sitting on the floor in her nightdress, all warm and pink and human.

'I was a bear a minute ago,' she said.

'A bear!' said her father. 'Well. No wonder you made such a mess.' He righted the dolls' house and began putting the things back into it.

'But I was, Daddy, I really was.'

'Well, you'd better be a tidy little squirrel now and pick up all that Lego before your mum sees it. You can pretend they're all nuts.'

'But I wasn't pretending!'

'Of course you weren't.'

'Do you believe me?'

'Of course I do.'

But she knew by the tone of his voice that he didn't. Changing into bears just wasn't the kind of thing that adults did. They would be far too worried about what other people were thinking. So when, a few weeks later, Tess turned herself into a cat, she promised herself that she would never, never tell anyone ever again. And she never did.

That boy, that scruffy Kevin character, he couldn't know. He just couldn't. It wasn't possible. All the same, there was something about the way he had looked at her that scared her and made her almost

24

believe that he did, somehow, know what she could do.

'Tess?'
'Yes?'
'You're not eating your dinner, sweetheart.'
'Oh. I was just listening to the news.' She hadn't been, but she did now.

'Meanwhile,' said the TV newscaster, his face impressively grave, 'the freak weather conditions continue. The snow storms that have been ravaging the Arctic regions for the past eight weeks show no signs of abating, and their area of activity continues to increase. The death toll in northern Europe now stands at more than seventeen hundred, and there are many more people unaccounted for. Evacuations continue across the Northern Hemisphere.'

The TV screen showed a picture of a line of cars driving through a blizzard.

'Inhabitants of Alaska and northern Canada continue their southwards exodus as weather conditions make their homes uninhabitable. Air-rescue teams are working round the clock to move people from outlying areas, and snow-ploughs are working twenty-four hours a day to keep the major routes clear. However, it is feared that there may be thousands of people trapped in snowbound vehicles on minor highways throughout the area, with no hope of relief from the already over-stretched services.'

'There's something fishy about all this,' said Tess's father.

'Fishy?' said her mother. 'How can there be something fishy about the weather?'

'I don't know, but it isn't natural.'

25

'How can the weather not be natural?' her mother asked. 'If the weather isn't natural, what is?'

'Well, it's not normal, anyway.'

'Normal is a different question entirely. No one is saying this is normal.'

'Shhh!' said Tess.

'The fourth land attempt to reach the weather-bound Arctic drilling station has had to be abandoned,' said the newscaster above pictures of army snowmobiles and tanks. 'Radio contact with the rig was lost soon after the storm conditions began, and successive attempts to reach it by air and by land have failed.'

An army officer appeared on the screen, dressed like a Himalayan mountaineer. Snowflakes whirled around him.

'It's just impossible out there,' he said. 'Conditions like these have never been encountered before. The temperatures are falling off the bottom of the thermometer and visibility is nil. With the best will in the world, it is not feasible to expose army personnel to conditions like those.'

Tess thought he looked scared.

'I still say it's fishy,' said her father.

Her mother sighed in exasperation. Tess stood up with her tray. 'I'm going upstairs to read,' she said.

'Don't you want any pudding?' said her mother.

'No, thanks.'

'It's lemon meringue pie.'

'I'm not hungry. Perhaps you could leave me a piece for later?'

Tess took the tray out to the kitchen and went back up to her room. No one was saying it, but it was on everybody's mind. If those snowstorms continued to spread, it would not be long before they closed in on

Ireland, as well. And then what would it matter if
that stupid boy did or didn't know her secret?

CHAPTER FOUR

In a private office in the Pentagon in Washington DC, the same army officer who had made an appearance on Tess's TV was sitting at a table with several other men. One was his chief of staff, General 'Whitey' Snow, and another was the chief of staff of the airborne forces, General Wolfe. The others were ministers and advisors from the American government. There were no members of the public or the press among them.

The officer, whose name was Colonel Dale 'Big Daddy' Dunkelburger, got up and wandered restlessly across the floor for a minute or two, then took his seat again in a leather chair at the head of the table. On a trolley at his right hand was a large, square tape recorder and, in front of him, covering most of the tabletop, was a huge map of the Arctic Circle.

Colonel Dunkelburger sighed and rubbed his eyes.

It had been a long time since he had slept, and it looked like being another long time before he would again. With an expression of grim resignation, he glanced across the table and nodded at General Snow.

The General stood up and cleared his throat. 'Gentlemen,' he said, 'the matter we are here to discuss today is one of the utmost seriousness and gravity.'

There was a murmur of assent from the assembly.

'Now,' the General went on, 'I know that all of us here are signatories of the State Secrets Act, and I know that you are all aware that the seal on the door of this office binds you to that oath. Even so, what Colonel Dunkelburger is about to reveal to you is so important that I want you to take another oath now, a personal oath, on whatever you hold most sacred, that what you are about to hear will not pass beyond these four walls, even if you might believe yourself that such secrecy is incorrect.'

One of the President's advisors shook his head and sighed.

'General,' he said. 'We all appreciate that there's something here that you consider to be pretty important, but don't you think that maybe you're being a little melodramatic about this? Most of us here have to deal with State secrets every day, and I reckon the oath we've all taken has been good enough so far.'

'I appreciate your point of view, Mr Dunwoody,' said the General. 'But I believe that when you hear the evidence that we have on these tapes, you may understand. We're talking about an issue of global importance here, as opposed to state security, and I believe that it might unleash a world-wide panic if it were to become public knowledge. I have no intention of calling the Secrets Act into disrepute, but it might not be sufficient in this case to cover all eventualities. I hope you can understand that and appreciate that no disrespect is intended.'

Dunwoody nodded and, one by one, somewhat self-consciously, the assembly rose and swore their own personal oaths. When they were finished, Colonel Dunkelburger reached into the inside pocket of his jacket and produced a small tape which he fed into the machine beside him.

'This, gentlemen,' he said, 'is the last message that our Arctic Surveillance station in North Alaska received from the polar drilling rig, a week after it was marooned by the storms. I think it's worth saying at this stage that we have no reason to believe that this transmission was received by anybody else apart from ourselves.' He switched on the machine. The reception was poor and full of crackling static but nonetheless the voices could be heard.

'Yeah, boys, we're still OK here.' It was the voice of a young man, a bit of a wiseguy, but putting a brave face on a difficult situation.

'Nothing to report?' said the radio officer.

'Yeah, a lot to report. A hell of a lot. But it's all snow, you know? A hell of a lot of it.'

'How's the platform holding up?'

'I guess it's OK. The winds are as high as ever, though. There's a lot of creaking and groaning going on, it's pretty scary sometimes, but I don't think there's been any more damage since last Tuesday.'

'You still got plenty of supplies?'

'Yep. We're having a ball, you know?'

'So morale is OK?'

'Good enough. We – ' Here there was a loud bang. 'Whoops! Someone in a hurry with the coffee.'

Now there were excited voices in the background, but none of it was picked up clearly by the radio mike apart from the louder exclamations. 'But it's massive, man!' and 'I swear to God it's moving.' Then the young man came back to the mike. 'Hey, I gotta go for a minute. The guys are kind of worked up. Cabin fever, I guess. I gotta go and take a look. Will you hold on to the line there for a minute?'

'Sure, Chris. But what's happening?'

'I'll get right back to you. Don't go away, now.'

There was a long pause, during which nothing could be heard except the hiss and crackle of static. Around the table, the listeners shifted in their seats as the tension mounted. Then there was a second bang, like the first, followed a moment later by a series of loud metallic groaning and grating sounds, and then there was nothing. The radio connection went dead.

Colonel Dunkelburger took the tape out of the machine and slipped it back into his pocket. 'We don't know any more than you do, gentlemen,' he said, 'and that isn't much. We have had no radio contact with those guys since. Any kind of air rescue is impossible in those conditions, as General Wolfe will confirm.' He looked towards Wolfe, who nodded sagely, and then continued. 'We have gale-force winds out there which are whipping around and back every couple of minutes. Nothing can fly accurately enough in there. And as you know, we sent in land teams, but those have failed as well.'

'Why don't you tell everybody why, Colonel?' said General Snow.

'Yes, sir. Uh, these were unsuccessful for a number

31

of reasons. The first two teams turned back because the snowmobiles they were using were too light and were just getting thrown about in the winds out there. The third team took specially modified machines which could handle the winds a little better, but we didn't have our back-up system worked out well enough and we couldn't keep the fuel supplies up. It gets pretty dangerous to run out of fuel in those conditions as I'm sure you can all appreciate, because no fuel means no heat, and without heat nobody can last long out there, believe me. It's cold. We got a couple of cases of frostbite, and we were lucky that it wasn't worse.'

'And the fourth team?' asked the presidential advisor.

'The fourth team was doing pretty well. They had top quality vehicles fitted with special heaters and back-up power supplies in case of emergency. We had teams running well to keep them supplied up front with food and fuel, and a shift system in operation. They had been on the route for three or four days.' He stood and leaned over the map, pointing to a dotted line which ran a short distance across it. 'We had our main supply depot here in Barrow, in Northern Alaska, which is about six hundred miles from the drilling station. The pack ice is hard right up to the shore these days, so we could send the expedition right out on to it. The leading members of the team had reached here, which is about four hundred and fifty miles from the rig.'

He reached into his other inside pocket and took out a second tape, exactly like the first, which he slotted into the machine.

'There were two 'mobiles out ahead,' he said, 'each with two men. The rest of the team were on supply runs and the nearest ones would have been a mile or so behind them. We're tuned into car two, here. Car one was off the air.' He sighed and wiped his forehead with the back of his hand. 'I'm sorry about this, gentlemen, but I don't want to hear this any more than you do, believe me. And you had better hang on to your chairs.' He switched on the tape.

This time the line was a lot clearer. 'Still moving along,' said a young man's voice. 'Ground's pretty level. Harry's taking a nap.'

'No, sir,' said Harry. 'Just resting my eyes as per orders.'

'Yeah,' said the first voice. 'It's tough on the eyes all right. Got little white worms running across mine. How come I can see white worms when everything else is white?'

'They got black edges?'

'Let me see. Yeah. I think they got black edges.' He laughed. 'But the little b. . . . .s won't keep still and let me look at them.' There was a pause, then the same voice continued. 'Any news your end?'

'Nope. Everything's pure white and deadly boring.'

'Oh, well. At least we're not missing – Hey! Woah! What the hell is that?'

'What's up?' said Harry. 'Hey! Stop, Bud.'

Bud's voice was suddenly full of terror. 'We are stopped, God damn it. It's that thing that's moving!'

'Mother of Christ. It's alive!'

There was a single scream that sent a chill of horror through the whole room, and then the radio went as dead as the first one. The silence spread to the listeners. After a long time, Colonel Dunkelburger cleared his throat.

'We never regained contact with that car or the other one. I called off the mission immediately and

33

brought the team back home as quick as I could. The way the weather is worsening, we can't maintain the base in Barrow any longer, and we've pulled all our men out of the area. I guess I should say here that we have no plans to make any further excursions into the region as long as current weather conditions continue.'

The Secretary of State broke into the silence which followed.

'If I can just try and clarify things, here,' he said. 'Are we to understand that there's something living out there in the middle of those storms?'

'I can't say, sir,' said Colonel Dunkelburger. 'We have no more evidence than what you have just heard.'

'But surely you have all kinds of intelligence at your disposal? You have instruments for detecting heat sources, don't you?'

'Nothing that could be accurate enough to pick out a living entity in storms like those. Besides, our experts tell us that no living species within our current spectrum of knowledge could survive on the surface in those temperatures for more than a few minutes.'

'So what are you suggesting?'

General Wolfe broke in. 'With due respect, Mr Secretary, we didn't come here with the purpose of suggesting anything. We came here because we thought that the evidence on those tapes should be made available to the Government.'

'Well,' said the Secretary. 'It goes without saying that you guys have the full backing of this Government to take whatever investigations or action that you think necessary.'

'That's much appreciated, of course,' said the

General, 'but I'm afraid there are no further investigations we can take. This country has three armed forces, but in these conditions, every one of them is blind. We're overflying the area constantly with all kinds of aircraft, armed and unarmed. We have every kind of surveillance equipment trying to get a look at what's happening in there, but we're not getting any information at all.'

'As I see it,' said Dunwoody, 'you're telling us there's a possibility that there are some kind of alien creatures inside those storms and there's not a thing you people can do about it?'

'We're not trying to tell you anything, sir,' said Colonel Dunkelburger, 'but the conclusion we have reached is pretty close to that, yes.'

There was another thoughtful silence, and then General Snow said, 'I think perhaps now you will understand the need for absolute secrecy.'

The next morning, Tess slept late and had a leisurely breakfast. The mood in the house was low, and Tess knew that it was not just because of yesterday's mix-up. Even her father could not raise his customary Sunday spirit.

It was this weather. There was no change, and the radio reports gave no indication that there was likely to be. The meteorologists admitted that they were baffled. Satellite pictures revealed nothing except what everybody already knew. The Arctic storms were as active as ever, and were gradually spreading southwards. There had been no rain since the day it all started, and now the radio gave the first warnings of possible water shortages. It wasn't yet necessary to introduce rationing, but people were being asked to reduce their consumption as much as possible.

The whole business made Tess gloomy. She was still a bit tired, too, from her wild antics of the previous day. But she wrapped herself up as well as she could and set out across the park with the sunflower seeds under her arm.

The scene was similar to the day before. Only those who refused to be defeated by the weather had made it to the park, and they were few and far between. Tess wound her scarf around her face and breathed through the wool. From time to time she jogged for a while to keep warm.

When she got to the wooded area she opened her bag and wandered through the thickets, scattering sunflower seeds as she went. She listened to the sounds of the birds and small animals, and laughed a little at their mixture of suspicion and delight. When the bag was empty, she checked the surroundings carefully and went quietly into her den.

Tess was completely adept at changing now. It had taken a lot of practice, and when she was younger there had been times when she couldn't make it work. It required a state of mind that was somehow more, and somehow less than just thinking. First, she would need to know what she wanted to be and have a clear picture in her mind of whatever creature it was. Next, and more difficult, she would have to try and imagine how it felt to be that creature from the inside. Then she had to let go. Letting go was the most difficult part, because the moment of changing was a bit scary. For that moment, brief though it was, it felt as though her mind was dissolving, and everything around her became vague and fluid and insubstantial. Once that moment had passed, everything was fine again. She took on the being of whatever she had become, and they were all as solid in their own way as her customary human existence. But there had been times, in the past, when she had failed to change because she had shied away at the last moment from that frightening instant of dissolution, and clung to what was certain and safe.

More recently she had discovered that thought, concentration and anxiety were all hindrances to the process of change. For several years now she had dispensed with them and simply plunged, spontaneously, into any shape she fancied. In the dark of previous dens, Tess had experienced the nature of most of the wild and domesticated creatures in Ireland, and most of the more common birds as well. She knew now, beyond all doubt, that she could be anything she wanted to be.

As soon as she was a squirrel again, Tess set out in search of the chipmunk. There was no sign of him in the immediate vicinity, so she scampered in the trees and hunted through the branches. But it soon became hard to keep her mind on what she was doing. All the other squirrels were frantic with activity, gathering the sunflower seeds she had scattered and bringing them home to their nests. For a while she resisted the temptation but in the end it proved too strong for her. She knew that she had brought those seeds and she knew that she had no need to make a winter store, but the instinct of a beast is strong, and soon Tess gave in and joined them.

It filled her squirrel heart with joy to find food so plentiful. She filled her little cheeks until they bulged, and scurried back to her den time after time. All around her the other squirrels and the birds and the fieldmice were delighted by the unexpected windfall and Tess knew that her pocket money had never been better spent.

Still there was no sign of the chipmunk. Every now and then Tess would remember him and take a leap up into the treetops to see if she could see him from up there. Then she would go back to work and forget him again.

The day drew on and Tess had a fine heap of sunflower seeds in her den. She realised that it would soon be time to go home, and it was then that she thought, for the first time, of the silver ring. Hurriedly, she unloaded her cheeks and skipped across to the dark corner where she had left it. The stone was there, big and solid, and she searched around behind it, but there was no sign of the ring. Tess sat down and thought as hard as a squirrel can think, but both squirrel mind and Tess mind were sure that she had left the ring just there, behind the stone. She searched again and, when she still didn't find it, she searched all the corners of the den, pushing aside the rotten leaves and twigs with her nimble squirrel fingers and feeling around where it was too dark to see. All at once she knew that the chipmunk had taken the ring. She stopped still and tried hard not to believe it but she knew that it was true. He had been such a friend, such a good friend, but now he had let her down, by taking her ring and disappearing. It filled her heart with such sadness that she didn't want to become Tess again, because she knew that most of the creatures of the earth feel sadness from time to time, but only humans collect it like a store of nuts and feel the need to make it last.

But she had to be herself again. There was homework to be done for tomorrow, and then another week of school before she could be here again, and free. She changed before she had time to think about it. With a human hand she reached behind the stone and felt around carefully, but there was no doubt now that the ring was gone. The little heap of sunflower seeds which had seemed so huge and satisfying to her squirrel self looked small, now, and pathetic. She brushed them into the palm of her hand and scattered them on the floor of the thicket as she set off for home.

CHAPTER FIVE

Monday dragged on, as always. Tess had brought her rodent book to school, and read it secretly beneath her desk during maths and religion, but since the disappearance of the ring it had lost its appeal. There were no references to wild chipmunks in Ireland, or any suggestion that chipmunks had any interest in collecting baubles.

The other girls in Tess's class had come to accept that she preferred to keep herself to herself. She knew that it would be hard to make up all that lost ground if she ever changed her mind and wanted to make friends, but she had created an image for herself in the school and for the moment she was content to leave things as they were. But that evening, when a photocopied letter was handed to each girl to bring home to her parents, she rather wished that she was free to join in the celebrations that followed. The letter read:

'Dear parent,
      Owing to the prevailing weather
conditions, the girls will not be required to
wear school uniform until further notice.
      Yours sincerely,
            M.L. Harvey (Principal).'

Tess almost got off the bus at the stop before her
own. She knew that there had to be a way through
to the park from there, and once she had reached it,
she couldn't go wrong. She pictured that stupid
Kevin's face as he realised she wasn't on the bus. He
could stand there and freeze for all she cared. But at
the last minute, Tess's courage failed her. She might
well freeze herself if she got lost and had to wander
around the streets for too long.

She hoped that he wouldn't be there, but he was,
on her side of the street this time. He was leaning
against the wall with his hands in his pockets,
watching for her. She noticed that his face brightened
for an instant the moment he caught sight of her, but
then it took on the familiar, shifty expression. Tess
thought of crossing the street, but she knew it was
useless. Instead she looked straight ahead and walked
briskly past. Kevin fell into step beside her.

After a minute of strong silence, he said: 'Ready
to tell me your name yet?'

Tess swung around and faced him. 'Look, why
don't you just clear off and leave me alone!' She was
shouting louder than she meant to, and a woman on
the other side of the street gaped at them as she
passed.

Kevin looked away, to hide the apprehension in his
face. After a minute or two, he said: 'What kind of
manners are those for a young lady?'

'What would you know about manners?' said Tess. 'With your whinging and scrounging.'

'Scrounging?' said Kevin.

Tess walked on, and he followed.

'Who's scrounging?' he said.

'What are you doing, then, if you're not scrounging?'

Kevin sighed deeply and took out a cigarette. 'You're being ridiculous, you know,' he said.

'Listen who's talking! I've already told you I don't want anything to do with you. You're not getting my name and you're not getting any money, either. If you want to get something, then get lost.'

Kevin laughed. 'That's a good one,' he said. 'Did you think of that one on the spot?'

Tess didn't know whether to be infuriated or flattered, and when Kevin stopped and turned to the wall to light his cigarette, she almost stopped as well. But she didn't get caught out this time. Instead she quickened her pace, almost to a run. Kevin caught her up. 'You won't help, then?' he said.

'No.'

'But you don't even know what I'm asking you for.'

'Whatever it is I haven't got it. And if I had I wouldn't give it to you.'

'But you have got it. In fact, you're the only one who has.'

'Rubbish.'

They were walking so fast now that they were nearly at the edge of the park. Suddenly, Kevin dodged in front of Tess and blocked her way. She tried to sidestep, but he threw away his cigarette and grabbed hold of her shoulders. She was shocked at the sudden movement, and surprised by his strength, but it was the look on his face that stopped her from

42

trying to break away. There was no slyness there now, no fear. He was looking at her straight on, and his eyes were bright and keen and completely serious.

'Is it really possible,' he said, 'that you haven't worked this out yet?'

Tess tried to think of something clever to say, but she couldn't. For some reason she knew it wasn't the time for being clever. Kevin spoke slowly, as though she were a rather dim child. 'Do you really believe that there are chipmunks in the Phoenix Park?'

Tess felt her mouth drop open. Her mind flew back to Saturday. She had been so careful. It was impossible that he had seen. He took his hands from her shoulders and blew on them to try and warm them. Tess remained motionless, open-mouthed, staring. Kevin put his hands in his pockets, and the sly gleam returned to his eye. And just as she remembered that same look in the bright little eyes of the chipmunk, Kevin took hold of her gloved hand and dropped something into it.

It was the silver ring.

Tess was afraid that her emotions would show on her face. All those years of silence and secrecy and guilt were over, and she was no longer alone. She would almost have hugged Kevin then, despite his scruffy clothes, but he began to talk before she had the chance.

'You'll help, then?' he said.

Tess was bewildered. 'But how? What?'

'I'm not sure, yet, said Kevin, gazing out across the park. 'But if you meet me tonight we'll find out.'

'Meet you? Where?'

'Connolly Station. One o'clock.'

'One o'clock?'

'Is that too early?'

'Too early?'

'Use your head,' he said. 'You'll have to get out, won't you? And you'll have to get there.'

'But I can't,' said Tess. 'How can I?'

Kevin blew on his hands again and shrugged. 'If you can't, you can't,' he said, and he began to walk away. 'But I'll be there anyway.'

She watched him as he went. She knew nothing about him, nothing at all. Then she remembered the little chipmunk racing with her, playing, staying close, and she felt that she did know him, at least as well as she needed to.

'Kevin?' she called.

He turned back. 'Yes?'

'My name is Tess.'

He smiled and gave her a thumbs up. But her heart was heavy as she walked towards her house. How could she possibly do as he asked?

CHAPTER SIX

Tess lay awake, listening to her parents getting ready for bed. She could hear their voices through the wall, but not the words. From the tone of their conversation she could tell that all was well with them, and the house was relaxed and comfortable as long as they were content. But it didn't make Tess any happier.

Kevin had asked her for help and she had let him down. The clock on the wall said twelve twenty-five. Even if she had the courage to cross the city at this hour, there was no way she could do it. The last buses would be on their way out of the centre of town and they would not be bringing passengers back in. A taxi, even if she could find one, would be too expensive. If she had meant to be there, she would have left an hour ago or more. But it was impossible. Couldn't he understand that? What parent would allow their thirteen-year-old daughter out in the dead of night to meet a boy they had never set eyes on?

If she had any friends in the area, she might, just might, have pretended to be staying with them. If she had gone with someone to a disco or a film, she could have risked her parents' alarm by going on from there and coming back late. But there was no one for her to go with and nowhere to go. She couldn't even sneak out. Just ten minutes ago her father had put his head around the door and listened, as he did every night. She had made her breathing as deep and regular as she could. It was dreadful, being an only child.

Twelve thirty-five. Poor Kevin. He would be there, soon, all alone among the homeless people and the winos, looking round for her, waiting. And here she was, lying in her comfortable bed, wretched, feeble, worthless.

She turned over on to her side, but she knew she wouldn't be able to sleep for a long time. The clock on the wall ticked with infuriating monotony. Outside, an occasional car passed along the road, and in the tree opposite a barn owl began to call.

Tess listened, slightly calmed by the familiar sound. It seemed strange tonight, different somehow. Her nerves were on edge. She sighed and turned again in the bed.

'What a fool,' said the owl. 'What a foo-ool.'

Tess sprang up, almost before she understood why. Of course! She would have laughed and shouted out loud if she hadn't been afraid of waking her parents. As quietly as she could, she opened the window and climbed up on to the sill. The freezing night air blew into the room. She wouldn't be able to close the window behind her, but it was too bad.

A moment later, a barn owl was speeding towards the centre of the city, high above the houses and offices. It was a young owl, healthy and strong, and singularly delighted by the power of flight.

Tess knew Connolly Station well. Although they had lived in Dublin for less than three months, they had often visited the city in the past to do some special shopping or to go to a show or a play, and as often as not they had come by train.

It was easy enough for her to find the station from above. The city was spread out like a map beneath her, and once she had found the railway lines where they crossed the North Strand, she could not go wrong. The difficulty would be finding somewhere to land and change her shape without being seen. But her attention was drawn from the problem as she flew down over the station, because she was joined by another owl. It swept in from somewhere above and behind her, and as it drew level it bumped into her and knocked her off balance, so that she fluttered wildly in the air for a moment or two. As soon as she was steady again, the other owl returned to fly beside her. Tess was afraid that she had broken some territorial rule and offended the other bird. It would not be a problem if it allowed her to fly away, but she was afraid that if it continued to be aggressive she would either fall or be forced too far away from the station to get to Kevin on time.

But it didn't collide with her again. Instead it flew alongside for a while, then moved a little ahead and veered across her so that she had to swing to her right. As soon as she did so, it dropped back beside her and turned its head carefully to look at her. It was then that Tess realised it was Kevin, and if an owl could have smiled, she would have done. Instead, she nodded her head in recognition, and he blinked three times, then flew on ahead. She followed as he swept over Busaras and the Custom House, then swung away from the river and back towards the north side. They followed streets which became darker and narrower until they came to a few blocks of dilapidated flats built around dark, rectangular courtyards. Above the first of these they flew in diminishing circles until they were sure that no one was around, then Kevin dropped into the courtyard and swooped straight in through an open window on the second floor. It was a lovely piece of flying. Feeling slightly reckless, Tess let go and followed.

By the time she had got her bearings in the room, Kevin had already turned back into human shape. Tess followed suit. As an owl, with her good night eyes, she had seen him quite clearly, but for a girl, the dark in the room was almost impenetrable. For a moment or two, she was quite unnerved. The place smelled bad, of mouldy mattresses and soot and stale beer. But there was something even worse.

'Kevin?' she said.

'Yes?'

'Can you see me?'

'Not really, no.'

'I'm in my pyjamas.'

She heard his laugh ring out around the room. It was hard and scornful, and it hurt.

'Shut up,' she said. 'I didn't have to come here, you know. You don't know what it cost me to get here.'

'What did it cost you?'

But she didn't tell him, because then he would know that it mattered to her not to let him down. Instead she said, as unkindly as she could: 'Is this where you live, then? Is this your house?'

48

He struck a match and lit a candle and a cigarette from it. 'I don't live anywhere,' he said.

'Don't be stupid,' said Tess. 'Everyone lives somewhere.'

'Who's everyone?' he said.

Tess shivered. In the candlelight she could see the stained mattress in one corner, surrounded by a jumble of newspapers and empty tins and bottles. There was an untidy heap of dark blankets in another corner, but Tess would not have touched them, let alone put one around her shoulders.

'Do you live here?' she asked. 'Seriously?'

'Of course not!' Kevin sounded bitter. 'What do you think I am?'

'Where do you live, then?'

'I already told you that.'

'Then who does live here?'

'No one. Some old tramps use it sometimes, when they can't get into the hostel.'

The cold was beginning to hurt. Kevin didn't seem to be aware of how bad it was. By the flickering light of the candle, she could see him looking from one corner of the room to another with that familiar nervousness. She was suddenly close to tears.

'What are we doing here?' she said. 'I don't understand any of this. How am I supposed to help you?'

Kevin shrugged. 'I'm not even sure myself, yet,' he said, 'but I know it's important. There's a rumour going around. The rats want to bring me somewhere.'

'Rats!'

'Yes. You got something against rats?'

Tess had. A rat was one of the things that she had never been and had no desire to be. But before she could say anything, Kevin went on.

'A rat is about the best thing to be in a city like

49

this. They have the run of the place, you know? They never go hungry.' He smiled at the distaste clearly evident on her face. 'They have a lot of fun, too. More often than not I'm a rat.'

He watched closely for her reaction. Tess tried not to show it. The idea filled her with unease. For although she had spent a lot of her time being all kinds of other creatures, she had never considered herself to be anything other than human. But if Kevin spent most of his time being a rat, then what did that make him? It made sense of the way he behaved when he was human, though; his nervousness, the sense that she had when she was with him of there always being an enemy somewhere close at hand.

'Never been a rat, huh?' he said.

'No.'

'Don't worry. You'll enjoy it. But there's quite a stir going on about this cold weather. At least, I think that's what it's about. Everybody's suffering, you know, not just the people. That's why I came looking for you. They want me to meet somebody. I don't know who it is, but it's a long way.'

As Tess watched him, the tense expression left his face, and there was a momentary confusion in his eyes as he said: 'I didn't want to go there on my own.'

There were suddenly too many questions. There was too much to share with this strange boy, and possibly too much to cope with. And it was too cold to face any of it.

'I have to go home,' said Tess. 'I have to get warm and think it over.'

'But there's no time to think it over. This thing is important, Tess. This weather's getting worse all the time.'

'Do you think I don't know that? Don't you realise I'm getting frostbite standing here?'

Kevin bit his lip. 'I'm sorry,' he said. 'I wasn't thinking.' He began to take off his coat.

'Don't be ridiculous,' said Tess. 'What difference does it make if you freeze instead of me? The point is, the whole thing sounds ridiculous to me. How can we possibly have any effect on the weather, whatever we do?'

'I don't know,' said Kevin, zipping up his parka again, 'but I do know this. Most of my life I've been going in and out of the animal world, and never before did they take any particular notice of me. But now they have. They know that I'm different and they're asking me for something.'

'I'm totally confused, Kevin,' said Tess, 'and I'm too cold to think straight. I have to go home.'

'But we can go straight away,' he said. 'Come on. You won't be cold once we get moving.' As he spoke, he was pointing towards a large hole in the skirting beside the fireplace.

'As a rat?' said Tess.

'Of course.'

Tess shook her head, and at the same moment changed back into an owl. She hopped out of the window and flew straight up and away towards the park. Gradually the activity warmed her and she began to feel better. The whole idea was crazy. All she wanted to do was to curl up in her own bed and forget all about it. But she was not allowed to. As she landed lightly on the edge of her bedroom window, she realised that Kevin was right behind her.

CHAPTER SEVEN

Kevin and Tess stood in her room, facing each other.

'Goodnight, Kevin,' said Tess.

'Oh. You're going to bed, are you?'

'Yes.' She wanted to close the window on the night and all that was in it and allow the room to warm up, but she couldn't do that until he was gone. Instead, she climbed into bed and wrapped the covers around her.

Kevin wandered round the room, examining her things. It made Tess uncomfortable. It always made her uncomfortable when someone less well off than she was came to the house. She had no pride in her standard of living, and in situations like this she felt rather guilty.

'You've got a lot of books,' said Kevin.

'Observant, aren't you?'

'Have you read them all?'

'Most of them.'

He took a thick volume out of the book case and opened it. 'You like mythology, then?'

'My dad does. He buys most of that stuff.'

'Do you read it?'

'If I'm bored enough.'

Kevin leafed through the book. 'This is a good one,' he said. 'I haven't seen this one before.'

Tess sighed and tried to drop him a hint by turning her face to the wall, but he went on: 'I spend hours in the library, you know.'

'Oh? When you're not rummaging through people's dustbins?'

She couldn't see him, but she could imagine the look on his face in the brief silence before he said: 'Yes. Or raiding their kitchens or waking up their babies at night. Rats are OK, you know, you shouldn't underestimate them. They have their own codes of behaviour, even if they're not like yours. They have a language, too.'

'All animals do.'

'No, not really. All animals have ways of communicating, but the rats actually have a language, a sort of visual language.'

Tess said nothing, and after a while, Kevin went on: 'I love all this stuff, though, all those heroes and gods and wonderful beasts. It's the best thing about people, if you ask me. Their imagination.'

'I didn't ask you,' said Tess, and as soon as she had said it, she regretted it. It was just one step too far.

Kevin hurled the book across the room. It hit the wall above her head with a loud crack and landed on the pillow in front of her nose. She sat up in bed.

'For God's sake, Kevin!' she said, as loud as she dared. 'You'll wake my parents!'

'Your parents? Your precious mammy and daddy? Who cares? Eh? As long as you're all right, all warm and cosy with your feather duvet and your central heating and your own private little life. The rest of the world can go hang, can't it, as long as you're all right, Jack!'

'Shh, Kevin, don't shout! I don't know what you mean, can't you understand that? I don't understand what you're asking me to do.'

'Nor do I!' said Kevin. 'But I know that it's important. And even if it isn't, I have to find out.'

He came over to her and sat on the edge of the bed. Tess's nerves were on edge, waiting for the sound of her father's feet in the hallway.

'You have to help me, Tess,' Kevin went on. 'You just have to. I can't do this on my own. For one thing, I don't have very much time left.'

'What do you mean?'

'It doesn't go on for ever, you know, this thing, this ability we have. Did you know that?'

'No.'

'Only until we're fifteen.'

'How do you know?'

'Someone told me. She was one of us, too, but now she isn't. She learnt it from another Switcher. After her fifteenth birthday she couldn't change any more. That's the end of it.'

The news came as a blow to Tess. She had always believed that her gift would be with her for the rest of her life, the one thing she could be sure of.

'We all meet someone who tells us,' said Kevin, 'and we all meet someone we have to tell. I don't know how it works or why, but it seems that it always does. Anyway, the point is, I'm nearly fifteen, you know? And I'm nervous about what's happening.'

54

'So you want me to come along and hold your hand?'

Kevin looked crestfallen, and suddenly Tess didn't know why she was putting up such a resistance and being so unkind. She lay back on the pillow to think about it, and Kevin sat quietly, glancing at her from time to time in his nervous, sideways manner.

Tess realised as she lay there that there was nothing to think about. If she refused and sent him away, she would never know what it was about and whether her gift had given her a part to play in some scheme or other. She would have to live with that uncertainty for the rest of her life. No matter how crazy it seemed, she had to go. There was no choice.

She sighed and threw back the covers. A look of delighted surprise crossed Kevin's face. He turned away quickly so that she wouldn't see it, but she could still see the way he felt by the spring in his step as he crossed the room. She pulled on her jeans on top of her pyjamas, and then two sweatshirts, a thick jumper and two pairs of socks. Then Kevin waited in her room as she crept downstairs, feeling like a burglar in her own house, to get her down jacket and gloves.

Back in the bedroom, Tess hesitated. Whatever anxiety she had about the risk she might be running for herself was nothing compared to the feeling that gripped her now. For some reason she knew beyond any doubt that she would not be returning to that room before morning, and that her parents would have to face the shock of coming in and finding it empty. She felt sick, but there was no longer any question of turning back. With hands that trembled more from tension than from cold, she searched through the drawers of her desk for some notepaper that her aunt had given her for Christmas. The she sat down and picked up her pen.

The paper had delicate impressions of swans in blue and gold. Kevin leaned over her shoulder as she wrote. 'Nice paper,' he said.

'Shh.'

> 'Dear Mummy and Daddy,' she wrote. 'I have to go away for a little while. I'm sorry, but I can't explain to you why. But you must trust me, just this once. Don't send anyone to search for me. It would only be a waste of time. I promise that I will take care of myself, and you must promise me that you will do the same and not worry too much. I will be back as soon as I can. Love you with all my heart, Tess, XXXXXXXX'

'Yuck,' said Kevin. ' "All my heart." '

Tess swung on him. 'Shut up,' she said, in a vicious whisper. 'Shut your filthy mouth. Just because you haven't got anybody.'

He shrugged and turned away, and Tess was sorry, because she realised for the first time that it was true. He had nobody. Nobody at all.

She pinned the note to her pillow and took a last look round the room. Then, side by side with Kevin, she walked to the window.

The two owls swept away again over the city. Kevin led the way back towards Connolly Station, but instead of returning to the flats, he headed for a small patch of wasteland in the same area, where houses had been demolished to make way for some new building project which had never materialised. They overflew it once or twice, checking out the area, and then they began to descend.

There was a crowd of young men gathered around a car a couple of blocks away, but they were not close enough to be a danger. The owls flew a little lower over the wasteground again and, to Tess's horror, her sharp night eyes saw that the whole area was swarming with rats. There was a high chain-link fence around the plot, but nonetheless the local people had managed to turn the place into a dumping ground for their rubbish. Mainly it was large things, old couches with the stuffing hanging out, broken TVs and fridges and mattresses with bulging springs. But there were black plastic bags there as well, spilling out their contents of empty tins and vegetable peelings and tea bags. A perfect breeding ground for rats.

As the owls spiralled cautiously downwards, there was a sudden flurry of rapid movement as the rats leapt for cover, and then there was nothing. Absolute stillness. Into this, the two birds landed, and before Tess could even take a breath, Kevin had dissolved before her eyes and become a rat.

It was strange to watch it happening. If Tess had been asked, she probably would not have been able to describe what it looked like, because it looked, in a sense, just the way it felt. She had the same dizzying sensation of the world losing focus and becoming fluid, as though the observer also were drawn into the process of change and somehow became part of it. She watched as Kevin trotted away a little distance, then stopped and looked back. Tess stood still, with her wings folded, looking around her with large eyes that missed nothing, even in the darkness. The rats were everywhere, poking their noses out of the tin cans and paper bags and carpet folds where they had taken cover. Kevin sat up on his tail and twitched his whiskers with that same nervousness that carried into his human form. Tess wanted to be with him, but she was stuck. She just couldn't bring herself to make that change.

It wasn't only as a human that she hated rats. Every creature that she had ever been hated them, too. The birds hated them because they would raid any nest they could reach and whisk away any hatchling or fledgling that got out from under its parent's eye. Cats and dogs hated them because they were thieving and provocative, and because if they were hungry enough they would take even a young pup or kitten from its bed. Other scavengers hated them because they were greedy and aggressive and invariably got the better of an argument. Even the large and tolerant beasts like horses and cattle found rats distasteful, because they respected neither peace nor privacy, and they fouled whatever fodder they were unable to eat.

Kevin came back towards her. The other rats, sensing that she was not a threat, had begun to emerge from their hide-outs. She turned her head slowly from side to side. She was not afraid. An owl is a match for any rat. She watched them carefully, allowing her owl instinct to savour the idea of snatching the plumpest of them and bringing it away with her to the nearest tree. But it was not to be. From the street came the soft click-click of a dog's claws on paving stones. The rats froze. As Tess watched, the dog appeared at the wire and stopped, looking straight at her. For a long moment, nothing moved. Then the dog, with a single, soft bark, announced its intention and ducked through a gap in the fence.

Looking back, Tess could never understand exactly why she made the decision she did at that moment.

It would have been as easy, and probably much safer, to lift off into the air and fly away from the scene, but she didn't. The sudden danger resolved her deadlock, and an instant later she was running for her life behind Kevin's retreating tail and leaping for the safety of a dark hole in the side of an upturned couch. Together with several other rats, they wormed their way between the springs and stuffing into the safety of the deep interior. From there they could hear the dog sniffing and scratching at the torn fabric, but they were quite confident that he couldn't reach them. Sure enough, he soon became bored and gave up. The rats wasted no time. Before he was out of sight down the street, they were out in the open again.

Suddenly, Tess found her mind full of vivid and disturbing images. The owl in the dog's mouth with feathers flying. Herself as a rat being shaken in his teeth, and the horrifying sound and sensation of her spine snapping. She stood transfixed, trying to clear her mind, until Kevin caught hold of her by the whiskers and gave them a tweak. It was then that she remembered what he had said about the rat language, and she realised that he had put those images into her mind. He was angry. But before she could work out how to answer him, they were approached by another rat, and then another, and her mind was fully occupied by their expressions and the images they were passing.

'Here among us, you two, huh? Days and nights, days and nights, us lot listening, looking, huh?'

Tess was surprised at how well she understood them.

'You two sleeping, huh? Days and nights, days and

59

nights. Stuffing fat bacon, huh? Trying to make a family, huh?'

Tess was shocked, but Kevin was angry. He jumped on the rat who had suggested it and bit his ear until he squealed. 'Ear gone, nanananana! Sit down, calm, days and nights, you two, empty streets, empty skies.'

Kevin was giving images now. 'Long canal, long towpath. Us two, many streets.'

Tess was grateful that he didn't let them know that the delay was largely her fault. 'Many streets, many streets,' she thought, 'yep,' and she was surprised when the others nodded and twitched their whiskers.

'Yep, yep, many streets. Many streets behind, many streets ahead, move, run, little old lady sitting beside a fire, looking you two, listening you two, run, huh?'

And run they did, straight away. Across the wasteground and down a hole which led under the foundations of the neighbouring house and through a series of underground passages lined with brick, earth and rubble.

Kevin went ahead with the rat whose ear he had bitten. The other stranger ran along beside Tess, watching her cautiously with what she interpreted as a rather stupid grin. From time to time the passageway grew narrow and the lead rat and Kevin would fall into single file until they were through. But Tess's companion didn't seem to understand. If she gained speed to go ahead, he gained speed as well, and if she slowed down to drop behind, he also slowed, all the time looking at her with that same, stupid expression. They survived a couple of tight squeezes, but managed to become completely stuck at one particularly narrow spot.

'Oops,' said her guide in rat language. 'Narrow, narrow. Us two, oooh, very, very thin, huh? Squeeze.'

Tess scrabbled with her claws and they managed after a brief struggle to break free. They ran on, and made up some of the ground they had lost. It was quite dark down there beneath the houses, and Tess realised that she was acting by an unknown sense which wasn't sight. She was aware of the spaces around her and the way the tunnels changed ahead and behind, even though she could actually see very little. After a while, they emerged into the open space of a basement, where light flooded through a grating from a lamp post on the street above. The rats stopped and looked around cautiously, before scuttling together across the empty space, which seemed huge after the narrow tunnels. At the other side they formed a line again to slip through a hole in the corner of the floor. Kevin was ahead of Tess and as he disappeared she noticed that his right hind foot had only three toes. But before she had a chance to wonder about it, her companion was back alongside her.

'Long nose,' he said.

'Huh?'

'Long nose.'

They were approaching another tight gap, and this time Tess stopped and thought as clearly as she could of the two of them going through it quite sensibly and politely, one at a time. But to her annoyance, her guide stopped as well, and said again: 'Long nose.'

She made a sprint for the hole, but he was too quick for her and there was no doubt that they would have got stuck again if Tess hadn't stopped in time. He grabbed hold of her whiskers and pulled her round to face him. She could just see the outline of his face in the darkness.

'Long nose,' he said, and he caught hold of his own nose and pulled it. She noticed for the first time that he did have an unusually long nose.

'Long nose,' she said, and was pleased to find that sarcasm was a readily available quality in the rat language. 'Yep, yep. Sunny days, happy rats, long nose. Me through the hole, you through the hole behind me, huh?'

He wrinkled his nose. 'Yep, yep,' he said, and she darted through before he had time to change his mind.

Kevin and his friend were waiting, but ran on when they saw the other two coming.

'Long nose,' said Tess's companion yet again.

Tess was beginning to get really fed up. 'Long nose,' she said. 'Small brain.'

'Huh?'

Tess mimicked his grin. 'Long nose, happy you, happy me, huge sack of oats in a big barn with no cats.'

'Nanananana. Long nose. You, huh?'

'Short nose.'

'Nanana. Short-nosed rat in a hotel basement, many many streets.'

At last Tess understood, and she felt slightly foolish. Long Nose was his symbol, his mark, his name in the visual language of rats.

'You, huh?' he said again.

Tess was at a loss. Her name was meaningless in this world. There was no way to translate it. And as far as she could tell, she was a completely ordinary rat with no outstanding features at all. Her mind

62

searched for images, but none of them seemed suitable.

'Owl, huh?' she said at last.

'Nanana,' said Long Nose. 'Nanananana. Owl carrying off young rats, us rats sad, us rats angry.'

There was another narrow opening ahead, and this time Tess managed successfully to communicate the idea of single file. She ran ahead of Long Nose into the dark gap, and was surprised to find that it stayed dark and narrow. It was sludgy and slippery underfoot, and there was a strong smell of drains. She waited for the tunnel to broaden out, but it didn't, and it soon began to seem as though it never would. Tess began to feel claustrophobic. The only reassurance was the sound of Kevin's pattering feet before her, and those of Long Nose behind. Gradually the smell grew stronger, and Tess realised that it was more than just drains. It was sewers. The stone passage they were in was sloping downwards now, and Tess found herself beginning to slither on the slimy stuff beneath her feet.

'This is the most foolish thing I've ever done,' she thought to herself. 'What on earth am I doing here? How could I have allowed myself to be talked into this?'

She had no time to dwell on it, however, because the next moment Kevin flashed her an image of a rat wearing a parachute, and then they were falling through the air in the darkness.

CHAPTER EIGHT

They landed with a splash, a shock of cold water that made Tess gasp and splutter. But she found that, before she knew it, she was swimming, and quite strongly too. For someone who had never swum before, either as a girl or any other creature, it was pretty exciting and completely took her mind off the nature of the liquid they were travelling in. There was just enough light for her to see the shapes of the other rats ahead of her and she swam up close beside Kevin before Long Nose had a chance to move in and monopolise her again. Kevin looked across and acknowledged her with a brief nod. His eyes sparkled and she caught the image he gave her of an underground train speeding along beneath a huge city. Then he gave her a second one, of four rats going twice as fast through their own underground system. If she had known how, she would have laughed.

Before long, the four of them came to a wider

canal, and they swam with a gentle current until they came to a shoal of sludgy stones and trapped paper, which allowed them to climb out of the water and into another system of pipes and drains.

Tess was beginning to get tired. The drains seemed to go on for ever, always sloping gently upwards and always wet and slimy underfoot. It took all her strength and concentration to keep close to Kevin, who seemed to find the going no problem, and the whole business was made worse by the irritating presence of Long Nose, who trod on her tail at every possible opportunity.

She called in Rat to Kevin: 'Boy and girl, out in the open, deep breaths, sleeping.'

He called back: 'Boy and girl squashed in drainpipe. Spaghetti.'

By the time they emerged, quite suddenly, into the cold, clear air, Tess was so exhausted that she felt she couldn't travel another yard. She wanted badly to be human, at least for a while, but before she could repeat her request to Kevin they were off again. They had come out on to another piece of waste ground which lay between two huge warehouses. Tess followed the others out on to a wide street. There was no sign of people or dogs, but they stuck to the deepest shadows all the same, running in single file close up to the walls and sprinting across the open spaces in between. At the end of the street lay the river. Ships were tied up beneath cranes, waiting for loading or unloading, but there was no activity now. All was still and silent.

The fresh air had given Tess a second wind and she was comfortable enough now as the little group followed the warehouse walls parallel to the river for several hundred yards. There were lights here, and they were much more exposed to possible danger than they had been in the drains, but Tess was happier nonetheless. The others, however, did not relax until they left the warehouses behind them and crossed through the wire fence which surrounded an area of huge coal heaps. Then they slowed their pace and picked their way among the loose slag at leisure.

'Dawn,' said Kevin, dropping back beside Tess.

'Happy us,' said Tess. 'Boy, girl, sitting on the coal, huh? Boy smoking cigarette, huh? Talking, huh?'

'Us four sleeping,' said Kevin. 'Curled together, warm.'

It was not an image that appealed to Tess, though it clearly did to him. She was still not entirely comfortable about being a rat and, besides that, it would be the first time that she had allowed herself to sleep as an animal. It was an idea that had always scared her a little, not only because she might sleep longer than she meant to and arrive home late, but because sleeping was a kind of forgetting and she was afraid that she might not remember who she was when she woke up.

Kevin nudged her with his shoulder and wrinkled his nose. Then he darted on ahead and, resigning herself, Tess followed.

The four rats slept throughout the day in a snug and well concealed hole beneath a portakabin at the entrance to the coal-yard. It was far from being a sound sleep, because the floor above their heads was walked on almost constantly, and the sounds of men's voices filtered through the wood. Lorries passed in and out all day, their tyres crunching on the coal dust, alarmingly close. But Tess didn't mind. Rat dreams were strange and frightening and it was a relief to be woken from time to time and to be able to remember where she was and why. Sometimes Kevin woke with her and they would exchange a few images and touch noses for comfort before they went back to sleep. Sometimes the rat with the bitten ear woke too and moved in small, irritated circles, trying to get comfortable again. Long Nose, it seemed, didn't wake at all, but snored and sighed throughout all the coming and going in ignorant contentment.

The best sleep came in the three or four hours between the closing of the yard and the arrival of darkness. Those hours passed like minutes but refreshed the four rats better than any before them. They spent a few minutes cleaning themselves when they woke, then emerged, bright-eyed and sleek, into the strange, orange gloom that covers cities at night. A few flakes of snow were falling, but there was little wind, and the rats were in no danger of getting cold as long as they kept moving. They were hungry, though, and Tess was about to discover that the hunger of a rat bore no relation to any hunger she had ever known. It began as a warm and rather pleasant sensation which made her feel energetic and strong, but within an hour it had grown larger and more demanding, and her feeling had changed to one of enormous courage and pride. She was sure that she would have stolen a bone from a dog at that moment, and longed for a chance to prove it.

'Eat, huh?' she blasted at Kevin.

He jumped at the force of her message but answered calmly: 'Basement, dark, black bags, flash restaurant, a few streets.'

Tess held on to the image of the diners in their expensive clothes, taking their time over their food. Her parents brought her to that kind of place from

67

time to time, but she was sure that Kevin would never have been in one, at least not while he was human. She decided that she would bring him out, when all this was over. She had her own account in the post office, and she would buy him some new clothes, if he would let her. It was a pleasant fantasy. She would be on familiar territory. He would be on edge, worse than usual, but she'd make him feel at ease and make sure he got the best the restaurant had to offer.

'Long Nose.'

Not again. Tess almost squeaked in annoyance. She was tempted to use the pent-up urgency of her hunger to jump on him and box his ears, but just in time she realised that he was probably hungry, too. By now they were back among the rat runs that honeycomb the foundations of the city, and Tess had allowed herself to fall back behind Kevin again and into the company of Long Nose.

'You, huh?' he said.

Tess was as stuck as before. To make time, she said: 'Him, huh?' and sent an image of the rat with the chewed ear.

'One black whisker.'

Tess hadn't noticed. 'Him, huh?' she said, indicating Kevin.

The image that came back was a disturbing one, an awful random mixture of rat features combined with the rat's version of what a boy is. Tess had no desire to have a name-image anything like that.

'You, huh?' said Long Nose again.

Tess said nothing.

'Huh? Huh?'

When she still made no reply, he gave her a

command that no rat will ever refuse, because too often their lives depend upon it.

'Freeze!'

Tess froze. But Long Nose did not. He walked all around her from her nose to her tail, muttering to himself. 'Huh? Huh? Nananana. Nope. Huh?' He tugged at her tail and her whiskers, prodded her nose and looked into her ears. He lifted her feet and counted her teeth and made her sit up on her tail while he examined her belly, all the while saying: 'Huh? Nope. Nanana. Nope.' At last he went round behind her and started fiddling with her tail again.

'Tail two toes short, huh?' he said.

Tess didn't catch the image. 'Huh?' she said.

'Three toes, four toes, huh?'

'Huh?' She turned around to see what he was doing, just as he bit off the last inch and a half of her tail.

Tess squeaked and swung round ready to attack, but Long Nose looked amazed and offered his throat in defence.

'Hurt!' she said. 'Tail, yowch!'

'Seven toes,' said Long Nose, holding up the end of her tail and measuring it against his front paw. 'You, Tail Short Seven Toes.'

Tess examined the wound on her tail and was surprised to see that it was hardly bleeding at all. Nor was it anywhere near as sore as she had expected. She could live with it, she decided, and would almost have forgiven Long Nose had she not turned round to find him contentedly eating the end of her tail for his breakfast. She shot him an insult that even he could not fail to understand, and ran ahead to find Kevin.

The rats feasted on the rubbish in the basement of the restaurant. There were other rats there, too, pleased to meet the newcomers and exchange the latest gossip. One of them, a handsome fellow who introduced himself to Tess as Stuck Six Days in a Gutter Pipe, showed her how to recognise rat poison and scatter bits of it around to make it look as if it had been eaten. Then he helped her to find the choicest bits of leftover food, such as fish spines, chicken hearts and slivers of soap. Tess accepted them as graciously as her rat nature permitted, but it seemed to her with her great hunger that anything she ate was as good as the next thing, and that was even better.

There was plenty for everyone and the place seemed to have a constant turnover of rodent customers who came and went in a leisurely fashion. Stuck Six Days in a Gutter Pipe wrinkled his nose suavely at Tess as he left, but the effect was slightly spoiled by the chicken leg in his mouth that he was taking home for the children.

When Tess had eaten all she could, she joined Kevin and One Black Whisker in a quiet corner where they were chatting with two unknown rats.

'Guides,' Kevin told her. 'Long Nose, One Black Whisker curled up asleep in the couch on the waste ground. Little old woman sitting beside a fire, many streets. Long Nose and One Black Whisker confused, lost.'

'Many street, huh?' said Tess. 'Boy, girl walking, riding on a bus. Owls, pigeons flying. Us rats going slowly. Us rats very tired. Us rats sleeping.'

'Boy, girl scratching their heads,' said Kevin. 'Looking at maps, shrugging their shoulders.'

70

'Us rats swimming in sewers, us rats in slimy black drainpipes.'

'Girl going into her house, huh?' Kevin's black eyes were cold and mistrustful and Tess knew her own must have looked the same. But he was right. There was no turning back now, and no way of knowing where to go without the guidance of the city rats. She showed Kevin her teeth for spite, but a few minutes later they were back on the rat highways with their new guides.

CHAPTER NINE

For three more nights Tess and Kevin travelled through the rats' city underground, changing guides twice more along the way. They ate from rubbish bins knocked over by dogs, from shop store-rooms and from the shelves of poorly guarded kitchens. When they reached the outskirts of the city they began to travel above the ground, and they stopped many times along the way in urban gardens to feed on fresh vegetables and tasty scraps from compost heaps. Rats, it seemed, were never short of food.

On the fourth day, dawn found them in one of the most affluent areas of the country. Green fields and trees surrounded impressive houses, both old and new, owned by those people who could afford the luxury of having the best of both worlds. Tess was aware that her parents had checked out areas like this before they settled on the house beside the park. The air was so fresh and the country smells so sweet that she found herself regretting their choice. What was puzzling her, though, was that the sort of area they were in didn't fit at all with the picture the rats had given her of the little old lady who was waiting beside the fire.

'Little old lady, huh?' she said to their latest guide. Her name was Nose Broken by a Mousetrap, and it was easy to see why.

'Yep, yep, little old lady,' she said, and darted through a hedge into a field of lush grass.

It was not snowing now, but there had been several light snowfalls over the last few days, and because of the relentless cold, whatever snow had settled had remained. It stuck to the rats now as they dislodged it from the grass, and melted in dark patches on their glossy coats. They stayed close in to the hedge to avoid the eyes of dogs or hawks or passers-by, and soon they crossed into a second meadow, and then a third. A road ran parallel to their route, between the meadows and the widely spaced houses on the opposite side, and the occasional car passed along it, driving slowly because of the icy conditions. After a while, Tess realised by the change in sound that the hedge they were following was no longer beside the road but running away from it and out into the open country.

'Road, huh?' she said. 'Little old lady house, huh?'

'Yep, yep,' said Nose Broken by a Mousetrap, and she led the way through the twisted roots of the hedge. They stopped on the other side. They were on the edge of a green track with high brambly hedges on each side. Blackthorn and ash trees grew overhead so as to make it almost a tunnel. It was a track for people and animals only, far too narrow for a car.

'House,' said Nose Broken by a Mousetrap, twitching her nose along the path.

'House, huh?' said Kevin.

'House, yep. Little old lady. Yep, yep. Careful. Cats. Many cats. Follow soak-away pipe. Passage through hollow walls, comes out above the fireplace. Cats can't reach.' She touched noses with each of them and said: 'Nose Broken by a Mousetrap visiting her grandchildren. No hair yet. Many streets.' And with that she was gone, back through the hedge and out of their lives.

'House,' said Kevin, and started running down the track. But this time Tess didn't follow.

'Freeze!' she said.

He did, instantly. Tess looked up and down the track. She sniffed the air and listened carefully for a while. They were well hidden from the road by a bend in the track, and the hedges were high on either side. With a sigh of relief, she Switched into human form, and after a moment or two, Kevin did the same.

Tess hollowed her back, stretched her arms above her head, and then swung them around like a windmill, all those things that a rat can't do. Then she sighed again and sat down against the base of a tree where the ground was free from snow.

'Shove up,' said Kevin.

Tess moved over, turning away from him, and he squeezed in beside her with his back against hers. 'What did you do that for?' he said.

'Do what?'

'Change.'

'We're going to see a little old lady, aren't we?'

'Yes. But she obviously speaks Rat, doesn't she? How else could she have sent the others looking for us, huh?'

74

'Don't "huh?" me,' snapped Tess. 'I'm fed up with being a rat. That wasn't part of the deal as far as I'm concerned. It's all right for you. You're used to it. Maybe too used to it.'

'Oh,' said Kevin, 'like that, is it? Well, maybe you're too used to being a rotten human. We didn't make the stinking sewers and slimy drainpipes, you know? You did. We don't leave rubbish thrown around all over the place. It's your lot who does that. You're lucky you've got us to clean up after you!'

Tess was staring at him, open-mouthed.

'What's wrong?' he said.

'What do you mean, "us"?'

Kevin looked at the ground and gathered a small lump of snow in his hand.

'What do you mean, Kevin?' Tess went on. 'What are you trying to say?'

'Nothing,' he said. 'It's just that I'm not good at being a boy. With rats you know where you stand even if it isn't always pleasant. But I don't understand people properly. They say one thing and they mean another. I don't know how to look at them and I don't understand the way they look at me.'

Tess looked around her. A weak morning sun was pouring yellow light through the branches and picking out specks of brilliance in the thin snow. Above their heads the birds were chatting quietly, not too concerned by their presence but aware of it all the same.

'I don't either, Kevin,' she said, gently. 'I'm not sure anybody does. That's just the way people are.'

'That's fair enough I suppose,' he said. 'But it doesn't give me a good reason to bother with them.'

'You keep saying "them", or "you", as if you don't

belong. But you do. You're the same as any of us when it comes down to it.'

'Am I, Tess?'

'Of course you are! We're all the same underneath.'

Kevin sighed deeply and tilted back his head so that it rested, just for an instant, against hers.

They walked together down the path until the house came into view. It was a tiny place and quite ancient, completely at odds with the surrounding wealth and grandeur. A few hens picked at the grass around the front door, and a troop of ducks that were puddling around in the mud beside an outside tap took offence at the presence of strangers and waddled away in a line, quacking contemptuously.

The little old lady heard them and came to the door.

'At last,' she said. 'I thought you'd never get here, so I did.'

'Pardon?' said Tess.

'I been waiting ages,' said the little old lady. 'You took your time, didn't you?' She threw a suspicious glance at Kevin and said: 'I thought you was a rat.'

'Huh?' thought Kevin instinctively. He looked crestfallen and hung behind Tess as they followed the old woman into the house.

'Never mind,' she said, pushing cats off chairs beside the fire to make room for them to sit down. 'I suppose you is a rat and you isn't. It's all the same in the end. All the same to me at any rate. Sit yourselves down, and don't take any notice of them cats. A knee is a knee to a cat and a lap is a lap, and whether it's a knee or a lap it's warmer than the floor. If you doesn't like cats,' she looked pointedly at Kevin, 'you can tell them where to get off, but politely, mind, because we doesn't tolerate rudeness in this house, does we, pussums, eh?'

She closed the hall door behind them and they settled, a little self-consciously, into the newly vacated chairs. The fire was crackling brightly, and a large black kettle on a hook above it was wheezing in a way that made Tess hopeful of tea. It seemed like a year since she had tasted it.

The cats didn't turn out to be a problem because as soon as the old woman sat down they began to gather on her lap, and before long there were four of them there, manoeuvring for position.

'Tell us your names,' said the old woman. 'Come on, don't be shy. No rules in this house except that you minds your manners and doesn't be anything nasty to scare the cats. And you needn't think you're so special, either, sitting there like that. We was all young once, you know. You isn't the only ones who was able to Switch yourselves.'

'We know that,' said Tess.

'You knows everything, that's your trouble. Teenagers always does. There's nothing anyone can tell them. Teenagers is arrogant, that's what they is. Isn't that true, pussums, eh?'

The four cats had settled comfortably now and sat gazing out at Tess and Kevin with narrow, malevolent eyes. Kevin was looking pointedly at the floor, and Tess knew that he wasn't going to be any help at all.

'Well,' she said. 'He's Kevin and I'm Tess.'

'Oh,' said the old woman. 'Kevin, is he? That's a good, solid name, now, Kevin is. You can't argue with that, can you?'

'I suppose not,' said Tess.

'But Tess,' the old woman went on, without pausing for breath, 'isn't a name at all. It's one of those ridiculous new inventions like a sticky label. They might as well have given you a number, miss, as a name like that.'

'But that's not true!' said Tess, beginning to get annoyed. 'It's a very old name.'

'A very old name? How can it be a very old name when you's only a little nipper, eh? I'll tell you a very old name. Lizzie is a very old name, and I isn't telling you how old it is, and as every young gentleman knows,' she leant forward and poked Kevin on the knee so that he jumped, 'it isn't polite to ask. But you can take it from me, it's a very old name. It's very nearly about as old a name as you can get.'

There was an awkward silence, during which the kettle's voice moved up a semitone. Tess glanced around the room, surreptitiously. Beside the fireplace was an old black oven, and above it Tess noticed a hole in the stonework of the chimney front which she recognised from Nose Broken by a Mousetrap's description. She could well imagine Lizzie sitting there in the evenings, having conversations with little twitching noses poking out, while the cats prowled below in impotent fury.

Behind them was a small table, and beyond that an old-fashioned square sink between cupboards with broken doors. There was a litter of bits and pieces everywhere, but Tess had the impression that, on the whole, the place was clean. Light streamed in from a large window behind the sink. Tess took a second look, unable to trust what she had seen. Hanging on a line above the window, like an eccentric pelmet, were a half dozen pairs of Lizzie's drawers.

Tess tried not to laugh. She looked at Kevin, but

he was rubbing imaginary dirt off the palm of his hand, and she realised that he was inwardly fuming.

'Is Lizzie your name, then?' she said, still battling with the giggles that were threatening to erupt.

'It isn't what I'd have chosen if I was given the choice,' said the old woman, 'but we never is, is we? There it is, as soon as we's big enough to know it, and then we's stuck with it, isn't we? We can't shake it off, can we pussums, eh? Born Lizzie I was, and Lizzie I'll be to the end of my days if there ever is an end to them.'

Tess realised that Kevin was swearing silently, in Rat.

'You has a very lazy tongue, young man,' said Lizzie, 'but a nasty, busy little mind. And you's very stupid if you thinks I can't know what you's saying.'

Kevin looked up, shocked. 'Sorry,' he said. 'I forgot.'

'You forgot, so you did. Teenagers always forgets. Teenagers thinks they's the only ones with eyes and the only ones with brains. I was a rat, young Kevin, before your father had an eye to have a gleam in. I was a rat in the days when those things wasn't done, and many other things besides. I was a rat in days when teenagers wasn't allowed. What do you think of that, eh?'

Kevin looked daggers at Tess and she glared back at him. It hadn't been her idea to come here. It was becoming clear to her that the old woman was mad as a hatter. Her parents would be at home, out of their minds with worry, and she had spent four nights in the sewers of Dublin to come and listen to total nonsense.

Lizzie put the cats down off her knee, one by one,

and got up. She reached out and gave the kettle a prod so that it swayed on its hook and hissed angrily.

'Get a move on,' she said to it. 'You's always slow when I's in a hurry. You does it on purpose.'

The hissing died down and a few weak puffs of steam escaped from the spout. 'These days,' Lizzie went on, 'anything goes, doesn't it, eh pussums? Anyone who wants to can be a teenager. You sees them everywhere with their hair all painted and their raggedy clothes and every one of them knows better than the next one. Oh, it's an awful thing. Dreadful. It's catching, too. It's an epidemic. And some people is never cured, never. Some people is teenagers all their lives. Isn't that right, pussums?'

Kevin stood up and turned to Tess. 'I've had enough of this,' he said.

'Oh?' said Lizzie, putting her hands on her hips. 'Had enough, has you? You hasn't had anything yet, so how is it you's had enough? If you's had enough, why did you come at all?'

'Come on, Tess,' said Kevin. Tess stood up a little uncertainly, looking from one to the other.

'That's teenagers for you,' Lizzie went on, her voice rising in tone to near hysteria. 'They hasn't even started and they's had enough. They only wants to sit in front of the TV or have a good time for theirselves being jackdaws and puppies and toads. They hasn't time to sit and chat. They always has to go. They's always had enough, even before they's had what they come for!'

Kevin wheeled on her, and the cats, which had occupied her vacated chair, scattered in all directions. 'And what about stupid old women? Who invites . . . who invite people to visit them and drag them right across Dublin and then tell them to mind their manners so they can stand there and abuse them?'

'You hasn't any manners to mind!' shouted Lizzie.

'Listen who's talking!' yelled Kevin, and he stormed out. Tess made to follow him, but in the dim hallway of the little cottage she hesitated and stopped. She could hear the old woman muttering to her cats, and she crept back and stood beside the hall door, where she could hear but couldn't be seen.

'They's all the same, Tibsy,' Lizzie was saying. 'They's all the same, isn't they, Moppet?'

Tess heard the springs of Lizzie's chair creak as she sank into it. 'But we's done it again, hasn't we? I's done it again. You gets offended sometimes, doesn't you? But you forgets. Them people never forgets. They didn't even let us tell them about the krools, did they? They was in too much of a hurry to get offended and be gone.' Her voice went quiet and Tess suspected that she was close to tears. 'Now what's we going to do?'

Kevin was halfway up the little path before Tess caught up with him. She was very relieved that he hadn't Switched, because she would have had a lot of difficulty finding a rat, and as for a pigeon or a hawk, it would have been hopeless. The fact that he hadn't changed meant that there was still a chance.

'Wait, Kevin,' she said.

'What for?'

'I want to talk to you for a minute.'

'Talk?' he said. 'That's all people ever do. Talk, talk, talk. They talk so much they get on each others' nerves and what happens then? They have to bloody well talk about it!'

'Don't be like that, Kevin.'

'Why not? What's the point of all that talking, eh?

81

Now you want to talk about that stupid old woman, and we wouldn't be here in the first place if it wasn't for her talking too much.'

'Will you just listen for a minute?'

Kevin sighed and turned to face her. His eyes were grim and determined, and her heart sank. He could disappear so easily, just vanish from her life into the skies or the underground passages of the city and she would never be able to find him again.

'Don't you see?' she said. 'The old woman is like you. She doesn't understand people either. She doesn't know how to behave.'

Kevin looked away from her. 'It just proves my point, doesn't it?' he said. 'It's a waste of time trying to understand people.' But Tess knew that he was disarmed now.

'All right, then,' she said, and then, in Rat: 'Girl going into her house. Rat crawling into the hollow couch.'

Kevin looked at her again, and she could see that his anger was dissolving.

'Maybe it will all turn out to be a wild goose chase,' she said, 'but we can't just give up without finding out. We have to hear what she has to say.'

'It's one thing hearing what she has to say and another thing understanding it! Where does she get that accent from, anyway?'

'I don't know. She's not from around here, that's for sure. Maybe she's from England somewhere?'

'More like Mars, I'd say. But if you want to hear more of it, go ahead. I'll wait here.'

'No. You come with me. Come on. She's sorry now.'

'And so she should be.'

Tess looked back towards the house. 'Do you know something, Kevin?' she said.

'What?'

'You care a lot more about people that you think you do.'

'Oh, do I?' His voice was full of contempt. 'Why do you think that?'

'Because if you really didn't care, if you really thought people were so useless, then they couldn't upset you, could they? Because you'd never expect anything better.'

Kevin didn't answer, but looked at Tess suspiciously. She began to walk back down the path towards the house and after a while he followed.

CHAPTER TEN

At that moment, in the sealed and bug-proofed room in the Pentagon, there was another meeting going on. Many of the same faces were there, but there were one or two changes. Colonel Dunkelburger was absent. And the newly elected President of the USA, Mr Dan Doyle, was there at the head of the table.

The meeting had been in progress for some time and the two tapes had been played by General Snow, and then played again.

'Maybe those guys in the snowmobile just woke up a polar bear or something?' said President Doyle.

No one ventured to answer. In the light of what they had just heard, the question seemed to answer itself. After a while, the President said: 'Well, what are we supposed to think? That there's some kind of aliens up there or something?'

Again no one answered. Quite a few of those

84

present had already come to the unpleasant conclusion that there was no other explanation.

'Hey,' the President went on, 'all kinds of things happen to guys when they're out in the snow too long. They get snow blind. They get cabin fever, that kind of thing. Hell, my great grand-uncle Zacchariah was holed up in the mountains for sixteen weeks once with nothing but a pair of wolverines for company. He was never the same again.'

General Wolfe cleared his throat. 'Er, that's quite understandable, Mr President.'

'Sure is,' said Doyle, brightly.

'But, the thing is, I guess maybe this isn't quite the same kind of situation.'

'No, I'm sure it isn't. But from what I can see, we got nothing at all to go on except a hell of a lot of snow. These things happen sometimes, you know? Two years ago we had a drought that went on a bit too long, and suddenly everybody was saying that the end of the world was nigh. People were saying the Russians were behind it, and maybe they were. But we didn't panic. We didn't go off bang and start losing our heads about it. I don't know about the rest of you guys, but I reckon that if the USA can win one Cold War, we can win another.' He slapped his knee and laughed aloud. One or two of the others tried their best to join him, but failed.

General Wolfe cleared his throat again. 'That's very good, sir,' he said, 'and there's no doubt at all that we all have to take that kind of attitude to this, uh, little problem we have out here . . .'

'Frankly, sir,' said General Snow, glancing disdainfully at Wolfe, 'we feel that this problem may be a bit more serious than that.'

'You think the Russians are involved?'

'No, sir. We have no reason to suspect that. In fact, from what we can make out, they're having a much worse time of it than we are. What I'd like to bring to your attention, if I may, is that these weather conditions are like nothing that's been seen on earth in recorded history. The satellites are sending us pretty uncanny pictures. Those storms are radiating outwards from the polar circle in something approaching perfect symmetry, and it's kind of hard to believe that whatever is causing that is a natural phenomenon.'

'Well, that may be,' said President Doyle, 'but I find it harder to believe that it's an unnatural one. I just can't go for these alien theories, gentlemen. I'm sorry.'

'That's OK, sir,' said General Snow. 'No one expects you to. But whatever we all of us personally suspect or believe, we need to decide on what kind of action we're going to take.'

There was a silence, while everyone followed their own thoughts, and then the President said: 'Maybe it's the FCOs.'

'FCOs, sir?' said Dunwoody.

'Yeah. You know. The gas they use in those little spray cans? Pfft. Pfft. Deodorants, that kind of thing. Maybe we should ban them. Would that help, maybe?'

'Er . . . that's CFOs, sir,' said Dunwoody, 'and we already banned them.'

'With all due respect, sir,' said General Wolfe, 'I think we have to be prepared to go a little further than stamping out deodorants to get to the heart of this mess.'

'Right. OK. I see you guys mean business. I like that. That's the true American spirit. So, what do you want to do? Do you want to throw a few nukes in there to be on the safe side? It's OK by me if you do. It'd be good for public morale. Show that we're doing something. Show the rest of the world that America cares.'

'It's . . . that's a very good idea, Mr President,' said General Snow, 'but I think it might be a bit risky.'

'Risky? Why? There's nobody up there, is there?'

'Not as far as we know. But the effects of atomic radiation can be a little unpredictable, as you know. The winds can blow it around the place and into inhabited regions. And besides that, there's the little problem that nuclear weapons aren't too popular with the public right now.'

'OK. Nukes are out, then. How about . . . let's see now . . . how about saturation bombing?'

General Wolfe's jaw dropped. 'Saturation bombing of the whole Polar region?'

'Too big, huh?'

'Way too big, sir.'

'Well, how about starting in the middle and work your way outwards? See what happens?'

'It's a little beyond our resources, sir,' said General Wolfe. 'And as a matter of fact, while we're on the subject of resources – '

'You looking for a raise? You got it. I like your attitude to this problem.'

'Thank-you, sir,' said Wolfe. 'Would you mind making a note of that, Mr Dunwoody? But what I was coming round to saying was that General Snow and I have been having some discussions. We feel that in order to get a better understanding of the Arctic situation we're going to need to get more satellites up there. We also need to get more planes in the air to overfly the area with radar, and we need some pretty damn fast research into anti-stealth detection equipment. We need more planes up above those storms and more planes down in the middle of them, taking pictures with radar and infra-red and every other thing we got at our disposal. We can't fight this enemy until we find out what it is, sir, and for that we need a bigger budget.'

'Ah,' said the President. 'Well, you know money is kind of tight right now. You're all aware we've got an increasing number of refug – er, visitors from Canada and Alaska staying with us for a while, and it's looking like there's going to be a bit of a crisis on the home front if this weather keeps up.'

'That's just my point, sir,' said Wolfe. 'We need funds to do whatever is necessary to avert that crisis.'

'Oh, yeah. I see. Well, I guess you guys had better produce some figures.'

General Snow nodded, and Wolfe opened his briefcase.

Lizzie was delighted to see Tess and Kevin back, though she did her best to hide it.

'Here they are again, pussums,' she said. 'You just never knows, does you. Forgot your tea, did you? Never mind, kettle's nearly boiling.' She poked it again and it swayed and spat water on to the fire where the drops fizzed and steamed.

'Find your chairs, find your chairs, they's still there, no cats back in them yet. Plenty of chairs, the cats hasn't worn them all out yet, make yourselves comfortable while I makes the tea. Come in, Oedipus, before you gets shut out.' She closed the hall door firmly behind a black tomcat and leant on it for an instant, smiling at Tess and Kevin as brightly as she could manage. Then she fell into such a frenzy of activity that it made Tess nervous just to look at her.

'Where's the milk, eh? Has you had it, Moppet? No, no, that's yesterday's milk. Where did I put it now, I wonder? Well, there's not many places it can be. Oops, kettle's boiling, let's just get these tea leaves out into the garden. Does you know that, Tessie?'

'What?'

'Tea leaves is good for the garden. Nothing better. Straight out the window on to the grass they goes and the hens scratches them in. Nothing better. I never puts no manure on that grass out there and there's no greener grass in the country.'

There was nothing Tess hated more than being called Tessie, but she bit her tongue and said nothing.

'Warm up the teapot, now,' Lizzie went on. 'Have to warm the teapot, does you know that, eh? Does you warm the teapot? Takes all the good out of the tea if the teapot isn't warm. I never gets a decent cup of tea anywhere except in my own house. All these teenagers, see? They never does anything properly. They hasn't any patience. Not yourselves, of course, yourselves is different. Yourselves has good manners. See how you sits there so quiet and not rude at all. Mind you, I's still sure they told me you was a rat. Hard to know the difference sometimes. Specially these days. Things was different when I was young. We was moving around, see, always on the go, we was. Here today, gone tomorrow. But the one thing we brought with us wherever we went was our manners.'

Kevin was looking steadfastly down at the floor between his feet.

'Not that we was gypsies, mind,' said Lizzie. 'We never had anything to do with that sort.' She paused for a moment and looked around, as though not quite sure where she was. Then her pale blue eyes brightened. 'I suppose that milk is still out in the pantry. Of course it is. It's cooling down, that's what it's doing. Don't go away now, little Switchers. I'll be back in a second.'

Tess nudged Kevin's shoulder. He looked up sternly, then dropped his guard and smiled. Lizzie came back and bumbled around in cupboards for a while, collecting an assortment of chipped cups and odd saucers. At last, after what seemed an age, she handed them each a piping hot cup of tea and sat down in her chair with her own.

Tess took a sip of her tea. It was hideously sweet, but what bothered her more than that was the hair in it that stuck to her tongue. She picked it out as politely as she could. It was short and white and rather thick. Lizzie's hair was white, too, but it was long and silky and tied in a tight french knot at the back of her head. There was no way this hair belonged to her.

Kevin seemed to approve of the tea. He sat back in his chair and sipped it slowly. 'Very good,' he said to Lizzie.

'Ah!' she said. 'You speaks then? I wasn't sure. I wasn't sure at all.'

It was the worst thing she could have said in the circumstances. Kevin scowled and retreated back into sullen silence.

Tess risked another sip of her tea. It tasted better now that the hair was gone, but there was still something about it that was slightly off-putting. 'I suppose we'd better get down to business,' she said.

'Business?' said Lizzie. 'What business? I can't stand business. Never has anything to do with it. All them fields out there is mine, you know, and there's a track worn to my door with business people coming to try and buy them off me. What does they want with them, says I? I never seen a farmer in a suit like they wears.' She laughed suddenly, long and loud. 'I tells them to take their business back where they came from and keep it out of my fields.'

'But they must be worth a fortune!' said Kevin. 'Why don't you sell them?'

'What does I want with a fortune?' said Lizzie. 'I has a fortune already. I has a house of my own and my cats and hens and ducks and my Nancy. I has green fields all around me and I likes it that way. I lets the farmer use the land and he brings me everything I needs from the shops. What's that if it isn't a fortune?'

'But you could live anywhere. Have anything you want.'

'I lives somewhere already, and I has everything I wants. I did enough travelling for a dozen lifetimes before I married and came here. What would I want to be taking to the roads for at this time of my life?'

For a moment all three of them were silent, and then Lizzie looked at Kevin and said: 'Now I knows you isn't a rat.'

Kevin clicked his tongue and sighed in exasperation. Tess sniffed the tea and had a nasty suspicion that she knew who Nancy was, but she decided to ignore it and think of more important things. 'I didn't really mean that kind of business,' she said. 'I meant the business of why we're here. Why you told the rats to bring us here.'

'Oh,' said Lizzie. 'That's something different altogether, isn't it? That's not business. That's a matter of altogether more urgency, that is.'

91

'Right,' said Tess, gently. 'Then perhaps it'd be a good idea if we talked about it.'

'Oh, not now,' said Lizzie. 'No, that would never do.'

'But you just said it was urgent,' said Kevin.

'There's some things in life,' said Lizzie, 'that just can't be talked about when the sun is shining and the birds are singing. There's some things that aren't fit to be seen, or heard, or said, or even thought in the daytime, no matter how urgent they is.' She threw Kevin a disdainful glance. 'If you was a rat, you'd know that.'

Kevin got to his feet in exasperation and stuffed his hands into the pockets of his jeans. 'Then I'm going out for a walk,' he said.

'Hold on,' said Lizzie. 'We'll all go in a few minutes, and you can meet Nancy. But let's have another cup of tea first. After all, it isn't every day I has a couple of young Switchers to visit me.'

CHAPTER ELEVEN

When Tess and Kevin had finished their second cup of tea, Lizzie brought them out to the back of the cottage to meet Nancy. She was a white goat, as Tess had suspected, and she was tethered by a long rope in a scrubby field which lay between the orchard and the ruins of what was once a large and rather grand house.

'I lived there once,' said Lizzie, 'many years ago. But it was too big for me all on my own. I prefers the cottage.'

Nancy stayed where she was as the three of them approached, and chewed her cud with weary patience as Lizzie prattled over her. Tess had something of the same distaste for goats that she had for rats. They were the poor relations of the other farmyard animals, always bony, always hungry, always eating what they shouldn't.

'There now, Nancy,' Lizzie was saying. 'Isn't you

a lovely goat? You's the best little goat in the world, so you is. You's my poppet. This here is Kevin, and this one is Tessie. They's Switchers, both of them. You can believe me or not believe me, it makes no difference to me, but they is. Don't you wish you was a Switcher, Nancy? I bet you does.'

Nancy spotted a few green bramble leaves that she had missed earlier in the day and barged her way between her admirers to go and collect them. Lizzie looked a bit embarrassed. 'She's very fond of me, really,' she said. 'But she's shy of strangers. Was you ever a goat?'

Kevin nodded, but Tess shook her head.

'Really, Tess?' said Kevin. 'Were you never?'

'No.'

'But why not?'

'Oh, I don't know. I never fancied it, I suppose.'

'Goats is all right,' said Lizzie, 'except that they has poor manners. Not Nancy, of course. Nancy has manners.'

But Nancy wasn't there to display them. She had disappeared around the other side of a clump of brambles and was straining as hard as she could on her tether.

'They has brains, though,' Lizzie went on. 'Goats has wonderful brains. Ten times as many as sheep has.'

'It's true, Tess,' said Kevin. 'Why don't you try it, eh? We could go for a spin.'

'You can't do that,' said Lizzie. 'That's bad manners. You's only just arrived.'

'But we wouldn't be long, would we Tess? Just a quick spin.' He turned a little further towards her so that Lizzie couldn't see his face, then he widened his eyes in a pleading way, and Tess realised that she was being very slow. He just wanted an excuse to get away from the old woman for a while.

'Oh,' she said, 'all right. I suppose it could be interesting.'

'Now I thinks about it,' said Lizzie, 'it's not such a bad idea. You two could do me a favour.'

'How?' said Kevin, slightly suspicious.

'Easy. There's a few gardens around here that could do with a bit of a trim by a pair of goats. They's an awful toffee-nosed crowd, those ones up the road. They sneers at me if I's out for a stroll. They thinks they's better than me what with all their fancy cars and posh clothes and their business and all. The way they talks! Pfoo! You can smell it.'

Kevin looked at Tess with mischief shining in his eyes. 'Come on. What are you waiting for?'

Tess hesitated, thinking of her own mother and her love for her garden, wherever she found herself. And her father had a fancy car and good suits and worked in what Lizzie scornfully referred to as 'business'. If they had bought a house here instead of near the park, it might have been her own garden they were intending to 'trim'. She looked at Kevin. He was waiting eagerly for her reply. They were living on opposite sides of the tracks, she realised. And yet, they were alike.

'You thinks about things too much, young lady,' said Lizzie.

'That's true,' said Kevin. 'She's right for once.'

'You bad-mannered little pup!' said Lizzie. 'Go on, the two of you. Get out of here and eat some shrubs while you still has the chance.'

Kevin winked at Tess and looked around. They were well hidden, there among the bushes and trees.

'Make sure you isn't white, now, whatever else

you does,' said Lizzie. 'I don't want anyone coming blaming my Nancy.'

Tess was converted. While Lizzie watched, they made their change. Nancy stared around the edge of the bushes, astonished by the sudden appearance of two goats, one brown and one black.

'Ooh,' said Lizzie. 'That did me the power of good, that did. Makes me feel young again.'

But none of the three goats understood a word that she said.

Tess and Kevin hopped over the stone wall which bounded the scrubby field and into a small orchard. Behind them they could hear Nancy bleating pathetically at the loss of her new friends. For a moment or two they dithered, drawn quite strongly by the call of one of their own kind, but then they moved off among the trees.

Tess knew immediately why the others had been so keen that she try out being a goat. She had been sheep, cattle, horses, and recently she had quite often been a deer along with the others in the Phoenix Park, but none of them had felt quite like this. She had realised quite some time ago that her ability to experience the lives and beings of other creatures had an effect upon her personality as a human being. Each time she changed, something of what she learnt of the animal character stayed with her. She had developed quickness of reaction and awareness of her surroundings from the timid creatures of the fields and woodlands: the mice and squirrels and birds. From the farmyard animals she had learnt patience and a kind of resignation. Now, as she felt the full-blooded mischievous nature of the goat, its sharpness and its love of life and wildness and freedom, she became aware of how tame and careful her life had always been. The values that she had absorbed in her succession of comfortable homes and high-class schools had prejudiced her more deeply than she supposed. She had always avoided those animals which had characteristics that she perceived belonged to people of a different, inferior class. She had never experienced life as nature's scoundrels because of her fear of their human counterparts. Foxes, bats, crows and magpies, rats and stoats were all villainous creatures in her imagination. She had seen herself as being on the other side of an ongoing battle between good and evil.

Now things were beginning to change. Some of that change was certainly brought about by the days and nights of existence as a rat, when she had experienced for herself how it felt to live outside the law, despised and hunted. But there had been good things about it, too. She had discovered a new sense of courage, and a willingness to stand up and put that courage to the test when she had to. It had been exhilarating. She remembered how she had felt when Long Nose had bitten off her tail. She had been utterly fearless at that moment. It had been a very different feeling from her prim and petty resistance of Kevin when they had first met, and she suspected that she would have more useful resources to draw on now if a similar occasion arose. Her time as a rat, and even more so this new, exciting exploration of goatness, had given her a new understanding of Kevin. He was the kind of boy that she knew her parents would view with contempt. They would mistrust his guarded and suspicious manner and be shocked by his outbursts of temper and foul language. He could not, by any stretch of the imagination be classified as 'our kind of person'. But

Tess had been into his world now, and experienced it from the inside. She knew how all those alien and conflicting feelings arose in him, and how he could not live the life he did without them.

As Tess mused, she and Kevin were wandering slowly through the orchard and browsing on the leaves and twigs that fell within their reach. There were windfalls lying on the ground, apples and pears, but they were small and hard and bitter because of the long spell of cold. The leaves had suffered too, and those that had not already fallen were fibrous and dry, but to a goat they were as delicious as mature cheese.

Tess was surprised by some of the things that she was learning. She found that it was a myth that goats would eat anything. On the contrary, her senses of smell and taste were so refined that she could tell in an instant whether a moth had laid eggs on a leaf or a bird dropping had landed there, even a month ago. She would leave anything that was the slightest bit tainted where it was on the tree, and eat carefully around it. She found that she had a rich and rare sense of her own independence, and that, much as she enjoyed the pleasure of Kevin's company, she would depart from him without hesitation if the need arose. Nancy was still bleating on the other side of the hedge, and although Tess recognised that the sound held within it the desire for company, she knew that Nancy was calling for more than that. For stronger than every other emotion in a goat's heart is the love of freedom. Even here, amid the luxury of the rich lands where food would never be scarce, her goat soul longed for the high, craggy places of the world, places which are of no use to mankind but are the wild, windy kingdoms of the goats.

She and Kevin browsed their way peacefully to the edge of the orchard where two strands of barbed wire reinforced a neglected hedge. On the other side of it, cattle were grazing.

Kevin turned to Tess, and the sly, mischievous glint was in his eye again. Tess knew that for the first time, she was returning it. Together they slipped through the fence as if it wasn't there and strolled out into the field.

The cattle stared, disconcerted, and swung to face them, blowing blasts of steaming air from their nostrils. For the hell of it, Kevin jumped at them, and they spun on their heels with surprising speed and careered away across the field. A goat can't laugh, but Tess's heart stretched with mirth as she watched them. Stupid creatures. She despised them.

From where she and Kevin stood, they could see the neatly trimmed hedges of the nearest house, and with another quick glance of agreement, they set out towards it. Behind them the cattle recovered themselves and followed cautiously, closely grouped for safety.

The garden they had seen proved to be impenetrable. The cattle were held back by barbed wire which prevented them from getting anywhere near the hedge, but this was no deterrent to the goats. Nor was the hedge itself, for it was immature and full of gaps. It was fortified, however, by a heavy chain-link fence that even a goat could not work loose, and the two sides of the property that had no hedge were guarded by a high stone wall. Tess and Kevin spent a while nibbling at the protruding sprigs of the hedge, but there was no damage they could do, so they left it and stepped out into the road.

A goat can see over great distances and hear sounds

from miles away if it chooses to do so. In the normal course of events, however, it doesn't waste its attention in this way, but holds it to a much smaller radius around its immediate environment. It was not greatly surprising to either Tess or Kevin, therefore, when they found themselves stepping right into the path of an oncoming car. Nor was it particularly dangerous, because a goat thinks fast and acts faster. They sprang out of the way, feeling nothing more than a brief moment of excitement which made them jump and dance for a few yards along the verge, just for the joy of existence. The driver, however, got the fright of her life when the two shaggy goats appeared from nowhere, and she swerved much more violently than was necessary to avoid them. When she eventually calmed herself down and reversed out of the hedge, there was a hole in it that would have taken the two goats a week to eat.

Lizzie was standing with Nancy in the scrub behind her house.

'Hush, now, Nancy,' she was saying. 'Shhh. Don't you worry about them two.' She peered between the trees. 'Where is they, anyway? They's gone out of sight, Nancy. They's disappeared.'

As it happened, they had disappeared from Nancy's mind at around the same moment, leaving an abrupt vacuum which she filled by lying down in calm detachment and chewing her cud.

'There's no sign of them at all, Nancy,' said Lizzie. 'I suppose they's forgotten us.' She was right.

The next house the two goats met was surrounded by a stone wall with a wide coping stone running along the top. The wall was high enough to deter a stray cow or sheep, and more than high enough to contain the little terrier who yapped at them from the other side of the gates. He was one of those pampered little dogs that are somehow never to be found in farmyards or houses that have children, and he had never in his life encountered a boot or a rough hand. To protect him against the cold, he wore a red tartan jacket which made him feel a lot bigger and stronger than he ought to have done.

Kevin hopped effortlessly up on to the top of the wall, and Tess joined him. The little dog began to yap hysterically, halfway between the garden wall and the safety of the house, halfway between rage and terror. Inside the house, his mistress turned up the volume on the TV to cover the noise he was making. He hadn't been outside for long, and the fresh air was good for him.

Kevin jumped down without warning and ran full tilt at the dog, who paused for an instant in astonishment, then ran yelping around the side of the house. When Kevin gave up the chase and returned to nibble the top off a young Japanese willow, the terrier took up a position on the corner of the house and stood there, watching, with his tail between his legs.

The hours passed. Lizzie pottered around the house and garden and waited for her visitors to return. Around mid-afternoon she hacked a couple of parsnips out of the frozen ground of her garden, and collected carrots and a turnip from the potting shed where they were stored in boxes of sand.

'They shouldn't be hungry by the time they gets back,' she said to Nancy, 'but in my experience them teenagers always is, no matter how much you gives them.'

She brought the vegetables into the kitchen and

ran water into the sink. Outside the window the sky
had clouded over, and as she stood there wondering
if it was going to start snowing, she saw a policeman
coming down the path.

'Watch out, pussums,' she said. 'You'd better make
yourselves scarce. Here comes trouble.'

CHAPTER TWELVE

Lizzie went out into the little hallway of her house and stood beside the hat-stand. The policeman knocked on the door. Lizzie sat perfectly still and waited. Moppet offered to sit on her knee, but Lizzie shook her head and held up a hand to stop her. The policeman knocked again. Lizzie reached out and rocked the hat-stand gently, so that it made mysterious creaking and rattling sounds. Then she waited again. After a while, the policeman knocked a third time and called out: 'Hello?'

Lizzie stood up and opened the kitchen door and closed it. Then she did it again.

'Hello?' called the policeman. 'Anybody home?'

Lizzie went into the kitchen and over to the window, where she made a big show of peering round the folds of the curtain. The policeman saw her, smiled, and lifted his cap.

'Who is it?' said Lizzie.

'No need to be afraid,' said the policeman. 'I'd just like a word with you for a minute.'

'What about?'

'Can I come in? It's awful cold out here.'

Lizzie went back out into the hallway, where she rocked the hat-stand again, tidied up a pile of newspapers and re-arranged the coats on their pegs. There was another knock.

'All right!' said Lizzie, impatiently. 'I's coming.'

At last she opened the door. The policeman made as if to come inside, but Lizzie stood solidly in the doorway and didn't move. He sighed. 'Garda John Maloney,' he said. 'I believe you're known as Lizzie?'

'That's right, yes.'

'Are you by any chance missing two goats?'

'Goats?' said Lizzie. 'I hasn't got two goats, so how could I be missing them?'

'I see. Your neighbours led us to believe that you kept goats.'

'I has one goat. Just one. Her name is Nancy and she's tied up out in the brambles where she always is. Who told you I keeps goats? If anyone has any complaints about Nancy they can bring them to me theirselves or else keep their mouths shut. Nancy has better manners than the rest of that lot put together.'

'No, no,' said the Garda. 'It's nothing like that. It's just that we've got rather a problem, you see.'

And they had, too. In a more built-up area, there might have been some chance of driving those two goats into a corner, but out there in the leafy suburbs, they hadn't a chance.

Tess and Kevin, communicating by a combination of goat gestures and Rat images, were having a ball. Three members of the Garda Siochana and a gathering of neighbourhood residents were red in the face with exertion and fury, but remained utterly helpless. The goats dodged and scrambled, jumped walls and pushed through hedges. They split up without hesitation when they had to, and met up again as soon as they could, and they avoided traps with uncanny and infuriating ease. A local farmer had been called in to help and he had arrived full of cool confidence with his two best sheep dogs. But ten minutes after he arrived, the farmer was coaxing the terrified creatures back into his Land Rover and wondering if they would ever have the courage to work again. Few dogs are a match for a full-grown goat, and a dog that has worked all its life with timid, flock-minded sheep is particularly helpless when it finds itself suddenly looking into the unflinching yellow eyes of one of their brazen cousins.

Lizzie's policeman rejoined the others, leaving her to carry on making her stew. It was simmering away nicely when she heard the two goats returning, their hooves clattering on the frozen ground as they came careering down her path. They swung at full speed into the yard at the side of the house and veered in through the open door of the woodshed. A few seconds later, Tess and Kevin emerged laughing, their eyes still shining with mischief. They had barely got inside the door of the house when three men came running down the path. They stopped outside the front door, blowing hard. One of them was the Garda who had visited Lizzie earlier in the day. The other two were local residents. Lizzie knew one of them, a short heavily-built man wearing a tweed jacket and white breeches. He was a banker, and he had tried on more than one occasion to get her to part with her land.

She got up from her chair and threw open the window. 'Clear off!' she said. 'We got no goats in here. We doesn't want you coming galumphing in here and frightening our chickens and our Nancy. Clear off.'

'But we know they're around here now, Ma'm,' said Garda Maloney. 'We followed them down your track.'

'Well they isn't here now, and we wants to have our dinner in peace. So clear off.'

Garda Maloney restrained his rising temper with some difficulty. 'I'm sorry, Ma'm,' he said, 'but those two goats have been causing havoc up on the estate up there.'

'Neighbourhood, Garda, if you don't mind,' said the banker. 'It's not an estate.'

Maloney sighed in exasperation. 'Neighbourhood,' he said. 'They've been causing havoc in the neighbourhood and I must insist that we have a look round.'

'Have you got a search warrant?' asked Lizzie and, before there was time for an answer, she shut the window and turned her back on it.

'Come on, Lizzie,' said Tess. 'Why don't you let them look? They won't find anything.'

'I don't want them poking around in my sheds and my garden, that's why. And I wants to have my dinner.'

'We'll show them around, then, me and Kevin. We'll make sure they don't go poking around. OK, Kevin?'

'Not me,' said Kevin. 'I don't like peelers. You show them around if you like.'

'Right then, I will.'

Tess went out and opened the front door to the three men. They had started out towards the yard, intending to have a look around whatever Lizzie might say. Tess joined them. 'I'll show you around the place,' she said.

Garda Maloney smiled pleasantly and said: 'Very good of you,' but he looked at her just a little too long, and all at once, Tess's blood ran cold. What a fool she was. What a complete and utter fool. Of course her parents would have told the police that she was missing, no matter what she had said in her note to them. She turned away and tried to collect her thoughts. 'Where do you want to look first?' she said.

'Everywhere,' said the banker. 'We'll start in here.' He looked into the woodshed, and the other neighbourhood resident, who was tall and thin and dressed in a ridiculous one-piece down ski-suit, peered in over his shoulder. Garda Maloney, however, seemed more interested in Tess. 'Are you a relative of the old bird, then?' he asked.

'She's not an old bird,' said Tess, thinking like a rat, thinking like a goat, wishing that she hadn't been so snobbish and knew what it was to think like a fox. 'She's my Aunt Lizzie. My great-aunt, actually.'

'Ah,' said Maloney.

Tess led the way purposefully towards the henhouse. Lizzie had been around feeding shortly before, and the hens were still gathered around the trough, pecking at the last crumbs of their mash.

The policeman watched them, absently. 'Just down for the day, are you?'

'Yes. My father will be here later to pick us up.'

'I see. You and your brother, is it?'

'Yes.'

He nodded, casually. He wasn't sure where it was he'd seen her face, or even whether he had seen it at

107

all, but there was something about her that was ringing a bell. He could check it out later, when he got back to the station, but in the meantime it was important that he didn't raise her suspicions and drive her off.

'Nice part of the country, isn't it?' he said.

'Not particularly,' said Tess. 'I'd prefer to go to the sea if I had the choice.'

She led them on around the back. Nancy had been milked and put to bed in her own corner of the cowshed. 'If there were any more goats around,' said Tess, 'she'd be going ape. They don't like being on their own, goats don't. But you can look around in the field if you want to. And the orchard's through there.'

'Like animals, do you?' said Maloney.

'Not particularly. But Aunt Lizzie does. She never stops talking about them. There's nothing she doesn't know about animals. And,' she added, conspiratorially, 'nothing she doesn't tell you. Whether you want to know or not.'

Garda Maloney was beginning to think that he was mistaken. This girl was far too relaxed to be on the run. He smiled at her and she shrugged and lifted her eyes to heaven. 'Family duty,' she said.

The other two were just closing the door of the potting shed. 'Nothing there,' said the sporty one.

'No,' said Garda Maloney. 'I think we'd better call it off. With any luck they're on their way back to wherever they came from. If they do turn up again you can let us know, and we'll have another try in the morning.'

'You'll have to get your marksmen with tranquillizer darts,' said Tess.

Maloney laughed. 'Yes, we'll certainly need

someone like that. Let's hope that's the end of them, though.' He followed her back to the front of the house and started with the others back up the track. 'Give my regards to your aunt,' he said. Tess looked heavenwards again and ducked in through the doorway.

Kevin and Lizzie were sitting in the fireside chairs. Lizzie was eating stew out of a jelly mould and Kevin was eating his out of a small, dented saucepan with a bent handle.

'We left the dish for you,' said Lizzie, pointing to the hob beside the fire.

'Never mind that,' said Tess, looking daggers at Kevin. 'That was a great bit of thinking, that was, Mr Rat, Mr Street-wise, Mr Hedgehog-brain!' Kevin stared at her in amazement as she went on: 'And you have the nerve to tell me that I'm all right, Jack!'

'What are you talking about?'

'I'm talking about you, looking after Number One. You don't like peelers, oh, no. What about me, then?'

'Children!' said Lizzie. 'Stop squabbling! Where's your manners?'

'Oh, shut up about manners, Lizzie,' snapped Tess. 'And we're not children. This has nothing to do with you. I'm talking to this selfish little swine.'

Kevin was growing darker by the minute, like a heavy cloud, waiting to burst. 'I don't know what she's talking about,' he said.

'I'm talking about the Gardai! I'm talking about missing persons, descriptions, photographs. I'm talking about being on their records!'

Kevin swore. Lizzie looked as if she might object, but changed her mind.

'You should have thought of that, Kevin,' said Tess. 'You should have warned me.'

'It isn't my fault! It was your idea. "Oh, la di da, come on, Kevin, let's show the nice gentlemen around." I didn't want to have anything to do with it!'

'But I don't think like you do. I wasn't brought up like that. It's your job to think of things like that!'

'And who do you think you are? Telling me what my job is!' He glared at her with such contempt that her anger evaporated and left a dull ache in the pit of her stomach.

'Come on, now, girls and boys,' said Lizzie. 'Stop arguing and eat your dinner while it's hot.'

Kevin poked around lethargically with his spoon. 'Did he recognise you?' he asked, sulkily.

'I'm not sure. I think he did, but I might have put him off the scent.'

'Not to worry,' said Lizzie. 'No sense in getting edgy, is there?' She handed Tess her stew in the dish they had saved for her. Tess looked at it gloomily. It had DOG written on the side.

CHAPTER THIRTEEN

Lizzie refused to let Tess and Kevin help her wash up, even though they really meant it when they offered. So they sat beside the fire and watched the flames licking round the kettle as she clattered around behind them.

'Funny thing,' said Tess, emerging from her own thoughts, 'but I can still feel the place where Long Nose bit off my tail. Ridiculous, isn't it, when I haven't even got a tail.'

'Like a phantom limb, I suppose,' said Kevin. 'You were lucky it was only your tail, though. If it had been your hand or your nose or something you'd be in a bit of a mess now, wouldn't you?'

'What do you mean?'

'Didn't you realise that? If you get injured it doesn't just go away, you know.'

Tess did know. She had often noticed that scratches and bruises from her animal exploits stayed with her when she Switched back to herself. But it had never occurred to her that something more serious might happen.

Kevin was unlacing his shoe. 'You probably didn't notice but I only have three toes on this foot. I got the other two stuck in a crack in a drain pipe once, and there was no way to get out except to just keep pulling.'

'Yeucch!' said Tess.

Kevin took off his sock. It was dark and stiff with dirt, and Tess was about to pass a comment on it when she saw his foot, and forgot about it. The last two toes, the smallest ones, were missing. It was slightly grotesque. 'Doesn't matter what I am,' he said. 'If it has toes, those two are missing.'

Tess thought about what he had said, about how it would be if she had lost a hand, or even a whole arm or leg. Kevin had started rubbing at the dirt between his remaining toes. 'Put it away, will you?' she said. 'It's disgusting.'

He shrugged and pulled his sock back on. Behind them, Lizzie closed a cupboard door with an emphatic bang.

Tess leaned back in her chair and closed her eyes. She was suddenly very tired. Up until now it had all been a kind of a dream for her. While she was a rat, it had been difficult to think about human matters, and then there had been the meeting with Lizzie and the reckless, capricious delight of their goat afternoon. But the episode with the policeman, and now Kevin's foot, had brought her back to earth. All through her childhood her strange ability had been something that was private and carefully contained. It was safe, that other world, and it had always been tidily separate from her 'real' life. But suddenly, over the last few days, it seemed to have moved beyond her control. She was no longer at all certain of who she was and what she was doing. Kevin was elusive and confusing. At times she was so sure that she had at last found the companion that she had been looking for all her life, and then something would shift and he seemed to be at odds with her, almost an enemy.

And then there was Lizzie. What was anyone to make of Lizzie? It had all seemed to make some kind of sense when they set out, as though there was a mission for them, but in the light of police searches and sleepless parents pacing the floor at home it seemed like madness. She didn't know what was real and what was not. She was suddenly, horribly afraid that they might all be mad.

'Tess?' said Kevin.

'Yes?'

He was looking at her carefully, and his concern was evident in his face. Here was yet another Kevin, one that she hadn't seen before now. But how did she know if she could trust him?

'Are you all right?' he said.

'I just don't really know what's going on.'

'I feel like that sometimes, too. But you know there's nothing to keep you here, don't you? You can go home right now if you want to.'

Tess looked across at Lizzie. She was drying the last of the cutlery with a grimy tea-towel, and Tess noticed that she was doing it rather quietly and thoughtfully, listening to their conversation. Her face was different, somehow, as though she were no longer trying to keep a distance between herself and the youngsters. The games were over. All three of them were ready, it seemed, to be serious.

113

'Maybe we should just hear what Lizzie has to say,' said Kevin, 'and then we can decide what to do. What do you say?'

Tess relaxed. She nodded and sighed, and settled more comfortably into her chair. As if in approval of her decision, a tabby cat hopped lightly up beside her and curled itself up on her lap.

Back at the Garda barracks, John Maloney carried his dinner tray over to a free table in the cafeteria. It was more usual for him to go home when his shift was over, because he preferred to cook for himself and was quite good at it. But today he was too exhausted to even think about it. His mind was littered with images of goats which did improbable things, and he couldn't shut them out, no matter what he did. He sat down and began to eat, but he couldn't taste the food. However hard he tried, he found he couldn't be concerned about whatever public menace those goats were causing. There were far more serious matters in police duty. But what irritated him was the feeling of having been defeated by a pair of dumb beasts.

Out of the corner of his eye, John spotted Garda Griffin leaving the check-out with his tray. He looked away quickly, but he knew he had been seen and that Griffin was coming to join him. Now he was in for a ragging. Oliver Griffin was one of those people who can never take anything seriously in life, or at least, pretend that they can't. John had worked with him for a while in a different part of town, and they had spent many a night on patrol together. In a crisis, Oliver was about the finest person he had ever worked with, because nothing, not even the most tense of situations, could deprive him of his sense of the ridiculous. There were times when John had found knots in his stomach being dissolved by unexpected laughter. But in the normal run of things, Oliver's eternal quipping was intolerable.

'Tough day, eh?' he said now, as he unloaded his tray. This was his breakfast. He had just arrived for the night shift. 'Job getting your goat?'

'Don't start, Olly,' said John. 'I'm not in the mood.'

'Ah, come on. It can't be that bad. Bit of sport for a change. Headline news. Big game hunting in Tibradden, County Dublin.'

'I wouldn't care if I never saw another goat in my life. If you'd had to deal with them you wouldn't be laughing.'

'Want to bet?'

John laughed despite himself and felt a lot better. 'The worst of it was,' he said, 'the little sods seemed to be enjoying themselves. You'd swear they were taking the mickey out of us.'

'Probably were,' said Griffin. 'And I hear you had an encounter with the Lady of the Manor.'

'Who?'

'Old Lizzie.'

'Oh, her. Do you know her, then? Some character, eh?'

'Yes. Sitting on a fortune and still living like a gypsy.'

'A fortune? What makes you think that?'

'All that land. All those fields around there. They all belong to her. About eighty acres, I think. Imagine what that's worth.'

'Phew!' said John.

Oliver finished his pudding and went on to his main course. John had seen it enough times now not to be surprised, but it still made him feel slightly queasy. 'Yes,' Oliver said. 'The developers are hovering round her like flies, but she won't sell. "I has all I needs," ' he mimicked, ' "and I needs all I has." '

The accuracy of the imitation had John laughing again. 'You must have been trying to buy the place yourself.'

'Na. I've known Lizzie for years. She's a great old character, really. There's more to her than meets the eye. I often stop in there for a cup of tea when no one's looking.'

'Naughty, naughty.'

'Public relations, John, public relations. And she's lonely out there on her own. Where's the harm in it?'

'I suppose so.' John put down his knife and fork and started peeling an orange, trying not to look at the red puddles of ketchup on his friend's plate.

'Besides,' Oliver went on, 'I feel sorry for her in a way, with half of Dublin's biggest speculators waiting around for her to die. Imagine thinking that the only thing the world wants from you is your death, eh? And like I said, she's not bad company once you get to know her. She still tells me to clear off whenever she sees me, but if you ignore her she gets quite friendly sometimes.'

'Hardly my idea of fun,' said John.

'Ah, don't be so cynical.' Oliver paused to slurp at his mug of tea, then went on: 'You can't get fun out of life unless you give it a chance, you know. I'll be sorry when Lizzie does snuff it, but I'll get a great laugh out of it, too. Can you imagine the faces of those Ballsbridge dudes when they find out she's left the lot to a home for retired donkeys?'

'Donkeys?'

'Well, she probably will, you know. Or goats. That'd be a good one. I wonder what the "Neighbourhood Residential Committee" would think of that?'

John smiled, despite himself. 'She couldn't do that, though,' he said. 'Her relatives would be entitled to collect, wouldn't they?'

'What relatives? Lizzie hasn't got any relatives.'

'Yes she has. I met her niece today, or her great-niece or something.'

Oliver was shaking his head with a certainty that infuriated John. 'Nope,' he said. 'Not Lizzie's, you didn't. She told me herself that she has no one left in England and she never had a family of her own here. "I's all alone in the world and I likes it that way. I's no time at all for people, I hasn't. They takes up too much space." '

'Well, you're wrong this time, Olly. I – ' He stopped abruptly. The gentle tapping of suspicion that he'd had when he first saw Tess had become a mighty hammering. 'Drink your tea, Olly,' he said as he stood up.

'Why? Where are you going?'

'We're going, Olly. Missing Persons.'

'I knowed it was going to happen,' said Lizzie. 'I knowed it as soon as I read about it in the newspaper.'

Kevin looked across at Tess and raised a quizzical eyebrow. Tess shrugged.

'I doesn't get newspapers to read,' Lizzie went on. 'I hasn't any interest in all them politics and wars all over the place. I gets the papers from Mr Quigley. That's the farmer who owns those cattle. He gives me his old ones to light the fire. I hasn't any time for fire-lighters. They smells like motor cars.'

Tess stroked the cat on her lap. She was relaxed now that she was sure she would soon be home. She didn't know what she was going to say to her parents, but she would think about that later.

'Sometimes I looks at them before I scrunches them up,' said Lizzie, 'and sometimes I doesn't. I always knows that if something's important it'll catch my eye. How can something be important if you has to go looking for it, that's what I says. So I wasn't surprised when I saw it.'

'Saw what?' said Kevin.

'About that drilling up there in the North Pole. I knew what would happen if they started all that carry-on. But people never thinks about what might happen. They wants oil and they wants money and cars and fire-lighters, and as soon as they's got them what does they do but want more of them? So I said to myself, I'll warn them. That's what I'll do.'

She got up a little stiffly and went over to the kitchen sink. The night had fallen, so she drew the curtains, and for a while the room was soft with firelight. Lizzie rummaged around in a drawer until she found what she was looking for, then turned on the light and came back to her seat.

'There,' she said, handing a piece of brown paper to Kevin. 'That's only a copy, mind. I always keeps a copy of letters. Not that I ever writes any these days. The real one was on good paper. The best you can buy, Mr Quigley said.'

Tess leant across and read the letter over Kevin's shoulder. At the top it said, 'To The Taoiseach And the Tanaiste of The Dail, KilDare Street, Dublin. From Mrs Elizabeth Larkin of TiBradden, Co. Dublin, OWNER of Much Land and VaLuable ProPerty.

'They has to know that you's someone,' said Lizzie,

118

proudly, 'before they takes any notice of you. They doesn't pay no attention to commoners.'

Tess and Kevin read on. The writing was large and untidy, with small letters and capitals all jumbled up together.

'YoU Cant alloW ThoSe comPanY PeoPle to Go driLLing UP in the NorTh PoLe. OR elSe YoU WiLL LeT ouT The krooLs and Then YoU WiLL Be SoRRY.
　　YoURS finaLLY,
　　　Lizzie Larkin.
PS PLeaSe Send a coPY to The comPanY ThaT iS doing The dRiLLing becauSe I don'T have There adReSS.

Tess sat back in her chair. She knew without doubt where that letter would have ended its life, and she wondered how many similar letters from cranks passed through government offices in the course of a year. She sighed and sat back. The cat made a tour of her lap and resettled itself.

'Well?' said Lizzie. 'What does you think?'

'It's a good letter, Lizzie,' said Tess. 'It's very good. But the trouble is, people don't . . . I mean people in government don't very often take much notice of letters.'

'Whoever they're from,' Kevin added.

'You's right, there,' said Lizzie, 'and you knows why that is, doesn't you?'

'Why?'

'Because they thinks they knows it all, that's why.'

Tess's face was among the first that John Maloney saw in the room where the files on missing persons were kept. 'There she is,' he said to Oliver Griffin. 'I knew I'd seen her before.'

'Who?'

'Lizzie's niece.'

'But Lizzie hasn't got a niece,' said Oliver.

'I believe you, Olly,' said John. 'Now let's go.'

'People in general,' said Lizzie, 'thinks they knows it all. And if they doesn't know it then they puts it in front of a microscope or a periscope and makes it bigger, and there's things in this world should be left the same size they always was and not interfered with at all.'

Tess looked at her watch. She would be home before her parents went to bed.

'They doesn't use plain common sense,' Lizzie went on. 'They sees things that is plain and simple and they goes to great lengths to make them as difficult and complicated as they can. They sees that the world is cold at both ends so they comes up with a cock and bull story about how we's all spinning around in the air like a football. But you can throw a football around all day and it never gets colder at the ends than it is in the middle.'

'I don't think it's the spinning that causes the Poles to be cold, Lizzie,' said Kevin. 'I think it's the way the earth tilts.'

'Tilts?'

'Yes. It's sort of leaning as it goes around, so some bits don't get as much sun.'

'And where did you find that out?'

'I read about it in the library.'

Lizzie got up angrily, spilling two cats on to the floor. 'That's exactly what I's talking about,' she said. 'What does a nice boy like you want to go poking

120

around libraries for? Nosing out all kinds of nonsense you has no use for? Then when you gets a chance of learning what you needs to know, there's no room left in your head for it.' She strode over to the fire. 'And you get a move on!' she said to the kettle, giving it a poke.

'Why don't you tell us anyway, Lizzie?' said Tess. 'About your krools.'

'My krools?' said Lizzie. 'They isn't *my* krools. They isn't anybody's krools. They's just krools.'

'Well, tell us about them anyway, will you?'

'We's too far south to know about them here, that's all. They knows about them in Finland and Norwiegerland, and they knows about them in Siberia, except they has a different name for them. They's big, cold, flat things like jellyfishes, and they sleeps in their own ice just like the grizzly bear sleeps in his own fat. They sleeps for thousands and thousands of years and while they's sleeping they doesn't bother the rest of the world. But if they gets woken up they gets hungry, and off they goes across the world, filling theirselves up again.'

Tess glanced at Kevin, hoping to share a silent joke, but he was gazing solemnly into the fire.

'What about the other cold places, Lizzie?' he said. 'Like the Alps and the Himalayas.'

'Those mountains, you mean? But they's cold because they's high up in the sky! Everyone knows that!'

There was a long silence. Tess moved her chair a bit closer to the fire. Outside the wind was getting up and she could hear the cat-flap on the outside door rattling. At last, Lizzie sighed and shook her head sadly. 'You doesn't believe me,' she said. 'I was afraid you wouldn't.'

The others said nothing, because there was nothing they could say. From time to time, the wind made the chimney give a great pull which sucked flames up to hug the kettle.

'You doesn't believe in krools,' said Lizzie, 'and I suppose you doesn't believe in them dinosaurs, either.'

'But dinosaurs are different,' said Tess. 'There's evidence for the dinosaurs. You can still see their bones.'

'We doesn't know what it was left them bones behind,' said Lizzie, 'and krools has no bones to leave, in any case. But if those dinosaurs was there, where are they now?'

Kevin was becoming irritable. 'Everyone knows that, Lizzie. They became extinct.'

'And does everyone know what happened to make them extinct?'

'There was a shift in the earth's crust and something changed in the atmosphere. That's what happened.'

'There was earthquakes,' said Lizzie, 'and they woke up the krools, that's what happened. And the krools was hungry when they woke up, that's what happened. And the krools ate up all the dinosaurs that wasn't already dead and buried. That, young clever clogs, is what happened.'

Tess felt a shiver run up her spine. It was the kind of shiver she sometimes got when she read a good poem or heard a piece of music that touched on some deep and delicate truth that everyday language didn't reach. There was another long silence, and then Lizzie said: 'It's snowing. I can smell it.'

The two policemen parked their car some distance

from the top of Lizzie's track. Before they got out, they emptied all the loose change from their pockets and put it in the glove compartment. Oliver took the car key off its ring and left the others under the seat. There must be nothing that would clink or jangle. They intended their approach to be silent.

Lizzie's kettle was starting to sing. This time she knew where the milk was and she had already emptied the teapot but even so there was plenty for her to bustle with. 'Switchers isn't what they used to be,' she said. 'There was things we knew in those days that you doesn't even begin to know.'

'But what could we do, Lizzie?' said Tess. 'Even if we did . . . I mean, even if it was true about the krools?'

'It is true,' said Lizzie.

'Even if it is,' Tess repeated. 'What could me and Kevin do about it?'

Lizzie thought for a moment, swirling hot water around the teapot. 'I doesn't know exactly,' she said. 'I's been thinking about it a lot, and I doesn't know exactly. But I know this. Switchers has powers that you hasn't even dreamed about. You hasn't even begun to know what you can do.'

'What do you mean?' said Kevin, suddenly interested.

Lizzie emptied the hot water into the sink. 'I knows all the things you two has been. I can see it. You could see it, too, if you was watching properly. And I knows that you hasn't done half the things I did when I was your age. You hasn't a notion of how much you can do.'

'What can we do, Lizzie?'

'Even I doesn't know that. But now it's too late I

123

wishes I had my time all over again. We all thinks we has all the time in the world when we's young. And sometimes we doesn't push ourselves hard enough. We doesn't use our imagination, so we never really gets to the bottom of ourselves. Sometimes we doesn't know what we could be until it's too late.'

Kevin was listening intently, but Tess's mind was beginning to wander. Lizzie sounded too much like her parents and her teachers, sounding off about how young people didn't make the most of themselves. She looked at her watch again. She would have time for tea, she decided, and while she was drinking it she could try and work out a way to get Kevin on his own and arrange another meeting. She didn't want to go home without being sure that she was going to see him again.

Lizzie poured water on to the tea leaves.

And then the knock came at the door.

CHAPTER FOURTEEN

'Lizzie?' called Oliver from the front door. 'Don't worry. It's only me, Garda Griffin.' He knocked again, without waiting. 'But don't waste my time now, you hear? Open up the door.'

'All right, all right,' said Lizzie, making her way through the hall. 'I's coming.' She turned on the outside light, opened the door, and peered shrewishly at Oliver. 'What does you want at this hour? Scaring old ladies in the middle of the night! You ought to be ashamed of yourself.'

Oliver stepped past her into the hall and went ahead of her into the kitchen.

'Sorry, Lizzie,' he said. 'But it's official business this time.' He was both relieved and disappointed to find that there was no sign of any young runaways.

'Well, I don't understand it,' said Lizzie, following him into the room and closing the door behind them. 'I never in my life heard so much fuss about a pair of goats. And look at you! You should have knocked those boots on the step before you came in. You's dragging snow all over my floor.'

'Sorry about that,' said Oliver. 'But this time it's not about goats. It's those two youngsters we're looking for. The ones who were here earlier on.'

'Why? What's they done?'

'Can I get through this way, Lizzie? To the back?'

'What you want to go out there for? There's nothing out there.'

Oliver went through the scullery and into the back porch, where he opened the door for John.

'What's he doing there?' asked Lizzie. 'What's going on? Why can't he use the front door like everyone else?'

'We're just being careful,' said Oliver. 'In case anyone slipped out the back.'

'Who's going to slip out the back? What's you talking about?'

'I don't think they're here,' said Oliver to John. 'But you'd better take a look upstairs, just in case.'

'No, he hadn't,' said Lizzie indignantly. 'And don't you talk above my head as if I wasn't there! I's smaller than you is, but I's older than the two of you put together and you has no right to barge into my house as if you owned the place.'

Oliver sighed. 'I'm sorry, Lizzie. You're right. We're just a bit worked up because we had trouble with your path in the dark. One of your trees has confiscated John's cap and won't give it back.'

'I'll have a word with it in the morning,' said Lizzie.

'It's all right. I'm sure we'll find it on the way back. We didn't use our torches on the way down because we didn't want anyone to see us coming.'

'You was sneaking up on us, wasn't you?'

'Who's us?' said John, casually.

'Me and Nancy and the pussums,' said Lizzie. 'They was sneaking up on us, pussums, so they was. Looking for that nice young boy and girl who was here. What's they done, anyway?'

'We don't think they've done anything very wrong, Lizzie, but the young girl has run away from home and her parents are very worried about her.'

'Oh, dear,' said Lizzie. 'And I thought they was such a nice pair of youngsters. Is you sure it was her?'

'Positive,' said John.

'Then they told me a pack of lies. I always says you can never trust them teenagers.'

'How long have they been gone?' said Oliver.

'Let me see, now. They left just after this young man was here looking for the goats, I think.'

'But maybe you're expecting them back?' said John.

'No. Why should I?'

'Well, I was just wondering why you have three cups set out on the table.'

There they were, three odd cups and three odd saucers with a jug of milk and a bowl of sugar beside them.

'Three cups,' said Lizzie. 'They's observant, isn't they, pussums, eh? Still, I suppose they has to be. That's what they's trained for. But maybe they's too clever, eh? Maybe there's things about an old woman's life that they didn't ought to ask?'

John felt a slight chill and looked around the room. The little old house was creepy enough at night, even with the lights on. He hadn't enjoyed the dark walk down the lane one bit.

'We have to ask, I'm afraid, Lizzie,' said Oliver. 'That's our job.'

'They has to ask, pussums. But maybe they'd prefer if they didn't know?' She went over to the table and poured a drop of milk into each of the three cups. 'I does this every night before I goes to bed. And in the morning, when I gets up, I does it again.' She poured the tea and spooned in sugar. Then she put one of the cups in front of her and one to each side. 'This one's for me,' she said, 'and this one's for my husband George, who went off over the sea to fight in the war and never came home. And this one here is for our little daughter Kitty who died before she was even born.'

John shuffled his feet in embarrassment. The cottage had suddenly become saturated by the most appalling sense of loneliness. Even Oliver was silent.

'So,' said Lizzie, brightly. 'Up you goes and take a look around upstairs. Go on with you.'

'That's all right, Lizzie,' said Oliver. 'It won't be necessary.'

'Indeed it will. You has a job to do and you's required to do it. And I has a reputation to protect. I won't let anyone have cause for doubt in case they says, "Maybe she was hiding those two young criminals all along." Go on. Up you goes.'

'They're not criminals, Lizzie,' said Oliver.

'Never mind.' She bustled them out towards the hallway. 'The bulb is blown in the hall but there's a switch at the top of the stairs. Go on.'

The two policemen obeyed, sheepishly, and thumped up the narrow stairs. They stayed there only long enough to poke their heads around the doors of the two small bedrooms, then they came down again.

'Sorry about all this, Lizzie,' said Oliver. 'We didn't mean to disturb you.'

'You's more disturbed than I is, by the looks of

things,' said Lizzie. 'Why don't you sit yourselves down and drink these cups of tea now they're poured?'

John blanched, and even Oliver's cast-iron stomach became momentarily queasy. 'It's very kind of you,' he said, 'but I think we should move on.' He reached down and picked up a ginger tomcat who had been asleep in Lizzie's chair. 'I see you have a new cat?'

'I has two new cats,' said Lizzie. 'So you needn't be minding about me and my little habits. I has all the company I needs.'

Oliver put the cat down and led the way to the front door. 'Did they say where they were going when they left?'

'They said they was going home. "Time we was going home," that's all.'

Oliver retied his scarf and pulled his coat tight around him. 'That's where Garda Maloney's going, too. Wish I was. Goodnight, Lizzie.'

'Goodnight.'

The two men lit their flashlamps and were soon hidden from sight by the blizzard. Lizzie closed the door and went back to the kitchen, passing on her way the army parka and down jacket that were hanging among her coats in the hall. 'That was a close shave, pussums,' she said. But she got no response, not even a glance. Every one of the six cats in the room was sound asleep. Lizzie looked at the three cups on the table. For a moment the loneliness still lying in the air closed in and settled on her heart.

Tess woke shortly before dawn. The fire had died down during the night and the room had become chilly. She yawned, then stood up and stretched, reaching out as far as her paws would go and catching them on the upholstery of the chair to check that her claws were sharp.

The other cats had gone on an inspection of the night and not yet returned. Someone was sitting in a chair pulled up close to the fireplace and Tess slipped down on to the floor with a view to finding a lap and getting warm enough to sleep again. But halfway there her other mind woke up, and she realised that it was Kevin.

She Switched, feeling rather glad that she hadn't made it as far as his knee before she realised. He jumped slightly as she appeared, then nodded briefly and returned his attention to the fire.

A few dry logs had been propped up in the embers, but they hadn't been there long enough to light. Kevin was leaning forward with his elbows on his knees, and it was clear that he was deep in thought. Tess pulled up another chair and spread her hands above the grate. 'Cold,' she said.

Kevin stirred and sighed but said nothing.

'I fell asleep,' said Tess. 'Cats are great, aren't they? There's nothing to beat a cat for comfort. I sometimes think that if I had to choose, I'd choose a cat.'

Still Kevin said nothing, but went on gazing into the fire. Tess looked at her watch. It was six-thirty. 'I meant to get home last night,' she said. 'But then I fell asleep. There's no point in going now because nobody'll be awake yet. Do you think Lizzie would mind if we made a cup of tea?'

Kevin threw her an icy look. 'Do what you want,' he said. 'Who cares?'

'You know what's wrong with you, don't you?' said Tess. 'You spent too long being a lizard. Personally I never found it much fun.'

Kevin's eyes blazed. 'And you spent too much time

130

being a flaming magpie, yakking away to yourself and getting on everybody's nerves.'

Tess swore in Rat, and Kevin swore back. The scores were level, and for a while they both stayed quiet. Small flames began to catch the base of the logs and creep up their sides. Behind them one of the cats came in through the scullery door, but went out again when she realised that neither of them was Lizzie.

At last, Kevin stood up and went over to the window. He pulled back the curtain and looked out into the darkness. Snowflakes were falling gently against the glass and little drifts had formed against the bottom of each pane. 'I don't mind if you go home, Tess,' he said. 'I won't blame you.'

'What do you mean?'

He let the curtain fall and came back to sit at the fire. 'I'd probably do the same thing if I were you,' he said.

'I don't understand,' said Tess. 'What else is there to do?'

'I'm going up there.'

'Up where?'

'To the Arctic.'

Tess stared, wide-eyed. 'What? To look for Lizzie's krools?'

'Why not?'

'Because . . . because it's crazy, Kevin, it's a laugh. You really believe they're up there? Giant slugs that cause ice ages?'

Kevin shrugged. 'I don't know.'

'Well, I do,' said Tess. 'Lizzie's not so bad when you get to know her, but she's not all there, you know. She's not the full shilling.'

'Is that right?'

'Of course it is. You saw that letter. She's harmless, but she's mad.'

'And what about us, Tess?'

'What about us?'

'Well, what would people call us if we told them what we do? What we are?'

'We don't tell them, though, do we?'

'Of course not. But why? What would they think if we did?'

Tess said nothing, not wanting to fall into the trap.

'Come on,' Kevin went on. 'What if you were to tell your parents where you've been for the last few days? What would they say?'

'They'd probably say I'd fallen in with a bad crowd and taken some funny drugs.'

'They might. But I'd say the chances are they'd take you to see a psychiatrist, wouldn't they? If you insisted on sticking to the truth.'

'Anyhow,' said Tess, 'that's different.'

'Why?'

'Because it is. Because we know the truth, and if the worst came to the worst we'd be able to prove it. But this business about krools is ridiculous.'

Kevin said nothing. The fire was burning brightly now and sending out sparks on to the hearth. Tess got up and filled the kettle at the sink. Outside in the trees, the first birds were beginning to complain about the weather. 'Besides,' she said, as she hung the kettle on its hook, 'even if it was true, which it isn't, what could we do? You and me?'

Kevin leant back in his chair. 'That's the whole point, Tess,' he said. 'That's why I'm going.'

'What do you mean?'

'Well, if you really want to know, I'm as doubtful about this krools business as you are. I wouldn't be going either, if it hadn't been for what Lizzie said about . . .' He paused.

'About what?'

'What was it that she said, exactly? Something about not knowing what we could do. Not knowing half of what we can do.'

'But we know that anyway, Kevin. Or I do, anyway. We're living in Ireland, you know? We can't go around the place being elephants and kangaroos and flamingos, can we? It'd be ridiculous.'

'I don't think that's what Lizzie was talking about.'

'What was she talking about, then?'

'I don't know. But when she said that, I had the strangest feeling all of a sudden. I can't really explain it, but it was as if I knew for certain that she was right, and that there was all this strength and power in me that I didn't know how to use. I felt like I was filled with it, just waiting to explode, except that I didn't know how to set it off. There was nowhere for it to go.'

Tess said nothing; not because she thought it was stupid, but because she was remembering times when she had felt like that herself.

'It's different for you,' Kevin went on. 'You still have a couple of years to play around with this thing, you know? Find out what you can do. But I don't. I don't have much time left at all.'

The kettle came to life with a long, low moan. Tess refrained from giving it a poke. 'I can understand that,' she said. 'But it still doesn't explain why you should want to go off on a wild goose chase up into the Arctic.'

'It does, though,' said Kevin. 'You remember the time when we were in the waste-ground and you didn't want to turn into a rat?'

133

'Yes.'

'Well, it's like that a lot of times in life, isn't it? Maybe you would never have taken that step if the dog hadn't come along and made you do it. But you did do it, didn't you? You could have flown away, but you didn't.'

'So what?' said Tess. 'To be quite honest with you, I'm not sure at this moment what good it did me.'

'Well, maybe it did and maybe it didn't,' said Kevin. 'And maybe not everything that happens ends up getting you what you want, or what you think you want. Maybe things happen for some other reason that we don't see straight away, or maybe they happen for no reason at all. You could spend your whole life worrying about why things turn out the way they do and you still wouldn't be able to fix it so that they always did you some good.'

'I didn't mean it like that,' said Tess, 'and you know I didn't.'

She gave in to her impulse to poke the kettle. It swung slowly backwards and forwards for a while, but instead of singing louder, it went silent again.

'I know you didn't,' said Kevin, 'and even if you did, it wouldn't matter. The thing is, I want to go. Everything in me wants to go, even though I know there probably aren't any krools.'

'But I don't think you're seeing things straight, Kevin. I mean, even if we . . . even if you did decide to go, how would you get there? All the animals are coming south, I've seen it on the news. The conditions up there are impossible for anything to live in.'

'But that's the whole point!' Kevin leant forward to look at her more directly, and his eyes were bright with excitement. 'Don't you see? Because sometimes

134

we don't know what we can do until we have to do it. And if we always stick with what's easy and what's safe, then we'll never be made to find out. I'm not sure that I'd want to save the world, Tess, even if I thought there was anything to save it from, even if I could. But I want to know what I'm capable of, before it's too late.'

Tess heard Lizzie's footsteps on the stairs. Somehow the cats did, too, because they began to come in from outside, one at a time, shaking the snow from their paws.

'What's you two doing up so early?' said Lizzie.

'Just chatting,' said Kevin.

Lizzie put her hand on her hip and used it as a lever to straighten her back. 'Ooh. I's getting as stiff as a poker, so I is. All this cold weather doesn't do me any good. Hasn't they fed you yet, pussums? Hasn't they even given you a drop of milk? They's sitting there with all their important chatting to be done and you's all starving with the cold and with the hunger.'

The cats purred and wound themselves around her ankles. She poked the kettle, which dribbled on to the fire but began, a bit reluctantly, to sing. 'And has you come to any decisions with all that chat?' she went on. 'Is you going to go sledging or play snowballs in the park?'

'I'm going north, Lizzie,' said Kevin.

Lizzie straightened up as though she were twenty-one again. 'I knew it,' she said to the cats. 'I told you, didn't I? He may not be all rat, I said, but he's got rat in him.'

Kevin laughed, and suddenly Tess felt remote from them, as though she had been excluded. She realised then for the first time that if Kevin went alone up to the North Pole, she might never see him again. It was possible that he would come back and look her up in her house in the park, but what if he didn't? And what if it kept on snowing, and they had to leave and go to Greece like the Sheehans? How would he find her then?

'And what about you, Tessie?' said Lizzie. 'What's you going to do?'

It hit Tess, then, with no warning, that expansive feeling which was so strong that it was hardly bearable. She was suddenly certain of her own strength and resourcefulness, and suddenly afraid of nothing.

'I, Lizzie,' she said, 'is going with him.'

CHAPTER FIFTEEN

Lizzie made pancakes for breakfast, which Tess and Kevin ate much faster than she could cook in the old black skillet. They drowned them in melted butter and golden syrup and ate them with their fingers, and nobody complained about the drips.

'Like Pancake Tuesday,' said Tess.

'Yes,' said Kevin, 'but let's hope we don't have to give up too much for Lent.'

Tess thought about the blizzards outside that they would be meeting for as long as they continued north. She still had no idea how they were going to travel, and her parents were trying to edge their way into her consciousness, threatening to destroy her resolve.

As though she were reading Tess's mind, Lizzie said: 'You thinks too much, girl. I's told you that before. And it's nothing but a waste of time. If you's finished with that pancake you better go over to the sink and wash your hands, because you isn't getting any more. I hasn't had one at all yet, and I's getting weak with the hunger watching you two stuff your faces.'

Tess got up and went over to the sink. Kevin followed. The water was icy cold and only hardened the butter on her fingers, but most of it came off on the towel. She handed it on to Kevin and looked out of the window. The snow had already made little ledges of itself on top of every level spot it could find. Every branch, twig and leaf bowed in submission beneath its weight. Tess could no longer remember the elated sense of power that she had felt before breakfast when she made the decision to go.

'Well? What's you waiting for?' said Lizzie. 'Off you go, get your coats on. There's no sense in standing around.'

Kevin went out into the hall and came back with their jackets. Tess put hers on, feeling like a small child who has been told to go out and play and has no choice in the matter. But it wasn't Lizzie, she knew, who was driving her to do it, or Kevin. It was her own pride. She was more afraid of letting herself down than of losing their respect.

'Lizzie,' said Kevin. 'There's something I want to ask you before we go.'

'Ask away,' said Lizzie, pouring batter into the pan.

'You know what you were saying about the power that we have? How we can do things we don't even know about?'

'Was I saying that? I suppose I was.'

'Well, can you tell us about it? So that we know what kind of things we can do?'

Lizzie shook the skillet so that the pancake slid around. 'I's been thinking about that,' she said, 'and I's decided that it isn't a good idea.'

'But why?' said Tess.

'Because I doesn't want to put ideas into your heads. Because if I puts ideas into your heads they might turn out to be the wrong ones. And there's nothing that gets in the way of a right idea more easily than a wrong one.'

'But can't you give us a clue, Lizzie?' said Kevin. 'A couple of examples?'

'That's just what I doesn't want to do. I has no idea what you's going to find along your way and I has no idea how you's going to deal with it. But I does know this. I'd lock that door this minute and holler as loud and as long as I could for Oliver Griffin and his ignorant pal if I thought you was going to be in any danger that you couldn't manage. I knows that I could do it if I was still a Switcher, and I knows without any doubt that you can do it, too. So get on your way before you starts thinking about things, and be sure to call in and see me as soon as you gets home.'

Kevin turned to Tess with a question in his eyes but she looked away and went towards the door. Her heart was numb with fear and she didn't want him to see it.

Lizzie came with them as far as the front step. 'Goodbye, now,' she said, as they walked out into the snow. 'Look after yourselves. And don't be too busy concerning yourselves with what is. There's times when it makes more sense to think about what isn't.'

Kevin turned to question her, but the door was closing in his face.

It was still early. Tess looked about her as they walked across Lizzie's front garden towards the narrow path. Apart from a few cat paw-prints, rapidly being filled in, there was not a mark on the snow. The birds were moving about in the trees and causing little avalanches among the branches, but they were not at all happy about the weather and saw no sense in going further afield before Lizzie came out to feed the chickens.

'What now?' said Tess.

Kevin shrugged. 'Fly, I suppose. There's no point in walking, is there?'

'Fly where?'

He shrugged again. 'North, I suppose.'

They moved closer together as they entered the narrow tunnel of the path.

'Just like that?' said Tess. 'Just fly north into a blizzard? Nothing worked out? No plans?'

'No plans,' said Kevin. 'No compass, no maps. And no hotels along the way, either, and no tents, no sleeping bags.' Abruptly he gave Tess a friendly shove so that she sidestepped into a shallow drift. His nose was red from the snowflakes blowing into his face, and he was grinning, so that Tess had the fleeting impression of a circus clown. 'We're leaving everything behind,' he said. 'We're on our own. No rules, not even Rat rules. Just the two of us, and all that out there.'

All that out there was still filling Tess's heart with dread, but Kevin's eyes were shining. 'Don't waste your fear, Tess. Save it up for when you need it, like the animals do.'

She smiled, despite herself, and he smiled back, more openly than he had ever done before. 'Pigeons?' he said.

Tess laughed, and they were friends beyond any shadow of a doubt, travelling with a common purpose. 'I hate pigeons,' she said. 'Why not be something bigger and faster? We can be anything we want. No one's going to see us in this snow.'

'Flamingos?'

'Eagles?'

'Swans?'

'Storks?'

'Albatrosses!'

'Yeah! Albatrosses.' And they were, squeezing awkwardly through the hedge, running with clumsy strides across the wide meadow beyond, and finally rising with slow, graceful wing-beats into the white heart of the blizzard.

Without thinking, without even wondering how they knew, they tilted their wings and were heading north. They flew high, to avoid the hazards of tall buildings appearing out of the snow, and they stayed close together, one slightly beneath the other, so as not to lose sight of one another. Their powerful wings settled into an easy rhythm that they could have maintained for countless hours, but even so, it soon became apparent to them that they would have to choose some other means of travel. The snow was driving into their eyes and blinding them, and the winds up there were gusty and erratic, and made them swirl and spiral in a way that made it almost impossible to stay close together. On several occasions they lost sight of each other, and had to circle and call until they met up again. It was possible for them to continue on, but it would be a slow and anxious journey.

The suburbs of the city were beneath them. The two birds passed quickly over a sprawling area of housing estates, then followed the line of the main road towards the centre of the city. It might have been the instinct of the birds to take refuge on the water, or it might have been an unrealised decision which their human minds had reached, but there was no doubt now about their destination. They were heading for the river.

As they came closer to the city centre and the buildings and traffic became more dense, Tess and Kevin could feel the slight rise in temperature. All those houses and offices were heated, and all the cars were burning fuel, and the excess heat was rising into the air. The snow seemed a little softer. It slid off their wings without sticking at all, and it didn't sting their eyes so badly. Nonetheless, it was a great relief when, surprisingly soon, the broad band of the river came into sight.

Tess was flying a little ahead of Kevin, and below him, but he was within her field of vision constantly. All of a sudden, there was a wobble and a flutter of darkness where he had been, and then she was on her own in the swirling snow. She wheeled in a great arc and turned back to see a black drake with a green head flapping towards her as fast as its little wings would carry it. Tess understood. Two albatrosses landing on the Liffey would undoubtedly cause a little more attention than they wanted.

The long spell of cold weather had caused parts of the river to freeze over, even before the snow had started to fall, but a channel through the middle had been kept clear by the current for most of its length. If anyone had been watching, they wouldn't have been too surprised to see two ducks coming in to land and floating along downstream for a while. They would have been a little more surprised, however, to see both ducks dive, one after another, and not come up again.

High above the Polar ice cap, Lieutenant Andy

142

'Scud' Morgan was flying a medium-range bomber with a full complement of armed missiles. The plane was on loan from the Pakistan Air Force, who had bought it from its manufacturers in the USA some nine months earlier. He checked the radio link with ground control to make sure that he wasn't being overheard, then he said: 'At least it doesn't smell of curry.'

'Huh?' said his co-pilot, Mark Hadders, who was sitting in the seat behind him.

'No garlands round the control panel. No incense burning under the seats.'

'Huh?' said Hadders again. He was cleaning his fingernails with a tooth broken from a pocket comb. The comb had about twelve teeth left. Scud Morgan hated Mark Hadders more than anyone on earth. He hated Mark Hadders more than he hated the Russians or the Iraqis or even the Cubans. Mark Hadders was a numbskull. Scud didn't know where he had got the nick-name 'Squash', but he was willing to take a good guess. The only part of Hadders' brain that worked was the bit that handled the aeroplane. The rest of it was completely atrophied.

But he had to talk to somebody. 'They didn't use the plane to clear some of their homeless off the streets,' he said, more loudly than he needed to.

'Why should they?' said Hadders. 'We don't. Besides, I think they're mostly Muslims in Pakistan. They don't go in for the incense and garlands stuff.'

'Dumb asshole,' muttered Morgan.

'Huh?'

'I said, "some hell-hole". Down there.' He pointed down at the floor of the cockpit beneath his feet.

They were flying above the storms, in bright sunshine. Beneath them there was nothing but unbroken cloud for mile after mile after mile.

'Anything on the radar, Jake?' said Morgan. The technician was behind them in the body of the plane, dozing over a bank of specially installed surveillance equipment. 'Couple of planes,' he said. 'That's all.'

'Theirs or ours?' There was no answer, so he said: 'Ha ha. Theirs or ours. Joke.'

There was still no answer. Hadders had finished cleaning his nails and was reading another of those dumb books that he seemed to go through like comics. Morgan had tried one once, but it made no sense at all. It was by some British woman who had been dead for a hundred years and whose brain had been dead for a hundred and fifty.

'They think we're crazy, you know?' he said.

Hadders sighed and rested his book on his knee. 'Who, Andy?'

'The Pakistanis, the Israelis, everyone who's cleaning up by hiring our own airplanes back to us.'

'No they don't, Andy.'

'Sure they do. And they're right, aren't they? We got sixteen hundred planes in the air, day and night, dodging each other like a swarm of mosquitos, and what are we fighting? A snowstorm.'

'Don't worry about it, Andy. We're not doing anybody any harm. Let them think what they like.' He picked up his book again.

'But I wasn't trained to not do anybody any harm!' said Morgan. 'I wasn't trained to spend eight hours a day pretending to be a weather satellite!'

'Come on,' said Hadders. 'Look around you, Andy. The sun is shining in a clear blue sky. At least we're not down there wearing snow goggles and dodging polar bears.'

'Anything would be better than this,' said Morgan. 'Sitting up here and getting bed sores on my rear end with some lunatic who reads ... what do you call that stuff, anyway?'

'Literature,' said Hadders.

'Hell, that ain't literature!' said Morgan. 'Literature is what they give you when you can't decide which hi-fi system to go for. I got piles of it at home.'

Hadders wasn't listening. He was mentally absent again, reading his book.

'Anything new, Jake?' said Morgan.

'Couple of planes,' said Jake.

CHAPTER SIXTEEN

Goats had the secret of mischievous fun, it was true, but the spirit of pure joy had been perfected by another species and made its own. Two of these creatures were now speeding down the River Liffey, keeping well below the surface except when they had to rise, briefly, to catch air. They were dolphins, and they were heading for the open sea.

There are other sea creatures as fast as dolphins, but there are none that enjoy their speed so much. There are other sea creatures that live among their own kind, but there are none that take so much pleasure in each other's company. And on land or sea, there are no creatures anywhere that get such enjoyment out of merely being alive.

Tess and Kevin sped downstream, catching the strongest currents to help them on their way. They stayed close together, weaving around bridge supports, making small detours to get a quick look at interesting bits of wreckage on the river bed. There were prams, bicycles, supermarket trolleys, there were sunken boats, and cars, and once they passed a bus, with its rows of silted windows gazing vacantly towards the surface.

Tess knew that if she had to choose now, she would not be a cat. There was nothing that compared with being a dolphin. Her awareness was acute, her intuition sharp, and her body flowed with the current, all comfort and sinuous strength. If there had been time, she would have stood on her tail in the water and laughed at the people crossing O'Connell Bridge or walking to work beside the river. She would have done it not because she wanted their attention and applause, but because joy, more than anything else in the world, is for sharing.

Many, many miles away, between Norway and Iceland, the nearest krool was sliding towards them along the top of the rapidly expanding ice cap. It knew nothing of dolphins, and nothing of joy. All it knew was cold, and an endless, relentless hunger.

From above, the krools were invisible. They were round and shallow, roughly the shape of an upturned saucer, and so huge that they could cover an average-sized town without leaving any trace of it. Because they were very much colder than the snow around them, it didn't melt when it landed on their backs, but gave them a coating of camouflage. So perfectly did they blend into the surrounding snowfields that they could not be seen at all, even when they were moving, unless you happened to be right in front of them.

And if you were, you were in big trouble. For krools will stop at nothing when the time comes around to expand their icy kingdom across the globe. They will slide over land or sea on the carpet of ice that they spread for hundreds of miles before them with their snowy breath, and as they travel they will eat anything of animal or vegetable origin which lies beneath the snow or above it. Trees, rocks, houses, and all the ice and snow which cover them, are swept into the great maw of the krool and processed by its phenomenal digestive system. It sifts out what is useful and discards what is not as a powdery mixture of ground ice and stone. And the more it eats, the larger and colder it becomes.

The only enemy the krool fears is heat. Even a small animal which might somehow survive the vanguard storms by burrowing a hole in the snow can cause a reaction of revulsion in the krool as it passes over, and give it a spell of indigestion. The heat of the drilling rig had enraged the krool who encountered it, and caused it to heave and shudder for several days before it regained its strength and went on.

Such instances, however, are rare. The krools give fair warning of their arrival, and those warm-blooded creatures who are unable to keep pace ahead of the storms are usually frozen corpses by the time the krools arrive.

At the mouth of the River Liffey, Tess and Kevin turned east into the Irish sea, then northwards up the coast. They stayed close to the shore, where the water was warmer, but even so it soon became clear that they would need more insulation than they had to cope with the cold seas ahead of them. There was only one possibility for a journey as long as the one they were about to undertake and, reluctant as they were to change out of dolphin form, they knew that they would have to.

The oceans, as any seaman will testify, exist in a different part of time from the land. If anyone were to ask Tess how long her journey through the Irish Sea and up into the Norwegian Straits took her, she would have been unable to answer. How long is an hour? An hour doing homework or an hour at the fun-fair or an hour when you're too sick to go out and play? How long is an hour for a whale? For the whole of that trip beneath the waves, time was a currency without value, as meaningless as pound coins are to a frog.

Tess's human mind was all but engulfed by the phenomenal intelligence of the whale, and it was as much as she could do to keep her purpose intact. Whales have a knowledge of the whole global ocean with its varying currents and temperatures and moods, not as a person remembers some place where they have been, but as they might know their own house or garden, without ever having to think about it. But more than that, they could know each part of their immense home and what was happening there, even though they were not in it, for the voices of whales travel far and their thoughts travel further.

This much Tess might have been able to remember, but it was only the tattered and tawdry edge of the truth, the way that words can only explain the edges of dreams and not their vivid depths. The whole of that world could not be held in the limited mind of a human being, and was lost to her for ever when the time came to leave the oceans behind. But the thing that Tess never forgot was the whales' code of honour. For the whales know the ways of the ocean from top to bottom and from end to end, and that means that they know where the whaling boats lie. It is not stupidity which makes whales easy prey for the gunners, but their knowledge that the ocean is their own, and that it is better to die than to move even by the width of a flipper towards the faint-hearted existence of the hunted.

Krools move with astonishing speed when they first wake up. The areas of the planet which are near the polar regions have no resistance to their advance, because they are affected by the presence of the krools even as they sleep. They are territories which are already claimed by the cold and merely need to be re-established.

As they move towards the equator, however, their progress slows, partly because they come into contact with the sun. By the time these krools had reached the line of sixty-five degrees latitude, which runs through the middle of Norway and Sweden, and through Siberia, Alaska and North Canada, they were already slowing down. Their snowstorms still preceded them by hundreds of miles, but would spread more slowly as they blew towards Southern Europe and the USA.

The krools on the Norwegian Sea were having a particularly hard time of it. They had long since passed the limit of permanent pack ice and were having to use enormous reserves of cold to freeze the surface of the sea before them as they went. It was a hungry time for them as well, because there was no nourishment to be had from the sea, whose citizens stayed well below the freezing surface. All krools are dangerous, but a hungry krool is the most dangerous of all.

CHAPTER SEVENTEEN

When Tess and Kevin reached the fresh edge of the ice cap, now lying between Iceland and Norway, they said goodbye to the world of the whales and turned themselves into seals for their re-emergence on to the surface.

Despite their layer of blubber, they were shocked by the intensity of the cold. Snow was still falling, but it was a very different kind of snow from the large, soft flakes which were still settling on Dublin. Here the particles were small and dense, as though the air itself were ice that had lost its solidity but nothing of its coldness. It froze their whiskers as soon as they flopped out of the sea, and it stung their nostrils and eyes.

Tess stood beside Kevin, both of them blinking against the swirling snow and wondering what to do. Her mind searched for possibilities, but there were only two. To turn back, or to go on. It was Kevin who made the decision. He touched her nose briefly with his, and began to shuffle himself forwards. Tess followed.

But seals are cumbersome on land, and unhappy. Their exertions warmed them but they were making little headway. After a while they stopped to rest, but as soon as they did, the cold began to bite into them again. So they moved on in a more effective manner, as polar bears this time.

Tess was torn between conflicting instincts. She wanted to turn back, to the solid safety of whales and dolphins and home, but at the same time she was afraid of being separated from Kevin in this white and terrifying world. She knew that nothing would persuade him to give up, even though she had long ago forgotten the feeling that had made her understand why. She had the awful sensation of being caught up in his life, his search for some intangible thing which she neither understood nor wanted. It made her feel helpless and worthless, with no choice but to trail along in his tracks and accept whatever was going to happen.

And there was only one thing, as far as she could see, that could happen. They would walk into the snow and ice until they could walk no longer, and then they would die. She wondered what had happened to the other polar creatures, the bears and Arctic foxes with their silver coats, and she hoped that at least some of them had managed to stay on land and keep ahead of the storms. She shuddered and shook a crust of snow from her coat. Her fur was thick, but not thick enough, she knew, to protect her for much longer.

Kevin was still walking with silent determination, but the snow was getting deeper as they got further from the edge of the ice, and it was soft and powdery, which made progress slow and tiring. Tess's eyes and lungs were sore from the bitter air. She dropped her head. White bears, white snow, white air constantly moving around them. The only change in all that whiteness was when, from time to time, Kevin turned around to make sure she was there, and then she saw his black nose and eyes.

It was almost a relief when night began to fall. To Tess, numb with cold and exhaustion, it no longer seemed to matter what form rest might take, as long as it came soon.

Kevin stopped. Directly in front of them was a miniature mountain, an iceberg which had been captured and imprisoned by the spread of the krools' carpet. Some of its facets were too sheer for snow to lodge there, and the ice showed through, darkly opaque, like crystal. To Tess it represented an obstacle, but to Kevin it was a godsend. Because around its base the snow had gathered into wide, deep drifts. He began to dig.

In the middle of the night, Tess woke. It was absolutely dark in the snowhole. If any moon or starlight filtered through the clouds above, it failed to make its way through the tunnel they had dug and into their tiny cave.

It was surprisingly, luxuriously warm in there, from the trapped heat of their furry bodies. Tess would have stretched if there had been room, but they had made the space just big enough for the two of them to sleep curled up, so that they wouldn't have to warm any extra air. She yawned and turned over so that she was facing Kevin, and now she realised why she had woken. It was a long time, who knew how long, since she and Kevin had talked together, and she wanted to do it now before daylight came and urged them into action. She Switched, and immediately felt a little frightened to be lying in total darkness with a large bear. She could smell bear fur and bear breath, and before it frightened her any further, she reached out and tugged at Kevin's thick, warm coat.

He started, then grew rigid, and then the coat between her fingers was cotton, a little damp.

'You idiot, Tess! Don't ever do that again!'

'What? What did I do?'

'I was a bear, you fool. You woke me up. I nearly ripped out your throat!'

'Wow.'

'I only just remembered in time!'

'Sorry,' said Tess.

Kevin said nothing, but turned awkwardly in the cramped space until he was on his back. Tess was afraid that she was going to cry and, as if he realised, he reached out his hand and touched her arm.

'It's OK,' he said. 'I shouldn't have shouted. I'm sorry.'

Tess turned so that she was on her back as well and their shoulders were squeezed tight against each other in the dark. For a long time they lay in silence breathing the warm, foetid air.

Tess's mind was a jumble. She knew that the most sensible thing to do was to turn back and go home, but she couldn't say it to Kevin. It would seem like a betrayal after they had come so far. And if they weren't going to go back, what did you say to someone when it might be your last conversation with them? There was an awful sense of the executioner's cell about the snowhole. And despite all they had been through together, Kevin seemed like a stranger again, lost in his own thoughts. But it was he who spoke first.

'What did she mean, Tess?'

'Who? Lizzie?'

'Yes. About what isn't?'

'I don't know.'

'But what could she have meant? It must have been important or she wouldn't have said it.'

'I don't know if that follows,' said Tess. 'Lizzie said an awful lot of things that weren't important.'

'Oh, come on, Tess. You're not going to start backing off again, are you? It's hardly time for it, you know.'

'Maybe it is the time for it. Maybe it's the only time. The last chance we have.' She expected him to be angry, but his answer was surprisingly calm.

'No, it's too late for that now. We've come this far because we believed what Lizzie said. It'd be completely pointless to give up now, just when we're getting to the heart of it.'

'The heart of what?'

Kevin shrugged, and they were squeezed so tightly together that Tess's shoulder rose with his. At another time she would have laughed, but at that moment laughter seemed to belong to a different life.

'Of what we are, I suppose,' said Kevin. 'Of survival, of freedom, of independence.' He sighed. 'But I don't know what the problem is. My mind feels as if it's shot through with steel cables, or something. Whenever I try to think about anything a bit different, like what isn't, I just find myself running along the same old lines. I can't seem to get anywhere.'

'I suppose we haven't done too badly so far,' said Tess, 'and most of the things we've done have been

155

your ideas. The dolphins and the seals and the polar bears and this hole in the snow.'

'Yes. But it's all practical stuff, isn't it? It's all what is and not what isn't. But the polar bears aren't going to take us much further, are they? We couldn't last much longer out there, and we can't hole up for ever, either. We need something else now. Some leap of imagination.'

He fell silent again. Tess noticed that her eyes were flicking around in the darkness, seeking something to rest upon. She closed them, and must have dozed for a moment, because Kevin's voice woke her from a dream.

'Have you got your watch on?'

For some reason the dream was important, but when she tried to remember it, it slipped away from her. It was all snow, anyway, ancient and endless. She felt her wrist. 'Yes.'

'Has it got the date on it?'

Tess was already looking at it. 'It says seven-thirty,' she said, 'but I suppose the time is different up here. I can't see the date. That bit isn't luminous. Why do you want to know, anyway?'

'I was just wondering when my birthday was. It must be quite soon.'

'What date is it?'

'The thirtieth. Can't be that far off now.'

Suddenly Tess realised why he was asking. She had an awful image of Kevin losing the ability to change and being stuck out there in the frozen wastes. He would freeze in no time in that stupid parka. He didn't even have gloves. And going back would be just as dangerous. He might be in the middle of the sea when it happened, or up in the air. It was important to know.

'Haven't you got a match?' she said.

'Good thinking,' said Kevin, fumbling in his pocket.

The first match he struck hurt their eyes so much that they couldn't see the watch. As the second one was burning down, Tess held the watch up close to it.

'The twenty-eighth,' she said.

Just before the flame died, she caught the look of dismay in Kevin's face. Their situation seemed even more hopeless than before, if that was possible. But Kevin said: 'Never mind.'

'Never mind?'

'I was just thinking we might have had a bit of a party, that's all. But we'll have to skip it.'

'A party? Are you out of your mind?'

'No. It's part of the tradition, apparently. The girl who told me about it had one. I didn't really know her very well. She wasn't like you. But she invited me to her party, and I went. The day before her fifteenth birthday.'

'Why the day before?'

Kevin laughed. 'You can't very well throw a party if you're an eagle, can you?'

'An eagle?'

'Yes. She was into discos and motorbikes and stuff. An eagle suited her, actually. It was her kind of thing.'

'You mean . . . You mean you can choose?'

'Of course!' said Kevin. 'Didn't you know that? Whatever you are at the time of your birthday, that's what you stay. You can't Switch any more, that's all. But there's nothing to say you have to be human.'

Tess stared into the darkness, trying to take it in.

'I've spent months worrying about it,' Kevin went on. 'Ironic, isn't it? Months trying to choose between a rat and a sparrowhawk and an otter, and now it

157

looks as if I won't have a choice at all when it comes down to it. I'll just have to take whatever I get.'

'No, Kevin,' said Tess. 'We could still get back.'

'How?'

'Somehow. I don't know.'

'I don't see how we could. But in any case, I don't seem to be too worried about it. I can't understand it, really, but ever since Lizzie said what she did, about us having more power than we know, I've had this kind of faith. I'm not worried about those things any more. They don't seem to matter.'

'But you can't just end up as a polar bear or a walrus! You're human, Kevin, you have to be human!'

He laughed again, and Tess felt her heart fill with despair.

'Why?' he said.

But she couldn't tell him. She couldn't explain that she wanted to dress him up and take him into a French restaurant, or that she would welcome him any time she got off the bus and found him waiting. Even if her pride would allow it, it made no sense out here, with the Arctic gales blowing all around them.

'I never was any good at being human,' he said. 'Even with my family, even before I knew what I was.'

'Why not?'

'I don't know. I just didn't have the knack. My brother did. He was older than me, and he got along OK with everyone. My father's a toolmaker, and he does a lot of work at home. Makes all kinds of bits and pieces that people want. My brother was always out in his workshop with him, helping him. But I couldn't take an interest in it. I always got everything wrong, no matter how hard I tried.'

'So what? That doesn't mean anything.'

'It did, though. It meant that I didn't fit in with the men in the family, you see. And my mother . . .' He stopped.

'What about your mother?'

'I don't know quite how to explain it. She was always there, always. She never had a job, she never went anywhere, she was there every day when I came home from school and she did all the things that mothers are supposed to do. But in another way she wasn't there at all. She wasn't there for me. Her mind was always on something else, on what she was doing or on what she was listening to on the radio, or on something that she kept locked away inside herself somewhere.'

Tess noticed that the snow cave wasn't as warm as it had been. The cold seemed to be creeping through her from below, and she turned on to her side to relieve the discomfort in her back.

'When I look at it now,' Kevin went on, 'I see that she just didn't have it, that thing, whatever it is, that attention that people give to each other. I don't blame her for it. But at the time I used to think it was my fault, that I just wasn't good enough to be worth bothering with. But then I got angry about it, and it worked, because at least when I was bad she took some notice of me. That was around the time I discovered I could turn into a rat. It was ages before I discovered that I could be other things as well. In those days I used to set off for school in the mornings and spend the day with the other young rats, and even when my parents knew I was playing truant, there was nothing they could do to stop me. If they left me to the school in the morning, I'd slip off somewhere at break and do a bunk. The other kids

159

hated me because I was different, and I hated them because they weren't.'

'I know the feeling,' said Tess.

'Yes. And as time went by I stopped bothering to go home. When I did turn up from time to time, they used to get into this awful flap and talk about borstals and reform schools, so I thought it was best to just stay out of the way.'

'Did you never spend time being human then, after that?'

'Oh, yes. I still turned up for their birthdays and Christmas, things like that. After a while they just accepted it and stopped asking questions. And I told you I spend . . . spent a lot of time in libraries. Sometimes I'd meet someone on the way and hang around with them for a while. But I never had a real friend. Not until . . .'

'Until what?'

'Phew. It's getting cold in here, isn't it?'

'Yes. We're not as warm as the bears were. What were you going to say just now?'

'It doesn't matter.'

Tess rested her head on the crook of her elbow. She was colder than she had realised, and beginning to feel drowsy again. She knew that it was dangerous. She remembered reading about it, about how the cold sends you off to sleep, and then you never wake up again. For a while she resisted and pulled herself awake to listen to Kevin's steady breathing in the darkness. What if they both fell asleep here? No one would ever find them. If the weather changed and the ice melted, their bodies would slide into the sea and be lost for ever. The thought of all those fathoms of dark water beneath them filled her with horror, but also a strange sort of resignation. They were so small in the middle of all this. Air, water, ice, and nothing else for hundreds of miles. Suddenly, there was no more resistance. She allowed her mind to drift away wherever it wanted, and there was a deep, deep sense of comfort.

The forgotten scene from the earlier dream returned. It was a landscape as bitter as the one outside their snow hole, but there was something moving across it, some kind of animal. And suddenly, Tess was wide awake.

'Kevin!'

He jumped at the urgency in her voice and she knew that he, too, had been asleep. 'What?'

'I've got it! All that stuff about what isn't.'

'Have you?'

'Yes. It's so simple, I can't believe we didn't think of it before.' She was determined to stay awake now, and she sat herself up so that the top of her head was wedged against the roof. 'Lizzie was right. We're completely caught up in the things around us, just trying to copy what already exists. But what about something that used to exist, and doesn't any more?'

Kevin was holding his breath, and Tess could feel his sense of excitement. 'Go on,' he said.

'Well, what about when there really was an ice age? There were animals that lived in those times, weren't there?'

'What, like dinosaurs?'

'Yes. Except that the dinosaurs didn't make it. They didn't adapt. But some other creatures did.

Kevin let out his breath with a gasp. 'Mammoths!' he said.

'Exactly! I saw them, Kevin, just now in a sort of dream. Walking through the snow. And why

161

shouldn't we? I'm sure we could. We know what they looked like. I'm positive we could get a feel for them.'

'Of course we could. It'd be a lot easier than a whale.'

There was no more to be said, and they fell silent, their minds full of new hope. After a while, Tess said: 'Kevin?'

'Yes?'

'We ought to be bears again. Until the morning. It's too cold in here. It's dangerous.'

'Yes, you're right,' he said, but he didn't Switch, and Tess had a feeling that he was waiting for something. 'Don't go to sleep again,' she said.

'No. I'm not. I was just thinking.'

'What?'

'Well, if I got stuck as a mammoth. If my birthday came.'

Tess said nothing, thinking about it, and he went on: 'I know there's nothing you could do about it. I wouldn't ask you to stay with me or anything. But maybe you could ... I don't know, just keep an eye on me somehow. So I wouldn't be completely alone.'

'Of course I would, Kevin. I'd do anything. I'd go to the ends of the earth if I had to.'

'I know you would,' he said, and then he laughed. 'You already have, in a way, haven't you?'

Tess's pride reared up. 'I didn't come here just because of you, you know,' she said.

'I know that,' said Kevin. 'But you're still the only friend I ever had.'

Before she could answer, he was a bear again and, with a sigh, she joined him.

162

CHAPTER EIGHTEEN

The two mammoths moved slowly but solidly across the snowfields. Their long, woolly coats provided perfect insulation against the blizzards, and their shaggy eyebrows and whiskery nostrils protected them from the effects of the freezing air. So little heat escaped through all that insulation that snow landing on their backs didn't melt, and even provided a further layer of protection.

It also provided a partial shield against the sensitive infra-red scanners in the planes that passed from time to time above their heads.

'Anything new, Jake?'

'Naa.'

They were flying low this time, through the white heart of the blizzard. There was little or no danger of encountering anything in the air. The high points in the pack ice were well charted, and their radar

screens would give warning well in advance of anything that might be in their path, but even so, Scud
found it nerve-wracking to be flying so totally blind.

'That freighter out of the way?'

'What freighter?'

'You said there was a freighter.'

'Hell,' said Jake, 'that was an hour ago. He'll be
over Stockholm by now.'

'Nothing else?'

'No. Wait a minute, though.'

'What?'

Even Hadders put down his book for a moment.

'Nothing. Infra-red's just picking up a couple of
animals down below. Small ones. I don't know how
they can survive down there.'

'Poor suckers,' said Hadders.

'Poor suckers?' said Scud. '*They're* poor suckers?
What about us?'

The only danger that the mammoths were aware of
was hunger. There was no source of food for miles
around, not even the rough Arctic vegetation on
which they had learned to survive in the past. Their
reserves of fat would keep them going for a while,
but for how long they didn't know. It took a lot of
energy to keep those massive bodies warm, and a lot
more to keep them moving.

But keep moving they did. Tess and Kevin had
passed another test. Kevin's faith had held, even if
Tess's hadn't, and circumstances had proved him
right. The mammoths were slow but they were
comfortable, and they were making steady progress
towards the north.

The hours passed. The human parts of their minds
chafed at the tedium of the changeless landscape, but

the mammoths had learnt patience over the generations, and plodded along tirelessly.

The krool sensed them coming long before they were able to see it, and its small, uncomplicated brain went into a momentary seizure. For although it was a poor thinker, its memory was as long and as ancient as its life, and it was well acquainted with mammoths. The prospect of encountering these two was not a pleasant one.

A dead mammoth is an agreeable snack for a krool, but a live one is a different proposition entirely. This particular krool had once had the experience of swallowing a whale which had been trapped beneath the ice, unable to breathe and dying. Its phenomenal internal temperature had crippled the krool, and it had never forgotten the agonizing days that followed as it battled with the heat the way a person battles with infection. Even two live mammoths would not be as bad as that, but they would nevertheless create a considerable disturbance in its system, and it would have to lie up for a while until they were digested.

In the normal course of events, a krool would not even consider eating a mammoth, which was one of the reasons why the mammoths had come to survive their last colonisation of the earth. A krool encountering a mammoth in the usual course of events would flatten the leading edge of its mantle so that the mammoth wouldn't know it was there and would merely continue on its way, traversing the krool's back until, after a few hours, it reached the other side. If this particular krool had not been so hungry, it would have left the two mammoths to go along their way. But it could not allow any source of food to escape, even if it caused a belly-ache. It lay still and waited.

Some miles away, Scud Morgan's bomber had completed an in-flight refuelling operation and started its return journey. In a few more hours it would make a radio-controlled landing on the salted runway of an air base in central England and its crew would get out of their air-bound prison.

Jake was dozing. Hadders was reading. Scud was flying as low as he dared, for the sake of producing adrenalin.

Tess and Kevin blundered straight into the waiting krool. One moment there was nothing ahead of them except untrodden snow and the next, a whole section of it lifted and towered above them, and they were gazing with horror at the black underbelly of the krool. For an instant, Tess thought that the world had collapsed and she was staring into nothingness, a gaping abyss. Then she saw the eye. A single, huge, unblinking eye, gelid and green, looking straight at her.

If Lizzie had been wrong, it would have been the end, not only of the two mammoths, but of Tess and Kevin as well. For the mantle was above them now and the huge, cavernous maw was opening as the krool pushed forward to swallow its prey. But if Lizzie had been wrong she would not have sent the two young Switchers out to test their strength against the krools. Lizzie knew, and quicker than thought, Tess knew too, that they did indeed have powers beyond their wildest dreams. Kevin had been right. If they hadn't been faced with the ultimate test of their skills, they might never have learned them. Because, if there had been time for thought, Tess would never have believed that what happened next was possible. The krool's mantle was dropping like a monstrous fly swatter. Not even a bird would have had the speed to dodge out from under it. But Tess Switched, quicker than she had ever Switched before, and suddenly the krool was rearing away again and backing off.

For Tess's heart had understood even more clearly than her mind what Lizzie meant by being what isn't. And it had acted before her mind had been able to doubt, and to stop it. In front of the krool's retreating underbelly was a huge and magnificent dragon, and then there were two of them, blasting flame at the hideous eye, which shrivelled and melted and dripped like warm treacle into the snow. The krool reared as high as it could go, a mile into the sky, but the dragons took to the wing and continued their pursuit until it collapsed and doubled back on itself like a monstrous, black pancake.

The two dragons leapt for the skies in a delirium of delight. They were faster, cleverer, more powerful than any creature on earth, and they swooped and soared, chased each other's tails and tumbled in the air in sheer elation. This was the feeling that their premonitions had promised them, the certainty of power beyond human imagination, the sensation of absolute freedom. For all the elements were theirs to enjoy. They were equally at home in water, earth and air, but they were not bound by any of them. They carried the secret of fire within them, and even the great ice wastes all around them could cause them no discomfort. They were the rulers of all they surveyed, and there was no creature on earth that could defeat them.

In the midst of their celebrations, they heard the plane passing above them in the clouds. Heard it first, and then saw it, with their infra-red vision.

Just as it saw them. The scanner beeped, warning of a strong signal. Jake sat bolt upright and stared at the screen.

'You got something, Jake?' said Scud.

'Holy God,' said Jake. 'What the hell is that?'

'What is it, Jake, what is it? You got something?' Hadders sat up and turned around in his seat.

'I've never seen anything like it,' said Jake, his eyes filled with wonder.

'What the hell is it, Jake?' Scud yelled.

Jake moved into military mode, sharp and efficient. 'We got hotspots, boys. Two of them. I don't know what they are and I don't know where they came from, but they're like nothing I ever saw before.'

Hadders had left his seat and was standing in the small space beside Jake, looking over his shoulder at the screen. 'Swing around, Scud,' he said. 'We're losing them.'

'Who's giving the orders around here?' screamed Scud. 'What the hell are you doing, standing back there telling me what to do?'

'You should see this, sir. We should get a better look before we go past.'

Scud gritted his teeth and swore, but he dipped his wings and swung around in the tightest circle the plane could handle. 'Come in, base,' he said into the radio mike. 'This is Delta Zero Five, are you reading me?'

General Wolfe was sitting at his desk in Mission Control when one of the technical assistants called him over to the computer terminal which was receiving Scud Morgan's pictures. 'God damn,' he said. 'What the hell is that?'

'Damned if I know,' said the aide. 'There's no plane in the world that flies like that.'

The shapes on the screen were descending in rapid circles, leaving a residue of heat in their wake that showed up on the monitor like the tail of a comet. The plane was passing above them and moving away again.

'Get on to the guys in that plane,' said Wolfe. 'Tell them to stay above those things and keep sending back pictures.'

'Yes, sir.'

By now there was quite a gathering around the terminal, watching the screens. 'I knew it,' said Wolfe. 'Didn't I tell you, huh? I knew there was something in there.'

CHAPTER NINETEEN

The plane above their heads was unsettling, but dragons are not easily intimidated. When they realised that it was not going to go away, they agreed to ignore it and go in search of more krools. They split up, one going east and the other west, flying low enough to be able to see the ground beneath them.

The plane above circled one last time, then followed Kevin. For a while he allowed it to drone along behind him, but then he grew irritated by it, and doubled back on himself, too rapidly for the plane to follow. Then he flew south at top speed for a while, and did not turn back to his original course until he was sure that the skies around him were clear.

Scud Morgan swore. Jake shook his head. Mark Hadders went back to his seat and his book.

A krool in a snowstorm is not easy to find, even for a dragon. Kevin scanned the ground as he flew, but it was only by chance that he came across his second krool. It was sliding southwards across Norway, more slowly now than in the preceding weeks, but still making good progress. It had fed well recently, cutting a great swathe through the forested regions in its path, and had grown to enormous dimensions.

Krools do not reproduce like most of the other creatures of the earth. They don't mate with others of their kind, and they produce neither eggs nor young. When they reach a certain critical mass, however, they divide, simply split down the middle and become two, like amoebae. Kevin was able to spot this krool from the air because it was in the process of doing just that.

Where it was splitting into two the camouflage of snow was shifting and revealing patches of the glutinous black flesh beneath. Kevin slowed, wheeled round and returned, spitting flame. But by the time he reached it, the krool had become aware of the hot little presence above and glued itself firmly to the ground.

The first krool had been so easy to dispose of that Kevin wasn't prepared for the battle which followed. The krool did nothing, merely sat tight, knowing that as long as it didn't reveal its underneath to the attacker it was almost invulnerable. Almost, but not quite. Kevin came in time after time, throwing flame constantly. Wherever he attacked the krool, it melted into black, oily liquid, but it was so huge that his best efforts made little impression on its bulk.

He stopped for a while, trying to work out a plan. It was tiring, the way he was acting, and he realised that he was using too much energy. If he became exhausted, he would have to rest, and then feed, and when he thought about feeding his mind became filled with pictures of what dragons best like to eat, which is people. And when he thought of people, he could think of only people that he knew, and he wondered if any Switchers before him had experienced the weird sensation of imagining a slap-up meal consisting of their relatives and friends.

To take his mind off these unpleasant thoughts, he returned to the krool and flew up the gradual contour of its body until he reached the highest point. Then he burned away in one spot, calmly and consistently, until he had produced a hollow full of bubbling black liquid like a cauldron. Still he carried on, until at last the heat melted a hole right through the krool and the liquid flowed away on to the ground beneath it. The beast began to convulse, flapping its skirts and heaving its great body so that the snow which covered it flew up in a thick cloud. Kevin hovered in the air and waited until the krool gave a final shudder and lay still.

High above, a satellite had picked up the heat emissions from the battle, and three planes were converging on the spot. But by the time they arrived, Kevin was gone, and their surveillance equipment picked up no signs of life.

But a few hundred miles away, above Greenland, another plane was about to intercept Tess's path. Her infra-red image had just appeared on the aircraft's monitor, and a rapid radio communication had put the crew on to the offensive. Wolfe didn't know what those things were out there, but he wasn't taking any chances. The first heat-seeking missile was armed and ready to go.

Tess's flight path was erratic and unpredictable, and the pilot of the bomber wasn't about to take chances. As soon as he got a clear radar fix, he fired off the missile and swung around out of the area.

Tess had known that the plane was there, but she hadn't expected that it would be able to detect her. She accepted her dragon ability to see objects by the heat they emitted, but she had no idea that there was an equivalent technology available to the military. So, when she picked up the image of the missile snaking towards her, she was completely off guard. If she had been expecting it she might have dodged, since dragons can perform fantastic aerial manoeuvres which no missile could possibly follow. Instead, instinctively, she changed herself into a swallow. The missile swept past, catching her in its current of air and swirling her around in the blizzard. Then, finding itself without a target, it ploughed blindly on, straight into the snow beneath.

The swallow was well clear of the centre of the explosion, but even so, chunks of snow and ice flew up to where she was recovering her balance high above. She flew upwards and away, but in no time at all the blood of the little bird began to freeze. She listened for a moment, and as soon as she was sure that the plane was not returning she Switched back into the warm and fearless form of the dragon.

The monitor in Mission Control slowly cleared and became blank as the heat from the explosion died away. A great cheer went up. General Wolfe leant back in his chair and clasped his hands behind his head in satisfaction. 'Whatever it was, we got it,' he said.

'Uh oh,' said a technician behind him. 'I'm afraid not, sir.'

'What?' Wolfe sat up again. There, on the screen,

was the hot spot again, as clear as ever. It was heading east with surprising speed. 'But it disappeared, didn't it?'

'It looked like it did,' said the technician. 'Maybe the heat from the explosion just masked it somehow. It's there now, anyhow.'

It was, and racing back through the snowstorms towards Kevin. He had heard Tess's call and was coming to meet her. From their positions all over the Arctic Circle, the military planes moved in.

It was nearly dark when the two dragons met above the Norwegian Sea, and it was time to call it a day. Their infra-red vision enabled them to see planes overhead, but no kind of vision would enable them to find krools in the dark. Kevin wanted to stay a dragon, but Tess had learnt that they were not as invisible as they had believed, and insisted on the safety of polar bears. Kevin capitulated. They dug in quickly and slept straight away, curled closely together for comfort.

As soon as the sun came up the next morning, the two hot spots were picked up on the monitors of a surveillance plane. They didn't appear gradually, as a plane does when it starts its engines and warms up, and they neither taxied to a runway nor rose vertically. One moment there was nothing on the infra-red screens above, and then there were two large, hot objects flying off at impossible speed in different directions.

This time, Tess and Kevin had a plan. It was a dangerous plan and would require all their courage and all their wits but, if it worked, it would be a brilliant way to get rid of the krools. All they had to do was to find them.

They had decided to fly low, so low that a krool would appear to them as a patch of slowly-rising ground which would then fall away again. In the middle of a blizzard such flying required steel nerves and lightening fast reactions, but the dragon has both, even at the speed of a jet plane.

When they had talked in the early hours of the morning, Tess and Kevin had agreed that there must be a vanguard of krools along the same latitude as the first ones they had found, to account for the even progress of the blizzards that preceded them. So the dragons flew in straight lines, due east and due west from where they had started. Several times in the first hour, Tess slowed and circled to examine a suspicious slope in the ground, but each time it was a false alarm. Above her the planes criss-crossed continuously, and she had already out-foxed three missiles before she found her first krool. As soon as she was certain of it, she rose some distance into the clouds above and circled steadily, waiting. Before long she saw the tell-tale heat of the approaching plane and heard its engine. As soon as it was within range, it launched its missile. Tess dived at full speed towards the unsuspecting krool. The missile spun after her, coming closer to her tail, until at the last minute, she Switched as she had done before and swung out of the way. It worked. The gathered momentum of the dragon dive flung the little bird out into the blizzard at terrifying speed, and away from the explosion. A few bits of exploded krool reached her as she shot through the air, but she was too busy trying to gain control of her dizzying flight to be concerned about them.

In Mission Control, the observers watched the clearing screen in tense silence. Then someone said: 'We got one this time.'

There was no cheer. This had happened before. 'Don't count your chickens,' said Wolfe, then groaned as the hot spot reappeared and resumed its eastward flight.

On the other side of Greenland, heading west, Kevin was playing the same game, with slightly more success. He had discovered a better way of finding his prey.

A krool crossing land leaves a distinct trail behind it where it has cut a mile-wide path through the vegetation and left nothing but a clean sweep of powdered snow, ice and rock. Kevin happened to notice this when he found his first krool of the day, and after that he stopped looking for their convex forms and searched instead for abrupt tree-lines or abnormally smooth stretches of snow. The method served him well. He found krool after krool, and each time he hovered above them and waited until the military arrived.

As the day wore on, General Wolfe grew increasingly exasperated. The events of the day were beginning to send shivers down his spine. It was becoming clearer all the time that whatever those things were, they were playing games with him. The phone was ringing from Washington a little too often and the questions were becoming embarrassing.

But the strangest thing of all was that whatever was happening out there was having the desired effect on the weather. Already the blizzards were dying out and clouds were disappearing from large areas that had previously been covered. In southern England and

Ireland, he was told, the sun was shining and the snow was beginning to melt.

It was just in time for Lizzie. For the first few days of the blizzards, Mr Quigley had been extremely helpful. He had come every day with whatever supplies Lizzie needed, and he and his daughter had shovelled the snow away from her door and made paths to Nancy's shed and the henhouse. But then, one day, he had come and told her that he had sold all his stock and managed to get a passage for himself and his family on a ferry to Cyprus, and he could not let the opportunity pass. He had brought her provisions for a fortnight and a hundredweight of rock salt to help against the snow, but beyond that he could do nothing more for her.

When the daily digging became too much for her, Lizzie brought Nancy and the hens into the house and let them have the use of the scullery. The mains water had long since frozen tight, so she filled the bath and the sink and a few old milk churns with snow. Then she brought in as many logs as she could stack in the hall, and closed the doors. She was dug in like an Arctic creature in her little snow-hole of a cottage, and was forgotten by the world.

The drifts rose until they covered the downstairs windows, and, since the power lines were down over half the country, Lizzie moved around in the dim light of the fire, saving her candles for emergencies. The first thing to run out was the oats she fed to Nancy and the chickens, and she had to start sharing her own rations with them. Then water began to get scarce. The plug in the bath had proved useless, and the snow which Lizzie had gathered so laboriously ran away as soon as it melted. She was reduced to scraping snow from the insides of the drifts outside the windows and melting it over the fire, and anyone who has ever tried this will know that it is a lot of work for very little return. By the time the sun appeared, Lizzie was exhausted, dispirited, and almost down to the last of her provisions.

If it hadn't been for the cats, she would probably not have known the snow had stopped until the next day. Her kitchen was as dark as a basement with the windows all covered in drifts, but it was too cold to sit upstairs where there was still light. The cats, however, went up and down quite often during the day to use the litter tray that Lizzie had set up in the spare room for them as soon as they could no longer get out.

It was when Moppet failed to return from one of these visits that Lizzie went upstairs to investigate and found him curled up on the windowsill in the sunshine. For the first time since Tess and Kevin had left her house, Lizzie's stiff old back straightened up. She went to the window, prised it open, and called out to the sky: 'You did it, you little horrors! You made it!'

CHAPTER TWENTY

Back at the edge of the Arctic Circle, the dragons were still at work. Tess had eventually discovered Kevin's method of detection for herself, and was making up for lost time.

In Mission Control, General Wolfe was getting fed up with throwing missiles at infra-red ghosts, but he had discovered that there was little else he could do. He had found volunteers to go in for close combat in fighter planes armed with machine guns and close-range missiles, but they had flown back bewildered. As soon as they came anywhere near to visual range, their targets disappeared. Simply vanished without trace.

Wolfe called them back. With outward confidence and inward despair, he continued with the missile attacks.

Tess and Kevin were in a mood of high exhilaration.

179

They were living by the skin of their teeth, dodging death one minute and tempting it the next. As a result, life had never seemed better or more precious.

And they were winning. Their phenomenal speed had taken them around the globe to meet again on the other side above Canada, where they played aerial tag and leapfrog together for a few minutes before turning round and starting back the way they had come, to pick off the krools they had missed.

Wolfe followed their progress on radar and infra-red. He now knew that he was playing into their hands in some way, but he also knew that the snow-storms were abating. He didn't know how he was going to explain it, but he was sure of one thing. He was going to take all the credit that was on offer when the time came.

The one in the west was circling again. 'Let him have it,' he said.

Fast as the dragons were, they couldn't make it back around the globe before nightfall. They could call to each other, though, and they did, before they came to land and settled as polar bears into their separate dug-outs for the night.

Tess slept fitfully, dreaming bear dreams and dragon dreams, and terrible dreams of Kevin trapped in the form of some awful creature for the rest of his life. A single bear produces very much less heat than two curled up together, and she woke before dawn, stiff and sore with the cold. She knew that the only way to get warm was to get moving, so she crawled out of the tunnel and was amazed to find herself standing in the middle of clearly visible snowfields, stretching away in all directions, glowing in the light of the stars which shone out of a cloudless sky.

A plane passed low over her head, blinking a single, white light. Tess shook her damp coat and began to trot northward.

In Mission Control, General Wolfe was popping caffeine pills to keep himself awake. The meteorological satellites were beaming down gratifying pictures of the cloud formations. A few isolated blizzards were still stretching southward like thick fingers, but otherwise the area below the line of seventy degrees latitude was clear.

But Wolfe knew that those things, whatever they were, would return in the daylight. He had spent most of the night in a fury of injured pride, and he wasn't about to give up. There were all kinds of theories buzzing around. Some said the hot spots were Iraqi war machines, developed for the purpose of freezing out the Northern Hemisphere and crippling the American and European economies. Others said they were UFOs making a bid to colonise the planet. Wolfe was willing to believe that they came from outer space, but nothing that had happened had succeeded in convincing him that they were not living beings of some kind. He hadn't forgotten those two tapes.

As Tess warmed up she began to make plans. The blizzards had died down, she knew, because of the krools she and Kevin had killed, but there would surely be others closer to the Pole which would need her attention. Even in the dark, however, she was reluctant to become a dragon now that the cover of clouds had gone, just in case some low-flying plane might get a sight of her in the starlight. So she Switched instead to a Canadian goose, and began to fly steadily north.

She was right about the krools. What she didn't know, however, was that they were no longer a danger. Apart from the unknown enemy in the skies, they were under increasing threat from their greatest enemy, the sun. Only in large numbers can krools be certain of producing sufficient freezing clouds to keep them covered and safe. A single krool cloud can be dispersed by warm winds and leave its maker helpless, melting in the sun. Already the second and third line of them were in rapid retreat, and the rearguard had retraced their tracks and slithered back into their icy beds.

Kevin woke at dawn, and the first thing he knew was that it was the day before his birthday. He had one more day and one more night.

He emerged from his den and stretched. It was still snowing, but the snow was softer that it had been, and kinder. He was feeling fresh, and ready for another day's action, but before that he wanted to have a look around, and he knew exactly how he was going to do it. In the blink of an eye he was a dragon again, moving rapidly up towards the top of the clouds.

The air force was waiting for him, and a passing plane let off a missile as he rose towards it, but he Switched and dodged it easily. It exploded beneath him, not far from his snow-hole. When he recovered his equilibrium, he Switched again, and set off at high speed towards the Pole. He flew so fast that he soon outdistanced the planes behind him, and by doubling and zig-zagging as he went, he was able to confuse the controllers on the ground until at last he found that he had a clear sky above him. Rapidly, he dropped a couple of hundred feet so that he could give himself the momentum he needed, then he launched himself like a rocket, straight up through the clouds and into the air above them.

It was similar to the way a spaniel will jump up above the long grass to get a look around, except that Kevin went up almost as far as the stratosphere. From there he could clearly see the pattern of clouds beneath, which told him the exact locations of the outlying krools. It took him scarcely a second to take it all in, and then he was dropping again, like a monstrous hawk plummeting down through the sky.

In front of the monitors in Mission Control, a dozen mouths dropped open in disbelief as radar relayed the astonishing feat.

'What the hell,' said General Wolfe, 'are we dealing with?'

Just across the Arctic Circle from Kevin, Tess had reached the safety of clouds and Switched. Kevin had been calling periodically throughout the morning and was delighted at last to get a reply. He called again, relaying his information about the whereabouts of the krools, and the two dragons set about finishing them off.

It was easy now. All they had to do was to sweep down along the fingers of cloud until they found the krools. After a while, Mission Control began to understand the pattern, and quite often the dragons found that the planes were already in position even before they arrived.

By late afternoon, Tess and Kevin had located every krool that lay outside the line of seventy degrees latitude. They met directly above the North Pole, where night had already fallen, to celebrate and discuss tactics. Kevin was full of the joys of victory, and was in favour of carrying on, but Tess wanted to stop and talk to him. She was as excited as he was, but for a different reason. For a while they argued in the air, until they became angry and began to burn each other's noses and ears with jets of flame, which sobered them up a bit. In the end, Kevin relented and they sprinted away from the planes gathering above them until they had left them behind. Then they geared down to geese in order to put the enemy off their tracks and flew on for a while. Finally, when the skies were clear of planes, they landed in a strange amphitheatre of ice in the middle of the Greenland Sea.

'Phew,' said Kevin, when they stood face to face at last. 'It's cold.'

'Yes,' said Tess. 'So we have to talk fast.'

'What's so important, anyway?'

'This,' said Tess. 'We've got the krools on the run, right?'

'Well, we've knocked most of them out, anyway.'

'Right. And I knocked out two today up in Northern Greenland that were definitely going backwards.'

'Did you?'

'Yes. Going at a hell of a speed, too. So listen. Maybe the job is finished, you know? And even if it isn't, I could always finish it off on my own if I had to.'

'But why should you?'

'Because maybe you can still have the chance to be what you want to be.'

'But there's not much choice up here, is there? Anyway, I quite like being a dragon.'

So did Tess, but if she had been a dragon at that moment, she would have burned his nose again. 'Don't be an idiot, Kevin,' she said. 'We've only survived so far because we can Switch! If you couldn't dodge those missiles and disappear at night you wouldn't stand a chance!'

Kevin sighed. 'I suppose you're right,' he said.

'But this way you still have a chance. With the speed we can travel as dragons, we could be in Ireland before morning. We might even have time for some bit of a party. At Lizzie's, maybe?'

'It's a bit risky, isn't it?' asked Kevin. 'They'll be able to follow us on radar, won't they?'

'So what?' said Tess. 'We've been dodging planes and missiles for two days, now. What could they possibly throw at us that we couldn't handle?'

Kevin said nothing. Tess rubbed her gloved hands together and blew on them. 'Come on, Kevin,' she said. 'It's too cold to stand around and think about it.'

'I suppose it is,' said Kevin. 'The only problem is, I still don't really know what I want to be. There was something nice about not having to choose, you know?'

'But you don't have to choose right now. You'll have all today and tonight to think about it. And in any case, you'll probably know when the time comes, won't you? The same way as you knew it was right to come up here?'

Kevin brightened. 'You know something?' he said. 'What?'

'For once in your life, you might be right.'

CHAPTER TWENTY-ONE

General Wolfe was on the edge of his seat. 'Come on, my tricky little friends,' he said to the moving blips on the monitor in front of him. 'You just keep right on going the way you are.'

The two UFOs were heading south, right out in the open above the Norwegian Sea. He had been following their progress for some time, watching the satellite pictures with growing anticipation. If they carried on in their present direction, they would soon be crossing the north-west tip of Scotland. And when they did, he would have a little surprise waiting for them.

At an air base in North Wales, Scud Morgan and his team were getting ready for take-off. They were in a line of planes similar to their own, crawling towards the runway, waiting their turn. The snow was still thick on the fields all around, but the skies were clear.

Scud was champing at the bit. 'Know something?' he said.

'Not a thing,' said Hadders, who was carefully checking over the instruments on the panel in front of him.

'I got a feeling we're going to see some action tonight.'

'I guess that's why they're sending us up there, Scud.'

'Yeah, course, I know that. But this feeling is more than that. It's in my bones, you know? Like, we were the first guys to spot those two aliens out there, weren't we?'

'I never saw any aliens.'

'What were they, then? They weren't planes. Everyone knows those two things weren't planes. You must be some kind of a nut-head if you think those two things are planes.'

'Nobody knows what they are,' said Hadders, 'and nobody knows how to stop 'em. But it seems to me that there's no sense in talking flying saucers here and getting ourselves into a stew.'

'A stew?' said Scud. He jammed on the brakes as he came up on to the tail of the plane in front, and the three of them lurched forward into their seat-belts. 'Who's getting into a stew? I'm not getting into a stew. Are you getting into a stew? Nobody gets into a stew in this bird, not as long as I'm in command, anyhow.'

Hadders sighed and continued with his last-minute checklist. 'All I'm saying,' Scud went on, 'is that I got this feeling. We were the first to see those two aliens, and I got an idea we're going to be the last.'

'Did you see any aliens, Jake?' said Hadders.

'Couple of planes,' said Jake.

There were no missiles aboard the bombers which lifted off, one after another into the star-lit sky. They were fully loaded though, but this time with another kind of weapon.

When Scud and his crew took off, Tess and Kevin were still well out over the Norwegian Sea. They were flying low, skimming close to the waves, enjoying their flight. The night air was clear and fresh, and they were beginning to believe that they had finally left the battlefield behind.

Once they had passed over the line of new ice that the krools had made, they got the occasional glimpse of a whale breaking the surface of the sea, and they knew that they were heading away from the cold, towards life again. Tess looked across at Kevin flying beside her, and it seemed that it was the first time she had been able to relax for days. What they had done was ridiculous, impossible. It made no sense at all, and yet it was true, and they had done it. The starlight shimmered from the metallic scales of Kevin's back as he turned to her and winked. She was a dragon, flying with another dragon across the sea beneath the stars, and she took time to drink it in and fix the images and sensations into her mind. Because she knew that whatever else happened, she would never feel like this again.

Within an hour, the thirty-five planes had reached their positions and were set in a holding pattern, waiting.

'You got a reading on them yet, Jake?' said Scud.

'Just what the satellite's sending.'

'They far off?'

'About fifteen minutes, I guess.'

'What's that on the radar, then?'

'Let's see. FT6R. That's Pete and Jeremy coming round again. Hi, guys.'

'Jeremy!' Scud spat. 'That's what you get for working with this British crowd. Whoever heard of a serviceman called Jeremy, for God's sake? Wouldn't you think he'd change his name or something? How can anybody fight a war when there's people called Jeremy flying around all over the place? How's a man supposed to think straight?'

'I'm not sure this is a war, Scud.'

'Read your book, Hadders. That's what some people do. Some people are born to read books and some are born to fight wars. I don't care what anyone else says, but when I'm in a plane, I'm fighting a war.'

Hadders broke one of the last spines from his comb and picked his teeth with it. 'You can say that again,' he said.

As the north tip of Scotland came into view, the two dragons did a quick loop-the-loop of delight. Wolfe, along with fifteen assembled advisers and assistants, held his breath. When the two UFOs resumed their course the print-outs on his table fluttered in the breeze.

They were over the land now, with the ragged western coast of Scotland to their right. Beneath them, the trees of huge forestry plantations poked their dark heads above the snow, and occasionally the sharp eyes of the dragons could make out the roofs of abandoned villages and isolated farmhouses. Tess was surprised to find that now and then she got a whiff of wood-smoke. There were people still surviving somehow, despite the depth of the snow. She was looking down, trying to get a glimpse of the heat of hearth-fires, and Kevin must have been as well, otherwise they would have not been taken so utterly by surprise by finding themselves flying straight into the path of an oncoming plane.

'They're going to pass right under us!' yelled Jake.

'And we're going to get 'em,' said Scud.

'OK,' said Hadders. 'Just take it easy, now. We all clear of other planes, Jake?'

'All clear. And we're on computer count-down, seven, six . . .'

'Hell, where are they? They got no lights or nothing.'

'Four, three . . .'

They were practically beneath the plane before they had time to blink.

'Two . . .'

Tess acted Goat, swung wildly to her left and upwards, Switching as she did so.

'One . . .'

But Kevin was just that little bit slower. He carried straight on, and he Switched, too.

'Zero!'

But he was too late. The napalm bomb dropped from the undercarriage of the plane and exploded in the air, scattering its flaming contents of sticky jelly through the sky and down on to the forest below.

'We got 'em!' yelled Scud. 'Did we get 'em, Jake, did we?'

'Get what?' said Hadders. 'I didn't see anything. Did you see anything?'

'I didn't see anything, but we sure as hell got 'em, whatever they were. Did we get 'em, Jake?'

'How should I know? I couldn't see anything.'

'But you got the machines. What do the machines say?'

'The machines say there's a big fire behind us, that's all.'

'Anything flying away from it?'

'Yeah. We are.'

'I knew it,' said Scud. 'I could feel it in my bones. We got 'em.'

Jake was still watching the satellite monitor in the back of the plane. 'I wonder,' he said.

'You bet we did,' said Scud. 'And you know something else?'

'What?' said Hadders.

'This is going to be cause for a celebration, pal. I'm going to buy you a brand new comb.'

By the time Tess had got control of her flight and swung round to see what was happening, the plane was gone and the forest was blazing. Above it, she could just make out a speck of flame which twisted as it tumbled down and was lost in the thick smoke and sparks which rose from the inferno beneath. Her bird mind was utterly calm and detached, but her human mind was screaming. 'Switch, Kevin, Switch!'

But it would have been no use. Nothing, not even the dragon, could have survived those flames. Kevin was done for.

Nonetheless she waited, an eagle hovering high above the forest as the fire reduced it to a skeleton of charred tree-trunks and melted the snow around its edges. She stayed long after the planes had stopped circling and gone away. She stayed until the dawn arrived, the dawn of Kevin's fifteenth birthday, but all it brought with it was military helicopters coming to examine the aftermath of the fire. They would find nothing.

With a heavy heart, Tess wheeled and flew away.

CHAPTER TWENTY-TWO

Tired and dispirited, Tess made her way back to Dublin. It was a difficult journey, and she tried several different birds before she finally settled on the Arctic tern. It was a tough little bird, she discovered, and coped well with the cold and the long hours on the wing, but even so, she was ready to drop by the time she spotted the Phoenix Park and came in to land.

The lights were on in her house. Tess stood among the trees across the street and looked around carefully. There was no one about. The snow was melting fast, but there were still deep drifts around the trunks of the trees and against hedges and walls. The prospect of warmth and rest was almost irresistible, but even as she made the Switch, Tess realised that something was wrong. Much as she loved her parents and longed for the comfort of home, what she needed above all else at this moment was understanding. The shock and grief she felt at Kevin's death struck her with full force now that she was human again, and it was something she would never be able to share with her parents. There was only one person in the world that she could tell, and that was Lizzie.

Reluctantly, Tess turned her back on the bright lights of her parents' house and returned to the shape of the brave little seabird. On tired wings she crossed the city and searched among the snowy fields and trees for the ruin of the big house and the little cottage beside it. When, after some time, she found it, she was relieved to see smoke rising from the chimney and paths cleared to the sheds. She landed on the roof of the hen-house and looked around for a while before she decided on the best way of getting into Lizzie's house without alarming her.

The other cats arched their backs and hissed when they heard the stranger come in through the cat-flap and scratch at the kitchen door, but Lizzie knew straight away.

'You's back!' she said as she opened the door. 'That was quick!'

Tess Switched, and the cats scattered into the corners of the room. Lizzie looked at her in concern. 'You's worn out, girl. What's happened?'

Tess flopped, exhausted, into a chair. The seat had been warmed by the cats, and for a long time Tess sat in silence, letting the warmth sink into her and waiting for her strength to return. Lizzie went over to the sink and set about making tea, but she did it quietly, and Tess forgot that she was there until the cup was pressed gently into her hand. She sat up and sipped the sweet tea, but still she could not speak.

'Rat-boy, huh?'

Tess looked up. Above the hob in the fireplace, a

twitching brown nose was poking out of the hole. An unusually long nose. Tears began to pour down Tess's cheeks. Lizzie took off her slipper and threw it at the hole. Long Nose squeaked and disappeared, but a moment later he was back.

'Nanananana,' he said. 'Tail Short Seven Toes curled up with Long Nose and Nose Broken by a Mousetrap. Us guys sleeping. Sun rising, us guys bright eyes, hungry and strong.'

Tess nodded through her tears. 'He's right, Lizzie,' she said. 'You and I can talk in the morning.'

'Off you go, then,' said Lizzie. 'But don't forget to come back to me, will you?'

'Of course not.' Tess gulped down the last of the tea, then put down the cup and Switched. As soon as she was a rat again, she felt better. Rats live together closely, but without attachment or sentiment, and although Kevin's death was still an absence, it was no longer a loss or a cause for grief. She shook herself and began to groom, to put herself back in order, but Lizzie picked her up and lifted her to the hole in the chimney breast before the cats could catch sight of her. There she touched noses with the other two, and quite dispassionately told them her adventures as she followed them through a twisting network of passages and underground tunnels. Long Nose loved the story, and made her tell the bit about the meeting with the first krool again and again, until eventually they arrived at their destination, a snug nest beneath the cowshed. Tess curled up close against Nose Broken by a Mousetrap, and the last thing she heard before she fell asleep was the sound of Nancy above her head, drowzily chewing the cud.

The next morning, Tess made her way back to the

cottage, and, in human form again, told Lizzie everything that had happened. The old woman listened carefully, slapping her knees with delight at each new development in the story. When Tess had finished, they both sat quietly for a few minutes, then Lizzie said, 'If I remembers right, you likes pancakes for breakfast.'

Tess looked over at her in astonishment. 'How can you think about pancakes, Lizzie? Aren't you upset about Kevin?'

'No,' said Lizzie. 'I isn't. There are those who say there's life after death and those who say there isn't. But until I gets there myself, I isn't in any position to say one thing or another.'

'But that isn't the point,' said Tess. 'I'm sad because I won't see him any more.'

'Then you's sad for yourself, girl, not for Kevin.'

Tess looked into the fire. The flames were just taking hold of the wood, leaping up towards the kettle, sending sparks up to disappear into the darkness of the chimney. Lizzie got up and began to crack eggs into a bowl.

'Maybe you're right,' said Tess. 'I don't know. But the thing I can't understand is why it should have been us. I mean, why was I born a Switcher, and Kevin. And you, why you?'

'But all kids is Switchers,' said Lizzie. 'Didn't you know that?'

'What do you mean? How could all kids be Switchers?'

Lizzie began to beat flour into the eggs. 'All kids is born with the ability. But very few learns that they has it. You has to learn before you's eight years old, because after that your mind is set and you takes on the same beliefs as everybody else. A lot of kids find

196

out they can Switch, but when their parents and friends say it's impossible, they believes them instead of theirselves, and then they forgets about it, like they forgets everything that doesn't fit in with what everyone else thinks. It's only a few who has enough faith in theirselves to know that they can do it despite what the rest of the world thinks.'

'So was it all just chance, then? Just coincidence?'

Lizzie was beating furiously at her batter. 'Chance?' she said. 'Coincidence? I doesn't know what the words mean.'

A movement in the chimney breast made Tess look up. One crooked nose and four small ones were poking out of the hole, and five pairs of eyes were fixed upon her. 'Grandchildren,' said Nose Broken by a Mousetrap. 'Tail Short Seven Toes telling krools, mammoths, dragons, little ones watching.'

The four small noses quivered in nervous anticipation. Tess laughed and, while Lizzie fried the pancakes, she told her story once again.

Tess's parents were astonished to see her arriving home. They had forgone the chance to escape the weather and flee to southern Europe and had stayed in the seized-up city instead, in case Tess returned. When the snow began to melt and the roads were cleared their hopes rose, but by the time she finally knocked on the door they had almost given up on her. They greeted her with tears and laughter, and there was much talk of forgiveness and all being well that ends well.

But they found it difficult to adjust to the changes that had happened to Tess. Because although the date told her that it had not been so long since she left her bedroom window in the form of an owl, by

197

another reckoning it was a year, a lifetime, an ice age. She could barely remember the child that she had been.

Tess had always been aloof, preferring her own company to that of others, but now it was more than that. She had become a stranger to her parents, and in all the years that followed they never learnt more about her absence than they had heard from Garda Maloney's report. All they knew was that she had been away with a boy, and that she would not or could not discuss the matter. It was clear from her withdrawn behaviour that in some way or other it had ended badly, and they believed that she would tell them about it when she was ready.

So, although they noticed that from time to time Tess wore a silver ring that they had never seen before, they didn't ask her about it. They left her alone and tried to resume the family life of old. Tess tried, too, but it was clear to all of them that she was acting mechanically and not from her heart. She made an effort at school, and succeeded in making one or two friends, but that was mechanical, too, and superficial. It helped to pass the time, but it did nothing to relieve the deep loneliness she felt. Nor did her occasional trips to the park, to join with squirrels or birds or deer for an hour or two. She was not a part of their world, she knew, and nor was she a part of the world of home and school. She was somewhere in between, and all alone.

And her sense of isolation increased whenever she turned on the TV or radio and heard them talking about the famous 'Northern Polar Crisis'. The krools, as she suspected, had retreated back into the ice cap and left no trace of their passing apart from the mysterious barren pathways which stretched for hundreds of miles through the vegetation in the Arctic Circle. A thousand theories were put forward, and it seemed that there was a new one getting aired every week. Each was as ludicrous as the last, but what really made Tess's blood boil was the unanimous agreement that General Wolfe and Scud Morgan were the heroes of the day. And no human being apart from herself and Lizzie would ever know the truth.

Tess's parents never reproached her, but she knew that they had suffered a lot when she disappeared. They didn't try to stop her going for her walks in the park, but they made her promise never to be away for more than two hours and never to go out at night without telling them where she was going. Tess knew that in their terms it was a reasonable request and she agreed. She was sure that in time they would come to trust her again, and she would have more freedom, but in the meantime she would have to live without seeing either Lizzie or her friends the rats.

So she had to look elsewhere for comfort. She saved up her pocket money until she had enough to buy the biggest cage in the pet shop and the nicest white rat they had. Her parents were surprised, because Tess had so often expressed her disapproval of keeping animals in captivity, but they didn't object.

But the rat turned out to be a terrible disappointment. It was terrified of the brown rat that she turned into, and terrified to leave its cage. When she did finally tempt it out into the room, it was timid and clumsy and slow, and no amount of persuasion would bring it to attempt the stairs. The worst of it, though, was that the poor, stupid creature could not even speak Rat. It had been born and brought up in a cage like its parents and grandparents, and it had never been allowed, much less encouraged, to use its intelligence. It had a few basic words-images, but beyond that it was mute, and no effort on Tess's part succeeded in teaching it. The white rat was a mental infant, and would remain that way all its life.

It was company, nonetheless, and quite often Tess would lie awake at night, listening to it exercising itself on the wheel and talking baby-talk while she mulled over her experiences and thought about the decision which would face her in another year or so, when she turned fifteen. Time after time she dreamed of the possibilities, weighing the peaceful lives of dolphins and whales against the briefer but more thrilling lives of rats and goats. Time after time she seemed to reach a satisfactory decision, only to remind herself of how. heart-broken her parents would be if she were to disappear from their lives for ever, without explanation. And on a particular night a few days after New Year, she had just reached the point, once again, of deciding to stay human, when something happened that was to make her think all over again, in an entirely different way.

It was the white rat's sudden silence that pulled her out of her reflections and alerted her to the change in the atmosphere. She watched it sniff the air, then turn around and gaze steadily into the darkness outside her window. The hairs prickled on the back of Tess's neck as she got out of bed and crossed warily to the window to look out.

There, on the same tree that the owl had once called from, was the most beautiful bird she had ever seen. It was familiar to her, somehow, and yet she was sure that she had never seen it before, or any other like it. Its bright feathers glowed in the light cast out from her room, and its tail hung down below it, way longer than its body. Then, suddenly, Tess remembered the page of the book where she had seen the bird pictured, and even before she noticed that it had only three toes on its right foot, she knew that it was Kevin. She knew that he had learned, in the nick of time, to find for himself the invisible path which lies between what is and what isn't. As he had fallen, burning, that autumn night which was the eve of his birthday, he had made his final, irreversible Switch, and become the only creature, either of this world or not of it, that could survive that raging fire. And when the helicopters had left the following morning, he had appeared again, rising from his own ashes; a beautiful, golden phoenix.

Tess's heart leapt, racing ahead of her into the night skies where she would soon be flying beside her friend. With a silent apology to her parents for breaking her promise, she reached for the latch and pushed open the window.

PART TWO

MIDNIGHT'S CHOICE

CHAPTER ONE

The white rat watched as the two golden birds rose up into the night sky and disappeared from view. A few minutes ago, one of them had been his owner, Tess. Then she had seen the other bird on the tree outside her window, and she had shimmered, changed, and flown away. For a moment or two the rat remained still, staring into the empty darkness in perplexity, then he twitched his whiskers, washed his nose with his paws and jumped back on to his exercise wheel.

As she soared up high above the park, Tess had no thought of what she had left behind her. In her young life, she had used her secret ability to Switch to experience many different forms of animal life, but she had never been a phoenix before. All her attention was absorbed by this new and exhilarating experience, and until she had become comfortable with it, she could think of nothing else.

She followed the other bird faithfully as he rose through the night sky, higher and higher. Each sweep of her golden wings seemed effortless, and propelled her so far that she felt almost weightless. Behind her, the long sweeping tail seemed to have no more substance than the tail of a comet. It was as though the nature of the bird was to rise upwards; gravity had scarcely any power over it at all.

Up and up the two of them flew, not slowing until they had risen well clear of the city's sulphurous halo and into the crisp, cool air beyond. Then the three-toed phoenix began to drift upwards in a more leisurely way and eventually came to a halt. Tess slowed down and began to hover beside her friend, using her wings to tread the air as a swimmer treads water. But when she looked at him, she noticed that he wasn't using his wings. He was merely sitting on the air, floating without any effort at all. With slight apprehension, she followed suit and stilled her wings. It worked. The two of them floated there, weightless as clouds, looking down on the city of Dublin below.

Back in Tess's bedroom, the white rat's wheel was spinning so fast that its bearings were getting hot. He didn't understand what had occurred when Tess had Switched and taken flight but it excited him, and the only way he had of expressing that excitement was in movement. So he ran and ran, the bars of the wheel becoming blurred as they passed beneath his racing feet, again and again and again.

A faint breeze moved the curtain and reached the rat's cage. He paused in his stride, then stopped so abruptly that the flying wheel carried him right round inside it three times before it fell to swinging him back and forth and finally came to rest. The white rat was frozen to the spot, every nerve on edge as he strained his senses to understand what that mysterious breeze had brought with it. He waited, and was just about to return to his futile travels when the message came again. There was no mistaking it this time. Somewhere in the city streets, someone or something was sending out a call which Algernon had no power to resist. He hurled himself against the side of the cage, scrabbling with his paws and biting the bars. When this failed he began to dig frantically against the metal floor, throwing food and sawdust and water in all directions in his desperation to escape. But the cage was too well made. The message grew weaker until at last the white rat resigned himself and curled up, exhausted, among the disordered bedding in the corner.

Once Tess had become accustomed to the strange sensation of floating, she turned her attention to her friend. Everything had happened so quickly that she hadn't even greeted him yet; not properly, anyway. There was so much she wanted to know, so much news to catch up on. There was no need for them to recount their adventures in the Arctic when they had fought the dreadful krools; nor was there any need to remember the awful moment when Kevin had Switched just a moment too late and got caught by the flying napalm. The last time she had seen him he had been a small bird, burning, tumbling into the flaming forest below, and there had seemed no possibility of hope.

She could understand the leap of imagination that had enabled him to escape by turning into a phoenix and rising again from his own ashes, but a lot of time had gone by since then and she was impatient to know where he had been and what he had done.

She turned to look at him, but when she caught sight of his golden eyes, all her questions suddenly seemed to be without meaning. Her mind stilled and became peaceful, merging into his in a kind of featureless calm. All at once, Tess felt that she knew all there was to know about the nature of the phoenix. It was ageless, timeless, the essence of all that was pure and beyond the reach of mortal concerns.

Far below, the life of the city continued despite the lateness of the hour. The last buses returned to the station and parked; taxis picked up party-goers and brought them home; lovers stretched the evening on into the small hours, strolling slowly home. Beneath the roofs, nurses worked night-shifts, presses rolled with the morning's newspapers, babies and small children woke and cried, bringing their parents groggily from bed. And still further down, in their own subsystem of homes and highways, hundreds of thousands of city rats were awake and going about their business. From her great height, Tess perceived it all happening. It was her city, her home, and yet she was so detached from it that she might as well have been looking down on an ants' nest. She sank into the ecstasy of the experience and all her cares melted away.

When Tess returned to her bedroom shortly before dawn and resumed her human form, the sense of joyousness remained with her. It was as though all the worries of the last few months had vanished and been replaced by a calm certainty that the future was assured. The choice of the final form that she would have to take when she reached her fifteenth birthday seemed to have been made for her.

Nothing that she had ever been before could

compare with the serene, weightless existence of the phoenix, and she could not imagine ever wanting to be anything else. Already she was beginning to miss it.

Although she wasn't particularly tired, Tess got into her pyjamas and snatched a couple of hours' sleep before breakfast. So it wasn't until her father woke her and she began to get into her school uniform that she noticed the state of the white rat's cage. There was always a certain amount of clearing up to be done there in the mornings, but Tess had never seen anything like this before. The water bowl had been knocked over and the floor was a mess of soggy food and sawdust. The top of the chest of drawers where the cage stood and the carpet underneath it were both littered with debris that the rat's scrabbling feet had thrown out, and the shredded paper of his bedding had been pulled out of the nest-box and slung over the wheel like festive streamers.

'What on earth have you been up to, Algernon?' said Tess.

In reply, the white rat hopped into the wheel for a morning stroll, but before he had done two turns the paper strips caught up in the axle and jammed it.

Tess tried to speak to him in the visual language of the rats that she had learnt during her adventures with Kevin.

'Sunflower seeds and shavings all over the place, huh? White rat digging, huh? White rat angry, huh?'

Algernon twitched his nose in bewilderment. Tess finished dressing, then took him out of the cage and put him on the floor while she sorted out the mess.

He was his usual timid self, never straying far from Tess's feet and investigating her school bag with the utmost care, as though something large and aggressive might leap out of it and grab him. By the time she had emptied the contents of the cage into a plastic bag and replaced it with fresh food and bedding, he was standing up against Tess's shoe, sniffing the air above him and longing to get back home.

'Tess!' came her mother's voice from the kitchen.

'I'm coming,' she called back, releasing the wheel from its bearings and starting to unwind the tangled paper. It broke in her fingers every time she tried to pull it clear of the wheel, and looked like taking a lot longer to unravel than she had expected.

'Tess!'

'Yes!'

'Your breakfast is ready!'

'All right, all right, I'm coming!' Irritation was apparent in her voice, and she felt disgusted with herself, aware of how rapidly the righteous mood of a few hours ago had passed. She made one more attempt to free the wheel's axle, then threw it down in disgust.

'Cage with no wheel in it,' she said to Algernon in Rat as she picked him up from the floor, a little roughly.

'Huh?' said Algernon. He loved his wheel. Apart from eating and sleeping, it was the only pleasure he had in life. But Tess had one eye on the racing clock and was growing angrier by the minute.

'White rat with no brain,' she said. 'White rat with hairless baby rats in nest.' She shoved him into the cage and closed the door.

'Huh?' he said again. 'Huh?'

Tess ignored him. She tied a knot in the top of the

plastic bag and turned her mind to what she was likely to need in school that day. They would be playing camogie: that would mean helmet and hurley . . .

'Tess! You're going to be late!'

She ran downstairs and snatched a hasty breakfast, then raced for the bus. As it brought her through the streets of the city she looked up into the sky, hoping to catch a glint of gold; some sign that it hadn't all been a foolish dream. Clouds had gathered since the early hours, and from time to time a ray of sunshine broke through them, but she knew that it had nothing to do with the phoenix.

The phoenix. As she thought about him, and about the time they had spent up there above the city, Tess realised that, although the bird undoubtedly was Kevin, it wasn't the friend she had known. In all their previous adventures together, no matter what form they had taken, they would recognise each other instantly. Rats, goats, dolphins, even mammoths and dragons had not served to disguise the individuality of the person who dwelt within them. But the more Tess thought about it, the harder she found it to identify the Kevin she knew and loved with that lofty, ethereal bird. When she remembered the way it had felt to be with him, the sense of joyous detachment and freedom, she longed to be back there again, away from the smoggy trundling of the traffic and the dreary day ahead. But it was, she realised, because of the delight of the phoenix nature and not because of any sense of companionship. The joy of that experience ought to be sustaining her, but instead it was being nudged aside by doubt. Where was Kevin? Where was all the rest of him, the mischievousness and the moodiness and the flash of anger that came

211

to his eyes? There was no sign of any of those things in the phoenix. It was like some kind of divine being, capable of nothing except existing; just radiating light and goodness.

Her mind wandered and returned to the problem of Algernon and his unusual behaviour. When she remembered how unkind she had been to him, she was sorry. Poor creature. He wasn't very smart, it was true, but he had the sweetest temperament imaginable. He was incapable of an unkind thought. How could she have been so cruel to him?

She closed her eyes and leant her head on the back of the seat. Taking a deep breath, she tried to think herself into the mood of perfect understanding that the form of the phoenix had given her the night before. But the only revelation she received was that she had, after all, forgotten her helmet and her hurley. She was going to be in big trouble.

CHAPTER TWO

Tess had a lousy day at school, and not only because she had forgotten her camogie kit. Her mind refused to apply itself to the work in hand, and at every opportunity she sank into euphoric day-dream memories of the previous night. Only when she was ticked off by one of the teachers did she return her attention to the present. Her class-mates found her even more strange and dreamy than usual, and one or two of the more cynical ones took the opportunity to tease her.

'Look at Madam Tess with her head in the clouds.'

'Oh. Better than the rest of us, that one. Wouldn't bother trying to communicate with her.'

'You'd need to be on your knees to do that.'

'You'd need a priest.'

'Come on, exalted one, hear us, we pray.'

'Oh, stuff it, will you?' she said at last.

'Stuff it, stuff it. Hear ye, the almighty one has spoken. We must stuff it, one and all.'

Tess moved away, but the harsh laughter continued to ring in her ears long after the other girls had forgotten the incident. She knew that they could never understand what she was going through, but their reaction made her uneasy all the same. Glorious as it was, the phoenix experience seemed to be increasing her sense of loneliness and isolation.

At home that evening, she went straight up to her room. The white rat popped his head out of the nest box where he had been sleeping away a dull day. He looked for his wheel, still bewildered by the change in his circumstances, then stood up against the bars of the cage, whiskers twitching, pink eyes peering around ineffectually for Tess.

She opened the cage door and lifted him out. He fitted snugly into the crook of her arm as she stroked his sleek coat and apologised to him for her impatience that morning.

'Poor Algernon. It wasn't your fault, was it?' Her mind drifted back to the skies above the city and she turned to the window. It was January and already dark, but she hadn't drawn her curtains yet. Although she could see nothing beyond the black squares of the glass, she knew that somewhere out there the phoenix was waiting for her. It would be another year before her fifteenth birthday, another year before she had to decide once and for all what form the rest of her life would take. But what was there to say that she couldn't make that decision sooner? Why shouldn't she make it tonight, if she wanted to? She could be free of school and home and all those human concerns that dragged at her existence. She could be out there with her friend and not a worry in the world. Once again the memory of the night before crept back, filling her with that glorious sense of lightness and well-being.

'Tess?'

Tess jumped. Her mother was standing in the doorway. 'Your tea is ready. Are you all right?'

'Yes. Just day-dreaming.'

'Anything wrong?'

'No. Nothing at all.' Tess stood up and slipped Algernon back into his cage, then followed her mother down the stairs.

As soon as she had finished her tea, Tess started on her homework, but when her father came home two hours later she was still struggling with a simple history project, unable to make her wandering mind concentrate. She put it away unfinished and joined her parents for dinner, the one meal of the day when they all sat down together.

The meal seemed to take for ever. Tess pushed her food around the plate and sighed a lot. Her father tried to chivvy the conversation along but it was a thankless task. As soon as she could, Tess made for the peace and quiet of her own room and settled herself to wait; she could do nothing safely until her parents were asleep. She could hear their quiet voices in the room below, and she wondered if they were talking about her, discussing her uncharacteristic loss of appetite or her dreamy mood. She wished, as she had done many times before, that she was not the only child, that she had sisters or brothers to share the responsibility with her.

The night was cold and windy, but Tess opened the window anyway and peered out. The darkness above the park was muddied by the street-lights, whose orange radiance leaked upwards like escaping heat. But beyond it, Tess could just make out a few faint stars appearing and disappearing as heavy clouds moved across the sky. As she watched, it seemed to her that one of them was a little brighter than the others, and golden in colour. She fixed her eyes on it, unsure whether it was drawing closer or whether her imagination was playing tricks. The star seemed to blink and turn. Was it moving? Did it have a tail which streamed out behind it, even a short way?

Tess's concentration was abruptly broken by a loud scratching noise from Algernon's cage. She turned and saw him trying to burrow into the corner where his wheel had been, throwing sawdust all over the cage and out through the bars.

'Poor old Algernon,' said Tess and then, in Rat, 'Wheel, huh?'

Algernon made no reply, but turned his attention to another corner of the cage and continued to scrabble away desperately. It was uncharacteristic behaviour, and it worried Tess. She picked up the wheel and began again to unravel the wound-up paper from around the axle. She had done most of the work that morning, and it didn't take long to free it and clear the last few shreds which were draped between the bars.

'Here you go, Algie. Is this what you want?' Tess opened the hatch in the top of the cage and reached in with the wheel in her hand. Before she could react, before she could even blink, Algernon had run up the bars of the cage, out through the hatch, and down Tess's legs to the floor. Tess stared at him in amazement. She had never seen him behave like that before. Something must have happened to him. His timidity was gone, and instead of bumbling round short-sightedly he was scuttling into the corners of the room and scratching at the carpet with his claws.

Quickly, Tess refitted the wheel and checked that it was spinning freely. Then she tidied up the floor of the cage, picked the stray shavings out of the food-bowl, and replaced the dirty water with fresh from the tap.

By this time Algernon was at the door, poking his paws into the narrow gap beneath it and gnawing at the wood with his teeth. When Tess reached down to pick him up, he jumped in fright, as though he had been taken by surprise. He had never done that before, either. He wriggled and squirmed as she pushed him through the small door of the cage, and threw himself against it when she closed it. Tess hoped it was the loss of the wheel that had upset him, and that once he found it back in its place he would settle himself down. His behaviour disturbed her more than she liked to admit, and she wondered if she should take him to the vet.

'White rat in pain, huh?' she said to him. 'White rat afraid of sore head? Sore belly?'

Algernon paused in his restless scurrying and looked at her. 'White rat go,' he said, his thought images dim and poorly formed. 'White rat go under city.'

His pictures of the rats' underground system were whimsy, like a young child's drawing of a fairy-tale land. But it was the first time he had used that image, or even given any intimation that he knew such a place existed.

'Brown rats in tunnels,' said Tess. 'Brown rats tough, fierce, biting white rat.'

'White rat go,' said Algernon stubbornly, his rest-lessness returning. 'White rat go, white rat go, white rat go.' He began to chew with his yellow teeth at the bars of the cage.

Tess sighed. 'Teeth worn down,' she said to him. 'Sunflower seeds won't open, white rat hungry.'

Algernon took no notice whatsoever. Tess returned to the window, but it was impossible for her to relax with the sound of Algernon chewing and scratching and rushing around his cage. Eventually she picked up a book and went downstairs, hoping that he would settle down in her absence. If he was still the same way tomorrow she could bring him to the vet.

Her parents were glad to see her coming down, and her father made room for her on the sofa beside him.

'Everything all right?' he said.

'Just Algernon. He's a bit restless. It's not like him.'

'I expect he needs a pal,' said her mother. 'What about getting another one?'

'As long as it's not female,' said her father. 'There's enough rats in the world as it is without breeding more of them.'

Tess laughed, reassured. The TV programme was humorous, the room was warm, and she had no premonition at all of the dramatic changes that were about to come into her life.

When the evening film was over, Tess brought an apple upstairs to share with Algernon as a bed-time treat. The rat however, had other things on his mind. The room was cold when Tess came into it, and the first thing she did was to go across and close the window. There was no sign of the phoenix beyond it, and she turned her attention to Algernon. He was upside down, hanging by his paws to the wire roof and gnawing on the metal clasp which kept the roof hatch secure. The water bowl had been knocked over again, and almost the entire contents of the cage had been hurled through the bars, littering up the room in a wide circle around the cage. Tess groaned and fought down a desire to punish the white rat. He was already disturbed enough, and scaring him further would not accomplish anything. Far better to try and find out what the problem was.

'Apple, huh?' she said.

In reply, Algernon dropped from the top of the cage, twisting in mid-air so that he landed on his feet, then proceeded to perform the most extraordinary feat of rodent gymnastics, leaping up the sides of the cage, across the roof and down to the floor again in a dizzying sequence of somersaults.

'White rat go, white rat go, white rat go,' he repeated as he swung wildly around.

Tess began to realise that the situation was much more serious than she had thought. It was clear now that the problem wasn't just going to disappear and there was no sense in trying to ignore it. Where did Algernon want to go, and why? She turned his repetitive visual statement into a question and, in reply, Algernon sent a most extraordinary image into her mind.

It was a little like the visual name the city rats had given to Kevin, a gruesome mixture of rat and a rat's conception of a boy. But this new image was vaguer, and tied up with other images as well; wolves perhaps, and bats, all in darkness. Strangest thing of all, and the most disturbing thing to Tess's human mind, was that this being was calling. It was calling for all the rats in the city to come towards it, and the reason for Algernon's behaviour was suddenly crystal clear. For Tess could tell without any doubt that if she had been a rat at that moment, she would have had no resistance whatsoever to that call.

CHAPTER THREE

Tess sat on the windowsill and stared out into the darkness, longing for the phoenix to come. Behind her, Algernon was still rattling against the sides of his cage, his anxiety growing into a kind of dementia as he found that all his efforts were useless. Tess kept her mind firmly closed to his pathetic babbling. The weird communication that she had tuned into with her rat mind disturbed her a great deal and she knew that she was turning her back on the problem. But the lure of the phoenix was too strong.

Her parents' door eventually closed, and in a surprisingly short time she heard her father's regular snores coming through the wall. There was still no sign of the golden creature, but as she looked out into the darkness, Tess realised that this didn't matter. She could still re-live the experience on her own. The wonder of being a phoenix had nothing to do with companionship. It was beyond companionship; beyond all worldly attachments.

She was just on the point of deciding to Switch when something happened which made her change her mind. In a last, desperate attempt to break free, Algernon hurled himself at the door of the cage with such force that it sprang open and he found himself sliding over the edge of the chest of drawers and falling towards the floor. Tess caught sight of him as he fell, but before she could get to him he had landed, picked himself up, and was racing towards the corner of the room.

Tess followed, irritated by the delay but concerned as well. Despite Algernon's limitations as a companion, she was fond of him and she would have hated to see him coming to any harm.

There was no fireplace in Tess's room but there had been one, long ago, and the chimney-breast ran up one wall. Beside it was a redundant corner, about the size of a wardrobe, and Tess had helped her father to put doors across it when they first moved in. She kept her clothes there, hanging from an old broom handle, and beneath them her shoes and boots were arranged on the floor.

Algernon ran straight towards this cupboard as though he knew exactly where he was going. Tess and her father had never got around to fixing bolts on to the doors, and they always stood slightly open. Algernon nosed through the gap and disappeared among the footwear. Tess followed and pulled the doors wide open, just in time to see the rat's pink tail disappearing down a tiny gap between the floorboards and the wall of the chimney-breast. There was only one way to follow him. Switching had become so much a part of Tess's nature that she no longer had to think about it. She didn't even stand still but, in one fluid movement, changed into a brown rat and went slithering down the hole in hot pursuit.

Beneath the floor and behind the walls, a maze of old rat passage-ways ran through the house. Tess hadn't known they were there, but she might have guessed. All old houses are riddled with rat-runs, even if they aren't in current use.

Despite Tess's speed, Algernon had already disappeared behind the first of the joists which ran beneath the floorboards. But to her surprise, Tess realised that she didn't need to follow him. Her rat mind had picked up on the command from the mysterious stranger, and there was no doubt that she and Algernon were heading in the same direction.

She scuttled down through the walls of the house, between the courses of bricks, until she came into a long, rat-made conduit which connected with the drains. At the end of that, she caught a glimpse of Algernon's tail as he turned a bend in a pipe. She accelerated, and after a few more twists and turns she found that she was gaining on him. Before long she had caught up, but when she tried to communicate with him, he ignored her, his mind fixed exclusively on the unknown destination ahead.

The most direct way of following the call led the two rats across the city by way of drains and underfloor passages. Tess was surprised by Algernon's speed and agility, and also by his apparent lack of fear. She realised as she ran beside him that this was what he had been deprived of as he grew up in his artificial environment. It was no surprise that he was dull-witted and inarticulate, since he had missed out on the rats' basic education in life. But all that was changing now. Who could tell how much his intelligence might increase, provided he could avoid the common pitfalls of city rats and stay alive long enough to learn his way around.

One of these hazards, poison, was very much in evidence in several of the gardens they had to pass through. Tess was on guard, but Algernon was far too preoccupied to be diverted by food, no matter how enticing it smelled. Where cats were concerned, however, his single-mindedness was a considerable handicap and, on two separate occasions, Tess had to rescue him; once by steering him away from the waiting jaws of a large tom, and once by charging a cat that was just about to grab him from behind. The cat was so surprised by Tess's aggression that she turned tail and fled, and by the time she had recovered herself, the two rats were long gone.

The rest of the journey was safer. When they joined the sewers, Algernon proved to be an excellent swimmer, and his regular exercise on the wheel had made him fit enough to cope with the slippery exertions of climbing back out of them. By the time they surfaced, in order to cross a small open square, he was a lot less white than he had been, but still not as camouflaged as Tess would have liked him to be. Because what she feared most for him had yet to be encountered, and that was the reaction of the other rats. She was not surprised that they hadn't come across any before now, because she was working on the assumption that all the others within range of the strange call had got a long head start on them. They were stragglers, she and Algernon, bringing up the rear. But she knew that before long they would be getting close to their destination, close to the moment of truth.

They dropped back into the underworld by means

of a hole in the ground beneath the cover of bushes in a corner of the tiny park. Tess called to Algernon again, warning him to take his time and watch out for cats, but when she opened her mind for his reply she caught nothing but a babble of rat images. They were close. Above them, they could hear the deep rumble of a car passing along a street. A moment later they were on the other side and, surprisingly, beginning to climb.

Abruptly, Algernon stopped. He was ahead of Tess and blocking the narrow passage which ran higgledy piggledy through a foundation wall between detached houses. She couldn't see beyond him, but she could hear the restless rustling of a great gathering of rats. Impatiently, Tess squeezed her way in beside Algernon, whose fluid body seemed to elongate as he made room for her in the narrow space. They were looking into the kitchen of a vacant house. Tess held her breath, astonished by what she was seeing. There were rats of all shapes and sizes: rats with grey coats, brown coats, black coats, sleek rats and mangy rats, thin rats and fat ones, all milling around in an aimless fashion. The dim light on their moving backs made Tess think of water, rippling and flowing. The kitchen was flooded with rats.

Her first concern was for Algernon. The hole in the wall where they were standing was about two feet from the ground. It would be easy to slip down the wall on to the floor, but not so easy to climb back up if there was trouble down there. A rat could scale that height in a flash, but not without a run-up. Already a few twitching noses were beginning to turn and look with curiosity at the two newcomers. Tess tried to pick up on the reactions, but the images she received were the visual equivalent of a roar in a football stadium – it was impossible to pick out any individual communication. She scanned the crowd, hoping to find someone she knew, but there was no one she recognised. She hesitated, and beside her Algernon was hesitating too. Whatever certainty had brought him here was severely weakened by the sight of so many rough and street-wise relatives.

Their decision was made for them. Without warning, another group of latecomers arrived in the passage behind them and, in their urgency to obey the call, they crowded forward relentlessly, pushing Tess and Algernon out of the hole in the wall and down into the restless mob below. Tess scrabbled through the crowd, desperate to stay close to Algernon and defend him against attack, but to her relief it proved unnecessary. The other rats grudgingly made space for him on the floor. Those closest to him inspected him curiously, but none had time or energy for aggression. All minds were firmly fixed on the powerful call that had brought them together.

Tess tuned into it as accurately as she could. It was a strange feeling, being drawn to something she could neither see nor hear, but which exerted such a powerful attraction on the rat part of her mind. It wasn't an active call; none of the rats was being asked to do anything except be there. It was as though they had been drawn by some sort of magnetism and were now held within its field of force, powerless to move away.

When she looked round, Tess saw Algernon struggling across the backs of the other rats towards the opposite side of the room. She tried to call him, aware that walking on another rat's back without permission is extremely bad manners. But if he heard her at all, he ignored her and carried on, oblivious to the warning clouts and nips that the other rats were giving him. Tess bared her teeth in exasperation and followed. There is no equivalent of an apology in the rat language; instead, Tess tried to convey a sense of urgency to the rats whose backs she crossed. It was of little use, however, since all but the eldest and wisest rats in the gathering were feeling a similar sense of urgency and had little patience with shovers. By the time Tess caught up with Algernon on the other side of the room, she was covered in little cuts and bruises and thoroughly fed up.

Algernon was scratched and bitten too, but he didn't seem to care. He was wriggling into a small hole that had been chewed in the bottom of the door which led into the hall. Tess followed. This narrow space was full of limp cardboard boxes and dusty trunks, long since abandoned. Rats were packed into every available space, level upon level of them, like the audience at a mega pop concert. A flight of stairs ran down from the floor above, and Tess noticed something which filled her rat mind with wry amusement. On the top step a cat was sitting, its face turned away in silent uninterest, as though it had no idea that it was surrounded by its worst enemy. Tess knew that the nonchalance was feigned, that beneath its smug exterior that cat was absolutely terrified. It was another measure of the single-mindedness of the gathered rats that they didn't set upon the poor creature and tear it to shreds. Despite herself, Tess hoped that they wouldn't change their minds.

Ahead of her, Algernon was slithering through the gathering again, over and under and around, any way that he could see of getting across the room. Tess followed, steeling herself against another series of bites and blows. From time to time she looked around her, hoping to catch a glimpse of friends from the past; Long Nose, perhaps, or Stuck Six Days in a Gutter Pipe. but she had no luck. They could have been anywhere. There was no way for Tess to tell how many rats had gathered, or if any were exempt from the call.

Algernon scuttled along beside the wall and Tess followed, determined to try and hold him still by force if once she managed to catch up with him. But as they slipped through the open door into the front room, a new message began on the stranger's mental wavelength. It was electrifying. Every rat in the place sprang to attention, some sitting up on their tails or standing on their hind legs in an effort to understand.

Tess was no less attentive than the others. The images coming into her mind were quite clear. The rats were to search beneath the city for a certain type of large, stone container. Some of these structures would be open to the human world, in huge basement rooms where they were regularly visited. Others would be buried in the ground where no humans could reach, and these were the kind that the rats had to go and find. If and when they succeeded they were to return and report.

That was all. As abruptly as it had started, the communication ended, and for a moment there was a profound silence. Then the visual babble began again, becoming pandemonium as a hundred thousand rats began to react. Tess resisted the temptation to join the confusion and looked round. Rats were pouring out of the room as though someone had let the plug out. She caught a glimpse of Algernon disappearing into a hole, like a piece of white paper being swept by the current into a drain, and a moment later she was alone.

CHAPTER FOUR

About a mile away, Jeff Maloney, the head keeper of Dublin Zoo, was being woken from a deep sleep by the phone. His irritation at being disturbed was worsened by the fact that he had only just got to sleep, following a long evening trying, unsuccessfully, to save a new-born calf in the pet section. Even now it was the first thought that came to his mind. The irony of it. The zoo had successfully bred hippos, elephants and rhinos, but when it came to a common Jersey cow, they had been powerless to save the calf.

As he crossed the sitting room, Jeff tripped over a dog first, and then a chair. He was swearing by the time he reached the light-switch, but it was nothing compared to the torrent of abuse that he let loose when the phone stopped ringing the instant before he reached it.

Tess stood in the middle of the floor and tried to

gather her thoughts. She sent out a few half-hearted calls towards Algernon and her other rat friends, but if any rat picked them up he or she was far too preoccupied to respond. It was all so confusing, and Tess's rat mind hadn't much space for rational thought. For a few moments she scuttled around the empty house with the vague idea of finding something to eat in order to calm her nerves. At the top of the stairs, the cat was still frozen in the same position, even though all the other rats were gone. Tess knew that the poor creature would climb walls rather than go in there again.

Think; she needed to think. Slipping back into the third of the rooms, she Switched back into human form. The smell of rats was strong, even to a human being's weak sense of smell. Tess wondered how she would feel if she opened the door one day and found her own house as full of rats as this one had been. Her parents would call in pest control; the house would be evacuated – perhaps the whole street. But no matter how hard people tried, they would never get rid of the rats in the city. There would still be rats there long after the human race had died out or moved elsewhere.

Tess shivered. She was still wearing her school uniform, but without a cardigan or a jacket. She was wasting time. As soon as she put her human mind to the problem which faced her she began to see her way forward. The image of the person that had called was still confused, but of two things she was sure. He was a boy, and he was a Switcher. The realisation brought a sense of excitement with it, because Kevin had told her that all Switchers must meet with another to pass on their knowledge. She had often wondered since whether this was true and, if so, when she would encounter this new friend. Now it seemed that the time had come. The only problem was that she still had to find him.

She concentrated hard, trying to remember how it had felt to her as a rat when the message had come through so strongly. Where, exactly, had it come from? Somewhere above, she realised, and behind her as she stood now. She turned round. Yes, that way. Not directly above, but ahead of her now; a house across the street perhaps?

Jeff Maloney was just getting comfortable in bed when the phone rang again. For a few seconds he hesitated, then decided not to ignore it. He took a different route across the sitting room this time, but unfortunately the dog had also decided to change location, and once again there was an outraged yelp as Jeff's foot came into contact.

This time he went straight for the phone, fumbling in the darkness for the receiver.

'Hello?'

'Hello. Jeff Maloney?'

'Speaking.'

'Garda barracks here. We have a report of an unusual bird at the edge of the Phoenix Park. We were wondering whether you had lost any.'

Jeff had visions of blundering around with nets in the night. It wouldn't be the first time such a thing had happened. 'What sort of bird?'

'I'll hand you over to the witness, hold on.'

There was a crackle, and then a sort of knocking sound, as though the receiver at the other end had been dropped on the floor. At last a rather drunken voice came on to the line.

'Hello?'

'Hello.'

'Hello?'

'Hello. Jeff Maloney here. You've seen an unusual bird?'

'By God, I have. Never saw anything like it. It must be one of your lads, come out of the zoo. I never saw anything like it.'

'Can you describe it to me?'

'It was golden, pure golden. I never saw anything like it.'

Jeff gritted his teeth, convinced that he was dealing with a hallucination. It wouldn't have been the first time that had happened, either. 'Can you tell me any more?' he said.

'I've never seen anything like it. It had ... sort of ... long tail feathers, hanging down. And it was golden.'

'Probably a hen pheasant,' said Jeff. 'We quite often see them in the park at this time of year. Was it sitting in a tree?'

'It was, by God, but it wasn't a pheasant, no way. It was golden, pure golden, I've never seen anything like it.'

Jeff sighed. 'A trick of the light, I'd imagine,' he said, as kindly as he could. 'Those street lights can have a strange effect sometimes.'

'Well, you can say what you like,' said the voice on the other end of the line, 'but that was no pheasant, hen or cock. I've–'

' – never seen anything like it, I know,' said Jeff, his patience finally deserting him. 'I appreciate your calling, and I'll check it out first thing in the morning on my way to work.'

'It'll be your loss if it's gone by then,' said the voice.

'It'll be my loss if I don't get a bit of sleep tonight, too. Goodnight, and thank you for your information.'

As he put down the receiver, Jeff heard the dog shuffling into the corner, well out of range.

The best way for Tess to get out of the empty house was to become a rat again. She made her way out by using a series of passages and air vents, then checked carefully up and down before leaving cover.

The street meant nothing to her. It was like dozens of others in the area, made up of two-storey brick-built houses dating from the fifties and early sixties. For some reason, she had thought that she would recognise the house where the Switcher was living as soon as she saw it, but now that she was out in the open, one house looked pretty much like the next.

A car came slowly down the street and Tess instinctively slipped into the damp and oily gutter, sheltering behind the wheel of a parked van until the coast was clear. When she came out from behind the wheel, it was in the shape of a small mongrel dog. She had often used this form when a certain type of investigation was needed.

It was no use, though. She patrolled the length of the street in both directions, catching every available scent from the sleeping households, but there was nothing out of the ordinary. She had hoped for some lingering residue of the Switcher's ability, a variety of animal smells coming from one of the houses perhaps, or one of an unusual nature. But apart from the still pervasive smell of rats, there was nothing out of the ordinary at all. The dog's nose couldn't help.

She craned her neck to look at the upstairs windows. Presumably, whoever had called the rats was still awake, which probably meant a light on somewhere. But the only lighted windows were in a house at the end of the street, and the voices which could be heard coming from it were of people much older than Switchers could be.

Tess considered changing into something smaller and taking a look around the inside of a few of the houses, but her instinct told her it was beginning to get late. She remembered the phoenix with longing, and became aware of the time she was wasting by trotting up and down the empty street. There would be other nights for investigating; all she needed to do was to find out where she was and she could come back any time. So she trotted along until she found the sign on the wall which told her the name of the street. To her dog mind it meant nothing, just a white square with bits of black stuck on it, like the bits of cars which were at her eye level and which had to be avoided if they were moving.

Tess looked along the street. There was no sign of anyone around but she still felt too exposed to Switch. The nearby houses had tiny front gardens with low walls; no cover at all. The best place she could find was the pavement between a transit van and the windowless corner wall of the end house. She slipped in there and sat down close to the kerb. Then, with a last glance around her, she Switched. She waited for a minute or two, then got up and strolled back to look at the street-name. There was still no sign of anyone awake. She had been lucky.

Back in bed once again, Jeff Maloney found that he couldn't sleep. He lay on his back first, then each side in turn, and finally on his stomach, but he just couldn't get comfortable. He thought about his last girlfriend and about his next one, whom he hadn't

234

yet met but who would be perfect in every way when he did. He thought about what he would do on his day off, and what he would do in his summer holidays, but nothing worked. Every time he got comfortably absorbed in his thoughts, the slightly slurred voice returned to his mind: 'It'll be your loss if it's gone by then.'

Eventually, with a sigh of exasperation, he threw back the covers and sat up on the edge of the bed. 'I should have been an accountant,' he said to himself.

It was as well that Tess, in the shape of a pigeon, was able to cross the city faster than Jeff Maloney could cross the park. At the time he was visiting the barracks and getting the exact location of the alleged sighting, Tess was joining the three-toed phoenix on the branch of the tree outside her window. But the distant glimpse that the zoo-keeper got of two flecks of gold rising into the night sky was enough to rouse his curiosity.

CHAPTER FIVE

The following morning, when Tess's father went into her room to wake her, he found her bed empty. As he looked round, his heart filled with anxiety, he noticed that Algernon's cage was empty too.

'Tess?' he called, checking the bathroom and going on down the stairs. 'Tess, where are you?'

'What's wrong?' called her mother from the bedroom.

'Can't find Tess. Don't worry, she can't be far away.'

She wasn't. He saw her as soon as he drew the curtains in the kitchen, out in the back garden on her hands and knees.

He opened the window. 'What on earth are you doing out there, Tess? You gave me the fright of my life.'

Tess looked up, revealing a nasty-looking graze on her cheek and another above her nose. 'I was looking for Algernon,' she said. 'I brought him out for some exercise this morning and he's disappeared.'

It was the only excuse she could think of. She had arrived back from the second spell of being a phoenix just a few minutes ago, and realised that she had no way of getting into the house. Her window was closed, and it would take too long to find her way into the right system of underground passages if she tried to get in as a rat. There hadn't been much time to think.

'But it's hardly even light yet,' said her father. 'Why on earth did you get up so early? And what's happened to your face?'

Tess's mother, always put on edge by the slightest sign of strange behaviour, joined her husband at the window.

'What have you done to yourself?'

For a moment Tess had no idea what they were talking about. She couldn't recall having done anything to her face. Just in time she remembered the bites and scratches she had received from the other rats when she was following Algernon a few hours ago. There were probably a lot more scrapes and bruises hidden by her uniform. She thought quickly.

'I was feeling around in the bushes there,' she said, pointing to a shady corner where several well-established shrubs were growing. 'Have I cut myself?'

'You certainly have,' said her mother. 'Come in, now, and let me have a look.'

'But what about Algernon?'

'You'll have to worry about him later. He can't be far away.'

Tess felt in her pocket. 'You'll have to let me in,' she said. 'I left my key in my coat.'

As her mother fussed over her face, Tess slipped

237

back into the warm, euphoric memory of the phoenix nature that she had abandoned just a few minutes before. She scarcely felt the antiseptic on the wounds, barely heard her mother saying, 'They're not as bad as they look. Just scratches.' She was floating again, high above it all, filled with brightness and peace.

'Wakey, wakey.'

'Hmm?'

Her father put a plate of scrambled eggs on toast in front of her on the table. Tess's stomach rose in protest, and she wondered why it was that the nightly sessions as a phoenix made her lose her appetite. She played with the scrambled egg but ate no more than a couple of mouthfuls.

'Are you worried about something?' her mother asked.

'Just Algernon. I think I'll have another look around outside.'

'No. You get yourself ready for school. I'll have a good look for him after you've gone. He can't be far away.'

That day was even worse than the one before. Tess had not slept at all during the night, and although the phoenix mood was invigorating and relaxing, she could only sustain its memory for short periods of time. When it was gone she was exhausted and depressed, and felt weak from lack of food. She was worried about what was happening with the rats as well, and between her various preoccupations found no energy or attention for her school work. On two occasions she narrowly avoided detention, and she promised herself that she would take a nap when she got home before she made any decisions about what she was going to do next.

But as the bus passed through Phibsboro that evening, she suddenly recognised the area of streets where she and the other rats had ended up the previous night. Before she had time to think, she had made her way to the front of the bus, and at the next stop she got off.

It would make her late home. Were other girls of her age never late home? Did they never make independent decisions to call on some friend or go into town for a coffee? Would her mother believe her if she used an excuse like that? 'I went to listen to Catriona's new R.E.M. tape, Mum.' Or, 'I felt like walking a bit of the way home.' Why shouldn't she? She was fourteen, after all.

As she was mulling these things over in her head she reached the corner where she had hidden in order to Switch the night before. The big blue van was still there, and she considered using another animal form for her first investigation but, looking around, decided against it. She had nothing to hide after all. She was just a schoolgirl walking along the street. Who would be likely to question her?

Without changing pace she swung round the corner into the street where, she was sure, the Switcher lived. She was slightly disappointed to find that it was completely empty, although if she had been asked what she was expecting to find she wouldn't have been able to say. She strolled slowly along, and was opposite the empty house, just stopping briefly to shift her schoolbag from one shoulder to the other, when a woman came out of her front door and turned into the street towards her. The house she had left was one of the three or four that Tess had targeted as being the most likely. As surreptitiously as she could, she watched the woman approach.

She was about the age of Tess's own mother, but shorter and much, much thinner. She walked with her face turned down towards the pavement, so it wasn't until she was almost level with her that Tess became aware of the most striking thing about the woman. She was deathly pale, paler than anyone Tess had ever seen before. She was so pale that her cheeks were like translucent paper, and Tess had to look closely to be sure that she wasn't wearing some strange kind of make-up or theatrical paint.

Careful as Tess was, the woman became aware of being examined, and looked up quizzically as she passed by. It was clear that she had been crying; her eyes were red-rimmed and puffy, and Tess looked away in embarrassment. She was so disturbed by the strange, pale woman that she almost missed seeing the red-haired boy who stood at the open door, watching after her. As he caught Tess's eye, he gave her the most charming of smiles, so delightful that she smiled back automatically, without thinking. She walked on a few paces before she was struck with an uncanny certainty that it was him. He was the Switcher. He was the right age and lived in one of the likely houses, but it was more than that. It was a feeling of affinity, of some shared experience even though they had never met. Tess stopped and turned round. She didn't know how, but she would find some way to introduce herself.

But when she got back to the door, it was closed. Tess stood there, stunned. The strength of her feeling made no sense to her. She and the boy had never met, so why should he expect her to turn round and come back? Why should the closed door feel so much like a rejection?

And yet it did, and the feeling of disappointment

didn't lessen with time. When she got back home, she was in a foul temper.

'But why?' she said to her mother. 'Why should I always tell you exactly where I'm going to be at any given moment of the day?'

'Because I worry.'

'Why do you worry? You don't trust me, do you?'

'It's not that, Tess. It's . . .'

They both fell silent, each remembering their own, very different sides of Tess's Arctic adventure. As far as Tess had been concerned, it had been imperative for her to go. She realised, however, that for her mother the time she had been away meant no more than a completely unexplained disappearance.

'It upset us, Tess. We were worried.'

'I know you were. But I came back, didn't I? I do my homework every night, I help with the washing-up. It's not as if I'm off carousing every night, is it? You should see some of the other girls in my school, what they get up to!'

Her mother sighed. Tess sighed back, in an exaggerated way, and went upstairs to change. When her father got home, she came down to dinner, ate the biggest meal she had eaten in months and went back upstairs again.

Long before the small hours of the morning, when the phoenix comes into its own, she was fast asleep.

CHAPTER SIX

The following morning, on her way to school in the bus, Tess tried to gather her thoughts. There had been such a whirl of activity in the last two days and nights that she had no idea what was happening and what she should do next. She hated herself for the way she had spoken to her mother, and felt guilty about wanting to leave her parents to be with Kevin and become a phoenix for good. But before she could work out what to do about that, she had to sort out this business about the new Switcher. She had a duty to tell him that his powers would go when he reached his fifteenth birthday, and perhaps to encourage him in some way to learn, as she and Kevin had done, the full extent of his abilities before it was too late.

She wondered how old he was. From the brief glimpse she had got of him, smiling in the doorway, it was hard for her to tell. Younger than she was or older? Not much in it, either way. And how much did he already know? The business with the rats disturbed her. His relationship with them was very different from hers or Kevin's. When they had been among the rats it had been as equals; they learnt from them, and were guided by them on more than one occasion. But this boy, the boy with the strange, mixed-up Rat name, seemed to have a power over them.

Why, though? What did he want? She remembered the message about the stone containers beneath the ground with a strong sense of unease. What was he after? Buried treasure? If so, was it right for him to be using his Switching powers for such purposes: getting the rats to do his dirty work so that he could become rich? Yet if it wasn't right, who was to say? What business was it of hers?

The bus pulled up outside the school and Tess joined the lines of dreary uniformity filing in through the gates. Not much different from the poor old rats, she remarked to herself wryly.

'Still no sign of Algernon, I'm afraid,' her mother said as she began to peel the potatoes that evening. 'I hope he hasn't been caught by a cat or something.'

'So do I,' said Tess. 'I suppose there's nothing we can do about it now.'

'Never mind. We can see about getting another one if he doesn't turn up.'

Tess nodded. 'Anything I can do?'

'You can make a salad if you've finished your homework.'

Tess fetched lettuce and tomatoes from the rack beside the back door and rummaged in the drawer next to the sink for a sharp knife.

'I'm sorry about yesterday evening,' she said.

243

'About being late and saying you don't trust me. I was a bit tired. And I was upset about Algernon.'

'No.' Her mother looked as though she had a lemon in her mouth, as though what she was saying was difficult for her, but necessary. 'I was thinking about it afterwards, and you were right. You're fourteen now, and what's past is past. I can't go on treating you like a child any more. You do need to have more freedom.'

Tess stayed silent, aware of having won a victory but unsure whether she wanted it or not.

'You have to begin making decisions for yourself,' her mother went on. 'It's only right at your age. You know the dangers of the city, and if you don't understand them by now then you probably never will.'

'It's not as if I want to go off and . . .' Tess lost her thread. Her mother's words were enormously generous, but they also placed a new responsibility on her. It was a big moment.

'I know that, I know that you're not going to get up to mischief. You see, despite . . . despite everything, I do trust you, and so does your father. We were talking about it last night. We think that as long as you keep up with your schoolwork and provided we always know where you are, you ought to be allowed to make more of your own decisions.' She paused for a moment and then added: 'Within reason, of course.'

'You won't worry, then?'

'If I do, it's my problem, isn't it?'

Tess put down her knife, wiped her hands on a tea-towel and flung her arms round her mother's neck.

'Thanks, Mum,' she said. 'You're great, you know that?'

Her mother smiled, a little sadly, and Tess saw her as though for the first time: just a woman doing her best in life, as human as everyone else.

The sense of closeness lasted until Tess's father came in a few minutes later. He exchanged the day's news with everyone, as he always did, then settled himself down to read the evening paper until the supper was ready.

'Look at this,' he said, pointing to an item low down on the front page. Tess went across and read over his shoulder. With the first glance at the headline her heart began to sink.

RARE BIRD CAPTURED IN THE PHOENIX PARK
In the early hours of this morning, head zoo-keeper Jeff Maloney, with the help of two assistant zoo-keepers, netted a rare bird which was discovered in a tree at the edge of the Phoenix Park. The bird had been sighted the previous night, but was gone by the time Mr Maloney arrived on the scene. Last night, however, he was well prepared and arrived in good time to find the bird roosting on an outer branch of the tree. The bird offered no resistance to being captured and was clearly quite at ease when handled. This suggests that it has escaped from some other collection, perhaps a private one, but so far no one has reported it missing.

The bird is said to be about two and a half feet in length with small wings and long tail feathers. It is golden in colour and, unlike some species of domestic and wild fowl which are also described as golden, it has no black markings whatsoever. At the time of writing, the experts at the zoo have failed to identify the bird.

By the time Tess had finished reading the report, she was leaning against the back of her father's chair, willing her shaking legs to bear her weight. How could this have happened? Why on earth hadn't he flown away? And the worst thought of all was: would it have happened if I hadn't been fast asleep at the time?

'There was some sort of activity going on outside here last night,' said Tess's mother, who was also reading the report. 'I thought it was some people come back from a party, getting excited about something and banging car doors. Do you think it was something to do with the bird?'

'It's possible,' said her father.

Tess's legs weren't responding as required, and she had slumped into an armchair in the corner. Now she dropped her head into her hands in despair. What would they do with him? How could she find him, let alone get around to setting him free?

Her mother checked the potatoes and drained them, then began to set out the meal. 'Are you all right, Tess?' she asked.

Tess stood up. There was no way she could just sit there and keep her emotions hidden, pretending that nothing had happened. 'I won't be having any dinner, if you don't mind. I have to go and look for someone.'

'What? Look for who? And your dinner's on the table – why don't you just have a bite before you go?'

'No, thanks.' Tess was already on her way out of the kitchen and collecting her coat in the hall.

Her mother followed. 'But Tess . . .'

Tess's emotions got the upper hand. 'But Tess, but Tess,' she said angrily. 'It's fine in theory, isn't it, saying that you trust me. In practice it's different, isn't it?'

There was a heavy silence between them, during which Tess could hear her father push back his chair and cross the room towards them. Then her mother sighed and turned away. 'OK, Tess,' she said. 'But be back before ten o'clock, all right?'

Tess nodded and shot out of the door, pulling on her coat as she went. As the door closed her father said, 'What was all that about?'

Her mother shrugged. 'She's a teenager,' she said. 'What do you expect?'

Outside the door, Tess buttoned her coat against a damp westerly wind. She had let down her hair when she got home, and now it began to fly around, getting in her eyes and obscuring her vision. She felt in her pocket. There was loose change in there, and her door key, but no hair band. She stuffed her hair down the back of her collar and looked around.

She had come out with no clear idea of what she was going to do. Her first thought was to go to Phibsboro to try and find the Switcher and enlist his help, but she realised now that she had no idea of what she would be asking him to do. Until she knew where the phoenix was, there could be no plan made for releasing him.

She walked along the street until she felt safe from watching eyes, then she crossed over into the shade of the trees, where she was hidden from the street lights. It was a short walk across the park to the zoo, but in human form she would have no chance of getting inside and looking around. She cut across an open space, checking to be sure that there were no people around, and made for the cover of a small stand of trees, where she Switched into an owl. Within a minute she was approaching the zoo, but it became apparent that her choice of bird was not of the best. The buildings were ablaze with light, which blinded her so badly that she became disorientated and had to make an emergency landing in a nearby tree. She considered trying a bat, even though she knew it was their time of year for hibernation, but when she thought about it further she realised that would not serve her purpose either. The bat's sonic system would tell her a certain amount and avoid the confusion of light, but she would have no way of seeing inside the buildings since the sound would bounce back from the glass windows and tell her nothing of what lay behind them.

She needed sight. What creature could find its way through the darkness but not be dazzled by bright light? A cat would do it, but then a cat might attract too much attention and be too slow to escape. The last thing she wanted was to be collared herself.

The answer came to her in an instant. When they had lived in a wooded area of the countryside, she had made the acquaintance of a pine marten, who had often come to visit even on days when she didn't Switch and go to find him. The pine marten had become a sort of family pet, and they left food out for him on the porch outside the back door. The house lights had never bothered him, and he seemed to be able to see perfectly well when he came to the kitchen door and poked his nose in.

As she Switched, Tess realised that the pine marten had other advantages, too. It was as fast as greased lightning if threatened, and it could climb; not only up and down trees, but on surfaces that were almost smooth. She shinned down the tree in which she had made such a clumsy landing, and raced across the grass towards the zoo. As she ran, she remembered how the long, sinewy body felt from inside; its wiry strength and its quickness and its cunning. The pine marten was afraid of very little in life. There were few dangers which it could not avoid with its remarkable speed and agility.

A guard stood at the entrance gate of the zoo. As Tess watched, a taxi pulled up and let out a group of men and women in smart clothes. The guard checked their identification, then made a call on a portable phone before letting them through and pointing out their destination with a series of gestures. While his attention was taken up with that, Tess slipped beneath a turnstile and into the grounds.

There was plenty of cover for a pine marten. The areas between the roads were covered in low shrubs which smelt enticingly of domestic fowl: ducks and peacocks and guinea-hens. With an effort, Tess brought her mind back to the business in hand. The new arrivals were making their way towards the hexagonal aviary, and Tess followed at a distance, on silent paws. Outside the aviary door a second guard was standing, and he, too, talked into a mobile phone before opening the door with a key and locking it again behind them.

Tess lay low and watched carefully. All around the outside of the building were wire pens which connected to the cages inside, so that on fine days the birds could be allowed out into the open. They were all vacant now; the sharp eyes of the pine marten could have picked out a roosting bird no matter how well camouflaged it was. If the phoenix was in there, and the flow of activity suggested that it probably was, she would have to find some way of getting close enough to the door to see inside. That was going to be tricky, with the guard standing there. A pine marten is as big as a cat, and there was no cover close to the door; no way to stay hidden.

Tess used both her minds together and eventually

249

came up with a solution. The outside pens were enclosed by strong wire netting, and if she could sneak around and scale the furthest one, round the other side, she would be able to cross the tops of them until she got to the front again, where she would be in a perfect position to see into the door the next time it opened.

Taking a long way round, she approached the pens. With a jump and a scramble she was up, and slinking silently along the top of the cages to the door. There she settled herself to wait.

It seemed like hours before the door eventually opened again and a group of people came out; many more than Tess had seen go in. A man at the back was talking loudly, and Tess knew that he was feeling very proud of himself even though she couldn't understand, with the pine marten's brain, what he was saying. She edged forward, stretching down to try and see through the door. No one looked up; all were too busy talking in excited voices. Tess stretched still further, her body becoming longer and longer as her front paws walked down the edge of the net and her back paws held tight, keeping her anchored. Still she couldn't see around the angle of the door, and in another minute the last of the people would be out and the door would close again. In a moment of desperate courage, Tess made a flying leap and landed on the ground between two of the departing guests, who sprang back in shock. She was only on the ground for a split second, but that split second was all she needed to get a glimpse inside the door. Then she was gone, racing away through the undergrowth and leaping up the netted wire which ran between the zoo and the main road through the park.

The various experts on birds and wildlife who had

been inspecting the strange new find were puzzled by the sight of the pine marten, but not as puzzled as Jeff Maloney was. Before he left for home that evening, he checked the enclosure where the pine martens lived, and was even more surprised to find that neither of its occupants was missing.

CHAPTER SEVEN

The sound of the morning paper being pulled through the letter box woke Tess. It was Saturday, and there was no reason for her to get up for another hour or two, but she jumped out of bed and pulled on her dressing-gown.

Her father was making coffee when she got into the kitchen. The paper was folded beside his place at the head of the table, but Tess got to it first. On the front page, beneath the main item on the failure of peace talks in the North, was a feature about the golden bird.

'Your mother was worried about you last night,' her father said.

'Why? I was back before ten o'clock, wasn't I?'

'And why do you have to be so mysterious about where you were?'

Tess felt her irritation rising. She wanted to read

the piece in the paper without a cross-examination. 'I was visiting a friend.'

'What friend? Since when have you had friends that you go to visit? You never bring them here.'

'I can't, not this one, anyway. He's not allowed out.'

'Oh? Why's that?'

'Maybe they're afraid he'll disappear.'

Her father began to say something more, but thought better of it. Tess returned to the paper.

US COLLECTOR TO BUY
PHOENIX PARK PHOENIX

Officials of the Dublin Zoo have today confirmed that the mysterious bird captured two nights ago in the Phoenix Park is to be sold to a private collector based in Missouri, USA. The figure involved has not been disclosed, but it is said to be 'fabulous'. Zoo officials say that it will allow for a complete refurbishment of certain areas of the zoo compound, as well as providing funds for the purchase and housing of a number of new animals: endangered species in particular.

The government has sanctioned the decision, on the condition that the 'phoenix' be kept for one week at the Dublin Zoo, and made available for public viewing. To this end, a special display unit is under construction, and the zoo will be open from 10 a.m. to 6 p.m. from Monday 16th to Sunday 2nd February.

The Head Keeper at the zoo, Mr Jeff Maloney, confirmed that there had been initial difficulties in finding out the diet of the mysterious bird. While this had caused serious concern, it has now been resolved. The phoenix has revealed a partiality for fresh apricots, cashew nuts and spring water, and is now feeding regularly. Its condition is described as 'excellent'.

Tess handed the paper over to her father and waited while he read the article. As soon as he had finished, she said, 'Can I go?'

'Of course. I'll go with you, if you like.'

Tess spent the morning in town with her parents, struggling against a growing frustration and impatience. She urgently wanted to get to Phibsboro and find a way of looking up the boy, but she couldn't push her luck with her parents. Saturday-morning shopping was a ritual, and so was Saturday lunch in town.

It was after two when they got home. Tess ran upstairs and changed into a new pair of jeans that her mother had bought for her, then came back down.

'What's time's dinner?' she asked, pocketing a banana and an apple.

'The usual time, I suppose,' said her mother. 'Why? Where are you going?'

'To visit a friend in Phibsboro. I won't be late.'

Before her mother could reply, Tess grabbed her jacket and raced out into the street. She ran across the corner of the park to the Navan Road and began to walk quickly, checking over her shoulder from time to time for the bus. By the time one came and stopped for her, she had walked half-way to Phibsboro, but she felt so anxious about the captured phoenix that every minute mattered. It was an expensive two stops, but worth it to her.

A few young children were playing soccer in the street where the Switcher lived. They looked Tess over suspiciously before resuming their game. The door of the red-headed boy's house was closed. There was no car parked in front of it and no sound of a

254

television or radio coming from within. Tess hesitated before knocking, aware of the eyes of the soccer players returning to her, aware that despite spending most of the morning trying to work out what she would say when that door opened, she still hadn't come to any firm decisions.

Her stomach was in knots. It would be so much easier just to turn and walk away. But without help, how was she going to go about releasing the phoenix? She hadn't even come up with a plan yet.

Tess knocked and waited. If there was no one there it would at least solve the immediate problem. She was just raising her hand to knock again when she heard the latch turn. The door opened a crack and the face of the pale woman peered out.

'Yes?'

Tess's mouth moved, groping for words that didn't come.

'Can I help you?'

'I was looking for . . . have you got a son? Red hair?'

The woman opened the door another inch but only, it seemed, to scrutinise Tess in an extremely suspicious manner.

'Who are you?' she said.

'I . . I'm a friend. I wanted to ask him for some help.' She would get herself into deep water if she wasn't careful.

'Martin hasn't got any friends. What sort of help are you looking for?'

Tess's mind went blank. The thin woman opened the door and folded her arms.

'It's a sort of project,' said Tess, lamely. 'To do with birds.'

For a long moment Martin's mother stared hard

255

at Tess, but gradually her gaze began to soften and be replaced with something slightly less hostile.

'Well,' she said at last, 'you can only try. He's in his room, sleeping, probably. Why don't you go on up and see if you can get him out of bed?'

Tess nodded and stepped inside.

'First door on the left at the top of the stairs. Let me know if you need anything, won't you? Like a straitjacket or a tranquilliser gun.'

Tess turned to share the joke with the woman, but she was merely looking up the stairs, her white face drawn with anxiety. With mounting apprehension, Tess started up.

The house was unusually dark. The window at the top of the stairs which ought to have lit the landing had been replaced by dimpled yellow glass; the type that is sometimes found in bathrooms. There was something eerie about the silence up there which made it difficult for Tess to muster the courage to knock on the bedroom door. Martin, he was called. She remembered his charming smile. Surely there was nothing to fear?

She knocked and waited. Nothing happened. She knocked again, and then a third time.

'Martin?' she called. 'Hello?'

Nothing. She knocked again, then leant against the wall, wondering what to do next. There was no sound from below, and she wondered what the boy's mother was doing down there. She had the impression that the rest of the house must somehow be as dark as this landing, and it gave her the creeps. She longed to turn back, to just slip quietly down the stairs and out of the door without telling anyone, but she knew that if she did that she would never have the courage to come back again. If she was going to make contact with Martin, it was now or never. Steeling herself, she reached out and quietly turned the door handle.

It wasn't locked. The door opened stiffly, rubbing against the dark grey carpet within. The curtains were drawn and only a suggestion of daylight made its way through them. In the opposite corner was a bed, and as Tess's eyes grew accustomed to the gloom she could just make out the shape of the boy, lying on his back.

'Hello?' she said, but quietly. The atmosphere was so heavy that she dared not speak any louder. There was no response, so she crossed the room, taking care not to disturb any of the clutter which covered most of the floor.

Martin showed no sign of hearing her approach. His face, when she drew near, was not as pale as his mother's, but there was a darkness around his eyes as though he were in the habit of not getting enough sleep. Tess wondered whether she was making a mistake in coming to wake him. Perhaps there were family troubles? Perhaps he was an insomniac and this was the only sleep he had managed to get in days?

'Martin?' she said, gently. Still the boy's eyes didn't open, and Tess realised with a shock that she could see no sign of movement from his chest to signify that he was breathing. What if he was dead and his mother didn't know? What if she did know?

Suddenly Tess had had enough of the darkness and enough of feeling afraid. With a new sense of purpose she strode across the room, knocking her knee against a stack of magazines as she did so, then pulled back the curtains. The rings squealed on the rail as though protesting against the flood of early-evening light.

'Martin!' said Tess, with as much firmness in her voice as she could manage.

The boy cried out softly as though he had been robbed of something precious, then opened his eyes.

'What is it?' he said. 'Who's there?'

'It's me. My name's Tess. I saw you on the street a few days ago, remember?'

Martin looked at her blearily for a moment, then sat up.

'Have you come to help?' he said.

'Help with what?'

Martin looked away for a moment, then turned back. Once again his face wore the sweet smile that had stayed in her mind's eye for so long.

'Do you need help with something?' she said.

He laughed and shook his head, and Tess had a strange sense of having missed some kind of opportunity.

'Are you sure?' she said.

'I'm sure.'

'Well, I do.'

'Oh?'

She stopped, remembering the difficulty that Kevin had encountered when he tried to convince her that he knew she was a Switcher. It was something that had been private for her all her life, and it was a subject not easy to approach. She had been defensive and dismissive. She had no reason to believe that Martin wouldn't feel the same way.

'It's a friend of mine,' she said at last. 'Sort of a friend, anyway. He's been taken prisoner.'

'By who?' Martin's face seemed to be open and full of concern, but Tess was aware of some darkness which flitted behind his eyes.

'By the zoo,' she said.

'The zoo?' said Martin, his voice full of incredulity. Tess had hoped that it might have been enough of a hint; that if he was a Switcher he would empathise with her having animal friends and open himself to her. But instead he went on, 'Are you serious? Are you the full shilling?'

Tess swore to herself in Rat. There was no easy way into this. 'Look,' she said, 'let's not beat about the bush, eh? I know who you are, I know what you can do. You don't have to pretend with me.'

The boy ran a hand through his thick red hair and looked at Tess with a bemused expression. 'What, exactly, do you know?' he asked. Again his face seemed open and friendly, but again Tess was aware of a shadow passing behind his eyes, as though there were someone else in there apart from the charming boy, looking out through his eyes.

Tess took the bull by the horns. 'I know that you're a Switcher. I know that because I'm one, too.'

'A Switcher?' Martin's face wore a puzzled frown. 'What's a Switcher?'

'You know very well, because you are one.'

'I know what I am, all right,' said Martin, and there was an edge to his voice as he said it which went along with the sinister shadow in his eyes. 'What I don't know, though, is what it has to do with you.'

'I've already told you. I need your help to rescue my friend. I don't know how I'm going to do it on my own.'

Martin looked thoughtfully at his feet for a moment, then said, 'Tell me about your friend.'

CHAPTER EIGHT

Tess wasn't sure where to start. She realised she was still standing up beside the bed, and took the opportunity to get her thoughts together while she looked for a chair. There was one beside the table, but she had to move a pile of books off it. She noticed as she did so that they were all horror stories, classics as well as modern writers.

'How old are you?' she asked, as she brought the chair over to the bed and sat down in it.

Martin resettled himself as well, propping himself up on pillows and pulling the covers up around his waist.

'Fifteen,' he said.

The wind was knocked out of Tess's sails, and for a moment she wondered if she was making a terrible mistake.

'You can't be!' she said.

'Well I am, almost. Why shouldn't I be?'

Tess breathed a sigh of relief. 'Because if you were, if you'd had your fifteenth birthday, you wouldn't be able to do it any more.'

'Do what?'

'You know very well, what. Change your form, become something else.'

The look in Martin's eye was, for a moment, openly hostile. In an instant, though, he had recovered his poise, and the charming expression of puzzled interest returned.

'Go on,' he said.

'Well, you need to know that, because whatever you are on your fifteenth birthday is what you'll stay. You need to have time to think about it.'

Martin shook his head. 'Not me,' he said. 'I already know what I'm going to be. I mightn't even wait until my fifteenth birthday.'

It was the acceptance that Tess had been waiting for, but she was careful not to show her satisfaction.

'I feel like that, too,' she said. 'But I can't do anything about it until I've got my friend out of the zoo.'

'Ah, yes. Your friend. You were going to tell me about your friend.'

Tess relaxed and began to tell the story of her meeting with Kevin and the adventure which had brought them to the Arctic Circle to battle against the krools. It was wonderful to be able to relive her experiences once more, with someone who understood and seemed to appreciate them. She told him everything, right up to Kevin's return and his capture by the zoo authorities, and then she fell silent. Martin was silent, too, and Tess had the impression that he wasn't sure whether to believe her or not. In any event, it was clear that he wasn't going to admit that

261

he was impressed. Outside a few birds were beginning their evening song, and on the street below the game of soccer was still going on. As the two Switchers sat there, each engrossed in his or her own thoughts, Martin's mother appeared in the doorway, looking anxious and eager to please.

'A cup of tea?' she said.

Martin nodded without a word, and his mother smiled in acknowledgement. 'Everything all right?'

Again the boy nodded. His mother departed, as though she had been dismissed. Tess was shocked. She turned to Martin, meaning to remark on the nature of his behaviour, but he was smiling so sweetly that she was disarmed.

'How did you find out about me?' he asked.

Tess told him about Algernon and her journey through the city in response to his call.

'What do you want with those stone boxes, anyway?' she asked.

Martin rubbed his chin and looked heavenward, musing. Then he said, 'Let's just say that I have a certain interest in archaeology, shall we?'

'But why?'

'Why not? There are probably hundreds of ancient structures beneath the city that have never been excavated. I'd like to know where some of them are, that's all.'

Tess wasn't entirely happy with the explanation, but she didn't feel she could push it any further. Besides, there were more important matters to be sorted out.

'Well, what about it?' she said.

'What about what?'

'About the phoenix. Will you help me to get him out?'

262

'How do you propose to do it?'

'I'm not sure, yet. Maybe we could come up with a plan together? I'm sure we could get some help from the rats if we needed to.'

'Hmm.' Martin hitched himself up in the bed and rearranged his pillows. 'The rats are fairly busy at the moment. Besides, I'm bored with all that squirrel and bunny stuff. I've grown out of it, you know?'

'Who said anything about squirrels and bunnies?' said Tess. 'I was a pine marten yesterday and it was brilliant! In any case, I can't see how squirrels and bunnies are going to help get Kevin out.'

'No. You know what I mean, though. It's all a bit tame, isn't it?' Martin was looking into space as he spoke, as though seeing something in his mind's eye that Tess had no conception of. She was about to ask him what he meant when his mother appeared again at the door with a tray of tea things. She had moved so softly that Tess hadn't heard her approach, and she hoped that she hadn't overheard anything she shouldn't.

Martin made no move to help his mother with the tray, so Tess got up and cleared a space on the table. She was shocked again by the drained, bloodless look on the woman's face and by the way her hands and arms trembled as though the effort of carrying the tray upstairs had been too much for her.

'Everybody happy?' she said.

'Yes, thanks,' said Tess.

'You can pour, I suppose?'

'Of course I can,' said Tess.

Martin's mother turned to leave, but before she did so, Tess thought she caught an expression of gratitude on her face.

'Why is she so pale?' she asked Martin, after a safe length of time had passed.

Martin shrugged, and a queer little smirk crossed his mouth. 'The doctor says she's anaemic. He doesn't know why.'

'Why don't you help her? You could have made that tea yourself, you know.'

Again Martin shrugged. 'Mothers,' he said. 'You know what they're like. They don't want you to grow up because then they have to let you go.'

Tess felt an intense irritation towards the slovenly boy, lying in bed waiting to be spoon-fed. She wanted to tell him to pour his own tea or go without it, but her nerve failed her. If she got on the wrong side of him he might refuse to help her, and she didn't believe that she could liberate Kevin on her own. Suppressing her anger, she filled two cups and handed one across. Martin took it without thanking her.

'Do you want to watch a video?' he asked. 'My mother will go and get one if you do.'

Tess noticed for the first time that there was a TV and video recorder in the corner of the room beside the window, placed so that Martin could watch from the bed.

'No, thanks,' she said, struggling now with her still-rising anger. 'And if I did want to watch one I'd get it myself.'

Infuriatingly, Martin giggled. Tess sipped her tea and looked at her feet. However weak he was, she needed him. She would have to get help from him even if she had to beg for it.

'Will you help me?' she asked.

'I might.' He thought for a moment, then seemed

to come to a decision. 'I'll tell you what. I'll consider helping you to get your friend out on one condition.'

'What's that?'

'Well. You've told me about your adventures, and what you've learnt to do with your powers. I'd like you to know what I've learnt as well. How does that sound?'

'Sounds great.'

'Good. Only I'd prefer to show you than tell you. Does that make any sense?'

'I suppose it does.'

'Right. Come here tonight, then, and we can do the rounds together, OK?'

'This evening?'

'Tonight would be better. When dear mother is asleep. Say, one o'clock?'

Tess groaned inwardly. Another sleepless night. Another night of worry about leaving the house and getting back in time. But it had to be worth it.

'It might be a bit later,' she said, 'but I'll be there.'

CHAPTER NINE

That night, soon after midnight, two figures walked quietly down a street in Phibsboro. A heavy frost was beginning to spangle the grass in the gardens they passed, and their breath curled billows of steam around them as they walked.

'Warm enough?' said Martin, as they turned the corner of the street where he lived.

'Just about,' said Tess, pulling her scarf up over her mouth and nose. 'You must be freezing, though.'

'I am,' he said, 'but I won't be for long.'

They crossed the street and walked past an off-licence with padlocked aluminium shutters over all the windows, then turned on to the main road which ran from the outskirts of Dublin in towards the city centre.

'Where are we going?' asked Tess.

'Nowhere in particular. Just walking.'

'Why?'

'You'll see.'

Tess stuffed her hands deeper into her pockets, feeling irritated by Martin's secretiveness. What could be so special, after all? She followed rather sullenly as Martin crossed one small intersection in the road, then another. A few cars passed, every second one a taxi, bringing people home from the pubs.

Ahead of them, at the next intersection, was a red brick building which sold carpets and upholstery fabric. Outside, a group of young men were gathered, smoking and swigging from beer bottles, tussling with each other and laughing. Tess slowed down, uneasy about passing them by.

'Shouldn't we cross over?' she said, coming to a halt on the footpath.

Martin turned to her with a smile, and as he did so it seemed to Tess that the darkness she had glimpsed behind his eyes earlier in the day had come right up to the front and was leering out at her in mockery.

'Why?' he said.

Tess faltered, all her courage leaving her. She had a strong desire to Switch, to become a rat and scuttle down the nearest drain, or a creature with wings, to fly her out of there. The boys on the corner had noticed them now and they became quiet, all their attention turned towards the two strangers. Tess pulled her coat tighter around her, aware as she did so that it had been bought in one of the swankiest shops in town. It told everything about her and her family. Even though she had no money on her, she was an obvious target for anyone with mugging on their mind.

'Martin,' she said, her voice pleading for reason.

From the corner of her eye she saw the group of lads gather together and begin to advance.

Martin smiled, or leered, at her again. 'Just watch,' he said. He began to walk forwards. It was too late now for Tess to break off on her own and cross the road. It was even too late to run. In a few quick strides she drew level with Martin, just as the first of the young men stepped into their path.

In that instant, Martin Switched. Tess saw and felt the strange fuzziness in the air around him as he lost substance and regained it again. She shivered; her mind was caught up in the moment of vacancy, then began casting around for the new form that Martin had taken. He had turned slightly away from her as he Switched, and it seemed as she looked at him that nothing had changed. He was still a boy in a light anorak, standing quietly in the edge of a street-lamp's glow. But as she watched, she became aware that there had, indeed, been a change. Even before she noticed the gang of boys backing off, Tess could feel some sort of power radiating from Martin. It attracted and repelled her at the same time, so that she didn't know whether to move away from him or towards him. As she stood still, trying to understand what was happening, the lads retreated towards the brighter light beneath the lamp-post and stood there uncertainly, huddled together.

Then Martin turned to face her. Tess's heart lurched. In a sense the boy in front of her was still Martin, but at the same time he wasn't. His face was deathly pale apart from his lips, which were strangely red and protruding, as though the teeth inside the mouth were too big to fit properly. The eyes which gazed out at her were dull and lifeless, yet they latched on to something within her, drawing her in, making it impossible for her to move away. As she gazed in a grim mixture of fear and attraction she knew what had happened, she knew what he was, but she just couldn't put a name on it. Until he smiled.

The only experience Tess could remember which had anything of the horror of this one was the time the first krool had suddenly reared up before her in the Arctic. That time she had reacted without thought; this time there was no reaction apart from complete paralysis. For when Martin, or the thing that had been Martin a few minutes ago, smiled, it revealed a pair of razor-sharp fangs, so long that they reached down over the bottom teeth and were hidden by the bulging lower lip.

'Well?' he said. His voice was smooth and seductive. Tess looked over at the lamp-post, and as she did so two of the boys there made a sudden dart across the road. She turned back to the vampire, still leering at her, showing his fangs. As a boy he had been a moderate sort of height, but now he seemed to tower above her, sneering down.

Tess looked at her feet. There was a scuffle as the other boys raced across the road to join their friends and she felt suddenly alone. A few minutes ago those lads had been her enemies, but now that she was faced with this monstrous creature they seemed to be allies and she felt abandoned by them and desperately alone.

'Are you going to back out on me?' said Martin.

Tess looked up, trying to avoid the lure of those vacuous eyes but failing. 'What do you mean, back out?'

'You promised to try my way, remember?'

Tess shuddered with revulsion. 'I . . .'

'You what?' The voice was like sleep, sucking at her mind, dragging her under. She struggled.

'I didn't know,' she shouted. 'You didn't tell me!'

The vampire's smile broadened. 'You didn't ask,' said the creamy voice.

Tess felt sick. What stood in front of her wasn't Martin. It was something that was dead and yet lived on, undead. She understood now why he had said that he wouldn't be cold for long. Vampires didn't feel the cold. They didn't feel anything at all, in any way. Tess knew beyond doubt as she looked into those dark eyes that there was no appeal under the sun that would release her from his power. She did not exist for him as an equal being at all. To him she was nothing more than an object, a victim, the source of his next meal.

Behind her she heard the sound of a car drawing up close to the kerb. Martin closed his lips over his teeth and glanced up over her shoulder to see who was behind her. Tess closed her eyes, released for a moment from that dreadful gaze, and fear welled up within her. She began to turn towards the car, ready to scream out for help, but even as she did so the car started to draw away. The garda in the passenger seat nodded towards Martin as his partner drove off. Tess called out, but it was too late. Beside her, Martin was exuding charm again, and before she could tear herself away he slipped a strong arm around her and began to walk up the quiet street which led away from the main road, into the darkness.

Tess tried to struggle but it was useless. The vampire was strong beyond imagining, and already his power was beginning to take over her mind again, drawing her in to the vacuum of his heart. At a corner beneath a tall sycamore tree, he stopped, and Tess leant against the wall, looking down at the ground. Leaves and sweet wrappers and crisp bags had gathered there during the last windy day. Martin leaned towards her. His voice was a harsh whisper in her ear.

'It's up to you. You can join me if you want to, but if you don't . . .'

He smiled again, that sinister smile that was as cold and distant as the moon. Tess knew what he meant. He was in front of her now, blocking any escape she might attempt. His breath was cold on her face and had a faint metallic scent.

Her mind felt slow and cumbersome, numbed by her fear. She could think of no creature on earth that would be a sure protection against the power that confronted her now; certainly there was none that could kill him. How can you kill what is already dead?

Slowly, inch by inch, his face was coming closer to hers, his head bowing, his teeth approaching her neck. The knowledge, when it came to her, seemed always to have been there, perfect in its logic. There was only one protection against a being like this, and that was to become like him. She resisted, waiting for the last moment, desperately searching her mind for an alternative.

His breath, colder than the frosty air surrounding them, touched her neck, freezing the area where he planned to bite. She was in an impossible position; whichever course she took seemed like a submission. She tried to dodge out to the side, but he was quicker. She thumped and pushed at his shoulders and knees, but he was like a statue: cold and immovable. His teeth met her neck; she felt the pressure of their points against her skin, and as they broke through she began to drift down, down, away from consciousness, into a dark oblivion.

'No!

At the moment that she shouted, Tess Switched. Martin drew back and regarded her, his cynical smile tinged now with an element of respect and comradeship. Tess returned it, feeling the new shape of her mouth as it accommodated those deadly teeth. She ran her tongue over them, careful of their sharpness, and lifted a hand to her face. The external change was small. She still fitted into her clothes; if she met someone she knew they would probably recognise her. But the internal change was enormous. Without ever testing it, she knew that she was possessed of fantastic strength and that no living person could stand up to her. And her mental strength was no less: a storehouse of power, just waiting to be used. The only problem was a deep and urgent hunger which could only be satisfied by one thing.

Without a word, Martin and Tess linked arms with each other. From a distance they were like two young lovers strolling down the street, as innocent as spring.

CHAPTER TEN

The city belonged to Tess and Martin. By night, there is nothing under the sky that vampires fear, for nothing can harm them. It is only by day, when they sleep away the hours of daylight, that fear impinges upon their dreams and makes their rest uneasy.

The two Switchers crossed the road and followed the route the gang of boys had taken, towards the centre of the city. At the next junction they veered to the left, heading for the docks and the darkness. They moved swiftly and silently, but if anyone noticed their strong strides and solemn deportment, they didn't stop to question them.

Tess gloried in the dark power she found within herself. She had experienced many kinds of strength in the past, in the different animal forms she had assumed, but she had never imagined that a human shape could make her feel like this. It was wonderful to be able to walk the city streets at night in full view of any watching eyes and know that she was invulnerable. She could do anything, go anywhere she liked; no one could stop her, no one could harm her in any way.

She turned towards her companion and the two of them exchanged grim smiles of complicity. But even as they did so, Tess knew that she wouldn't care if she never saw him again. Let them hunt together tonight; let her learn from him whatever she had to know. After that she was on her own, gloriously alone, for ever.

Literally for ever. For all eternity. Because vampires live for ever, spreading their condition like a disease to everyone they feed upon. Unless they are unlucky, that is. Unless someone discovers their existence and tracks them down to their hiding place and drives a stake through their heart. But who, these days, believes in vampires?

Tess laughed to herself, quietly, and discovered the new sound of her voice. She liked it; it was dark and husky, as different from her human voice as Martin's was from his. She knew that it would be as hypnotic to a potential victim as a mongoose's dance is to a snake. All she needed now was an opportunity to try it out.

Although it was the early hours of the morning, the streets were not empty. Taxis serviced the night-life of the city, twisting through the quiet streets. Occasionally a police car cruised past; occasionally a speeding biker, revving hard. Drifters idled their way home from pubs and night-clubs, and homeless people beat the streets to keep themselves warm. Every time they came within a few metres of another human being, Tess felt her hunger gnaw at her, as though she had come in from a long day at school and smelt dinner roasting in the oven. But her companion kept well away from anyone else on the street, and she decided to stay close. The two of them let everything pass them by, like lions walking peacefully through a herd of small game, their attention fixed on better things.

'Why the docks?' said Tess, as they first came in sight of the river.

'Good hunting ground,' said Martin.

'But we've passed plenty of possibilities,' said Tess. 'What's so special about the docks?'

'Dark, for one thing,' said Martin. 'And for another thing, who wants to drink the blood of boozers and dossers? It's weak and impure. Gives me a headache.'

Tess looked at him carefully, but he didn't appear to be joking. He pulled up his coat collar as he stepped on to the bridge and, aware of the bright street lights all the way across, Tess followed suit.

On the other side of the river they turned right. A few cars were parked beside the road, and in one of them two men were sitting. Tess glanced through the window as she passed by. One of the men was reading a newspaper, the other was pulling absently at the crease in his trousers.

'No good?' she said to Martin as they walked on.

'Cops,' he said. 'Plain clothes. Not bad, if you like cholesterol.'

Tess peered into his shaded eyes and he grinned at her. This time he was joking.

'My tastes aren't that refined,' he said. 'Not yet, anyway. Too much light, though. Be patient.'

They walked on until they came to the first of the ships moored up against the river wall, then crossed over the road and turned up a dark side-street.

'Now we're in good hunting grounds,' said Martin.

He slowed the pace a bit and became more watchful, looking casually but carefully into parked cars and checking out the yards that opened off the street. On the corner, a man and a woman were sitting in a high-bodied van. They looked anxiously at the two Switchers as they passed. Martin took no notice of them.

'Dealers,' he said. 'Small fry, though. They use drugs themselves, just deal to feed their habit. If you could get the guy who supplies them, now, you'd be on to a good thing.'

'Why?'

'Because they're usually clean, those fellows. Too careful to get mixed up in the stuff themselves.' He chuckled to himself in a manner that Tess might have found sinister on another occasion, then went on, 'I've had a good guzzle or two on that kind. Very clean, they tend to be. Very well fed.'

'Why don't we wait here, then?' said Tess. 'Someone's going to come and supply those two in the van, aren't they?'

'I doubt it. That's what the cops are thinking, too. That's why they're there. But the big fish are too smart to get copped that easily. They're somewhere else, you can be sure, laughing their heads off at this lot.'

Tess shrugged and kept pace with Martin as he strode through the streets, always seeking out the darkest ones. As they turned yet another corner, they caught a glimpse of a woman in high heels running across the junction at the other end. Tess's hopes rose. She knew that the two of them could have been on her in a few powerful strides, like greyhounds on a hare, but once again Martin shook his head.

Tess was beginning to lose patience. 'Why not?' she said. 'What on earth was wrong with that one?'

'Nothing, as far as I know,' said Martin. 'But why run when you don't have to? It's undignified.'

'What do I care about dignity?' said Tess. 'I'm hungry.'

Martin stopped abruptly and swung around to face her. 'Hungry?' he said. 'What do you know of the hunger of a vampire, eh? I mean the real hunger, not your pathetic peckishness?'

Tess felt her lips draw away from her teeth in an automatic, defensive sneer.

'You'd better not be hungry,' Martin went on. 'Not really hungry, I mean. We can live for a long, long time on these streets without raising anyone's suspicions, but not if we let our appetites run away with us.'

'I don't know what you're talking about,' said Tess.

'I'm talking about the difference between keeping the wolf from the door and having a real feed. The fact is, you can't be that hungry, any more than I can, because you've had your breakfast and your dinner and your tea at home, haven't you?'

Tess was about to tell him that she hadn't, in fact; what she had eaten that day was breakfast, lunch and dinner, but she decided against it. 'More or less,' she said.

'Right,' Martin went on. 'But if you hadn't, and if you didn't have them yesterday, either, then you'd be really dangerous.'

'To who?'

'To us. Because when you pulled someone in and started feeding, you wouldn't be able to stop.'

'So what?'

'So they'd find a dead body, drained of blood, wouldn't they? With two tiny incisions on the neck.'

'But no one believes in vampires these days.'

'No. But they soon would if it happened often enough, wouldn't they?'

Tess shrugged. 'Who cares, anyway?'

'I do,' said Martin, with cold determination. 'I plan to live in this city for a very long time. A very, very long time. And I don't plan on being discovered. That means we have to go carefully, drink little and often, so as not to make people suspicious.'

Tess looked up and down the street, sighing with incredulity. 'You're mad, do you know that?' she said. 'You're going to feed off a different person every night and you think you can get away with it? You think your victims are going to shake your hand and say, "You're welcome, come again?" Don't be ridiculous! All right, the police won't believe the first person who complains, but they'll believe the tenth and the eleventh and the twenty-first!'

The creamy quality slipped back into Martin's voice. 'You haven't read the literature, have you?'

'What literature?'

'All there is. On vampires. Our victims forget, didn't you know that? They pass out as we feed and go to sleep. When they wake up they feel a bit weak and fuzzy-headed, but they have no memory of us at all. And who's going to notice a couple of pinpricks on their throat? Specially if we're careful.'

Tess looked Martin straight in the eye, still wishing she could win the point but knowing she was beaten. At last she smiled mischievously, and nodded.

'Understood,' she said.

They resumed their patrol, silent and agile as cats on the frosty street. They turned again, following the darkness wherever they could and then, as they passed the open doors of an abandoned coal-merchant's, Martin stopped and sniffed the air. Tess joined him and immediately caught the same scent. There were two people nearby. Very nearby.

Stealthily, the two vampires slipped into the yard. In the nearest corner, hidden from the street by the open corrugated iron door, a car was parked. Quite a new car, clean and without a scratch. Martin crouched low and crept up to the driver's door, Tess on his heels. Under the cover of almost perfect darkness, they peered into the car, their vampire eyes penetrating the dim interior. Tess had expected the couple to be kissing, but they were sitting apart in total silence as though they had just had an argument. The man, in the driver's seat, was grey-haired and well-dressed. He was staring straight ahead of him, smoking a cigarette. The woman was much younger, with long brown hair and a heavy sheepskin coat. Her face was turned away from him, gazing out of the passenger-side window towards the wall of the yard.

Martin winked. Tess nodded and slipped around to the other side of the car. No midnight feast had ever been more eagerly anticipated than this one.

CHAPTER ELEVEN

The following morning was Sunday and Tess slept late. She slept so late that her father slipped into the room to check that she was all right before he went off to play a round of golf with a friend from the office.

'It's normal for a teenager,' her mother told him when he expressed concern. 'She'll be up and about soon.'

But when Tess had still not come downstairs by lunch-time, her mother made a cup of tea and brought it up to the bedroom. The first Tess knew of the day was the rattle of the runners on the curtain rail and the subsequent blaze of winter sunlight that fell upon her face. To her, still sleeping off the vampire feed of the night before, the sudden burst of light on her skin felt like a bucket of boiling water. She yelped and sat up, scrabbling for the bed covers.

'Tess!' said her mother. 'What on earth is wrong?'

Tess said nothing, but threw herself back down on the bed, pulling the duvet up over her head.

'Come on, Tess,' said her mother brightly. 'I've brought you a cup of tea.'

Tess's voice was muffled beneath the duvet. 'Leave me alone. I don't want to get up.'

'But it's one-thirty! If you don't get up soon you'll miss the daylight altogether!'

'What do I want with daylight?' Tess's voice sounded slightly husky to her mother.

'Are you ill, sweetheart? Have you got a sore throat?'

'No. I'm not ill. I just don't want to get up, all right?'

Her mother stayed in the room for another minute or two before deciding not to make an issue of it and returning downstairs. Tess listened to the receding footsteps, then turned over and tried to go back to sleep.

It was too late, though. She was awake now in a groggy, leaden sort of way. The events of the previous night slid into her mind, producing a strange mixture of guilt and delight. She knew that what had happened was wrong, but the memory of the hypnotic power of her vampire eyes and voice still thrilled her, and the sensation of that keen hunger being satisfied. She wondered where the couple from the car were now, and laughed out loud to think of them waking together and wondering how they had come to fall asleep in the first place. She thought of Martin sleeping in his blacked-out room and wondered whether she, like him, could get out of going to school.

Carefully, inch by inch, Tess drew the cover from her face. The light didn't feel so bad, now that the

281

initial shock had passed. She reached for the cup of tea that her mother had left on the bedside table. As she sipped it, she ran her tongue around her mouth, feeling her teeth. They were neat and even again now, the canines back to their normal, blunt condition. But Tess's mind was still functioning along nocturnal lines, and it wasn't until daylight began to fade and her father returned from his game of golf that she finally dragged herself out of bed and went downstairs for a late, late breakfast.

'Anything special on at school, tomorrow, Tess?' said her father as they sat down to dinner that evening.

Tess had been withdrawn and sullen since she got up. At the best of times she got irritated by her parents' questions about school; now she saw this as a feeble attempt to draw her into a conversation that she didn't want.

'When is there ever anything special going on in school?' she answered, filling her mouth with roast beef.

Her father sighed and put down his knife and fork. Tess failed to heed the warning and reached out to turn the page of the magazine she had laid open beside her plate. He whipped it out from under her nose and flung it with a slap on to the floor. Tess's mother jumped at the uncharacteristic display of anger.

'I've had about enough of you, Tess,' he said. 'You mope around all day and treat your mother and myself as second-class citizens.'

Tess experienced a moment of anxiety. Her parents were so rarely critical that she hardly knew how to react. For a moment she was vulnerable, staring at the place where her magazine had been, struggling with shame. Then before she knew what was happening, the cold calm of her vampire mind came to her defence. Without looking up, she cut another forkful of beef.

'Do I?' she said.

'Yes, you do. You're doing it now.'

'Am I?'

Her father thumped the table with his fist, and Tess giggled inwardly at the sight of her mother jumping again, this time spilling her glass of water into her lap. But if her father noticed, he didn't pay any attention. He glared at Tess and said, 'I asked you a civil question and I expect a civil answer!'

'You asked me a boring question about a boring subject because you have a boring need to make boring conversation over dinner.'

Tess's words were met by a stunned silence.

'Boring dinner, I should have said,' she added, pushing a heap of mashed carrot and turnip towards the edge of her plate.

Her father stood up and pulled the plate away, knocking over his own glass of water in the process. Tess laughed as her mother leapt up and threw her already sodden napkin into the puddle. Then, slowly, she got to her feet and confronted her father. His face was stiff with fury.

'Until further notice,' he said, 'you are to stay in the house. I don't know who it is that you're meeting when you go out in the evenings, but whoever it is, they're clearly a bad influence on you.'

'Maybe,' said Tess. 'Or maybe I'm a bad influence on them. It all depends on which way you look at it, doesn't it?'

Her father stared at her, still unable to believe what he was hearing. Her mother was fussing with the highly-polished surface of the table, trying to pretend that nothing was happening while her life fell apart all around her.

'Get up to bed, young lady.'

'That's exactly where I was going.'

'And don't come down again until you're in a more reasonable humour, you understand?'

'Don't worry,' said Tess, heading towards the door. 'I won't come down until I'm Daddy's little darling again. Is that what you want?'

Her father's hands were clenched into fists, and they were shaking.

'Get out!' he yelled. 'Get out of my sight!'

Taking her time, Tess went out of the room and closed the door quietly behind her. Then, as an afterthought, she came back in, picked up her magazine from the floor and walked out.

Tess lay on her back on the bed in the darkness and stared up at the ceiling. Her father had been a fool to challenge her; there was no way he could win. As soon as he was asleep at night she would be gone, out of the window and away across the city, feeding herself with the best that Dublin could offer. And in the morning she wouldn't go down to breakfast even if he asked her; even if he begged her. What could he do? He couldn't force her to get up and go to school. She would lie in bed and sleep away the day, refusing to eat or drink. By the time a week had passed he would be putty in her hands; her mother, too. She would be like Martin: ruling the roost, getting whatever she wanted whenever she wanted it.

Tess smiled to herself in the darkness, then Switched and ran her tongue over her fangs. This was so easy, so perfect. She thought back over all her previous worries about what she was going to do when she reached fifteen. It all seemed so absurd now, and the answer so simple. It was good that she had met Martin and learned his secret. Perhaps she would meet him again tonight and hunt alongside him? But then again, perhaps not. They had no need of each other, after all, and the more she thought about hunting alone, the more she liked the idea.

Her mind stilled, alerted by soft footsteps on the stairs. Her mother, by the sound of it, coming to make her peace. Tess felt the familiar hunger and was surprised as the image of Martin's mother, pale and haggard, entered her mind. Of course! She smiled to herself, suddenly understanding the cause of the woman's mysterious anaemia.

The footsteps reached the top of the stairs and came on across the landing. Tess felt her mouth beginning to water at the prospect of an unexpected snack. Her mother was outside the door. The handle began to turn.

Not yet, though; not yet. Just in time, Tess got a grip on her vampire instincts. It was too early in the evening and too risky with her father in the house. Far better to wait for a more convenient occasion. Or an emergency, when other sources were hard to come by. Tonight, after all, she was eager for the hunt. There might well be times in the future when she felt more inclined to dine at home.

The light from the landing burst in and blinded Tess as the door opened. In the nick of time she Switched, keeping quite still as she did so, her face turned towards the wall.

'Tess?'

Her mother came cautiously into the room as though she was afraid that her daughter would pounce on her. Tess turned towards her, and watched as she picked up a chair and brought it over to the bedside.

'What's going on, Tess?' she said, sitting down in the chair and leaning forward with her elbows on her knees. The tone of concern in her voice almost disarmed Tess, but she recovered her guard just in time.

'Nothing's going on,' she said. 'Absolutely nothing.'

'Then why were you so unpleasant to your father?'

Tess sighed in exasperation, as though she was talking to an idiot. 'I wasn't rude to my father as a matter of fact,' she said. 'For the first time in my life I was honest with my father. It's the same every evening. He comes home from work and he says, "How was school, Tess?" "Did anything interesting happen in school today?" "Anything happening at school these days?" '

'But what's wrong with that?' said her mother.

'What's wrong with that is that he couldn't care less what's happening at school. If I told him the place burnt down and I carried the piano out on my back he'd just say, "That's good. What's for dinner?" '

'Oh, Tess. That's not fair.'

'It is fair. The truth is always fair.'

'And how do you come to be such an expert on the truth?' Her mother stood up and moved over to draw the curtains as she spoke.

'Leave them,' said Tess.

'I was just going to close them, that's all. Keep the heat in.'

'I like them open. Leave them.'

Tess's mother walked back to the chair, but she

286

didn't sit down. 'Now, you listen to me, Tess,' she began.

'I'm listening.'

'There's a possibility that you might be right about your father . . .'

'I am.'

'. . . Some of the time, that is. But as it happens, you were wrong today.'

'Oh?'

'Oh. Yes, oh. Your father has arranged to take the day off work tomorrow. He was about to ask you if it would be all right for you to take the day off school.'

Tess's eyes widened and she looked at her mother for the first time as she went on, 'He was planning for us all to get up at crack of dawn and go over to the zoo.'

'The zoo?'

'Yes. The zoo. There's going to be an awful crowd there tomorrow.' She paused, looking into Tess's blank face. 'Have you forgotten?'

'Forgotten what?'

'They're going to let the public in to see that bird they caught the other night.'

Tess sat up on the edge of the bed and stared into the middle distance. How could it have happened? How could she possibly have forgotten the phoenix? Not just for a few moments, but absolutely. She was quite certain that if her mother hadn't reminded her she would never have remembered it again. For the first time since she had assumed the vampire form, the horror of what she had done became clear to her. A desperate confusion flooded her mind as the phoenix memories returned and began to edge out the cold vampire complacency.

Her mother waited for a few moments, then said,

'Now. I've spoken to your father and he's still willing to go if you promise to think about your behaviour this evening. He doesn't want an apology: just a nice day out tomorrow and a bit more consideration in future. What do you say?'

Tess looked up, her face quite changed now. She nodded. 'I have to go,' she said.

'You don't have to,' said her mother, 'but it'd be a shame to miss the opportunity.'

Tess shook her head. 'I have to go,' she said again. Her mother put an arm around her shoulders and gave her a quick squeeze, then crossed the room towards the door. Tess found her shoes and began to put them on.

'And I will apologise,' she said.

As Tess watched TV with her parents that evening she had no awareness of what was going on beneath her. The city's rats, with Algernon somewhere among them, were digging, scratching, burrowing away, radiating outwards like the spokes of a wheel, still following their master's orders.

Most of the city underground had already been covered, since it had been dug up for foundations, and for sewerage, gas and electric systems. But directly beneath Tess's house, the rats were moving, breaking new ground as they pushed outwards into the unknown territory which lay beneath the park.

CHAPTER TWELVE

Before seven o'clock the following morning, Tess and her parents were standing outside the Dublin Zoo. Despite the early hour and the hard frost which had coated every leaf and blade of grass with silvery rime, there was already quite a queue of people there before them. The first ones in the line were wrapped in sleeping bags and blankets, and one or two gas stoves burned with yellow-blue flames beneath the street lights, brewing tea for cold campers.

Tess joined the line, pulling her pony tail out of the collar of her jacket and tightening the draw cords at her throat. Her father gave the pony tail an affectionate tug in an effort to break through the awkwardness which still lay between them. She gave him the best smile she could manage, but it wasn't great. Apart from anything else, Tess was desperately tired. She hadn't Switched at all the previous night; in her confusion she had decided to sleep on the problem in the hope that things would make more sense in the morning. But in the end she had found it impossible to sleep at all, and had spent the entire night in a terrible conflict with herself; swinging between her love for the phoenix and its ethereal existence and her desire for the bittersweet pleasures of the vampire. When her mother had come to call her at six-thirty, she had felt an enormous sense of relief, but it hadn't lasted long. Already the vampire side of her mind had begun to eat into her resolve to visit the phoenix. What was the point, after all? Why should she stand for hours in the freezing cold just for the sake of getting a glimpse of a namby-pamby bird that she had already seen?

The lights came on in the zoo, but there was still no sign of any activity at the gates. Tess shuddered as the frost bit deep into her tired bones. In an effort to close the contradictory voices out of her mind, she began to look around at the crowd. There were all kinds of people there, from new age 'crusties' with long-haired children to pin-striped businessmen who blew on their hands and stamped their polished brogues against the cold tarmac. The majority, though, seemed to be the type of people that Tess imagined would shoot birds rather than watch them; they wore waxed jackets or faded green anoraks with jeans and walking boots or green Wellingtons. The most noticeable thing about them was that they didn't seem to feel the cold as much as everyone else, but stood around in small groups chatting to each other as though they were quite accustomed to being out in the frost before dawn.

Tess examined the lines of parked cars and tried to match the people to their transport. There were a couple of brightly-coloured vans, a dormobile with dim lights on inside, several saloon cars with recent registration plates, a Morris Minor and four Land Rovers. As Tess watched, another one arrived, its diesel engine growling sweetly as it slowed and pulled into a space at the head of the line.

'I suppose it's too early to start on the breakfast?' said Tess's father.

'Of course it is,' said her mother. 'We've got three hours to wait before the gates open.'

'What do you think, Tess?' said her father, with a conspiratorial nudge of his elbow.

'I don't mind,' she said. She was still watching the Land Rover, expecting it to be loaded to the gills with Labrador dogs and men in deer-stalker hats.

'Just a cup of coffee?' said her father, in a wheedling voice.

The back door of the Land Rover opened and a huddle of children spilled out, stretching and yawning, their breath rising in misty clouds around them. The driver's door slammed and a man in a cloth cap walked around the bonnet, then went back to his own side to turn out the headlights.

Tess's mother conceded. 'All right. Just a small cup, though.'

The passenger door opened and swung back and forth on its hinges as a small figure manoeuvred around with considerable difficulty, until she was sitting sideways on the seat. The man in the cloth cap hurried round to help, and a moment later the elderly woman descended, stiffly but safely, on to the road.

Tess recognised her immediately. It was Lizzie, the eccentric old woman who had once been a Switcher herself, and had sent Tess and Kevin to the Arctic to do battle with the krools. Without thinking, Tess raced away from her parents and across the road, narrowly avoiding a minibus that was crawling along, looking for a space to park. Lizzie dropped her walking stick in surprise as Tess appeared at her side and flung her arms around her.

'Careful, girl! Careful of my old bones!' Lizzie suffered Tess's embrace for a moment or two, then extricated herself. 'This cold has me rusted up so I can hardly move!'

Tess stepped back and beamed at her friend. 'I never dreamt that you'd come,' she said. 'How did you know?'

'How did I know what?'

'How did you know that it was . . .' Tess stopped just in time, alerted by a fierce warning glint in Lizzie's eyes. The oldest of the four children, a girl of about nine, bent down to retrieve Lizzie's stick and handed it to her. The others stood in a shivering huddle on the road. Behind them, another Land Rover pulled up and waited for them to move.

But Lizzie was in no hurry. 'This is Mr Quinn, my neighbour,' she said. 'I told you about him, didn't I? He keeps his cattle on my land, and he helped me out that time when the weather was so bad. At least, some of the time.' She cast a surly glance at Mr Quinn, who cleared his throat and looked the other way. 'This here is Tessie,' Lizzie went on, 'who came snooping round my place last year with her young friend. What was his name again?'

'Kevin,' said Tess, nodding in greeting towards Mr Quinn. She was embarrassed now that her initial delight at seeing Lizzie had evaporated. Worse than that, she was unsure how she was going to explain the eccentric old woman to her parents.

'And as for how I knows,' Lizzie was saying,

292

looking pointedly at Tess, 'I read it in the newspapers like everyone else.'

Tess nodded, shamefaced. The driver of the waiting Land Rover honked his horn and the small group began to make their way towards the opposite pavement, all of them moving at a snail's pace to accommodate Lizzie's arthritis. Tess's mother was waiting for them on the footpath, and Tess cast around in her mind for some way of explaining Lizzie. There was no time to think, and she had to say something.

'Mother. This is Lizzie.'

The old woman stretched out a thin crooked hand, which Tess's mother accepted, a little reluctantly.

'Elizabeth Larkin,' said Lizzie, pompously, 'of Tibradden, County Dublin. I offered your daughter my hospitality during that cold snap we had that time.'

Tess's mother would never forget the 'cold snap', when her daughter had gone missing without warning and not returned until the thaw set in. Tess watched her face. She had never told her parents anything about what happened when she went away the previous year with Kevin, and they had never asked. She could see her mother's perplexity as she took in this information, knowing that it would do nothing to explain her disappearance but merely add to the mystery. Tess was afraid that she would ask Lizzie for more information but Lizzie was, as usual, a step ahead of her.

'This is my neighbour, Mr Quinn,' she said. 'He has most kindly brought me in to get a look at this funny pheasant, and I mustn't keep him waiting around. So nice to meet you.' With an authoritative air, Lizzie struck her cane on the frosty pavement and began to make her way towards the end of the rapidly lengthening queue.

Tess looked after them, surprised by the strength of her feelings for the old woman. When she had first seen her a few moments ago, she had felt that she had an ally, that she no longer had to face the current confusion alone. Now she wasn't so sure. Her heart was heavy as she and her mother made their way back to her father, who had stayed behind to hold their place.

'Who on earth was that?' he said.

'Lizzie. A mad old woman I met last year.'

'Where did you meet her? When?'

Tess was irritated by the questions. It hadn't been enough just to say hello to Lizzie. She badly wanted to talk to her. In the end it was her mother who had to fill the silence and answer her father's questions.

'She put Tess up during the snowstorms, apparently. Why didn't you tell us about her, Tess?'

Tess shrugged. Her parents looked at each other. Tess had always been secretive about her disappearance, and they had learnt not to pry. Nevertheless, the silence was full of tension. After a few minutes Tess said, 'Why don't you two have a cup of coffee? I fancy a wander around. I won't be long.'

Without waiting for a reply, she ducked out of the queue and made her way back along the side of the straggling crowds until she found Lizzie, standing a little to one side and leaning on her stick. People were streaming into the park now, some of them on foot, others in cars or coaches which pulled up beside the gates to unload. Tess was puzzled by the numbers. The capture of the bird had created a lot

294

of publicity, but she wouldn't have expected so many people to turn out.

As though she were reading Tess's mind, Lizzie spoke.

'People is looking for something,' she said. 'There's nothing left to believe in, and people wants something new.'

Tess nodded, looking round at the faces in the crowd. There was something in what Lizzie had said; a deeper emotion than simple curiosity shone in the expressions of the people all around her. There was an eagerness, almost a hunger, to witness the mystery that was residing in the zoo buildings ahead.

Lizzie left firm instructions with the youngest of Mr Quinn's children to hold her place in the line. The child nodded, an expression of utter terror on her face. Her father ruffled her hair and offered to help with the job, and the child relaxed. Lizzie's body might have been old and frail, but she had a powerful personality and Tess could well understand how a small child might be intimidated by her. She smiled encouragingly and wondered, as she often did, whether that child had discovered the ability to Switch and, if she had, where it might lead her.

The sun was just rising as she and Lizzie made their slow way towards a stand of sycamore trees on the other side of the road. Sunlight might be beginning to overpower the streetlights, but it would be a long time before it made any significant impression on the crisp white frost underfoot.

'You's worried, girl,' said Lizzie as she propped herself carefully against the scaly trunk of one of the trees.

Tess sat down on a protruding root and nodded. 'Do you know who this bird is?' she said.

'Of course I do!' said Lizzie. 'He would have had something to answer for if he hadn't come to see me!'

'I suppose so,' said Tess, though somehow she couldn't imagine the phoenix answering to anyone, no matter what the call. 'The question is, though, how do we get him out of there?'

Lizzie nodded slowly and looked over towards the zoo. 'I suppose he has to come out, sooner or later.'

'But of course he has to come out! How could you think of leaving him in there?'

'Well, he can't come to any harm, can he? He'll always rise up again, won't he, whatever happens? He'll be rising up again after you and me and the zoo is long since gone and forgotten.'

'But he can't stay in captivity all his life! Or all his lives, whatever way you want to put it. And we've only got a week to get him out!'

'I wouldn't say it bothers him too much where he is,' said Lizzie. 'He is what he is; here, there, or anywhere else he might happen to be.'

Tess tried to resist what Lizzie was saying, but when she thought about it, she had to admit that it was true. The bliss of the phoenix existed in being, not in doing. Why should it matter to him where he was?

But Lizzie, true to form, had not finished confusing Tess yet.

'Still, he has to come out, all the same,' she was saying, 'though I isn't sure it'll be enough to make the difference.'

'Make what difference?'

Lizzie sighed and shifted uncomfortably. 'I's sure you knows already, girl, but if I has to explain it then I will. As best I can, that is.'

'Go on.'

'There is a great light in this city, and within the next hour or two people are going to be pouring in through these gates to see it. Every person who sees it is going to be affected by it. You mark my words: that bird in there will change people's lives.'

'Really?'

Lizzie nodded. 'For a while, anyway. But the truth about this world is that wherever there's light there has to be darkness, and as soon as that bird came into existence some nastiness was born to balance it out. What's more, I's as sure as I can be that where the evil is based isn't a million miles from here.'

She looked pointedly at Tess, who felt her mind cloud over with suspicion. What did the old woman know? What business was it of hers, anyway? For a moment the sunlight which was beginning to break through the branches overhead felt intolerable to her. Then, as quickly as it had come, the feeling passed away, leaving Tess in a turmoil of confusion.

'But what should I do, Lizzie?' she said, trying to hide the desperation which was edging into her voice. 'How do I choose?'

Lizzie shrugged. 'We all has to choose at some stage, girl,' she said. 'But it may not be as difficult as you thinks it is. Sometimes it isn't choices that is difficult, but the way we looks at them. It's not always what we are that needs changing, but the way we thinks. You know what I mean?'

'No!' said Tess. 'I have no idea what you mean.'

Lizzie was about to reply when her attention was caught by Tess's father running towards them across the grass.

'They've opened the gates early,' he called breathlessly. 'We'd better get back in line.'

Tess stood up and took Lizzie's elbow to help her

back to Mr Quinn and his family. She seemed to move infuriatingly slowly, and Tess could see her mother nearing the gate as the crowd flowed forward.

Lizzie stopped abruptly. Mr Quinn was making towards them across the road.

'You get along now, Tessie,' she said. 'And mind you take care, you hear?'

'Are you sure you'll be all right?'

'I'll be all right, and so will you if you takes care. I trusts you, girl. If you trusts yourself half as much, you'll know what to do when the time comes.'

She shook herself free of Tess's grasp and latched on to Mr Quinn. Tess wanted to hear more, but it was too late. Her father was moving in another direction, and was just about to be swallowed up by the crowd.

'That all sounded very serious and profound,' he said, as she caught up with him. 'Far too obscure for an old dunce like me. What was it all about, anyway?'

'I haven't the faintest idea,' said Tess, 'but I wish I had.'

CHAPTER THIRTEEN

'It must be because of all these people that they're opening early,' said Tess's mother as they approached the turnstiles. 'I'm sure the adverts said the zoo would open at ten.'

Tess looked back. The line stretched as far as she could see, back along the road between the zoo and the main gates of the park. A few gardai had arrived and were standing at intervals beside the queue, but so far there was no need for them; all was quiet and orderly.

Tess's father paid a harassed young woman in the nearest of the wooden kiosks at the gate, then grumbled about the price.

'Better be worth it. Awful lot of money just to look at one bird.'

'You can see all the rest of the animals as well if you want to,' said Tess.

'Leave him alone, Tess,' said her mother, good-naturedly. 'His life wouldn't be worth living if he couldn't find something to complain about.'

Once inside the zoo gates, there were several directions that a visitor could take, but not one person deviated from the line which dragged slowly on towards the centre of the compound. To Tess's surprise they passed by the aviary where she had used the pine marten's sharp wits to get a look at the phoenix, and headed on towards another building beside the café. It was a huge grey warehouse of a place with nothing in the way of architectural imagination to recommend it. Tess had been inside it once before, when it had housed a rather boring exhibition of model whales and dolphins. Now it had clearly been given over to displaying the phoenix. As they drew near, a man was in the process of changing the queuing time notice beside the door from 'two hours' to 'three hours'.

'Glad we got here early,' said Tess's mother. 'We'd have been waiting all day if we'd got up an hour later.'

Inside the entrance to the building a pair of uniformed security guards were making cursory checks of everyone's hand luggage. The family's picnic basket got a slightly more thorough examination before they were allowed to move on, and Tess noticed two or three shooting sticks leaning against the wall, waiting for their owners to reclaim them as they left.

'They're not taking any chances, are they?' said Tess's father as they moved forward with the crowd.

'I suppose that bird must be fairly valuable,' said her mother. 'It seems to be the only one of its kind.'

'We don't know that,' said Tess. 'I think it's ridiculous. Why couldn't they leave it alone to get on with its life? For all they know it might have a family somewhere.'

She peered around the side of a heavily-built man in front of her, but the crowd was still too thick to see anything. For a long time they didn't move at all, and the guard at the door had stopped any more people from coming in behind them. Then, after what seemed an age, the line began to dribble forward again.

The phoenix's cage was in the corner diagonally opposite to the entrance door. A wall of hardboard partitions ran down the centre of the building and prevented anyone seeing around the corner until they got there. The wait was infuriating; the long, slow crawl to that corner. But when they turned it, the endless queuing all seemed worthwhile.

The light hit them before they saw the bird itself, and it produced a powerful sensation. The glass-panelled cage was lit from above by a double row of fluorescent tubes, but the radiance that flooded out of that corner was far greater than what they could produce. Tess knew as soon as she saw the light that in some way or other, it was being produced by the bird itself. And its effect was extraordinary. The moment she came within its aura, and long before she saw the phoenix itself, Tess felt her mood shift; elevate, as though she had received some wonderful news or been given an unexpected gift. When the phoenix first appeared at her window she had felt like that, but she had assumed her joy came from knowing that Kevin had survived. Now she knew it was more than that. The bird had some sort of mystical power of its own, and as Tess looked around her in wonder she could see that it was affecting everyone in the building in the same way. There was still a certain amount of shoving going on behind them, but all those who had stepped into the light were completely at ease; in no hurry at all despite their proximity to the source of the light. Even the zoo staff, there to keep the visitors moving, were relaxed and smiling, in no hurry to move people along.

Tess giggled to herself, imagining the sign outside the door being changed again from 'three hours' to 'four hours', then from four to five, and five to six, as progress slowed to a contented standstill inside the building. She could visualise the crusties getting out their Jews' harps and bongo drums as they settled in for the day, and the waxed jackets and pin-stripes sitting down among them, clapping their hands and chanting.

But the line did eventually move on, slowly but surely, and a few minutes later the golden bird came into view. It sat on a solid wooden perch, suspended above a lush forest of green and red foliage growing from large pots on the gravel floor of the cage. The sight of that gravel, laid down above the compacted earth floor on which she and the other onlookers were standing, meant something to Tess, though at that moment she couldn't understand what. It seemed absurd to be noticing such details when the phoenix was sitting there in front of her in all his glory.

She fought down a sudden urge to Switch and join him there and then, to become a part of that glorious radiance that shone through the glass panels of the enclosure. Instead, she tried to catch the bird's eye, to let him know that she was there and had not abandoned him.

It wasn't easy. His gaze moved slowly and evenly

302

across the crowd, first one way and then the other. His expression was inscrutable and, when Tess did finally succeed in making contact with those calm, golden eyes, she could see no sign of recognition at all.

It disturbed her, and for a moment her buoyant mood deflated. Was she nothing to the phoenix? Was she just another pair of gawking eyes in the middle of this latest crop of uplifted faces? There was a certain arrogance about the bird's demeanour as he hung there above them all, passing his benevolent eyes from one to another, as distant as a priest handing out communion. The fat man moved sideways, blocking her view, and at the same time a sullen anger tugged at the edge of Tess's mind. If he was so detached, why shouldn't she be, too? Why should she care about him being stuck there for all eternity if he didn't even bother to acknowledge her presence? She could turn away now and never turn back, just slip off into the darkness of that other existence, to hunt the city streets in the hours of darkness and never be bothered with him again.

The crowd shuffled forward and she was edged along with them. The fat man stepped aside to get a better view and the light fell directly on Tess's face once again. As it did so, all thoughts of darkness were washed out of her mind and she was swept back into the jubilant mood of the encompassing gathering. The gaze of the phoenix passed over her again and she was perfect, glowing with an inner light as radiant as his own.

Outside the dull grey building, no one seemed in any hurry to move off towards their homes. If it hadn't been for the zoo officials who kept everyone moving

303

along, people might have just sat down where they were, prepared to enjoy the weak winter sunshine for as long as it lasted. As it was, most people allowed themselves to be guided back to the gates, where a cordon of posts and plastic chains separated the exit from the dense crowds still coming in.

The grass was green again now, except for those shadowy places beneath the trees and hedges where the sun couldn't reach. Tess kept an eye out for Lizzie, but when she eventually spotted her a few metres from the entrance to the exhibition building, she was too far away to call out. She noticed the puzzled expressions on the faces of the incoming visitors as they observed those who were coming out, beaming with pleasure. In sudden excitement, Tess realised that something extraordinary was happening here. Whatever power the phoenix held within itself was infectious. People were being changed by it. It was pulling them out of their dull, everyday lives and inspiring them with some sort of new spirit.

As though he were echoing her thoughts, Tess's father suddenly stretched his arms up above his head as if he was trying to reach the sun and said, 'Do you know what?'

'What?' said Tess.

'I don't think I'll bother going on into the office after all. They can manage without me for one day. Let's go home and get the frisbee, then find a quiet spot somewhere and have our breakfast.'

'Does that mean I can stay off school, then?'

Her mother laughed, her voice bubbling with the same inner excitement that everyone seemed to be feeling. 'We may be in a good mood,' she said, 'but we'd hardly go as far as playing frisbee without you!'

★

'Oh, wouldn't you?' Tess thought to herself as she sprawled luxuriously among the remains of their picnic breakfast an hour later. Her parents were playing frisbee some distance away, fooling about like young children in the sun. She was about to get up and join them when she noticed a familiar group of people making their way towards her across the park. It was Lizzie, with her escort of Mr Quinn and his children. As she stood up to go and meet them, Tess saw Lizzie turn to the others and give them some sort of command. They dropped back and sat down on the grass to wait for her, while she came on alone.

Tess bounced over to her, eager as a puppy, but something in Lizzie's expression made her hesitate. The old woman looked marvellous, as though she was twenty years younger. Even her stiffness had eased, and she hardly used her cane at all as she came forward to meet Tess. But there was something in her eyes apart from the reflected glow of the pho-enix's radiance. It was clear to Tess that Lizzie had something on her mind.

'Well, young lady?' she said as Tess approached. 'What does you think of all that?'

'Oh, Lizzie. It's wonderful, isn't it?'

'Oh, it's wonderful, all right. Of course it's wonderful. Look at all these people all over the place, wonderfulling away the day.'

Tess looked round at the growing crowds enjoying the space and the fresh air of the park. The grass was becoming almost crowded as people continued to file in and out of the zoo, and swelled the numbers lying about under the sun.

'Well? What's wrong with that?'

'There's nothing wrong with that, unless someone has work to do.'

'Oh, come on, Lizzie! I didn't think that you were the sort to get wound up over a few people taking a day off work!'

'I isn't talking about that lot!' said Lizzie, sounding exasperated. 'I's talking about you!'

'Me! But you're the one who goes on about young people filling their heads up with useless rubbish and having no room left for what they need to know. How can you turn round and object to me taking a day off school?'

As she was speaking, Tess noticed Lizzie glancing past her and turning slightly away. 'Don't look now,' she said with a nonchalant kind of expression, 'but here comes trouble.' She lowered her voice and spoke rapidly, determined to say what she had to before they were interrupted. 'I isn't talking about school, you little fool. I's talking about work. Real work. You's here lounging around in the sun, lapping up all this light everywhere like a cat laps up cream . . .' Her voice lowered even further and Tess glanced round to see her parents approaching, their faces beaming with welcome.

'You has to do something with it!' Lizzie hissed. 'You's wasting time and you's wasting what that bird has given you! You has work to do.'

'Hello again,' said Tess's father breezily, extending a warm, ruddy hand towards Lizzie. 'I'm glad you found us. I was hoping to get a word with you.'

'How do you do, Mrs Larkin?' said Tess's mother, smiling from ear to ear.

'I's doing fine, thanks, Mrs. And how's you doing yourself? I's sorry I hasn't time to be standing around and chatting, but Mr Quinn there is a busy farmer, and he's waiting to drive me back to Tibradden. You's most welcome to call if you's in the locality.'

Before Tess's parents had a chance to reply, Lizzie had turned on her heel and begun to walk back across the park.

CHAPTER FOURTEEN

Tess's parents watched with benign expressions as Lizzie and the Quinns departed. To their euphoric minds Lizzie's behaviour was quite forgivable, no more than mildly eccentric. For Tess, however, the aspect of the day had changed entirely. She knew in her heart that Lizzie was right. There was something she ought to be doing. The problem was, she couldn't think what it was.

'Come on,' said her father, 'where's that frisbee?'

Frisbee would be fun, even though she was no good at it. But playing frisbee wasn't what she ought to be doing. She scanned the horizon of the park, looking for clues. For the most part, her view was blocked by trees, but here and there the buildings of the city showed through or above them.

'Catch, Tess!'

She swung round, just in time to see the bright-green frisbee go sailing over her head and disappear among the branches of a copse which stood in a hollow some distance away. It was a mighty throw, and the wind had caught it as well. Tess watched as her parents raced past in pursuit and began hunting through the dead grass beneath the trees. She went over and began to help in the search, but her attention was taken by a number of small, neat piles of earth which were spread around the area. They were like molehills, but Tess knew there weren't any moles in Ireland. Everything today had a strange, dreamlike quality and Tess tried to concentrate; tried to make sense of what was going on. She might have found the scene humorous if it hadn't been for the persistent nagging from the back of her mind about the task that awaited her.

The first time the idea came to her she disliked it so much that she ignored it. Coming back a second time with the ring of truth, it wasn't so easily put aside. She tried to reason the thought away, was still trying as her parents gave up and came back to her side.

'No use,' said her mother. 'It seems to be lost.'

'Sorry about that,' said Tess.

'No, no,' said her father. 'It was way, way too high. There was no way you could have caught it.'

'Did you notice the molehills?'

'Molehills? But there aren't any moles in Ireland!'

The idea came back and Tess finally accepted it. 'Never mind,' she said. 'I was thinking of paying a visit to someone. Would that be OK?'

'Who is it?'

'A friend of mine called Martin. He's off school these days.'

'Is he sick?'

'Yes, he is. Sort of.' As she said it, Tess realised

that this wasn't a lie. From her current viewpoint, out here under a cloudless sky and filled with the vibrancy of life, anyone who chose to spend their days sleeping behind closed curtains had to be sick.

Tess's father looked slightly disappointed, but he was far too happy to remain so for long.

'Don't be too late back,' was all he said.

It was early afternoon as Tess walked down the narrow street in Phibsboro. The sun was still shining, but apart from a shallow strip of brightness on the opposite pavement, the street was covered in shadows cast by the surrounding houses. Frost still lay in some of the remoter corners of the small front gardens and Tess shivered as she made her way up to Martin's front door.

As before, her knock was followed by a long silence. She waited, half hoping that no one would come and she could return to the sanctity of the park with a clear conscience. But Martin's mother did come, eventually, from some dreary corner of the house that Tess chose not to imagine.

Her face brightened when she saw Tess standing at the door, but not enough to bring colour to the pasty skin.

'Hello?' she said. 'Have you come to visit Martin again?'

'Yes. Is he in?'

His mother's face clouded over again. 'Where else would he be?' She glanced around at the stairs and then, to Tess's surprise, stepped out of the house and joined her on the front step, pulling the door to behind her.

'I probably shouldn't tell you this,' she said, leaning close to Tess and speaking in a low voice, 'but we had the social worker here this morning. She went up and talked to himself in the bed, but she didn't get much sense out of him. When she came down she told me that if he didn't start going back to school soon he'd be taken away from me and put into Borstal. Something like that, anyway.'

She looked at Tess closely for a reaction. Tess tried to ignore the smell of cheap margarine that lingered on the woman's clothes, and put on several expressions, one after another. She started with dismay first, then sympathy, then disapproval, but none of them really worked very well because all she could honestly think was that it would be a waste of everyone's time. She seemed to have done something right, though, because Martin's mother nodded gravely and went on, 'I don't know what's wrong with the boy. He hasn't been the same since his father died.'

'His father died?'

'Didn't you know that? I thought everyone must know. It affected him very badly, right from the start. He never cried, not once. He just seemed to close down like a clam. I suppose I should have taken more notice at the time, but I always thought that he would be all right in the end.'

She paused and listened at the crack in the front door for a minute before continuing, 'I've tried every-thing. Everything. I've done the rounds of the town with him; taken him to every counsellor and psy-chiatrist and psychologist in the phone book. He won't take any notice of them, though. He goes once and makes a fool of them, then refuses to go to any more appointments.'

Tess nodded, trying to look sage and concerned. Martin's mother sighed.

'The fact is, I'm at my wits' end. My own health isn't the best and I'm worn out trying to cope. But I don't want them to take him away. He may not be perfect but he's all I've got.'

She looked into the middle distance, her eyes glossing over with distress. For a long time she stood quite still, while Tess grew colder and colder and felt more and more awkward; then, at last, she seemed to pull herself together.

'I'm glad you've come again,' she said. 'I have to admit that I didn't think you would, but I'm glad you did. Martin seems to like you. He was quite cheerful for a while after your last visit. I don't suppose . . .' She stopped, looking searchingly at Tess as though she wasn't sure whether she could trust her or not.

'You don't suppose what?'

The woman sighed, her deathly white face relaxing into its usual defeated slackness. 'I don't suppose you'd talk to him? Try and make him see reason?'

Tess looked away. There was no point in trying to explain that she had come with exactly that purpose in mind. 'I'll do my best,' she said. 'But I wouldn't raise your hopes too high if I were you.'

In the stuffy darkness of Martin's room, his hands and face showed up against the bedclothes like pale moths in the night. In the corner opposite, the greeny-blue light on the video clock flashed on and off: 00.00. 00.00. The curtains had been reinforced by a grey army blanket so that the only light coming in from the day was a feeble line of paler grey above the curtain rod.

Tess waited in the doorway until her eyes became accustomed to the gloom and she could hear Martin's

312

slow, regular breathing, then she crossed over to the bedside. The boy's face wore a smug, satisfied expression and the hairs on the back of Tess's neck prickled as she became aware once again of the dark power which slumbered within that innocuous frame. But she had power as well: the inner freedom that the phoenix had given her. That was why Lizzie had been so keen for her to come soon, before it wore off. If she couldn't stand up to him, who could?

She called to him, gently. He stirred and sucked his teeth but didn't wake. She called again, a little louder. He sighed and woke, his eyes searching the room until they found her face. For a moment he looked bewildered, as though her presence there didn't fit with the dreams he had been having. Then he recovered his confidence, smiled his sweet smile and sat up.

Tess smiled back. 'Sorry to wake you. But it's a beautiful day outside.'

'Is it?' Martin yawned and stretched. Tess moved over towards the window, but he said, 'Whoa, hold on. One step at a time, eh?'

He reached out and switched on a heavily-shaded lamp which stood on the bedside table, then he leaned back and stretched himself again.

Tess cleared a chair and pulled it up beside his feet. 'Your mother's bringing us breakfast,' she said. 'Well, lunch, actually.'

Martin laughed and rubbed his bleary eyes. 'I was out until nearly dawn, but the pickings were mean. I hope she's making a fry.'

Tess made no answer and there was an awkward silence for a few minutes. Then Martin sighed and cuddled himself back down into the bedclothes.

Tess looked over at the mop of red hair which

313

shaded his marble-green eyes and felt a sudden surge of affection for him. He couldn't be that bad, he just couldn't. He was only a boy, after all.

'You didn't tell me that your father died,' she said.

Martin shrugged, pulling the covers tight for a moment over his toes. 'Did my mother tell you that?'

'Yes. Just now. Downstairs.'

'She tells everyone about it. She thinks it's like, some kind of big tragedy in my life which made me go wrong. She thinks it explains everything, but it doesn't. It doesn't explain anything. It didn't make any difference to me at all.'

'I find that hard to believe. How could you lose your father and not be affected by it?'

'How could *you*, you mean?' Martin's voice had a sharp edge that Tess hadn't heard before. 'You're talking about yourself,' he went on, 'not about me. Everyone does that. You'd miss your father so you assume everyone else would, too. But I didn't, not one bit. I didn't miss him 'cos I hated him.'

His face wore a sullen, bitter expression as he spoke, and his eyes were like glinting granite when he turned to Tess and said, 'Do you understand?'

Tess kept her face straight, determined to hide the unease his words had produced in her heart. 'Not really,' she said.

'Do you want me to tell you about it?'

'If you want to.'

'It's very gory. Do you like gory stories?'

Tess shrugged, torn between ghoulish curiosity and what she liked to think of as her finer sensibilities. 'I don't mind.'

'No, I'm sure you don't.' Martin's tone was sarcastic. 'But I'll tell you anyway. I like talking about

314

it. I've talked about it to every shrink in Dublin, so it doesn't bother me one bit.'

He stopped, listening. There were slow footsteps on the stairs, and a moment later his mother elbowed the door open, struggling beneath the weight of a heavily-laden tray. Tess jumped up and unloaded the plates, then, while Martin's mother got her breath back, reloaded the tray with yesterday's empty cups and dishes.

'I'll bring it down for you,' she said.

'No. You stay here and have your chat. If you need anything else, give me a shout, all right?'

When his mother was gone, Martin began tucking into his plate of rashers and black pudding.

'We used to live in the countryside, you know. Just outside Dublin.'

'Did you?' Tess thought he had changed the subject, but he went on, 'Yes. We had a run-down old cottage and a few acres. My dad used to breed greyhounds and sell them to people from England. That was all he thought about: greyhounds, grey-hounds and greyhounds.'

He paused for a minute to chew, then went on. 'It was a weird kind of life. One minute we'd be living on bread and margarine, wondering how we were going to last another week, and the next thing, he'd sell a dog or a pup for silly money to some English trainer and we'd be rolling in it. New clothes for me and my mother, Chinese takeaways every night of the week, him off to the pub buying rounds for the parish. Then back to bread and margarine again. I didn't mind, though. At least it was exciting.'

Tess poured out tea and handed him a cup. He took a few sips, then perched it on the bedside table beside the lamp and returned to the fry.

315

'Then what?' said Tess.

'Where was I? Oh, yes. I was into top gear by that time with this animal thing. What did you call us? Switchers, that's right. Well I used to be off in the woods and fields every spare minute trying out all kinds of things. I suppose it was good while it lasted. Then one of our neighbours gave me a donkey foal. Have you ever seen one?'

'Only in the zoo.'

'Yeah. Not many people keep donkeys these days. But the foal was . . .' He felt silent, staring ahead of him, and for a moment Tess fancied that he was vulnerable, that his guard had finally dropped. But if it had, it wasn't for long.

'Fact was that I was dead soft in those days. I doted on that little donkey like a right eejit. Spent half my time out in the shed with it, sometimes being another donkey, sometimes just being myself.'

'Bet you didn't tell that to the shrinks.'

Martin laughed. 'Be a lot more probable than some of the things I did tell them. They wouldn't know the difference anyhow. I didn't meet a single one who was the full shilling. I don't know how they're supposed to cure anyone else.'

He gave his full attention to his breakfast until Tess said, 'Go on. About the donkey.'

'There's not much to tell. Except that my dad said we had to get rid of her.'

'Why?'

'He said he needed the shed for his hounds. And she couldn't live out on the land because he sold the hay every year and then exercised the dogs there. He said I could have a pup from the next litter instead of the donkey and it would be worth twenty times

316

what she was, but that wasn't the point. Not then, anyway.'

Martin stopped to finish his breakfast. Outside, the birds were beginning to tune down as the short day drew towards an end, and Tess wished that she could see a last glimpse of sunshine. She looked over at the curtains, then decided against it, unwilling to disturb the atmosphere.

Martin wiped up the last of the grease with a piece of soggy toast, then put his plate down beside the bed, balancing it on his upturned trainers.

'So, anyway,' he said, wiping his mouth on the hem of his T-shirt, 'one evening my dad borrowed a cattle trailer and we brought the donkey out to some friends of his in Naas. Fifteen quid is all they gave me for her. It wasn't that, though. I didn't care about the money. The worst thing was that they had grey-hounds, too, and I was sure they only wanted my donkey for dog food.

'I wouldn't care now, but it bothered me then. There was nothing I could do about it, you see. I felt completely helpless. And then they got down the bottle of whisky and my dad sat there the whole evening drinking and laughing his head off. Have you seen people get drunk? Have you seen how stupid they look, and how clever they think they are?' Martin's sour expression accentuated the anger he was feeling. 'I hated him. I hated him so much I wished he was dead.'

He gulped down his tea and held the cup out to Tess for a refill. 'Ready for the gory bit?'

She nodded, putting aside her half-eaten fry. Martin's face held a strange kind of delight as he started up with his story again.

'It was pitch-dark when we started home that

317

night, and there was only one headlight working on the van. My dad took the back roads home because he didn't want to run into the cops with all that drink in him. He was driving too fast, as usual. I always wore my seat belt when he was driving, never with my ma. He didn't wear his, specially since they brought in the law that said you had to. He wasn't a violent man, but he'd go out of his way to get on the wrong side of the law if he could. That was just the way he was.

'So when this black cow appeared in the middle of the road, he didn't have a chance. I don't remember hitting her. I just remember seeing her on the road, coming out of nowhere, then waking up in the van with blood all over the place.'

Martin looked over to check Tess's reaction, but she was giving nothing away.

'I didn't know if the blood belonged to Dad or to the cow, and to tell you the truth I didn't care. The van was on its side in the ditch, and Dad's door had swung open during the crash and bent double under the wing. That was how the light came to be on inside the cab and I could see all the blood. Dad was covered in it and he wasn't moving. I was hanging over him, caught in the seat belt. All I could think of was getting out. I didn't care what had happened to him. I was really cool and calculated, manoeuvring myself around so that I could get a foot on the gear housing and lever myself out without standing on him. In the end I managed it. Then I just stood on the road for ages – hours, maybe – watching this sticky mess of a cow thrashing about on the road. And all I could think was that I didn't care. I had wished he was dead and now I didn't care whether he was or not. I knew then that I was a bad lot; always had been, always will be.'

'I don't believe that,' said Tess.

'Then you're a fool,' said Martin. He looked straight at her, the cold shadow of his night-time self at the forefront of his eyes. 'After it happened my mother couldn't bear to live out there any more. She sold the house and the land; turned out to be worth a fortune as a development site. We moved here. Too soon, perhaps, some of the shrinks said. I didn't speak to anyone for weeks, maybe months. I do now, though. I'll talk to anyone who wants to listen to me. Why not? It makes no difference. No one can touch me.'

Tess could think of nothing to say. For a long time they sat in silence until at last the gloom became too much for Tess.

'Can I open the curtains now? At least take a look at the day before it gets dark?'

Martin nodded. 'I was waiting for you last night,' he said. 'Where did you get to?'

Tess shrugged and went over to the window. 'Nowhere in particular. I went to sleep. Had to get up early this morning to go and see the phoenix in the zoo.'

'Oh, yes. Your phoenix. I keep forgetting about him.' Martin winced as Tess began to dismantle the blanket barricade and daylight lunged into the room. 'How is he?'

'He's . . .' Tess dried up, lost for words which would describe the glorious experience of the morning. 'He's perfect,' was all she could think of.

'That's good,' said Martin.

'But you should go and see for yourself. We haven't got all that much time; they're planning to move him

319

to America at the end of the week, so you'd better go as soon as you can. There's an awful crush there at the moment, but if we got up really early in the morning . . .'

Martin cut across her words. 'Naa. I don't think I'll bother.'

It was the first direct blow, and Tess felt her sense of well-being begin to diminish. She turned, her back to the window. 'What do you mean, you won't bother?'

Martin's face was screwed up against the light at Tess's back. 'I won't bother,' he said again. 'Why should I?'

'Why should you?' said Tess. 'Well, there's two reasons, actually. One is that the phoenix is probably the most beautiful thing you'll ever see. It'll change your life, I guarantee it.'

Martin nodded complacently. 'And the other reason?'

'The other is that you promised me you'd help me get him out. You have to come and look at where he is, so we can work out a plan.'

Martin shook his head with an expression of disdain. 'I didn't promise you anything.'

'Yes you did. You said that you'd help me if I tried your way first. I did that; I kept my side of the bargain. Now it's your turn.'

But again the boy shook his head. 'I didn't promise anything. I said that I might consider it, that's all. And I still might.'

Tess waited expectantly as Martin swung his legs out of the bed and stood up, taking his time.

'But I won't,' he said.

It was like being kicked in the teeth. Tess turned away to hide the fury that was rising like a rush of blood to her face. The phoenix light within her was eclipsed by that rage, and she floundered between enemies, one without, the other within. He was playing with her, teasing her, that was all. He had never had any intention of coming towards her way of seeing things; not one single step.

CHAPTER FIFTEEN

Tess couldn't face Martin's mother now that she had failed so miserably in her mission. Instead she slipped quietly down the stairs, out of the front door and away down the street.

The last of the sunlight held no warmth, but it had that sweet, golden hue of evening which made it seem more substantial than it had been earlier in the day. Tess was reminded of the light emitted by the phoenix, and she tried to settle her thoughts and recapture her earlier mood.

She had left Martin's house in a hurry, not because she was afraid of him but because she was afraid that her own feelings of anger and betrayal would overwhelm her. As she warmed to the stroll through the darkening streets, the strange contradictions of her situation began to become apparent to her. She was being swung like a pendulum between two opposing forces, one dark and bent upon nothing more than

322

satisfying its own desires, the other light, peaceful, beyond human yearnings and frailties. The first saw itself as all-important, with others being no more than a means of satisfying its needs, while the second had no need of others, but was perfect within itself. The choice ought to have been simple, according to the morality that Tess had been taught both at home and at school, but when faced with those opposites in reality, was far from being so. Because the phoenix, for all its light-giving qualities, was powerless when faced with opposition. How otherwise could it be caught so easily and held captive, at the mercy of those who held the keys? It might continue; it might rise again from its own ashes, and again, and again. But what use was that if it couldn't move about freely and spread its influence?

The vampire, on the other hand, would always be free to stalk the earth, even if it was restricted to the hours of darkness. It had the power to mesmerise, to bring others under its control. And in a confrontation, as Tess had found out, the only defence that existed against the creature was to become as he was. This had happened to her in the street under the trees, and in a slightly different way it had just happened again. The only response Tess had found to Martin's coldness was a coldness of her own, despite all her good intentions. Under threat, the phoenix force had diminished and the vampire force had grown.

Tess tried to remember what Lizzie had said. 'It's not what we are that needs changing but what we thinks.' Was that it? In any event, the words made no sense. Tess felt as though the seams of her mind were about to give way under the stress of the inner conflict. She wished that she had never met Martin, or Kevin either. She wished, for the first time in her life, that she had never discovered her power to Switch and that she was safely on the course that her parents wanted for her; towards a good education and a secure job. Life would be so simple, then; the only choices she would be faced with would be her Leaving Cert subjects.

She felt like screaming and began to run, trying to drown out the pursuing voices, both the light and the dark. When she got back to the house she barely greeted her mother, who was frying burgers in the kitchen, but went straight through to the sitting room and turned on the TV. A children's programme was on; it seemed fatuous, but lulled her like an old song and, exhausted from the excitement of the day and from lack of sleep, Tess dozed off.

She dreamt that the room was full of rats, a moving carpet of silky grey-brown. The rats were trying to get her attention, sending out strange picture calls, but she was refusing to listen. They were becoming more and more agitated, and some of them had begun to climb up on to her bed.

She woke and opened her eyes on to darkness. For a moment she didn't know where she was, then the familiar shape of the bay window reminded her that she had fallen asleep in the sitting room. One or other of her parents had brought down her duvet and pillow; she was snug and warm, wrapped up on the settee. She glanced at the luminous hands of her watch. Three a.m. With a sense of relief, she turned round to go back to sleep.

Something wriggled on the settee beside her. At the same time, something small and heavy ran across the top of the duvet. This was no dream. Tess threw off the cover and sat up, reaching out blindly for the switch of the standing lamp beside the settee. In the dim orange glow cast from the street lights outside the window, she could see her duvet moving on the floor as the rats beneath it squirmed around, looking for a way out. As her initial terror passed off, Tess relaxed, and was immediately bombarded by rat minds throwing images at her. It hadn't been a dream. The rats had come, and they had brought a message from their master.

For a long moment, Tess considered refusing his demand. She was afraid of what she might discover; afraid of the vampire's night-time power. But something stronger than fear lured her. Whatever her final decision might be, she needed to know everything there was to know.

She reassured the clamorous rats and sat for a while trying to compose herself; trying, without success, to draw upon the residual serenity somewhere within. She failed to find it, but discovered instead a small corner of her heart which still hoped to save not only herself, but Martin as well, from the eternal alienation of a vampire existence.

Despite the anxiety which wrenched at her guts there was no question of changing her mind. She took a deep breath and Switched, hating the transition as always but welcoming the alertness of the rat, and the vibrant certainty of its being.

The others led the way. There must have been about fifty of them, steaming down through a hole in the floorboards that Tess was sure wasn't there yesterday. One by one they dropped down through the joists beneath the floor and on to the uneven, muddy shale of the foundations. It was the last bit of open space that they were to see for quite a while, for the next minute they were underground, racing nose-to-tail through a newly-dug tunnel.

It was more like something a mole would dig than a rat and Tess remembered the little piles of earth she had seen in the park. Here was the answer to that mystery, at least. The earth that had been excavated would have to have been put somewhere. Below ground, the tunnels were economical, just wide enough for a rat to pass through at full stretch with no concession made for whiskers. Every few feet, subsidiary tunnels branched off the main one; some going up, some going down, some heading off on the same level, at right angles. As they sped along, the rats explained the system to Tess; how it had been devised so that every patch of ground beneath the city and the park could be searched. They would not, however, describe for her what they had found, despite their obvious excitement.

For the most part, the journey was easy going, if a little dull and claustrophobic. But on two occasions the entire party was brought to a halt by subsidence in the tunnel ahead. When that happened, the lead rat had to dig a way through, passing the fallen earth back from rat to rat until it reached the end of the line or the entrance to an excavation tunnel, whichever came first. The delays only served to heighten Tess's sense of expectation, so that by the time they eventually arrived at their destination, about half a mile from the edge of the park, she was bursting with curiosity.

The first she knew of their impending arrival was when the file turned in to a subsidiary tunnel on the right-hand side. It ran along straight for a few yards, and a single tip-head passage forked off to the left, sloping gradually upwards. Soon afterwards, the route began to slope downwards, gently at first, then more sharply. The earth was quite wet at that depth and the tunnel, which was clearly well-used, had turned into a mud-slide. The rats at the front tried to use outstretched paws to brake their descent, but the pressure of those careering down behind added to their speed, so that when they reached their destination they went shooting out into space like champagne corks.

Rats are hardy creatures, however, and take no notice of the occasional tumble. One by one they picked themselves up, licked their paws, polished their whiskers and were ready for action again.

And there was plenty of it. It was pitch dark down there beneath the ground, but between the sounds she could hear and the images she picked up from the minds of the other rats, Tess was able to get a fairly clear picture of what was going on.

They were in an underground chamber of some kind. Parts of the roof were still held up by pillars which supported crossed arches, but in other places these had given way and the chamber had filled with earth and rubble. Tree roots had reached down into the cavity, and one of the predominant sounds was of rats' teeth, gnawing through them to clear them away.

It was clear to Tess's human mind that this must have been the crypt of some long-forgotten church which had once stood above it. It was a dramatic find. Tess was sure that no one knew the place existed. Her human mind was aware of a brief thrill of excitement before the realisation of what she was here for sank home. There were two or three stone tombs in the chamber. One of them was standing in the open, the others were half buried by the subsidence of the roof. The rats were busy digging them out. Earth and small stones were flying everywhere, and the rats swore at each other a great deal as they got pelted by the debris. But despite this, the work was progressing at good speed.

Tess knew now that it wasn't treasure Martin was looking for. She knew as well that, despite what he had said, he hadn't the slightest interest in archaeology. She was just arriving at the obvious conclusion when a large shape appeared from nowhere, right there beside her. It made huge, hollow sounds with no meaning at all, and the rats' first instinct was to leap for the tunnels, which caused a great deal of useless falling around the place. The truth dawned on all their minds at the same moment. Their master had been among them for a while in rat form. Now he had assumed his own shape and was talking into the darkness in a language the rats didn't understand. They sniffed the air for a while, twitching their whiskers and passing information backwards and forwards to each other. Then, as though of one mind, they started back to work again.

Tess stayed where she was, close to the base of one of the great stone tombs. She could sense the vampire's mind trying to search her out, and shielded herself as well as she could. She needed time to decide what to do.

One or two of the nearer rats sensed Tess's fear and asked her what the problem was. She shut out their communications and tried to concentrate. What was she going to do? The only way out was back along the rat tunnels and Tess had a dreadful feeling that if she tried to go against the tide she would meet with little sympathy from the other rats. No other alternative seemed to offer any better chance. If she became a phoenix she could flood the crypt with light, might possibly even succeed in driving the vampire back into rat form and away down the tunnels, but it would not be a permanent solution to anything. Sooner or later she would have to find a way out, and when she did they'd be waiting for her.

The vampire mind was beginning to exert irresistible pressure upon her weak rat personality. Tess Switched quickly, before she lost the initiative, and found herself human again. There seemed to be no other choice, and at least this way she could think straight.

Or so she hoped. Without the extra nocturnal senses of the rat, Tess was helpless there beneath the ground. The darkness was total; silent for a moment as the rats adjusted to her altered presence, then full of their unseen scuffling and scratching. And, worse than that, there was someone in the enclosed space who was watching her without being seen.

'Where are you?' she said to the darkness. There was no answer, and if someone was breathing, the sound was lost behind the restless activity of the rats. Tess had never known claustrophobia before. She experienced it now: a brief, breathless panic at being enclosed on all sides. But the feeling didn't last long. A moment later it was replaced by sheer terror as she thought about the being that was closed in there with her. In that minute, her body seemed to become dysfunctional, as rigid and useless as a Cindy doll propped up against the cold stone wall.

She had been wrong about thinking straight. The truth was that she couldn't think at all. A low snigger slid out of the darkness, but she couldn't tell where it came from. Tess's fear suddenly converted into fury and, completely without thinking, she let fly with a series of the foulest swear-words she had ever heard.

The reply was another mocking laugh. All around them the rats continued working in the darkness.

'What are you afraid of?' said the vampire, his voice like poisoned syrup.

'What do you think I'm afraid of?' Tess was still shouting, her voice ringing back at her from the cold stone and damp earth. For an instant she wondered if she could be heard above the ground. There might be people around the park, sleeping overnight perhaps, to be early in tomorrow's queue to see the phoenix.

'But you have nothing to be afraid of, Tess.' The rich voice was amplified somehow by the enclosed space so that it seemed to be coming from all directions at once.

'Not much, I don't.' Tess jumped as a pebble flicked out by the eager digging of one of the rats bounced off her temple. She took a deep breath, aware of a trembling throughout her whole body. 'You're doing what you did before, aren't you?'

'What did I do before?'

'In the street the other day. You've got me trapped into a corner so that I'll have to Switch and become like you.'

The air seemed to be getting thinner. It smelled of rats and of ancient corruption. For the first time Tess thought of the original function of these tombs. She shuddered, and a new determination entered her heart. 'I won't, though,' she said. 'I have more tricks up my sleeve than you could imagine.'

It was a lie. Tess hadn't the faintest idea how to get out of this one, but her words seemed to have some effect, because the vampire fell silent for a while.

A rat scuttled over her foot. In the reprieve, she reached out with her rat mind to talk to it, and to her surprise a familiar signature of baby images came back. It was Algernon, camouflaged by the darkness; just another of the guys. Her mind flowed out to him, filled with relief at meeting someone familiar in this ordeal. Algernon's baby-talk returned; he was exhausted but proud of himself to be here working for the master. Reaching down to her feet, she found his little form beside her shoe. She closed her hands around him, anticipating his warmth against her face and neck, the pleasure of pets, the giving and receiving of comfort. But this new Algernon was no one's pet. He jerked wildly and jack-knifed in her hands, swivelling his head round and sinking his teeth deep into the flesh of her hand. Tess cried out and whipped her hand away, flinging Algernon out into the darkness in an automatic reaction. Straightening up, she felt the damp wall behind her again. Algernon's allegiance had changed. There was no comfort to be found in this place.

The shock of the betrayal seemed to deprive Tess of the last of her energy. Her breathing had become rapid and shallow as though there wasn't enough oxygen in the fetid atmosphere. She wondered briefly whether or not the vampire needed air and decided that he probably didn't. Nothing down here in the darkness seemed to be in her favour.

There was a flurry of squeaks as a fall of fresh earth and stones sent a party of miners scattering in all directions. In the relative silence that followed before they started work again, Tess came close to panic, gripped by a vision of the whole place caving in and burying her alive.

Martin's cold voice shifted her attention. 'Do you know what we're doing here, Tess?'

'Overseeing your archaeological dig, I suppose.' At the back of her mind, Tess knew much more, but the idea wouldn't come forward. It refused to be put into words.

'Yes. But do you know why?'

The understanding niggled its way out and, in a ghastly moment of realisation, Tess did know. He must have seen the expression on her face, even though she couldn't see him, because he said, 'Don't be so shocked. Everyone needs a place to sleep, after all.'

It was always the way, according to the legends. Vampires slept beneath old churches in coffins or in mausoleums exactly like these. She heard Martin's hand slap against the cold stone.

'This here is my bed,' he said. Tess didn't hear him move, but a moment later his voice came from another part of the chamber, near where the rats were working.

'And this, if you agree, will be yours.'

Tess shuddered at the thought. 'No way.'

'No? Perhaps you'd better hear me out, first?'

'If you like. But nothing you can say is going to convince me.'

'Convince you of what?'

'Convince me to become a vampire.'

The voice was smooth as ever, and tinged with a touch of triumph. 'But I don't need to persuade you to become a vampire, Tess. You are one already.'

CHAPTER SIXTEEN

'Don't be ridiculous,' said Tess, aware that she was speaking into a darkness that was impenetrable to her eyes. 'I'm not.'

'Don't believe me, eh? You really haven't done your homework, have you?'

'Perhaps I have, perhaps I haven't. But I know one thing for certain, and that is I'm not going to discuss anything down here in this dungeon. There's no air. I can't breathe properly.'

Martin considered for a moment, then said, 'Fair enough, I suppose. I need to take a look at the surface anyway.'

There were various exit tunnels, but Martin, in rat form, led Tess up the least arduous of them. On the surface they found themselves among trees and, after a careful check around, they Switched back to the way they had been beneath ground.

The place they were in seemed familiar. Tess knew

the park well, but it was a good while before she got her bearings and realised that they were very close to the place where she and her parents had been playing frisbee earlier that day. The dip in the ground where they stood made sense now that she knew there was a cavern beneath and that the roof had begun to subside, but there was no sign at all of any church. If there had been one, it must have been destroyed or abandoned and the stones cleared away to be used in other buildings.

She glanced across at Martin, hoping he had chosen to be human for this encounter, but there was no such luck. The pallor of his cheeks and the shape of his mouth made it clear what he was, even in the darkness. Even so, she was glad to be out in the open where she would have more chance of escape.

'All right, then,' she said, 'let's hear what you have to say.'

The vampire began to approach, but Tess held out a hand like a traffic policeman. 'Stay where you are. I can hear you perfectly well from there.'

He laughed. 'If it makes you feel better. But you don't need to worry. I've already fed tonight.'

The trees rustled in the wind. The clear weather of the previous days had given way to heavy cloud rolling in from the west. Tess had no coat and she had left her hair-band on top of the piano at home, so her hair was blowing around all over the place. They were small worries, though, compared with what she was confronting.

'Well?' she said. 'Explain to me just how it is that you think I'm a vampire.'

'I don't think. I know. Have you forgotten what happened that night in Dorset Street?'

'Nothing happened. I Switched, that's all.'

'You Switched all right. But you were too slow. Don't you remember my teeth on your throat?'

Tess remembered all too well: the icy pinpricks, the feeling of being sucked under.

'It took you too long to make up your mind,' Martin was saying. 'I tasted your blood. I made you mine.'

Tess's jaw stiffened. There was steel in her veins. 'What do you mean, "yours"?'

'You really don't know, do you? I thought you were just acting stupid, but it's true, isn't it? You really haven't read the stories.'

Tess scowled at him, aware that her position was growing weaker by the minute. Martin hissed at her, 'Everyone whom the undead feed upon become theirs, didn't you realise? Oh, you'll go on living, all right. You might even lead a normal enough life, provided you can stay out of my way when I'm hungry. It's not the same for you, of course, but most people never even know that they have been my victims. Until they die, that is. Then they know. As you will know, when you become like me. One of the undead, one of my minions, until the end of time.'

Tess was silent, absorbing the horror of what he had said. That fact wasn't new to her, after all, even though she hadn't remembered it. It was basic to the myth; the main reason that was always given for the need to wipe out vampires.

'Your phoenix,' Martin went on, 'is doing a great job in spreading his sweetness and light, but do you think it will last? Do you think people will go on dancing on the grass and being delighted with each other? Give them a few days and they'll forget it all, go back to their drab and selfish little existences as if nothing had ever happened. But in the meantime I'll be going from strength to strength. Some of the older people I've preyed on will be joining me quite soon, and then they'll start recruiting for themselves. So in fifty years' time I'll have an army of followers, and every one of them a vampire, practically impossible to defeat. You should be thankful to me, Tess. I've made you immortal!'

The word caused a freezing tide to race up Tess's spine. To be immortal, to live for ever, that was what all this was about. The trees huffed again and Tess looked up at them. They were so strong and serene, so much of this world, the here and now. For the moment she needed to be like them, living in the present and not in the world of future possibilities. It comforted her to see herself not as she might be but as she was: a schoolgirl, about to enter her Junior Cert year. The trees moved in the breeze. The winter grass lay tangled at her feet.

'This is ridiculous!' she shouted. 'I'm not immortal and nor are you. You're just a boy, Martin, however you've dressed yourself up with your special power! Tomorrow you'll be lying in your bed watching a video!'

Her voice was high and full of emotion but his, when he replied, was as deep and calm as a bogland lake.

'I won't, though. That's why I called you here tonight.' Despite the darkness and the distance between them, Tess could make out the cruel smile of satisfaction on his face as he went on, 'I'm glad you told me about that fifteenth birthday stuff. I might have been caught on the hop if you hadn't. It's tomorrow, you see. My fifteenth birthday.'

He waited, watching her reaction as she struggled against a fate which seemed to be blocking her at every turn. When she made no answer, he continued, 'I want you to be with me, Tess. I'm going to be the master of this city and you can rule it by my side, but only if you come with me now; share my hideout down below. No one will ever find us there. We'll be safe. We'll be able to come and go as we please.'

His voice was persuasive, reaching beyond her defences to the part of her mind that was vampire. She found herself wondering why she was bothering to put up such a resistance. What was so wonderful about her life, after all? She existed in a state of almost total isolation; there was no one she could share her secrets with apart from Martin, and even he would be gone soon. It was clear now that she wasn't going to have any more adventures like the one which had taken her and Kevin across the planet in search of the krools, and even if she did, no one would ever know about her powers. She still felt resentful when she saw members of the US armed forces taking credit for ending the climatic threat, when it had been she and Kevin who had done it. She missed him, as well, even after all this time. She had been so delighted to see him return as a phoenix, but what good had it done her? She was as lonely as ever, and he was locked up in the zoo. It seemed to make so much sense, here in the darkness, just to let go of all resistance and slide along with the current. No one would ever tell her what to do again. The world would be hers for the taking.

But it would be a world of perpetual night. She would never see daylight again.

'No!' she said, surprised by her own decisiveness. 'I'll never agree to it.'

Martin shrugged, calm as ever. 'Suit yourself. You're mine anyway. But if you don't come now, if you wait for your death instead, you'll be nothing special to me then. You'll just be one among millions, serving me, spreading my power. It's up to you.'

'Yes. It is up to me,' said Tess, her voice strangely different, as calm now as his was. Because as he was speaking, the conflict of the last few days had suddenly become sparklingly clear in her mind. There wasn't just one kind of immortality being presented to her; there were two.

'But what if I don't die?' she went on. 'Then what will you do?'

'What do you mean, if you don't die? Everyone dies.'

'What if I became a phoenix instead? What would happen then?'

Now it was Martin's turn to be stunned into silence. For a long time the two of them stood facing one another while the trees leant over them, nodding in the breeze as though discussing the possible outcome. Then the vampire straightened up and moved a single step forward.

'If I hadn't already gorged myself tonight I would settle the issue here and now. But it doesn't matter. Your dayglo friend won't win out. How long do you think he can go on burning away like that before his gas runs out?'

'I don't know. What difference does it make, anyway? He'll rise up again, whenever he needs to.'

'You think so? What if there aren't any ashes for him to rise out of, eh? Does anyone know what happens then?'

'Ashes are only metaphorical. He'll rise again no matter what the circumstances are.'

'How do you know? Has it ever been tested?'

'You don't need to test things like that. You just know them.'

'Do you?' As he spoke, the vampire seemed to be swelling and moving towards her, like a shadow with a light receding behind it. 'Well, I don't.'

A black cloud passed over Tess's head and vanished into the night. She stood still for a moment, searching the empty skies. Then something began to tug at the edge of her mind. Something urgent and demanding, making her restless and fidgety. Something she was supposed to do? Something she'd forgotten? She let down her guard and the message flooded in. It was being sent in Rat, and to her rat mind it was utterly irresistible.

'Top speed to the zoo. Phoenix is the enemy. Tear it to pieces.'

Tess took a few strides in the direction of the zoo, but realised that it was useless to try and go above ground. Now she knew why the dirt floor and gravel in the exhibition building had seemed so important to her that day.

That was the only way in.

339

CHAPTER SEVENTEEN

Tess Switched and made a dive for the nearest tunnel. Despite the huge underground mesh of interlinking passages, she had no problem finding the quickest route to the zoo. Rats work according to a precise logic of their own, and although it would have made no sense to her human mind, the way was clear and simple.

By the time she reached the well-established network of runs beneath the zoo, the place was stiff with rats. They had come from all corners of the city, some above ground but most of them below, and they were still pouring in. Despite the apparent chaos, work was already proceeding in an orderly manner. Tess asked around and soon got the low-down on what was happening. New tunnels were being constructed beneath the exhibition building and back-up parties were ferrying the freshly-dug soil and rubble out to the surface, emerging among the bushes and spreading the debris around carefully to avoid detection.

Tess joined one of the earth-shifting teams. She made sure that she pulled her weight and did nothing to delay the proceedings, but whenever she got the opportunity she dodged forward a place in the line, working her way towards the head of the tunnelling team.

She had no idea what she was going to do. Her human mind was struggling desperately to rise above the instinctual mire of rat behaviour, but it was about as successful as a moth in a jar of honey. Occasional insight broke clear, but it was always the same: she had made an awful mistake, betrayed Kevin, and there was nothing she could do to stop the impending horror.

As she worked, still edging her way closer to the lead diggers, she kept a close eye open for any rats that she knew. If she could find Algernon, or Nose Broken by a Mousetrap – even stupid old Long Nose – she might be able to win them over. Between them they might spread the word and talk some sense into the rest of the rats. But she had about as much chance of meeting them as of meeting a long-lost friend in a football crowd. There were hundreds of rats working on her particular tunnel, but not one of them was known to her. With an increasing sense of dread, she worked on.

There seemed to be nothing else to do. Even if she deserted the rat legions and went out on to the surface she would still be helpless. She had long since ruled out the possibility of releasing the phoenix on her own, since there was no way of getting into the exhibition hall apart from this underground route. The only thing she could do was to be there when the final confrontation happened, and to pray that the vampire was wrong about the weakness of the phoenix power. She could hardly stand to think about what would happen if he wasn't.

The going became more difficult as the tunnellers began to bore into the heavy rubble foundations of the building. Reports were coming in from various separate reconnaissance teams. There were two men in the building, apparently, keeping watch on the phoenix. Of the several dozen tunnels that were under construction, eight of them were on target, right beneath the phoenix's cage.

The rats abandoned the useless tunnels and gathered where they would be ready to pour into the good ones as they were completed. The ground beneath the glass cage babbled with images as the rats reported their progress to each other, their vivid communications passing easily through mud, stone or concrete. But above their heads, where Jeff Maloney sat playing cards with a highly-paid guard from a security company, there was no way of knowing that anything was going on.

Extra workers were drafted in to dig holes in the tunnel walls so that large stones being moved out of the foundations could be lodged instead of being dragged all the way out. The lead tunnellers, Tess among them, wove their way around the biggest stones, loosening the smaller rubble and shoving it back to the next in line. Then, suddenly, the leading rat froze as a tiny shower of loose sand and earth dropped down on to her nose.

Jeff Maloney turned his head at the sound of a few white quartz pebbles moving in the phoenix's cage. The lights were turned off so that the bird could sleep, and the only illumination in the building came

342

from a small lamp on the table where the two men were playing their game. The phoenix was on its perch, high above the potted shrubs, sleeping soundly. Only the dimmest radiance gleamed from its feathers.

'Probably a mouse,' said Jeff.

'What was?'

'That noise. Didn't you hear it?'

The security guard shook his head. 'You keep mice as well?'

'They keep themselves. And rats. The animal food attracts them, and all the rubbish the visitors leave. Nothing you can do about them.'

There was a dozy pause, then Jeff said, 'Whose go is it?'

Beneath their feet, Tess and her team were waiting for the other tunnels to be ready. To be sure of working, the attack had to be coordinated properly. A constant stream of visual messages passed between the members of the rodent army. They were almost ready.

Jeff and the guard swung round, instantly alert, as a half-dozen holes opened in the ground beneath the phoenix and pebbles began to pour into them. Jeff leapt to his feet and jumped for the main light switch. Cards fluttered across empty space as the guard threw down his hand and grabbed for the pistol he carried beneath his jacket.

Then the floor of the cage disappeared as a flood of rats welled up like a spring from below. Before Jeff could disentangle the key of the cage from the handkerchief in his pocket, the rats had streamed up the foliage and were beginning to take leaps at the perch where the phoenix still sat. In the nick of time he spread his wings, rose into the air and hovered there, just below the ceiling.

'Get help!' yelled Jeff.

The security guard, who had become glued to the floor at the sight of so many rats, needed no second bidding to get out. He raced for the main door, threw the bolt, and disappeared into the darkness outside.

Against the glass wall of the cage, Tess sat and watched as Jeff Maloney unlocked the door and slid it open. He was the one who had caught the magnificent bird, and despite his horror of the swarming rats, he had no hesitation in going to its rescue. He strode into the cage, oblivious to the outraged squeaks of the rats beneath his feet and, kicking clear a space for himself, stood on the edge of the tallest plant pot. From there he took a lunge at the perch, making it swing so violently that it dislodged the rats who were squirrelling up its suspension chains in their efforts to get at the floating phoenix.

The bird was still too high for Jeff to reach. With a Tarzan-like leap, he grabbed the perch and swung himself up, grabbing the phoenix by its three-toed foot before the chain links snapped and he dropped back to his feet on the carpet of rats, breaking several backbones.

Tess pushed her way through the throng as Jeff leapt out of the cage and raced across the building. She was at his heels, but others were there before her, climbing up his clothes, swarming all over his body and up the arm he was holding above his head with the phoenix at the end of it.

The bird flapped desperately as the rats reached it and the first set of teeth sank into its leg. Jeff struck out frantically with his free hand, but he was losing the battle. He was up to his knees in rats, wading through a sea of them, and as quickly as he could knock them from his clothes and face, they were being replaced by others.

Outside, the security man had failed to find help and was running back towards the building. He arrived just in time to see Jeff give in and let go of the phoenix in a desperate attempt to save himself. Through a gap in the clawing and clambering madness, Tess saw the phoenix dart out through the open door and soar away above the zoo.

Both Jeff and the guard were far too busy with the rats to notice a small, dark bird emerging from their midst and setting off in pursuit of the phoenix. They were thrashing and kicking around them like a pair of windmills. But to their surprise, as soon as the phoenix was out of sight, the rats did a complete about-face and vanished back into the ground, leaving the dead and the dying behind.

CHAPTER EIGHTEEN

The phoenix swept up and out over the park, each beat of its small wings giving it height, so that it appeared to move in a series of great bounds. Tess's swallow wings worked at double speed as she tried to keep up. The easiest way would have been to become a phoenix herself, but the human part of her mind could see that would be a foolish move. The other bird had become dim enough by now to be difficult to see, even above the relative darkness of the park, but Tess assumed that if she became a phoenix she would be as bright as ever and would draw attention just when they needed to shake it off.

The phoenix took another upward leap and the swallow flapped after it. A few minutes more would be enough. They were almost over the middle of the park now, and would soon be too high for anyone to see. Then Tess could Switch into phoenix form and become comfortable. After that, once they were safely clear of the city, they could rest and decide what the future might be.

Once more the phoenix leapt skyward. Once more, Tess drove her small wings to the limit. It was enough, surely. Below them, the park was a black island of emptiness in the middle of a lake of orange light. Even if someone down there did spot her now, they were surely beyond any danger.

But even as she prepared for the Switch, visualising the form she was about to take and remembering how it felt, a dark shape appeared out of nowhere and collided with the phoenix, knocking it off balance and sending it tumbling down towards the earth.

Tess closed her wings and dropped like a stone. Beneath her, the phoenix flapped and turned in the air, slowing its descent and finally recovering control. It began to climb again and Tess swooped beneath it, struggling to stay close. Out of the darkness the shadow reappeared and this time Tess could see that it was a huge bat, its wings stretched taut as it glided with deadly accuracy straight into the phoenix.

Again the phoenix fell, righted itself, began to ascend. Again the huge bat took aim and slammed into it. Tess fluttered wildly, first up and then down, her only objective being to stay as close to the phoenix as she could.

The battle was hopeless. Each time the bat hit the phoenix, the bird lost more height and, Tess thought, as it got closer to the trees below, it seemed to lose heart as well. Eventually it gave up and spread its wings to glide down between the branches and come to rest, sitting on the air a few feet above the ground.

Tess plunged after the phoenix, banking and twisting through the trees. Even before she had quite landed, she Switched back into human form, desperate for the full use of her human mind to work out what was going on. She stumbled as she landed, and found herself face down in the cool, damp grass. The wind was still waffling round in the trees and for a long moment Tess lay still where she had fallen, breathing in the damp scent of the earth and wishing she could stay there for ever. But out of the corner of her eye, she caught a glimpse of movement as the dark shape of the bat flitted into the copse, its leathery wings purring through the air. As it landed, it seemed to expand, and by the time Tess stood up it was the vampire that stood there, pale face set into a grin of satisfaction.

'He's a pushover,' he said.

'No!' Tess found herself standing between the two adversaries, just a few feet from each of them. The phoenix made no further attempt to escape, but hung in the air, his feathers casting a pale glow over the group.

'No?' said the vampire. 'But why not? You were so certain that Humpty Dumpty could put himself back together again. Are you not so sure now?'

'Of course I am! That's not the point.'

'What is the point then, Tess?'

The voice was soft as sleep, reaching out to her, drawing her in. With a tremendous effort of will she wrenched her attention away from it and fixed her eyes on the phoenix. It was still floating above the ground, unaffected by the strengthening gusts of wind that blew through the copse. Its eyes were on a level with hers, its gaze steady and fearless.

'Which way, Tess?'

Her eyelids drooped. Her gaze lost its focus, then shifted back to rest upon the vampire as he spoke.

'You have to make up your mind, you know. Come with me willingly and I'll leave your friend alone to go back to the chicken coop. How's that for a deal?'

It seemed reasonable, especially when she looked into the deep, soulless eyes and remembered the night they had hunted together, the entire city theirs for the taking. She was tired of struggling for what seemed to be right all the time. There was no reward for that, in the end. She had lost her best friend, and the creature that hung in the air beside her wasn't him, even if it once had been. Why shouldn't she become a vampire? What was the point of resisting? But as she began to turn, her attention drifting towards that dark, eternal power, the phoenix seemed to brighten for a moment, and the glow which emanated from him was reflected in the vampire's eyes, which glowed like a cat's in a car's headlights. The connection broke. Tess gasped and turned back to the phoenix. It continued to hang on the air, silent and motionless. As Tess opened herself to its influence again she began to feel warmth and life flowing through her, as though some lost flame had been rekindled within. Without knowing why she did it, she lifted her right arm and stretched out her hand towards the phoenix.

'No, Tess,' came the rich, silky voice of the vampire. 'Think again. Is that really what you want? All that twinkle, twinkle, little star stuff? Come with me, come on. Before it's too late.'

He was holding out his hand. All she had to do was take it. Her left hand reached out.

The wind came straight at her like a slap in the face, sobering her, bringing her, for a moment, back to reality. She was standing in the woods like a scarecrow, one hand stretching towards a golden light, the

349

other towards perpetual darkness. It was like a crazy dream, where the only thing that was real was the wind in her face, carrying the fresh flavours of all the places it had been, reminding her how alive she was right now.

To either side, eternities were pulling at her and she was stretched between them, standing on a razor's edge. She needed help, and cast around for some of those words of wisdom she was forever being crammed with in her religion classes. But the only words that came to her were Lizzie's.

'Trust yourself, girl. You'll know what to do when the time comes.'

'But I don't!' she yelled at her mind's image of the old woman. The two forces were working against each other now, so powerfully that Tess could no longer tell whether she were being torn apart or crushed between them. The dark shadow of the vampire was expanding, looming above her. On the other side, the phoenix was brightening, its light growing all around it until the two seemed about to meet over her head. And at that moment, Tess felt her left hand grasp the vampire's fingers and her right catch hold of the phoenix's three-toed foot.

A charge like an electric current went through her body and numbed her brain as the two forces met within her, on equal terms now, and began to do battle. Wild fantasies played through her mind as the protagonists took shapes for themselves, using the raw material of Tess's imagination. Angels and demons fought there, armies of light and dark, red and blue, good and evil. Characters came forward and spoke to her, each taking one side or the other, each as persuasive as the one before.

In the midst of it all, Tess swung from one allegiance to the other. One moment she was certain that the phoenix was the better choice and the next there seemed no doubt that the vampire was. What was it Lizzie had said about choice? 'It's not always what we are that needs changing, but the way we thinks.' What was that supposed to mean? How on earth could it help her?

The struggle worsened. The opponents seemed to be tearing at her sense of herself, destroying her confidence. If she did not choose soon, one way or the other, she would surely be damaged by the conflict. But what could she do? What was wrong with the way she was thinking?

As if in reply, one strong, clear thought began to emerge. Throughout the whole of the struggle she had not once had the impression that either the vampire or phoenix cared about her; about Tess, the individual. All either of them wanted was to attain superiority, even if she was sacrificed in the process. Suddenly she knew what Lizzie meant. Tess was burdened by choice only because she felt that she must choose one or the other. But the truth was that she didn't have to be either. If she could just rise out of this turmoil and feel the wind on her face once again, it would be worth all the fears and the pains and the longings of being merely mortal.

A new determination entered Tess's heart. She was part of the light and the dark and their struggle, but they were a part of her, too. She would not be vampire and she would not be phoenix. Later, if and when life made sense again, she would worry about her fifteenth birthday. But for the moment she could only deal with the present. She took a deep breath and, with a mighty effort, she gathered all her forces together and broke free of the grips on her hands.

'I just want to be human!' she yelled.

Jeff Maloney heard that extraordinary shout as he plunged into the copse where he was sure he had seen his precious bird descending. What he saw was totally unexpected. There were three teenagers in there on the grass: two boys and a girl, all of them strewn around the glade as though they had just been dropped from a height. For a moment Jeff was so surprised by the sight that he forgot what he was looking for.

'Hello?' he said, shining his torch on them, one after another. The girl looked exhausted, as though she had just survived some horrendous ordeal, and Jeff might have suspected the boys of some savagery towards her if they had not looked as dazed as she did. One of them, a mousy-looking fellow, was looking around him as though he was seeing the planet for the first time. The other, red-headed, was as white as a sheet, like someone who has just been in an accident.

'What's going on?'

Tess screwed up her eyes against the flashlight. 'Who's there? she said. Beside her, Kevin was shielding his eyes with his arm and looking over at Martin, who had buried his face in his hands. They looked odd, all three of them, but Jeff could see that they were all right, and his mind went back to his search. He turned his flashlight off and looked up into the trees.

'Anyone seen a bird come to land here? A golden one?'

The girl and one of the boys shook their heads

352

solemnly. The other boy seemed not to hear, but let out a sudden shout. 'Dad! I'm sorry, Dad. I didn't mean it!'

Tess struggled to her feet and went over to Martin. He was crying now, his whole body shuddering.

'I didn't mean it,' he gasped between sobs. 'I was going to go for help but I couldn't. The cow was in the road, heaving about the place. The stupid cow!'

Tess rested a hand on Martin's shoulder, frustrated by her helplessness in the face of his pain.

'I didn't mean to kill him, Tess.'

'You didn't kill him. It was an accident.'

'I did. I did kill him. I wished he was dead and he died. I killed him.'

He broke down again and Tess fell silent, knowing that words were useless.

Jeff Maloney was glued to the spot, torn between concern for the boy's distress and the urgent desire to search for his bird.

'Has there been some sort of an accident?' he said to Tess, quietly. She shook her head.

As Jeff lingered, still unsure what to do, two of his colleagues from the zoo ran up. They had been following the light of his torch for some time. Their arrival solved his dilemma.

'The bird is around here somewhere,' he said. 'I saw it come down. Will you keep on searching?' He nodded towards Martin and Tess. 'I'm not sure what's going on here, but I want to get this lot home.'

The others agreed and Jeff approached the huddled figures on the ground. His voice was friendly and reassuring.

'You're all right now. Tell me where you live and I'll drive you home. My car's parked on the road just back there.'

As Jeff spoke, Martin became silent and tense beneath Tess's hand. It was one thing to reveal his pain to her, but quite another to be caught, vulnerable, in front of a stranger. Before Tess knew what was happening he was on his feet.

'Leave me alone,' he yelled at Jeff. Then he raced away between the trees.

Tess set off in pursuit. There was barely light to see by, but she could just make out Martin's slight figure weaving through the tree trunks. He was fast, but as Tess ran after him she knew that she was, too. It was as though the resolution of that dreadful conflict had made energy available to her that she hadn't known she possessed. And every ounce of it had to be used in making sure she didn't lose her friend in the darkness. Because he was a friend, now. She had held her own ground, pulled the opposing forces together instead of allowing them to pull her apart, and in doing so she had not only made herself whole, but the others as well. Kevin, she knew, could look after himself, but she wasn't so sure about Martin; not now that his defences were down and he was exposed to all that old pain. He had closed off his feelings when his father was killed, safe within the vampire's cold shell. But now he would have to experience all that shock and fear and sorrow as though the accident had just happened. He was in danger, not only from the stress itself but from the possibility of reverting to the familiar protection of the vampire existence. It was vital that Tess should stay with him.

Ahead of her, he dodged left and right around a tree stump, heading for open ground. With renewed confidence, Tess made straight for the stump, certain that she could jump it and gain ground. She timed

354

her run perfectly and jumped well clear of the decaying wood, but as she landed, her feet went from under her and she came down hard, flat on her back.

The wind was knocked right out of her and for a few moments she found herself gazing at the blank face of the starless sky, wondering if her end had come. Then, just as it seemed she could hold on no longer, her chest relaxed and she pulled in a long, cool breath.

'Are you all right?' It was Kevin, leaning over her, his face filled with concern. He must have been right behind her. She tried to smile but there were more urgent priorities and for another minute she had to gasp for air, until her breath caught up with itself.

Kevin looked out across the park, but it was already too late. By the time Tess recovered sufficiently to sit up, Martin was long gone into the darkness.

'I landed on something,' said Tess, still panting. 'It slid along the ground and I skidded.'

Kevin kicked around in the grass, then bent and picked something up: a flat disc the size of a dinner plate. Tess reached out and took it from him.

'My frisbee!' she said. 'My useless, flaming frisbee.'

CHAPTER NINETEEN

It was ten past eleven, according to Tess's wristwatch, and the first rain was just starting to dampen the breeze. Kevin reached out a hand and helped Tess to her feet. It was the first chance she'd had to get a good look at him and she found herself grinning with delight.

'You haven't changed a bit,' she said, tugging at the lapel of his faded khaki jacket.

'Not on the outside, maybe,' he said, tossing back his long, wispy fringe with a familiar shake of the head. 'But I've changed an awful lot on the inside.'

He looked around him and, from the expression of wonderment on his face, he might have been standing at the foot of the Himalayas. 'I never thought it could happen. I wanted it to . . . you've no idea . . . but I never dreamt it could.'

'It probably wouldn't if it hadn't been for Martin.'

'I suppose so. There had to be an opposite. But if it hadn't been for you . . .'

Tess shuddered, remembering more than she wanted to about the battle that had been waged inside her mind. Whatever else might happen to her in life, she didn't want to go through that again.

'We shouldn't stand around, though,' she said. 'It mightn't be over yet.'

'What do you mean?'

'It's Martin's fifteenth birthday tomorrow. There's no guaranteeing that he'll stay the way he is now. It might all be too much for him; he might decide to become a vampire in spite of everything that's happened. And if he does . . .'

'If he does, what?'

'Come on. I'll tell you as we go.'

Tess looked around to get her bearings, then they set off, walking as fast as they could in the direction of Phibsboro. Here and there, torches flashed among the trees and desolate voices drifted on the wind as the zoo staff continued to hunt for the phoenix.

'Tough on them,' said Tess, but Kevin just laughed until he choked. By the time he had recovered his composure they had reached the city streets and, as they walked along, Tess told the whole story and explained about the vampire's method of spreading its influence.

'So you see,' she concluded, 'if he does become a vampire, then I will, too, when I'm dead.'

'You could still opt for the phoenix.'

'I might, if it came with recommendations. But you don't seem to have any regrets about being human again.'

'No, I don't,' said Kevin. 'The phoenix was glorious. I don't have to tell you – you know how it feels.

But it was too .. I don't know how to describe it. Too perfect, or too high and mighty or something. Too lonely.'

There was an awkward silence as they both became aware of the personal meaning in his words. Kevin coloured with embarrassment, but made no attempt to retract what he had said. They had missed each other more than either of them cared to admit, yet neither was prepared to reveal their fondness. In the end, Kevin changed the subject.

'So, if he does go vampire, we'll only have one option, won't we?'

That word 'we' was one of the finest sounds that Tess had ever heard. She realised how lonely she, too, had been over the past months.

'What's that?' she said.

'Well. You know where he'll be sleeping during the day, don't you? We'll just have to dig our way in there and do the old stake through the heart job.'

He spoke as if it were an everyday occurrence, like swatting a wasp with a newspaper. But the prospect filled Tess with horror.

'I hope we find him first,' she said. 'I prefer diplomatic solutions on the whole.'

It was nearly midnight when they reached Martin's house in Phibsboro. There were no lights on, but Tess took a chance and knocked on the door. As they waited, the rain worsened and blew against them, soaking into their hair and dripping down their necks. Tess wriggled with discomfort but Kevin didn't seem to notice, partly because he was still overawed at being human again. He gazed round at the dull houses as though he was in Disneyland. Tess sighed and knocked again.

'It's no good,' she said. 'If he's in, he's not answering. Wait here, will you?'

She was on the point of Switching into a rat when she remembered the compelling power that the vampire still held over all the rats' minds in the city. On impulse she tried a mouse instead, and found immediate entry into the house by way of a missing chip of concrete underneath the front door.

The hall was vast to her tiny eyes, stretching upwards and outwards into a dark oblivion. It was full of smells, alive with them; some appealing, others threatening. Mouse life was about weighing up the balance of the scents in the air all around. If danger weighed too heavily, then a change of plan was required. If it didn't, a chance was worth taking. But at that moment, it was all too much for Tess's already exhausted mind, so she Switched into a cat instead and padded swiftly and silently up the carpeted stair-case. Outside Martin's room she Switched back to human shape again and, with her heart in her mouth, pushed open the door.

Inside it was too dark to see anything. The video clock, still mindlessly flashing, distracted her attention and left dizzying green patches on her retinas. She held out a hand to block it from view.

'Martin?'

If he had got home, he couldn't have been there for long; certainly not long enough to get to sleep. She listened carefully, but there was no sound of breathing. Her skin crawled as she suddenly imagined the vampire there beside her, leaning across in the darkness . . .

With a hand that trembled slightly, she felt around behind the door frame until she found the light switch and flicked it down. The bare bulb blinded her for a moment, but even as she squinted and blinked she could see that the room was empty. The bedclothes were crumpled and the floor beside the bed was cluttered with the familiar collection of socks and tea cups and video cases. Everything was as usual, except for Martin. Tess swore to herself in a whisper. Because if he wasn't there, where was he?

She turned out the light, became a cat again, and was just about to go back down the stairs when her sharp eyes noticed another door along the landing which stood ajar. The black hair along her spine stood up as she remembered Martin's anaemic mother. If he was taking a late-night snack she would rather not know about it. But she had to. If there was any chance at all of getting to him before dawn, she had to take it.

Martin's mother was alone in the room, sleeping on her back in a battered old double bed that she must once have shared with her husband. Her face was deathly white in the dim light which entered from the street and for a moment Tess feared the worst. But as she slipped across the floor, her paws making no sound on the nylon carpet, Tess's sensitive ears picked up the faint rise and fall of shallow breath. She was alive, but undoubtedly weak. The implications were obvious. If Martin remained human, she would recover; her anaemia passing away as mysteriously as it had come. But if he chose to live out his existence as a vampire, then one more feed could finish her off and she would become like him: the first of many.

Would she take that other stone coffin, the one that Martin had reserved for Tess? Would Tess and Kevin have to bring two stakes down into the crypt with them, to be sure of finishing the job?

The black cat turned and bounded down the stairs, becoming a mouse between the bottom step and the floor and tumbling along the ground a few times as it slowed down. It flowed like toothpaste under the door and disappeared beneath the foot of a girl who hadn't been there a moment before. Luckily there was no one there to see the first part, and the only person who saw the girl appear was not surprised at all.

'Well?' he said.

'Not there.'

He sighed. 'Looks bad, doesn't it?'

'Maybe. Maybe he just needs time on his own to try and come to terms with things.'

Kevin looked around as though he hoped to see beyond the buildings into the darkness. Out there somewhere was either a boy coping with a private grief or a being on the point of entering perpetual night.

Tess shivered. Kevin slipped out of his parka and hung it over her bony shoulders.

'Your turn,' he said, before she could object.

It was heavy with rain, but still warm. Tess glanced up and down the street, hoping against hope to see Martin strolling down the pavement towards them. But from one end of the street to the other, nothing moved.

'I suppose there's no point in standing here,' she said. 'We might as well go home.'

CHAPTER TWENTY

It was well into the early hours of the morning by the time Tess and Kevin got home to her house on the edge of the park. Kevin shivered as he waited for Tess to turn the key in the lock. She looked at him and shrugged, abandoning them both to whatever trouble lay in store for them, then pushed the door open.

Immediately there was a noise from the direction of the living room: the flutter and slap of a newspaper being hastily thrown aside. A moment later Tess's father appeared in the hall, his face taut with worry which was rapidly turning to anger. He stopped dead in the middle of the hallway when he saw Tess's companion and an awkward silence hung on the air as she closed the front door behind them and slipped out of Kevin's jacket.

'Dad, this is a friend of mine, Kevin.'

Her father nodded, wrong-footed, uncertain

362

whether the occasion called for civility or righteous indignation. Before he could make up his mind, his wife appeared at the head of the stairs in her dressing-gown.

'Oh, there you are, Tess. Where on earth have you been?'

Tess hung the sodden jacket on a spare hook inside the door. 'It's a long story, I'm afraid.'

'You're not getting out of it that easy,' said her father. 'I don't care how long the story is, I want to hear it.'

Tess's mind threatened to go on strike. The best she could dredge up was the same excuse she had given them in the park earlier that day.

'We had to go and call on that sick friend. The one I was telling you about.'

'Oh, I see.' Her father's tone betrayed his scepticism. 'The sick friend again. And you were there until one-thirty in the morning, were you?'

'Not exactly. But we ran into a few difficulties.'

'Clearly. And for some reason you decided to bring one of them home with you.'

'Seamus!' said Tess's mother reproachfully. 'Don't talk about Tess's friends like that. Not without giving them a chance, at least.'

'Right,' said Tess, looking cryptically at Kevin. She needed help, but from the look of him she was unlikely to get it. He was standing with his hands in his pockets, dripping on to the hall carpet and looking self-conscious. Tess felt sure he was going to get sulky and clam up, the way he had with Lizzie, but to her surprise he pushed his wet hair out of his eyes and said, 'The phoenix escaped from the zoo. We met the zoo-keepers searching for it.'

'Yes,' said Tess. 'I saw it escape and I followed it.'

'Then she slipped on a frisbee and knocked the stuffing out of herself.'

'Oh, Tess. Did you?'

'Yes. But I'm OK, honestly. It just delayed us a bit. And now it's too late for Kevin to get home. So can he stay the night?'

Tess's father looked from one to the other, suspiciously.

'Is all this really true? It sounds very unlikely.'

'It's true. Every word of it,' said Tess.

'And what about your sick friend? Where does he fit in?'

Tess felt sick herself at being reminded of Martin. He could be out there in the night, feeding on some poor innocent's blood, preparing to return to his new underground bedroom. She glanced at Kevin as she said, 'We missed him in the end. We'll have to try again tomorrow.'

Tess's mother came down the stairs, the long hem of her dressing-gown covering her bare feet. She stood in front of Kevin and looked closely at him, as though trying to see into his soul. Then she said, 'Does your mother know where you are?'

'No,' said Kevin, looking her straight in the eye. 'But then, she never does. She doesn't take any interest, really. She certainly won't be worried about me.'

'Are you sure?'

'Positive.'

She examined him for a few seconds longer, then sighed. 'Well, whatever else you do, you'd better get out of those wet clothes before you catch pneumonia. Do either of you want a bath?'

Tess shook her head, but Kevin nodded eagerly.

'Yes, please. I can't remember the last time I had a bath!'

Tess cringed and her father looked astonished, but her mother laughed and gestured to Kevin to follow her up the stairs. She exchanged a complicitous smile with Tess over the bannisters which made her heart swell with pleasure. At least she had one ally in the house.

When she had towelled herself down and put on dry clothes, Tess sorted out a genderless tracksuit and left it outside the bathroom door. Then she went to help her mother, who was making up the bed in the spare room for Kevin.

'What about this sick friend of yours?' she said. 'You're being very mysterious about him.'

'Oh, there's nothing so mysterious, really.' As she spoke, Tess realised that despite their conspiratorial understanding of a few minutes before, they could never understand each other about some things. 'He's under a lot of stress,' she went on. 'His father died in an accident and he hasn't really got over the shock of it yet. He needs a lot of support.'

'You should have told me before,' said her mother. 'I'm all in favour of you being helpful like that. Perhaps I could help, too? Bake a cake or something? Would he like that?'

Tess fought back the deluge of ironic laughter that threatened to swamp her faculties. She pictured her mother walking into the vampire's lair, entirely unsuspecting, holding out a perfect specimen of her famous Lemon Drizzle.

'He might,' she said. 'We'll have to wait and see how things turn out.'

They finished making the bed, then her mother turned on the electric blanket and went back to her

365

own room. On her way downstairs, Tess met her father coming up with two cups of cocoa.

'Oh, thanks, Dad.'

'For what? These are for your mother and I. It's late enough as it is, and I'm supposed to be at the office early in the morning.'

'Oh.'

'There's plenty of milk in the fridge if you and your boyfriend want to make some.'

'He's not my boyfriend!'

'Good.' Her father's face softened and he moved both slopping mugs into one hand and reached out with the other to muss up Tess's damp hair. 'But whoever he is, don't be staying up all night, you hear? I don't know about him, but you have to be on the school bus at half past eight.'

School past, school future; both of them seemed light years away. But she nodded at her father and made a show of looking at her watch.

'Don't worry, Dad. We won't be up much longer.'

'Goodnight, then.'

'Goodnight.'

Tess had made cocoa and a pile of sandwiches before Kevin eventually finished soaking in the bath and came down. He was a fresh, pink colour, and his hands and feet were wrinkled like prunes. Together they raided the cupboards for crisps, biscuits and fruit, then they brought the whole feast up to Tess's bedroom.

'You've redecorated,' said Kevin, looking around him.

'Last year.' Tess put down the tray and slotted an R.E.M. tape into the cassette deck. 'My dad wanted to cheer me up.'

'Cheer you up? Why?'

Tess blushed and turned away, not wanting to tell Kevin how upset she had been when she thought he was dead, and how strongly it had affected her life. The music began with a boom, and she grabbed for the volume control before it could wake her parents.

Kevin started into the sandwiches. Tess had made one with apricots and cashew nuts and put it on the top of the pile, and for a long time neither of them could do anything except laugh. When they finally recovered themselves, Kevin said, 'It's so good to be human again. You have no idea, Tess.'

'Really?' she said. 'I thought it was wonderful, being a phoenix.'

'It was, for a while. But it's like, what do you do once you're perfect? Nothing to be afraid of, nothing to strive for. Hardly living at all, really, is it?'

Tess shrugged. 'If you say so,' she said. 'But I'm still not sure how it happened, how you came to Switch back even though you're over fifteen.'

'I didn't get it to begin with, either, but I think I do, now. I think that I could only exist as a phoenix as long as Martin existed as a vampire. We counterbalanced each other in some way.

'That's right,' said Tess. 'Lizzie said something like that. I just didn't understand it at the time.'

'And it was you who changed us, Tess. By deciding that you wouldn't become like either of us.'

'But how do you know I decided that?'

'I could feel it. I was part of the fight, remember?'

'Does that mean that Martin isn't a vampire, then?' said Tess.

'I don't know,' said Kevin. 'That would be the proof of the theory, I suppose, if it did. But I certainly wouldn't like to bank on it.'

They both fell silent, contemplating what he had said. Then Kevin said, 'Who lives in the cage?'

'No one.' Tess explained about Algernon and the vampire's control of the rats. As she spoke, they both became aware of the black, empty gaze of the window, and Kevin got up to draw the curtains.

'Do you think he's out there?' said Tess.

Kevin thought for a minute, and there was no sound apart from the tinny beat of music being played more quietly than it was meant to be.

'I don't know,' he said, 'but I feel as though I ought to. There should be some way of knowing, shouldn't there? Not logically, perhaps, but instinctively.'

Tess sat still, trying to work out what she felt. 'There's some kind of danger out there in the dark,' she said.

'I know that. But there always has been, hasn't there? And there always will be – places where it's not safe to be. Trouble is, it's like traffic accidents; you never know until it's too late.'

The mention of accidents reminded Tess of what she and Martin had been talking about. 'The crazy thing is, I don't blame him for what he did. I mean, shutting himself off like that and becoming cold and mean.'

Kevin surprised her. 'I do,' he said. 'It was his choice.'

The music played on, and it seemed like no time at all before the tape came to an end and Tess had to get up and turn it over. Kevin sat quietly in the chair, lost in his own thoughts. It didn't matter to Tess that he wasn't communicative; she didn't feel much like talking herself. It was enough that he was there.

The night slipped past. From time to time, Tess

thought about going to bed, but she knew that she wouldn't be able to sleep. Although neither of them said it, they were both waiting for the dawn and Tess noticed that, just as she did, Kevin regularly glanced up at the thin wedge or darkness where the curtains met.

Long before it began to get light, they heard Tess's father get up and go downstairs for breakfast. Soon afterwards he came up with tea for his wife. Tess waited for the regular knock on her door which woke her every morning, but it didn't come.

'He's letting me lie in,' she said quietly to Kevin.

'Lucky you.'

Tess laughed. 'I'm still not tired. But I keep telling myself how ridiculous it is to be sitting up like this.'

Kevin nodded, then looked again towards the window. Tess followed his eyes. The first hint of blue had crept into the blackness. She got up and drew the curtains, then switched off the light. When their eyes adjusted, they realised that there was more light in the day than they had thought.

'Is this dawn?' said Kevin. 'Does it count?'

'What difference does it make?' said Tess. 'We've no way of knowing what has happened, in any case.'

'I suppose not.'

'What are we going to do?'

'I don't know. Go looking, I suppose. With a good sharp stake of course.'

Tess shuddered, then sighed. 'I can't sleep. I just wish we had some way of knowing.'

As if in answer, there was a scuffle of tough little claws beneath the floorboards. Kevin froze, remembering the terrible attack the rats had made upon him when he was a phoenix. Was the vampire around, somewhere? Had he been hovering around all night, listening to them, and sent the rats to finish off Kevin before he could carry out his threat?

He stood up and looked around, horribly aware of his helplessness now that he no longer had the power to Switch. If the rats came for him here, there would be no way that he could escape.

Tess glanced over at him, understanding the situation immediately. Her mind went into overdrive as she searched for a solution. A terrier, perhaps? At least she could hold them at bay for a while.

But the nose that came poking through the gap in the wardrobe doors was very far from being aggressive. It was pink with white whiskers and it was twitching nervously. A white snout followed and a pair of weak, red eyes which peered anxiously around the room.

'Algernon!' said Tess.

The white rat heard her and moved cautiously into the room, sniffing the air and examining every object he encountered with grave suspicion. His nose was bumpy with scars and bruises, and his paws were swollen from digging.

'Poor Algie.' Tess bent down as he reached her foot, and stretched out a hand towards him. She was wary, remembering the fierce bite he had given her in the crypt, but this time there was no need to worry. Algernon jumped slightly as her fingers touched his grubby coat, then turned his head to sniff at her. Before she could get a hand around him, he ran up her sleeve and perched himself on her shoulder, pushing his twitching nose into the nape of her neck and up over her face.

'Apple, huh?' he said to her. 'White rat eating. White rat sleeping curled up in bed. Lots of shredded paper. Warm and cosy.'

Tess laughed in delight. 'White rat tired of tunnels and drains, huh?'

'White rat sleeping in cage. White rat running round on wheel.'

Kevin had been listening and now he bit a chunk out of an apple and handed it to Algernon, who sat up on Tess's shoulder and took it in his front paws. Eating didn't stop him from talking at all, since he didn't need his mouth to do it.

'Rat-bat-wolf-boy disappeared. Brown rats falling asleep on their feet. Sleeping in drains and tunnels. Whole city silent.'

Tess and Kevin said nothing, each of them dwelling on their own thoughts. Algernon finished the piece of apple and scuttled from Tess's shoulder into his cage. Tess was aware of a great sense of contentment. Lizzie had been right again and had helped her to do the right thing. Kevin was back, her parents seemed to be accepting the fact that she was growing up, and at that moment, Tess couldn't imagine why anyone would want to be anything other than human.

'We'll still have to look for him, of course,' she said. 'He's going to need a bit of support for a while.'

'We can leave the sharpened stake at home, though,' said Kevin. 'Do you think we should go now?'

Tess shook her head. 'I'm done in. This evening, maybe. The only thing I want to do now is to sleep all day.'

Kevin nodded. 'Good idea.' He stood up and stretched, then set off for the spare room. At the door he turned back, grinning widely.

'Just promise me you won't make a habit of it,' he said.

371

PART THREE

Wild Blood

CHAPTER ONE

When her parents told her their summer plans, Tess waited for the right moment, then turned herself into a swift and flew out over the city to visit her friend Lizzie. Human again, sitting at the old woman's fireside, Tess poured out her troubles.

'They're going on holiday without me!' she said. 'They're sending me to stay with my cousins in Clare. For three weeks!'

'I don't know what you's complaining about,' said Lizzie. 'The country is a great place for children.'

Tess stifled her irritation. 'I'm not a child, Lizzie.'

'Maybe you is and maybe you isn't. But you's still a Switcher, and that's all that matters. You'll have a great time down there in Clare.'

'I'm still a Switcher, all right. But not for much longer. That's why I came to see you. I'm going to have my fifteenth birthday while I'm down there.'

'Hmm.' Lizzie rubbed the chin of the tabby cat on

her lap. 'That is a bit sticky, I suppose.' The cat began to purr like a soft engine.

'There's no way of telling them how important it is, you see,' said Tess.

They fell quiet, each of them mulling over the problem in her own mind. At the dawn of their fifteenth birthdays, all Switchers lose their power to change their shape, and have to decide on what form they'll take for the rest of their lives. Lizzie knew that, because she had been a Switcher in her younger days, but Tess's parents knew nothing of their daughter's powers or her problems.

'Has you decided yet?' asked Lizzie. 'What you'll be?'

Tess shook her head.

'Then maybe it'll be easier for you without them around,' said Lizzie. 'And maybe Clare is the best place you could be.'

'Why?'

'You has wild blood in your veins, Tess. All Switchers has. And you might get a bit of help from your ancestors down that way.'

'My ancestors?'

'Be sure to give them my regards if you happen upon them, you hear?'

'What do you mean, my ancestors?'

The cat on the old woman's lap had been joined by two others, and three different purrs were creating guttural music. Lizzie seemed to be orchestrating it, with a stroke here and a rub there. Tess thought she had nothing more to say, and knew better than to try and push her. But eventually Lizzie looked up. Her sharp old eyes were full of life and humour.

'Does we believe what we sees, eh?' she said. 'Or does we see what we believe?'

CHAPTER TWO

On her first night in her aunt's country farmhouse, Tess had a strange and frightening dream. In the dream she was in a dark and magical place and she was watching Kevin, who had turned into a rat. Strange beings, huge and vague, hovered in the background, watching them. Tess knew that Kevin was afraid but she didn't know what to do, and a terrible urgency pervaded the dream so that a feeling of terror washed through her, again and again.

The fear woke her and she sat up in the bedroom she shared with one of her cousins. There was a strange, roaring sound which seemed to be coming from all around her, and for a long moment Tess lay frozen, holding her breath. Then, with a flood of relief, she realised what it was. Rain. It was thundering down on to the roof above her head, streaming into the gutters, sloshing away in the down-pipes and the drains. She breathed out.

The dream made no sense. Kevin was well past fifteen and could no longer Switch. Whatever dangers he might encounter in life, becoming a rat again wasn't one of them. Tess snuggled back into the bed and wrapped the covers around her. Gradually the fear receded and the sound of the rain was like music, lulling her back to sleep.

The following morning Tess woke to the sound of the cattle in the field beyond the yard grumbling together as they waited for their breakfast. The rain had stopped. In the other bed, her cousin Orla was still asleep, wheezing slightly with the asthma that had tormented her for most of her eleven years. Although Tess saw her cousins regularly when they visited Dublin, it was many years since she had visited them at their own home, in the wilds of County Clare. The sounds and smells of the countryside were so delightful that she forgot, for the moment, that she didn't want to be there and was still annoyed with her parents for going off on holiday without her. She stretched luxuriously and languished for a few minutes, listening to the birds. Then she got up and went down to help her Uncle Maurice with the milking.

A white cat with sky blue eyes was sitting on top of the oil tank in the yard. It watched Tess closely as she crossed to where her Uncle Maurice was letting out the dogs, Bran and Sceolan. He was surprised to see her.

'You're up early,' he said.

'Can I help?' asked Tess.

'You can, girl, indeed you can.'

He was heading for the feed-shed as he spoke, and Tess followed. But when he opened the door he stood frozen to the spot. Despite his large bulk in the doorway, Tess could see all that she needed to. The floor of the shed was strewn with dairy nuts, spilled from the paper sacks which were stacked against the wall. The smell of rodents was almost overpowering and Tess wasn't at all surprised to see that Bran and Sceolan weren't in any hurry to go in there. Indeed, a moment later they turned tail and fled, as Uncle Maurice's temper erupted.

'Damn and blast those flamin' rats!' he yelled, striding into the shed. As Tess watched, rooted to the spot, he punched feedbags, kicked walls, opened the infiltrated feed-bins and slammed their wooden lids. Even the restless cattle stopped complaining and waited politely, fearful that the violence might be turned upon them. But at last it abated. In silence, Uncle Maurice filled buckets and emptied them into the mangers. In silence, Tess helped. But her uncle's anger still resounded in the slamming of bolts as he opened the door of the milking parlour, and the cattle gave him a wide berth as they came in to take their places.

The sun was climbing high in a cloudless sky by the time the breakfast dishes were washed and put away. Tess asked if she could go out for a walk, and her Aunt Deirdre consented. The two boys, ten-year-old Brian and three-year-old Colm had already gone out to try to catch the bad-tempered little Shetland pony that grazed among the cattle, but for a few awkward moments it seemed likely that Orla was going to tag along as well. To Tess's relief, her aunt wouldn't allow it.

'What would you do if you couldn't catch your breath out there, child? What would poor Tess do?'

Before Orla could appeal the decision, Tess slipped out of the back door and headed off quickly across the broad, green meadows of the farm. She was delighted that she hadn't been made to come up with an excuse for wanting to be alone. It was never easy to lie about it, but it was vital that she had time to herself.

To her annoyance, Sceolan, the younger of the two dogs, attached himself to her heels, and no amount of stern instruction could persuade him to go back. But before they had gone too far he spotted Bran and Uncle Maurice gathering sheep and raced off to make a nuisance of himself. Tess pretended she hadn't seen them and walked on, climbing gates and walls until she came to the end of the clean meadows. The highest of them had been bulldozed in the distant past and the piles of cleared stone made untidy walls. Beyond, the rough land began; the area that Tess couldn't wait to explore.

She looked back at the house. She had already covered a good distance and it was unlikely that anyone was watching, but she could still see Uncle Maurice and hear him swearing at Sceolan, and she felt much too exposed to Switch. So she walked on, over ground that became rockier and more difficult at every step. Beneath her feet the limestone was full of fossils. Here and there huge flakes of it broke away and revealed the shapes of shells or mud patterns; the rock's own memory of its origins, deep beneath some ancient sea. The sense of great age gave the whole place a mysterious air, and a thrill of adventure coursed through Tess's bones.

Ahead of her the land rose gradually for another quarter of a mile, then reared up abruptly in a towering cliff face that her cousins referred to as The

Crag. At its foot she could see ash trees stretching out of a forest of hazel; a perfect place to explore and try some of her favourite animal forms, perhaps for the last time. She quickened her pace and before long she had come to the edge of the woods.

But they looked quite different from close quarters, and not friendly at all. Before moving to Dublin, Tess had spent most of her life in the countryside, but it had been broad, rolling farmland; small, closely-tended fields surrounded by straggly hedgerows. This was quite different. This was a wild and alien place. Small blackthorn bushes stood like squat sentries at every entrance, challenging her to brave their sharp weapons. Beyond them the interior of the wood was darkly green, full of shadows and silence.

Tess stepped back and made her way along the awkward stony ground at the woods' edge, hoping for an easier way to get in. Sometimes a stone wobbled or a stick cracked beneath her feet, and it seemed to her that she heard corresponding footsteps inside the woods. She stopped. The silence was complete. But as soon as she walked on she could hear them again, quite clearly this time; whispering footsteps on the soft woodland floor.

Again she stopped; again there was silence. Just ahead of her an entrance seemed to present itself; an opening like a dark tunnel, not obstructed by thorns. Tess hesitated. A blackbird gave an alarm call, a panicky rattle that seemed to tail off into a sinister laugh in the dark interior. Afterwards the flutter of bird wings sounded more like bats, and made Tess's skin crawl. She breathed deeply, trying to collect herself. It was only a wood, that was all. A quiet wood at the foot of a mountain. It couldn't possibly be dangerous.

But at that moment, as though to prove her wrong, something moved, gliding swiftly and silently among the shadows. Tess stepped back, unsure what she had seen. Whatever it was had walked on two legs, upright like a person. But it was vague and shadowy, too tall to be human and much too fast. What was more, it seemed to have antlers on its head.

Tess had seen enough. Her courage failed her and she began to walk quickly back the way she had come, glancing round frequently, her nerves on edge. Not until she was safely inside the boundaries of the farm meadows did she relax enough to stop and look back. From where she stood she could hear the anxious complaints of the gathered sheep and the irritated tones of Uncle Maurice's voice. The mountain was silvery-grey, its flowing lines graceful and soft, the woods at its feet grey-green and innocent. Tess wondered how she could have been so stupid. Surely there couldn't have been anything in those woods. It must have been her imagination. What was worse was that she had just wasted one of the last opportunities she was likely to have to make use of her Switching powers.

She would have gone back in the afternoon, or perhaps taken another route into the mountains, but her aunt, perpetually overstretched, collared her to look after Colm while she brought Orla to a local homeopath. Tess wanted to take Colm out for a walk or a game of football, but he was determined to stay in and watch his new *Star Wars* video, and when it was finished he wanted to watch *The Empire Strikes Back* as well. Tess watched with him, enjoying the films despite herself, and after lunch Uncle Maurice went out to meet someone on business and Brian joined them in the sitting-room. Colm didn't appear to understand a word of what was going on, but it didn't matter to him. He loved the little robot R2D2 and curled up with glee every time it uttered its electronic language of squeaks and bleeps. Tess laughed at his pleasure. There were worse things than having small cousins. Nonetheless she was uneasy. Time was running out.

That evening, Uncle Maurice was in an unusually cheerful mood. When he had finished his dinner he pushed his plate aside and said, 'Well, I've cracked it.'

'Cracked what?' said Aunt Deirdre.

'The sale of that piece of land. There's a developer in Ennis who is going to buy it off me to build a holiday village.'

Orla was always slow at eating, and this evening was no exception. Her plate was more than half full, but she put down her knife and fork in a very conclusive way. She looked across at Brian who, it seemed to Tess, had suddenly gone pale. He glanced back at his sister, and Tess thought she detected an expression of alarm in his eyes.

'You know. A place where tourists can come and buy a house, or rent one,' Uncle Maurice went on. 'Great spot for it. I'll be getting the deeds from the solicitor in the next couple of days. I'll need your signature, Deirdre.'

Aunt Deirdre nodded passively. But Orla said, 'Do we have to sell it, Daddy? Can't we keep it?'

'That piece of land is no use to us at all,' her father replied. 'You know that as well as I do. And think what we could do with the money!'

'But what about Uncle Declan?' said Orla. 'Couldn't we . . .?'

She got no further. If looks could kill she would have shrivelled in an instant beneath her father's furious stare.

'I'll not have that name mentioned at this table,' said Uncle Maurice, his voice conveying a growing danger. 'And as for the land, when one of you is running this farm let you run it as you want. In the meantime I'll make the decisions.'

His statement met with silence. Tess couldn't understand what was going on, but it was fairly clear that it was not a good time to ask. Her aunt was as white as the wall behind her. The rest of the family prayed that the fuse would go out before it lit the powder. And for once, it did.

After dinner, Tess went with Uncle Maurice and Brian to do the evening milking. Tess put out the nuts while Brian let the cows in. Bran and Sceolan made little rushes at their heels, but it was only for show. The cows knew exactly where to go and needed no encouragement. When the first lot were all in their stalls, Tess went round with the bucket of udder wash. Brian came along behind her, attaching the cups. Uncle Maurice stayed up near the machine's motor, checking that everything was going smoothly and doing a chemical test on the milk.

When the machine was set up and doing its work, Tess leant against the railings beside Brian.

'Why was Orla upset?' she asked. 'About your dad selling the land?'

Brian looked at her searchingly, as though he was trying to decide whether she was trustworthy. 'I suppose she thinks it's our land as well,' he said.

Tess nodded. 'Is it a big piece of land?'

Again Brian looked at her strangely, as though the information he was about to give was privileged in some way. He glanced around him, then shrugged.

'He has been wanting to sell it for years. Ever since he took over the farm from his father.' But if Brian planned to say more he didn't get round to it, because at that moment Uncle Maurice came marching towards them.

'Are you checking them?' he asked, knowing that they weren't.

Brian moved off and Tess followed, making sure that the cups were properly in place. The conversation had left her with more questions than answers, but her uncle seemed to be keeping a close eye on her and she couldn't get close enough to Brian to ask more. Some of the cows had finished their nuts, and turned to look at her as she worked around them. And although she had never found it very interesting to be a cow, she found their placid temperaments calming and she enjoyed their dry, philosophical humour. They had no language as such, but their expressions and movements told their stories. Best of all, Tess enjoyed the secret she learnt; that although Uncle Maurice considered himself to be their lord and master, they regarded him fondly as a rather bossy calf, who drank more milk than he ought to but was, like all young, ignorant things, tolerated.

When they had finished with the first lot of cows they moved quickly on to the second, and then the third. It wasn't long before the milking was over, and afterwards, while Brian and his father hosed down the floor of the shed, Tess went out into the yard.

The sun had dropped on to the horizon, where it sat like a vast, dazzling headlight. It lit the mountain

385

in a way that Tess hadn't seen before, accentuating its faults and folds so that it looked pliable, more like flesh than rock. It made her feel strange, tingly, and the feeling intensified when she noticed a black bird approaching through the sky above the meadows. At first she took it for a crow, but as it grew closer she realised that it was far too big. It could only be a raven, and along with that realisation came another which sent shivers through her bones. She didn't know how, but she was quite certain that it was looking for her. As it flew over, it turned its head and looked down with one black eye, then wheeled above the farmyard, dropping lower, watching her all the time. The tingle turned to a bone-deep chill as the bird looked her straight in the eye, then swept up into the heights again, its huge wings making a whipping sound in the air. She watched it as it soared high and turned back towards the mountain, then she realised that she was not alone. Brian and Uncle Maurice had come out into the yard and were looking from her to the retreating bird with curious expressions. Then, as though in a conspiracy of silence, they turned and walked away from her, back towards the farm buildings. Tess wanted to call after them and ask them if they had seen what she had, but Orla emerged from the house.

'Want a game of Monopoly?' she said.

Tess stared at her, readjusting her mind to everyday existence. Her spirit was in turmoil, still disconcerted by the raven's visit but at the same time longing for the freedom to investigate. With an effort she managed a faint smile.

'Just one, then,' she said. 'If I can be the ship.'

CHAPTER THREE

That night, it seemed to take forever to get dark. Now that there was no rain, the silence outside was profound; a mystery waiting to be explored. In the other bed, Orla wheezed painfully but, since she hadn't moved for more than an hour, Tess assumed she was asleep.

Something, a late bird or an early bat, fluttered past the window. Tess sighed and turned on to her back, willing the night to come. She wished that there was someone she could talk to. Not just anyone, but someone who would sympathise with what she was going through. Martin would understand; the boy who had learnt how to become a vampire but had opted in the end to be human. Lizzie would be all right as well, even if she did talk in riddles. But the person that Tess missed most of all was Kevin; her first and best friend. She wished she could see him now. She could imagine him sitting beside her, listening thoughtfully, understanding her frustration, knowing how it felt to be facing those last few days, knowing how difficult it was to come to a decision.

She realised that she was worried about him. Martin would settle down, sooner or later. He didn't admit it, but he was working hard at school, and he rarely needed to visit the counsellor who had eventually helped him to come to terms with the trauma of his father's death. His mother adored him and, although he was unlikely to be conventional, Martin would undoubtedly find a way to fit in and look after himself. But Kevin wasn't so lucky. When he had returned from his adventures and could no longer Switch, he had tried to rejoin his estranged family. It hadn't worked. They no longer understood each other, and Kevin couldn't fit in. Instead, he joined the increasing number of young people living on the streets.

He said it was different for him; said that he had spent much of his life scavenging as a rat and this was a kind of continuation of it. But from where Tess was standing it didn't look so noble. The streets and derelict buildings of Dublin provided a mean and cold existence for a boy, and although Tess helped him out as much as she could, she was afraid that if he didn't find a way of supporting himself he would sooner or later be compelled to turn to crime. And if that happened, Tess had no idea what would become of him.

Her thoughts were disturbed by a scuttling sound behind the wainscot. She sat up carefully, silently. There was an untidy hole in the boards where the radiator pipe had been brought through, relatively recently. As Tess watched, a brown nose and a set of twitching whiskers appeared, followed by a pair of bright, black eyes. Tess smiled, wondering how it was that her life had been populated by rats ever since she had first met Kevin. She was just about to address the newcomer in the visual language that she had learnt from the Dublin city rats when a door opened downstairs and Uncle Maurice's voice carried up the stairs, complaining about the film which had, apparently, just ended. The rat nose disappeared, but Tess's spirits lifted. Soon her aunt and uncle would be in bed, and she would be free.

When the human sounds finally came to an end, the rat sounds began. Tess heard the scuffles above her head as they left their nests in the roof-space and she listened to the rattle of loose plaster in the walls as they travelled down through the house. Before long, apart from Orla's breathing, all was quiet again. Still Tess waited until, eventually, she was sure that the household was asleep. Then she slipped out of bed and went to the window.

A gibbous moon was out, riding high above the mountains, making them seem closer than they were. A few small clouds hovered, becalmed, back-lit by the moon. Tess was torn between her desire to investigate the mysterious and beautiful woods and her fear of the gliding figure she had, or thought she had, seen. It would be better, perhaps, to return in daylight. In the meantime, a visit with the farmhouse rats would go a long way towards alleviating her boredom.

She was just on the point of turning back into the room when Orla spoke, sending an electric tide through Tess's blood.

'Tess?'

Tess caught her breath. 'Yes?'

'Can't you sleep?'

389

'No.'

'Nor me.'

Tess had a sudden vision of the two of them playing Monopoly until dawn. She prayed that Orla wouldn't think of it. But Orla had other things on her mind and Tess heard the familiar hiss and gasp as she took a dose from her inhaler. When she had let go of the medicated breath, Orla said, 'What are you looking at?'

Tess shrugged. 'I don't know. The moon. The mountains.'

Orla was silent for a moment and then, in a voice that betrayed a slight apprehension, she said, 'Do you believe in the Good People, Tess?'

'The Good People? Who are the Good People?'

'Fairies,' said Orla.

Another cold flush began in Tess's spine, but she caught herself and laughed it off. 'Fairies? You've got to be joking.'

But Orla didn't laugh. In the silence that followed her breathing became easier. Tess got back into bed and, seething inside, she waited. Her thoughts began to chase each other in irritated circles, but after a few minutes she was distracted by an unexpected sound.

At first she thought that someone had put on a video downstairs. The noise she was hearing was very like the musical bleeping of R2D2's electronic voice, and it was being answered by the polite, BBC tones of the other robot character, C3PO. But as she listened, Tess realised that the sounds were not coming from downstairs but from one of the other bedrooms.

She looked across the room. Orla was breathing freely and there could be no more doubt that she was asleep. Tess slipped out of bed again and crept out on to the landing. A dim light was always left on there, in case any of the children woke in the night. The sound of the *Star Wars* robots was still going on, and it was quite clearly coming from the bedroom which Brian and Colm shared, beside the bathroom. Furtively, Tess put her ear against the door and listened.

The boys must have been playing a tape. First there was a flurry of R2D2 bleeps and blips, then C3PO said, 'Oh, really, R2. We can't possibly do a thing like that!'

Another trill followed, like electronic birdsong, and C3PO replied again. 'Not tonight, R2. It would be far too dangerous!'

Tess was tempted to knock and join the boys, but she refrained. Better to stick to her own plan, now that she finally had the freedom to do it.

With the relief of a prisoner being released, she Switched. Even as she became a rat and began to adjust to her surroundings, processing sounds and smells, her human mind was wondering how she would survive when she couldn't Switch any longer. Like stepping back into prison, it would be. For a life sentence.

She put it out of her mind and concentrated on the present. Her rat body was supple and strong. She went silently back into Orla's room and slithered through the hole where the radiator pipe emerged. Then she was running and sliding down through the walls of the house. When she was human, Tess always thought that she could remember how it felt, but it wasn't until she became a rat again that she knew she was wrong. No memory could capture the immediacy of ratness or how it felt to be so small and yet so strong; so vulnerable and so brave. Why

391

would anyone choose to be human, she wondered, if they could be a rat instead?

The first room that Tess came to was the sitting-room. She didn't go in. It didn't look like a promising place for foraging. There was only one rat in there as far as she could see. He was quite elderly and was having serious trouble with half a packet of fruit gums which were sticking his teeth together. He was scraping angrily at his jowls with his paws but was having no success. Tess noticed that he was missing one of his teeth; a top one, at the front. She wondered whether it was a casualty of an earlier fruit gum battle, but decided not to embarrass him by asking. She turned and slipped away before he saw her.

In the hall-way she encountered one of the strangest rats she had ever met. She was scurrying rapidly down the stairs carrying a bread-crust that Colm must have dropped on his rambles, and as she passed Tess she flashed an unusual greeting. Tess was pretty expert at the visual language that rats used to communicate with each other, but she had never been greeted like this before. The image was of a huge gathering of rats with Tess in the centre of it, being welcomed with joy on all sides. It was more than unusual. It was grand, larger than life, almost poetic. Tess watched as the other rat squeezed through a tiny hole at the bottom of the first stair, then she turned towards the kitchen. But part of her mind was still on the peculiar message, and she had blundered into the middle of trouble before she realised her mistake.

A mother rat had claimed the kitchen for her large, adolescent family and, for as long as they were in residence, it was a no-go area for other rats. Tess realised her mistake when the youngsters looked up from foraging around the bottom of the table legs and she found herself observed by nine practically identical faces. She turned to leave, but it was already too late.

There is nothing on earth more savage than a mother rat protecting her young. If they are threatened she will attack anything: a dog, a human, even a tractor. If she cannot stop the enemy, she will die in the attempt. In the scale of things, Tess was a pretty minor threat.

The mother rat hit her from above, leaping down from the sink where she had been keeping a careful look-out. Her weight, greatly supplemented by gravity, knocked the wind out of Tess and she was flattened for a minute, scrabbling uselessly at the slick lino floor with her claws. Above her, the mother rat crouched with bared teeth.

'Nanananana!' Tess sent rat images as clearly as her shaken mind could manage. She had a Rat name, that had been given to her a long time ago beneath the Dublin city streets, but now her mind hit upon a more appropriate nickname.

'Town Rat not hurting young rats,' she said. 'Town Rat not taking their food. Town Rat stupid; very stupid.'

She had managed to regain her feet by now, but kept her head on the floor and her throat bared in a gesture of absolute submission. Rats, Tess knew, obeyed nature's rules, one of which is that, among members of the same species, submission ends aggression. The only creatures that Tess had ever known to break that rule were human beings, but for a moment or two she wasn't sure that it would work. The mother rat took a menacing step forward and loomed over Tess. She must have been eating soap up there on the draining board; she stank of it.

393

'Nananana,' Tess pleaded. 'Town Rat going. Going very fast. Not looking back!'

The mother rat sent no images in return but continued to stare hard at Tess. Then, with no warning at all, she turned and walked away. Tess stayed where she was until the young rats converged on their mother in a clamour of admiration and anxious hunger. Then, with no pretence at dignity, she fled.

In the hall-way, at a safe distance, Tess stopped and groomed. With her teeth she chewed and combed her sleek, chestnut coat back into order. Then, after listening carefully for a while, she washed her face with the back of her paws. Finally, her self-respect intact again, she set off to have a look outside.

At the edge of the yard she searched long and hard with her eyes and ears, but there was no sign of the white cat. The last of the clouds had drifted away, and the sky was clearer than any she had ever seen. Despite the strength of the moon she could see stars; some close, some infinitely distant, like bright dust scattered across the night. Nearer, the mountains stood silvery and silent. They seemed to glow as though the eerie light originated with them and not with the moon. As she looked on, Tess was surprised to find that her rat mind was as capable of wonder as her human one. Where they differed was in their response to it. The human part of her was filled with impatient curiosity; a desire to explore and to understand. Her rat nature, by contrast, was content to experience the wonder, absorb it, and return to the important things in life.

Which, to a rat, usually meant food.

Tess's nose and ears soon told her where it was to be found. From the feed-shed at the end of the milking parlour she could hear delightful sounds:

hasty activity, gnawing and crunching and chewing, rodent jubilation. Hunger roared in her belly. To make herself look bigger and fiercer, she puffed up her coat, prepared to fight her corner if she had to. Then, twitching and bristling, she went to join the party.

CHAPTER FOUR

But everything has a price. Breakfast the next morning was governed by Uncle Maurice's anger and, although Tess had been too tired to join him for the morning milking, she guessed what was on his mind even before he opened his mouth to speak.

'I've had enough of those flamin' rats. I'm getting rid of them once and for all. I don't care what it costs, I'm getting the exterminators in.'

Tess didn't know how pest control professionals went about their business, but she did know that they succeeded. If Uncle Maurice carried out his intention, most of the rats she had encountered the previous night would soon die a painful death. She shuddered at the thought, and Uncle Maurice caught sight of her.

'There's no point in being sentimental about it,' he said. 'It's all very well, you town folk coming in

and thinking the countryside is full of cuddly creatures. Real life isn't like that, you know.'

Tess looked down at the table. She would never be
able to tell him the reason why she was so horrified
by his plans. Or what 'real life' meant to her.

'How come the cat doesn't keep them under
control?' she asked.

'We have no cat,' said Uncle Maurice.

'But I saw . . .'

'I said we have no cat!'

Tess decided not to push it. After a moment, Aunt
Deirdre breached the silence.

'I don't know about those exterminators,' she said.
'Are you sure the chemicals they use aren't
dangerous? They might be bad for Orla's asthma.'

'Orla's asthma, Orla's asthma! I'm sick and tired
of hearing about Orla's flamin' asthma. The rats have
to go, right? If you can come up with a better suggestion, let me know.'

He stood up, pushing his chair back with such
force that its feet grated on the flagged floor and
made everybody's skin crawl. Then he was gone.
Brian, who was his father's right-hand man, got up
with an air of resignation and followed. One by one
the other members of the family, even little Colm,
let out a sigh of relief.

Orla was excused from washing-up because the deter-
gent gave her eczema. She entertained Colm in the
sitting-room while Tess and Aunt Deirdre cleared up.
Tess waited for the effects of Uncle Maurice's out-
burst to clear and, when she felt her aunt had cheered
up sufficiently, she plucked up courage.

'Who is Uncle Declan?'

Her aunt's mood collapsed again, as if she was a

balloon that had been punctured. 'Why do you ask that?' she said, and Tess thought she detected a touch of anxiety in her voice.

'No reason,' she said. 'Orla mentioned him, that's all.'

'I have no idea why she mentioned him,' said Aunt Deirdre. 'He isn't relevant at all. I have no idea what she was talking about.'

Tess waited, assuming that an explanation would follow, but it didn't. On the subject of Uncle Declan, Aunt Deirdre had said all that she intended to say. In silence she finished washing the dishes and in silence Tess dried them and put them away. Afterwards she slipped off again, quickly, before Orla could ask to come.

By the time she crossed the outermost boundaries of the farmland, Tess had already come up with a plan. Despite her fear she was desperately curious about the woods at the foot of the crag and she decided to use an alternative form to investigate. A bird of some sort would be ideal for getting a good look between the trees, and provided she didn't encounter that sinister raven, she should be safe enough.

A movement at the edge of her vision made her look up. A bright, red-brown hare was sitting on a rock a few yards away. Sensing Tess's eyes upon it, it froze, sitting upright on its haunches, still as the stones around it. Tess ached to Switch and join it, but she was still on the wide open hill-side. She could see no one, but there was no guarantee that no one could see her; from the height of the crag if not from the farmhouse. In the bright sunlight the fears of the previous day seemed absurd. Surely it would be safe

398

enough to slip inside the edge of the trees, just long enough to Switch?

There was nowhere else. Her nerves on edge, Tess crossed the brittle rocks until she had reached the woods. Everything was quiet. She took a deep breath and, making herself as small and as nonchalant as possible, she manoeuvred her way past the sharp thorns and into the shadows beyond.

Straight away Tess knew that the woods were full of magic. The air was as fresh as spring water. There was a brightness about the leaf-filtered light that her eyes could barely contain, and a thousand vivid shades of green reflected it. Nothing was inert; the bark of the trees was like living skin, and the rocks were covered with velvety moss, like soft, green pelts. Between them the richly-scented earth was concealed by the leaves of wild strawberry and garlic.

Tess's fears evaporated and, overcome by the strange atmosphere, she moved forward. Here and there, in dry hollows produced by overhanging rocks or exposed roots, little heaps of empty hazelnut shells had been left by mice or squirrels. The entrances to more permanent homes had been dug out of earthen banks, and musky scents drifted on the air above them like signs, warning or welcoming. There was no evidence anywhere of human visitors; no discarded wrappers or tissues or cans; no paths; no fences; no carved initials on the trees. This was the wildest place that Tess had ever encountered.

Her heart filled with excitement as she wondered what shape to take on first. As if in answer to her question, the hare that she had seen earlier came into view again as it slipped silently away into the heart of the wood. Tess took a last breath of the cool, moss-scented air and Switched.

It was a long time since she had been a hare, and she had forgotten the lean, lithe strength of it, as different from a rabbit as a wolf was from a poodle. Her long hind legs were hard and tight, coiled springs waiting to unleash their power. She listened carefully for a moment and then, unable to resist, sprang into the air. She kicked and twisted, and barely touched the ground before leaping again, mad as a March hare. Once started she couldn't stop. Her claws tore holes in the moss and released the trapped scent of the soil, but soon this was overwhelmed by the rank smell of the garlic, bruised beneath the hare's strong feet.

'Tessss.'

She stopped, frozen to the spot, her big ears listening. Although her hare's brain could not interpret human speech, the sound of her own name was unmistakable to Tess. For a moment it seemed that the sound must have been her imagination, but then it came again, a sibilant, far-carrying whisper which seemed to originate all around her at once.

'Tessss.'

Someone was watching, someone who knew who she was and what she was doing. Her instinct was to Switch, and fast; a bird would be the best way to escape. But as though it knew her thoughts better than she did, the raven chose that moment to swish above her head, so close to the treetops that it almost touched them.

'Tessss.'

Her hare brain was urging her to run and she would have complied if her human brain could decide which direction to take. But suddenly, in her panic, she had no idea where she was, and which direction led to the crag and which led away from it. She found herself running, dodging between the trees, thwarting the hare's instincts and heading for light and open space. A moment later she was back at the edge of the woods, and as she burst out past the blackthorn she Switched. But the voice was still there, still behind her.

'Come in, Tessss. Come in.'

The thorns snagged at her clothes and her skin, but her momentum was too strong for her to be able to stop or even slow down and she landed hard on the stony ground beyond, winding herself badly. As she picked herself up and began to examine the thorn-wounds on her arms, the unmistakable sound of delighted laughter rang out through the woods.

Back in the farmhouse kitchen, the smell of fresh baking made Tess feel ravenous. Brian was pouring tea into mugs.

'What have you done to yourself?' asked Aunt Deirdre, pulling up Tess's blood-stained sleeves and examining her scratched arms.

'I'm OK, thanks,' said Tess. 'I just had an argument with a bush.'

Brian snickered and Tess made a face at him. She bit into a steaming scone and wondered why it was that food always tasted so much better after a spell in the open air. Through the window she could see Colm splashing about with a bucket of water and a plastic jug. The family weren't so bad, really, and for the first time since she had arrived Tess felt comfortable and relaxed.

'I went up into the woods,' she said. 'Over there at the bottom of the crag.'

Aunt Deirdre glanced at her sharply. 'You might be better to stay away from there,' she said.

Tess's skin crawled. 'Why?'

'She's scared of the fairies,' said Brian. 'Take no notice of her.'

A sudden flash of white at the window made Tess look up. The white cat was there again, sitting on the outer sill, staring in.

'There it is,' said Tess. 'I knew I'd seen a cat.' She turned to Brian, but he was giving her that look again, like the time in the milking parlour; a worried, mistrustful look.

'Pay no attention to it,' said Aunt Deirdre. 'It's only a stray. Would you like another scone?' But before Tess could reply, the domestic storm erupted again. Without warning, the door to the hall burst open and Uncle Maurice swept in, dampening the mood instantly and putting everyone on edge. Brian jumped up to get him a mug of tea.

'Four hundred quid,' said Uncle Maurice, bitterly. 'Four hundred, flamin' quid, just to get rid of a few flamin' rats!'

'My god,' said Aunt Deirdre, but it was more in the way of a practised response than a genuine expression of surprise.

'Four hundred quid,' Uncle Maurice said again. He seemed dazed.

'And what do they do for it?' asked Aunt Deirdre.

'They get rid of the flamin' rats, don't they?'

'I know that. But how?'

'How should I know? Poison them, gas them, I don't know.'

Tess felt sick. She would have to warn the rats in time.

'When are they coming?' she asked.

'Whenever I ask them to,' said her uncle. '*If* I ask them to. If I can find four hundred quid!'

'We'll have to find it,' said Aunt Deirdre. 'I'm sure they were in the house last night.'

'And there are two of them drowned in the water butt,' said Brian. 'There must be millions of them around the place.'

Uncle Maurice shook his head. 'We can't be living with that, sure,' he said. 'Four hundred quid or no four hundred quid, they'll have to go.'

When Tess had finished her tea, Aunt Deirdre asked her to hang out a load of washing on the line. She was just pegging out the last few things when Orla called her from inside the house.

Tess ran in.

'Your boyfriend,' said Orla, handing her the phone.

Tess scowled at her and shook her head. 'Hello?' she said.

'Is that Tess?'

'Kevin! That's amazing. I was just thinking about you.'

'I bet.'

'Well, it was yesterday, actually. But I was, honestly. Wishing you were here.'

'Well, then. Your prayers are answered. I'm on my way.'

'Oh, yeah,' said Tess, sarcastically. 'Sure you are.'

Kevin laughed. 'I am. I really am. I'm coming for a holiday. A guy I know has a van and he's coming that way. I've borrowed a bike and a tent off Martin. Do you think that I'd forget your birthday?'

Tess's heart warmed towards him. 'You're brilliant, you know that?' she said.

'Yeah. But unfortunately I'm not rich. I'll only have a few quid left by the time I've bought a bit of grub. Any jobs down that way?'

403

Tess knew that getting money out of Uncle Maurice was like trying to get blood out of a stone. But, for some reason, the figure of four hundred pounds popped into her mind.

'Not unless you can . . .' She stopped, thinking it through.

'Can what?' asked Kevin.

'Come to think of it,' said Tess, 'there just might be. If we play our cards right, that is.'

She looked up the stairs and at the closed door of the kitchen.

'Now, listen . . .' she said.

The day passed easily for Tess in the knowledge that Kevin was coming, and Uncle Maurice's moods didn't seem to dominate her own. She helped to treat the gathered sheep for foot-rot and dose them against worms, and afterwards volunteered to help mend a fallen wall.

Before long she began to wish that she hadn't. The stones were awkward and heavy, and Uncle Maurice seemed to assume she had prodigious strength.

'Flamin' goats,' he said. 'They're what has all the walls knocked on me.'

Tess said nothing, but heaved up another stone. Her one attempt at repairing the wall had resulted in a badly bruised toe, and she now left the building to Brian, who was surprisingly skilled at it. He took the stone from her and she stretched to ease her aching back.

'There they are, look,' Uncle Maurice went on. 'Up on the crag, see?'

Tess followed the direction of his pointing finger. Sure enough, she could just make out the multi-coloured forms of a herd of wild goats. The higher parts of the crag weren't quite as steep as the lower ones, but nonetheless the goats seemed to be standing at impossible angles as they browsed on the wild foliage.

Tess's heart went out to them and she longed to be there, climbing with them, breathing the rarefied air up there above it all. She cast her mind back to the morning's events and decided that she wasn't going to let fear cramp her style. They were among thousands of acres of farmland after all, and there were ways of getting up into the mountains without going anywhere near those creepy woods. A goat was one of her favourite creatures, and she wasn't going to miss out on the chance to be one again, perhaps for the last time.

But the opportunity took a while to arrive. After lunch they went to visit Uncle Maurice's parents, and then it was dinner time, and then there was evening mass. By the time Tess found herself alone again, night had fallen, and she was lying in bed, waiting once again for the household to sleep.

When, finally, all was quiet, she got up and, taking care not to wake Orla, crept over to the window. The moon was high and white. Beneath it the mountains gleamed like mercury, their strange, fluid forms giving the impression of melting. The beauty of the night took her breath away.

As she watched, mesmerised, she saw, out of the corner of her eye, a glimmer of bluish light some-where around the base of the crag. She looked at the place where it had been, and immediately it flashed out in another place, just at the edge of her vision. A shiver ran down her spine. She blinked and rubbed her eyes to clear them, but again the spark-like lights flashed, first from one side, then from another. Like shooting stars, the flashes were gone before she could get a proper look at them, and they never seemed to appear where she happened to be looking at the time, but always at the edge of her vision.

She turned away from the window. She had intended to take on the form of an owl or some other nocturnal creature and make a night-time trip around the area, but now she wasn't so sure. There had to be an explanation for what she had just seen; a trick of her eyes, perhaps, or of the moonlight. But her rational mind was already way out of its depth and could make no sense of it at all. There was something in those woods that Tess couldn't begin to under-stand, and she had no intention of going out there in the dark, no matter what forms she had to choose from.

Much as she hated to admit it, Tess was afraid.

CHAPTER FIVE

But in the morning, things, as they so often do, seemed quite different. Tess woke early, and the delight of the birds in the trees around the house made the fears of the night before seem like a childish dream. The morning was fresh and bright, and it was impossible for Tess to go back to sleep. Hardly daring to breathe, she slithered out of bed and began to gather her clothes. But it was already too late.

'Where are you going?' asked Orla.

Tess tried to hide her irritation. 'Do you never sleep?'

'Not much,' said Orla, truthfully. She coughed and sat up on the edge of her bed. Her legs, emerging from beneath her nightdress, were like pale twigs. Tess turned away. It must be awful to be so ill.

Orla began to pull on her jeans. 'Can I come with you?' she asked.

'Sorry,' said Tess. 'You know your mother doesn't allow you to come.'

'That's OK,' said Orla. 'She doesn't have to know, does she?'

Orla's face was lit with an illicit joy, and Tess felt panic closing in. Emotionally she felt compelled to take her cousin with her and look after her, but the last days as a Switcher were so precious to her that she couldn't bear to miss out on the chance to make use of them, not even for those few hours.

'Don't worry about my asthma,' Orla was saying. 'I'll bring my inhaler. I'll be fine.'

But Tess shook her head, hating herself as she did so.

'I'm sorry,' she said. 'You can't come.'

Orla stared at her in disbelief. In her chest something began to harden, and the first organ-squeak of a wheeze entered her breathing. 'Please let me,' she said and then, when Tess made no response, she went on, 'I'll take you to meet Uncle Declan.'

'Who is this Uncle Declan?' said Tess.

'You'll see,' said Orla. 'Just let me come. Please?'

Tess found that her curiosity about Uncle Declan had evaporated now that she knew he was someone who could be visited.

'Sorry,' she said again. 'Sorry.'

Bran and Sceolan whined from behind the closed door of their shed as Tess passed through the yard, but she didn't let them out. Her steps were heavy with guilt, but the morning was so inviting that they soon lightened. The dew was still lying in big, spangly drops on the grass, making the fields pastel-coloured and soaking Tess's trainers. She looked down at them as she walked, wondering what kind of feet she would be looking at after her birthday, the day after tomorrow. She imagined hooves there, horse-hooves, and remembered the feeling of head-tossing horse-ness; all pride and contained strength. She saw dog-paws, trotting tirelessly through endless miles, then cat-paws, graceful and silent. They were all so familiar and so precious. She realised as she walked that part of the difficulty in choosing what to be was having to give up all the other things. She didn't want her time as a Switcher to end. The realisation threatened to drown her in tears and she looked up, struggling hard against a growing sense of despair.

At least Kevin was coming later on in the day. The thought went some way towards cheering Tess up, and she set off again, turning to her right, away from the woods and towards another area of the stony wasteland beyond the farm boundaries. The new route took her over one of the walls that she had been mending the day before with Brian and Uncle Maurice. On the other side of it the sheep sprang up from their woolly huddle and stood glaring suspiciously, leaving behind a large patch of dry, warm grass. As Tess passed among them they waddled out of her way, shaking the sleep out of their fleeces and their small brains. The ewes, recently shorn, seemed puny beside their fat, woolly lambs. There was one certainty, at least; one animal that Tess would never choose to become. Maybe it would be easier to decide the end result by a process of elimination?

She wouldn't be a cow, that was certain, nor a pig. Not a gerbil either, or a caged bird, or any of those poor creatures that lived half lives in the service of human beings. Still deep in thought, Tess arrived at the further wall of the sheep meadow and climbed over it into the grey scrubland beyond. She was just coming to the decision that she would be a wild thing, in a wild place like this one, when a snort as loud and sudden as a pistol shot rang out through the still morning air.

Tess jumped, then froze to the spot until the source of the extraordinary sound became clear. Not far away from her was a small herd of wild goats. Some of them were standing on the rocks, others lying nearby, but getting up now and stamping and staring across the open space at the intruder. Tess kept still, aware that they were on the point of scattering and that one wrong move would set them off. Carefully she turned round and looked back. The house was a good distance away but she was not out of sight of it. The wall, however, was quite high and she could drop down and hide behind it if she was careful.

A moment later, the disturbing presence of the human girl was gone and a new goat emerged, as if from nowhere. The wild ones stared at it in astonishment for a few moments before overcoming their mistrust and moving hesitantly towards it. Tess waited, adjusting to the new situation and the altered senses, remembering how it felt to be a goat. The first to approach her was an elderly nanny. Her bones protruded, her coat was long and straggly and clearly she had seen better days. But her age had bestowed two things upon her. One was an enormous pair of horns and the other was an indisputable authority in the group. She approached Tess with an expression of lofty disdain, defying her to make a challenge. Tess did not take up the offer but made herself as unthreatening as possible, waiting for the older goat to make the running. She knew that each species in the animal kingdom had its own protocol, and she knew that in no case could introductions be hurried.

But on this occasion, the proceedings were brought to an abrupt end.

Tess heard the ominous rumble of stones at the same time as the other goats. Unfortunately, however, she had her back to the danger, and the entire herd had launched into a gallop like racehorses coming out of the starting gates before she had the faintest idea what was happening.

She followed. A goat's eyes, like most other herd animals', are on the sides of its head and not at the front, and Tess had often wondered why nature had not provided human beings with the same system. It had a few drawbacks in terms of close focusing, but it was brilliant for observation, since it provided nearly 360 degrees of vision. What this meant for Tess was that even as she ran she could see all around her without turning her head. And what she saw struck terror into her heart. For behind her, rapidly eating up the remaining ground, were a brown dog and a black one. Bran and Sceolan.

Uncle Maurice was up. He had set the dogs on them.

Tess ran as she had never run before. There was no time to think, or to plan any kind of a strategy. The chemical fear that surged through her body was like dynamic fuel. She had to expend it. She had to run.

The dogs were close behind her as she bolted across the scrubland. She was barely keeping ahead of them. Her hard little feet glanced off the bare rocks, wobbled loose ones and sent small ones flying. Her mind worked with lightning precision as she sped across the rough ground, leaping over bushes and avoiding the dangerous grikes which criss-crossed the

411

limestone like small chasms, incalculably deep. But the dogs were as fast, and as clever.

Ahead of her the other goats began to prove that they were not sheep and to separate off into pairs and small groups, all taking different routes, improving the odds. Tess, still at the back, followed on the heels of two youngsters of an age comparable with her own. They made a dart to the left, towards the woods and the crag and, without thinking, Tess stayed close, shadowing their progress. To her horror, the dogs stayed with them, too. She could hear their breath and sense their steady, sinister purpose. What was worse, she knew what it was to be a dog; how determinedly they could run, and how tirelessly.

Ahead of her the two young goats shot into the woods and disappeared. A moment later Tess was in there, as well, and close behind them. Then, quite suddenly, the other two jinked to the right and back towards the open. The movement was brilliantly designed to put the dogs off, but unfortunately it put Tess off, too. She couldn't follow fast enough and knew that she couldn't afford to hesitate, either. Alone now, the dogs still on her heels, she plunged on between the trees. And with a dreadful shock, she realised why the other two had turned back. They knew, and the dogs did, too, that this way was a dead end. It was only a matter of time before Tess's progress would be halted by the foot of the crag.

Her fear increased. She looked right and left but couldn't find the right opportunity to turn. Nor, with every nerve focused on flight, could she muster the presence of mind to Switch. They were going so fast that they were already approaching the cliff, and for a few awful moments it seemed to Tess that all her worries had been for nothing, since she wasn't going to make it as far as her birthday. As the grey rock-face began to show itself between the trees, the dogs moved out to flank her on either side, prepared for any swerve she might take in either direction.

There was only one choice left open to Tess. She would have to stand and fight. She had no idea what the odds would be, since she was young and her short horns had seen no action. But she was determined that the dogs wouldn't see the end of her without some fairly tough resistance. All at once the rock was rising sheer before her, and she was skidding to a halt in a flurry of moss and leaf mould when she heard an unexpected sound behind her; a savage snarl followed by an indignant yelp.

Tess spun round to see what was happening. To her amazement there were now three dogs instead of two. The newcomer was not a sheepdog like Bran and Sceolan but belonged to a far older breed. It was an Irish wolfhound; grey as the limestone, skinny and muscular as the goats. It was on the offensive; hackles raised, snapping and snarling at the astonished sheepdogs.

There was no competition. Bran was too old to put up a good fight and Sceolan was too young. As well as that, they were away from their own territory and on unfamiliar ground. They did their best to maintain their dignity, but backed down nonetheless and were soon trotting through the woods the way they had come.

The wolfhound watched them go, then turned back towards the place where Tess was standing. And, as it regarded her quietly with its brown eyes, she realised that she had made a terrible mistake. The hound had rescued her, or at least given her a reprieve, but it had not been done out of gallantry.

The look in those eyes was keen and hungry. This was not a well-fed farm dog out for a bit of sport but a lean, mean hunter, looking for a meal. Tess might be out of the frying pan, but she had jumped straight into the fire.

But she had, at least, that moment to act, and she did. The instant before the hound sprang she Switched into a blackbird and rose with a terrified chattering up through the branches and into the clear sky beyond. Once there she Switched again, and with sharp kestrel eyes she watched as the thin hound sloped off among the trees. As she hovered, still watching, her ears began to pick up a sound in the background that meant something. She was still shaken, and it was a moment or two before she could allow herself to let go of the fear of the chase and concentrate on the information. But the instant she did, a new shock went through her bloodstream. The sound was the hysterical yipping of a dog that had cornered its prey. Bran and Sceolan had found another victim.

CHAPTER SIX

Still in the form of a kestrel, Tess climbed the skies until she could get a clear view of the surrounding wasteland. She did not have to rise very high in order to see where the noise of the dogs was coming from. For a moment she hovered, taking in the scene. The old nanny goat, the one who had first approached her near the farm wall, was facing Bran and Sceolan, who, despite having run down their quarry, weren't about to tangle with those well-practised horns. What Tess couldn't understand, though, was why the old goat had chosen that spot to make her stand. The ground there was wide open, and there was no way the dogs could have cornered her. It didn't make sense.

Then she saw. The goat's kid, one of the smallest of them all, had fallen into a deep grike and was trapped there, suspended between the sheer walls. And at the same time that she saw him, Tess's sharp hawk-eyes saw something else. Neither the goat nor her kid were in any immediate danger from the dogs, but Tess was not the only person to have heard the frantic barks. Uncle Maurice had heard them too, and was crossing the fields with a swift stride. Over his left arm, open at the breach, was his shotgun.

Tess began to act without stopping to think. Somehow, she had to get there before him. In the blink of an eye she had flown to the edge of the woods, then she folded her wings and stooped, dropping like a stone towards the rocky ground below. The fall was breathtaking, a kind of death-dive, and if Tess hadn't learnt to trust the instincts of her animal forms she would have been terrified. But the bird's senses were more accurate than any computerised landing system and, at the last possible moment, she opened her wings and broke the fall. Ducking sideways, she swept into the shadowy edge of the trees before landing and Switching, all in one motion.

Then she was running, as fast as she dared on the dangerous going. She was glad of her trainers. At home in Dublin she had a pair of fashion shoes with huge, chunky heels, but as she sped across the rocks she promised herself she would never, ever wear them again. You never knew when you might need to run; to save your own life or someone else's.

She glanced towards the farmhouse as she went. As far as she could make out, she was roughly the same distance from the goats as Uncle Maurice was, but she was travelling faster and would almost certainly get there first. He lifted a hand and waved at her, calling out something that she didn't hear but could guess. She looked away, pretending that she hadn't seen him, and raced on. Out of the corner of her eye she could see that he was increasing his pace, and before long he was across the boundary wall and moving rapidly over the rough ground.

Tess ran all the harder. Now she could no longer avoid hearing her Uncle's shouts.

'Tess! Stay away now, do you hear? Leave them alone!'

She was nearly there. Sceolan ran up to greet her, proud of himself, but Bran stayed where she was, holding the old goat, who stood with her horns down like drawn swords.

'Tess!' It was more of a scream than a shout, and now Uncle Maurice was running, scrambling over the flaking and wobbling rocks towards her and the stranded goats. But Tess was there first. Her heart was pounding, because she was running and because she was afraid. She was flouting Uncle Maurice, she knew, but there was nothing else she could do. If she obeyed him, stood by and watched while he shot the goat and her kid, she would never be able to live with herself.

Bran backed off and the old nanny ran a few steps when Tess arrived on the spot. She ignored them both and went for the trapped kid. As she knelt and grabbed it by the scruff of the neck it let out a harrowing bawl of terror, but a moment later it was free and speeding off across the rocks with its mother close at its heels. A few yards away, Uncle Maurice came to a halt. He raised the gun, but Bran and Sceolan were both in his line of fire, bounding after the goats.

Tess called them off and by the time they returned, willingly enough after their long ordeal, the goats were at a safe distance. Uncle Maurice lowered the gun and stared at Tess in impotent fury. Then he shook his head angrily, turned on his heel and marched off the way he had come. Apologetically, the dogs took leave of Tess and followed him.

She could understand why Uncle Maurice hated the goats. They knocked down his walls and stole the grass he needed for the sheep when grass was at its scarcest. She knew, as well, how she must appear to him; an interfering townee full of sentimental misconceptions about country life. She watched as he made his way home, the dogs at his heels.

They were going back to their everyday lives. So were the goat and her kid, who were already far away, two dots on the grey landscape. Everyone had a place in the scheme of things. They knew what they were and they accepted it and got on with it.

But not Tess. She was not of either world; the animal or the human. With a heavy heart, she sat down on a slab of limestone and waited for the trembling in her limbs to subside. Her birthday loomed, more like a funeral than a celebration, an end instead of a beginning. She didn't know who she was or who she wanted to be. When she tried to think of her life stretching ahead of her, nothing came. There was no picture, no purpose. Nothing fitted. Like a reflection of her dark thoughts, the raven flew over again.

Tess stayed out for as long as she could, delaying the time when she would have to go back to the farm and face the music. She would have liked to have spent more time as a goat, but the sour taste of the morning's experience stayed with her and she felt too downhearted to do anything adventurous. She spent an hour or two exploring the bottomless grikes from the thrilling perspective of a mouse, but eventually hunger drove her homewards.

It was nearly mid-day. She found Aunt Deirdre and Orla podding a bucket of peas.

'Can I help?' she asked.

Orla avoided her eye and said nothing.

'Have you had breakfast yet?' said Aunt Deirdre. She didn't sound very friendly, either, and Tess realised that her uncle had probably given them all a report of her rebellious behaviour.

'Not yet,' she answered.

'You'd better get yourself something,' said Aunt Deirdre, but she still didn't look up from what she was doing.

Feeling more like an outcast than ever, Tess made tea and toast to the rhythmical snap and rattle of the peas.

'Will you have a cup?' she asked the others.

'I don't mind,' said Aunt Deirdre, and at last Orla looked up and nodded and then, before she looked away again, she winked. Tess felt better, knowing that she had at least one ally in the house.

Soon afterwards, Uncle Maurice and the boys came back with a trailer-load of turf for the range. Tess went out to help with the unloading, but her uncle walked straight past her as though she wasn't there. Behind him, Brian shrugged and grimaced and, in the pick-up, Colm shrugged and grimaced in imitation.

Tess went back indoors. She had intended to explain about Kevin coming and to make much of his character and his abilities, but there was no point in trying to do that now. She was in Uncle Maurice's bad books and there seemed, for the moment at least, to be no way out of them.

So, instead, she got out of the way and lay on her bed and read a book. Before long, Orla joined her.

'I'm sorry about this morning,' said Tess. 'I know it was mean. The truth is, I just wanted to be on my own.'

Orla nodded, suggesting a forgiveness that Tess didn't feel she deserved. 'I saw what you did,' she said.

A chill ran down Tess's spine; the ever-present fear of discovery.

'What did you see?' she asked.

'With the goat and the kid,' said Orla. 'I was watching. Daddy gets so mad with the goats when they come anywhere near the good land. I was sure he was going to shoot them, and then I saw you come running out of the woods.'

Her eyes were glowing as she remembered the scene and Tess suddenly felt like a hero instead of a criminal.

'I was so afraid you wouldn't get there first. I was jumping up and down and shouting.'

Orla was gazing at the ceiling as she spoke, still full of the pleasure of victory. But abruptly her face changed as another memory supplanted the first. 'Daddy was very cross.'

She said no more, leaving Tess to imagine the scenes on his return to the house. For a long time they stayed quiet. Orla's breathing seemed to be worsening again, or maybe it was just that, because of the stillness, Tess was made more aware of it. From outside came the regular clatter of sods of turf being thrown into the fuel-shed. Then Orla spoke again.

'My grandmother told me that one time when her father was a young man his dog put up an enchanted hare.' She paused, perhaps to see whether or not she had Tess's attention.

'How did he know it was enchanted?' said Tess.

Orla sat up, all eagerness now to tell the story. 'He didn't at first,' she said. 'His dog caught hold of her by the heel but, good and all as the dog was, he wasn't able to keep a hold of her and she kicked free.'

Tess leant up on her elbow, aware of a strange thing that was happening to her cousin. Although her voice was as weak and breathless as ever, it seemed to have taken on a different intonation, even a different dialect. It was as though, in entering the story, Orla had moved backwards in time to another age, when stories were one of the only forms of entertainment. Lizzie's reference to ancestors flitted across the surface of Tess's consciousness, then was gone again. As Orla went on, the flow of words was smooth and seamless.

'She was wounded, though, the hare, and it was easy enough for the dog to turn her away from the woods, which is where she wanted to go. On she ran, and it seemed there was no cover in the world for her except for Josie Devitt's house.'

Orla stood up and moved to the window as she spoke. 'It's gone now, that house, but it used to stand over there.' She pointed and Tess joined her at the window. 'On that bit of grassy land there, where there's a clearing in the rock.'

Tess nodded, and Orla continued. 'Well. It happened that Josie was out and about on the land at the time, but the half-door of his house was open on account of the weather being fine for the time of the year. So up and over went the hare when she came to the house; up and over the half-door and disappeared inside. But the thing was, when my great-grandfather opened the door to let the dog in after her, there was no hare there at all, but only an old woman, and her leg all cut and bleeding.'

Orla stopped, and Tess thought she was pausing again. 'Go on,' she said. 'What happened?'

Orla shrugged. 'That's the story,' she said. 'That's all of it.'

Tess leant back, disappointed somehow.

'Do you believe it?' Orla asked.

Tess was tempted to explain that it was impossible; that she knew for a fact that no one could change their shape after the age of fifteen, but she refrained. Instead she said:

'I don't know. The old people were full of stories like that, weren't they?'

But Orla surprised her. 'I don't care,' she said. 'I believe it. It was a fairy hare and that's why I was glad you rescued the goat and her kid. They might have been fairy goats.'

'Well they weren't,' said Tess, feeling like a killjoy. 'They were just ordinary goats.'

'How do you know?' asked Orla, a hint of pique in her voice.

'Because there's no such thing as fairies, that's why. They're just old stories. From a time when people . . .'

'When people what?'

'When people were . . . less sophisticated, that's all.'

Orla was silent for a moment. Then she said, 'More stupid. That's what you mean, isn't it?'

'No. Not really,' said Tess.

But it was.

CHAPTER SEVEN

Outside, the dogs huffed and then barked in earnest, their voices trailing off around the side of the house. Tess jumped up and looked out of the window, but all she could see on that side of the house was Uncle Maurice straightening up from the turf pile and heading around to see who was there. Colm, still cradling a sod of turf, followed on behind.

'Who is it?' Orla asked.

Tess shrugged and went out to the landing, Orla close behind her. The window there was above the front door, but it was already too late. Whoever had come was directly below, now, and too close to the house to be seen.

There was a knock at the door. Tess stood at the top of the stairs and listened as Aunt Deirdre answered it. She hoped that it wouldn't be Kevin. Not yet.

But it was. Tess knew it even before he spoke, by

the length of the silence while he waited for Aunt Deirdre to say that she had been expecting him. When, instead, she said, 'Well? What can I do for you?', Tess heard him stammer into life.

'Oh . . . Oh, well . . . em . . . I was wondering . . .'

'What were you wondering?'

Tess cringed. She knew she ought to try to rescue the situation and she was on the point of going down when Uncle Maurice came around the side of the house and took over the proceedings from his wife.

'What's going on?'

There was no way, now, that Tess could help. She closed her eyes and crossed her fingers.

But Kevin was thinking on his feet. 'I was wondering,' he said, 'whether you might be having a problem with rats? There's a lot of them about this year.'

'Are you from Pestokill?' said Uncle Maurice.

'No. I work for myself.'

'Oh yeah? And whose rats have you got rid of so far?'

'Oh, loads,' said Kevin, vaguely. 'Mostly in Dublin. I thought I might be more use down the country.'

There was a silence and Tess could imagine Uncle Maurice examining Kevin, weighing him up.

'Where's your gear, then?' he asked.

'On my bike.'

There was another long silence, and Tess felt she could almost hear her uncle's mind, calculating away. She knew what the next question would be before it came.

'How much?'

Kevin didn't hesitate. He had already discussed it with Tess over the phone. 'A hundred quid. Results guaranteed.'

424

There was another silence from Uncle Maurice, but it was shorter this time.

'How long will it take?'

'Not long,' said Kevin. 'I have a special technique. If you take me on, you'll have no rats here tonight.'

'And how will I know if they're gone?' he asked.

'How do you know you've got them?'

'Hmm,' said Uncle Maurice. 'Smart, aren't you? I'll tell you what. I'll give you a chance, all right? No money up front, though. I'm not thick. But if all the rats are gone from the house and buildings by this time tomorrow, you'll have your hundred quid. How does that sound?'

'Sounds fine,' said Kevin. 'I'll start now, if that's all right with you?'

'Fine by me. What do you need?'

'Just for you to put the dogs away. I'll do the rest.'

Tess turned back to the window and watched as Kevin scrunched across the gravel to where his bike was leaning against the wall. She noticed that the white cat had appeared again and was sitting on a low branch of the apple tree beside the feed-shed.

Kevin began to rummage in a small, dingy rucksack. At the corner of the house Colm, still clutching the sod of turf, stood staring at him, open-mouthed. Kevin winked at him and pulled out the thing he had been looking for. It was a small tin whistle.

Up at the window, Tess cringed. That was going too far. If this didn't work, Kevin was going to look like a complete idiot. For a moment she was glad that she hadn't acknowledged him. Below her, Uncle Maurice said to Aunt Deirdre, 'Pure nutcase.' Beside her, Orla was staring, wide-eyed.

'Who is he?' she said. 'What is he going to do?'

'I don't know,' said Tess. But the next moment,

Kevin demonstrated. He began to play the whistle, fairly tunelessly, and at the same time he began to call.

The part of Tess's mind that was and would always be rat tuned in instantly to the powerfully projected images; images that no ordinary human mind could receive. She was reminded that before Kevin reached the age of fifteen and lost the ability to Switch, he had spent more of his time being a rat than being a human being. His mastery of their visual language was total; far better than hers, and the messages he was sending were compelling.

'Out, out!' is what he was saying. 'Men coming with poisons, gases, traps. Rats dying in this place, rats dying in pain. Usguys leaving this place, huh? Huh? All of usguys leaving.'

Colm began to dance, clumsy in his wellingtons, curly locks flopping over his eyes. A moment later, though Tess had not noticed she was gone, Orla appeared beside him and began to dance as well. Infected by their enthusiasm, Kevin started to hop and skip, and Tess was sure that his playing became better; even tuneful. But she didn't listen to it for long. Beneath its cheerful tootling the more serious communication was continuing.

'Rats waking up, quick, quick! Rats coming out into the daylight, escaping deadly danger behind, yup, yup.'

Tess could hear her aunt and uncle snickering downstairs inside the front door, but a moment later they went deadly quiet.

Because it was working. Sleepily, shaking themselves awake, the rats were beginning to emerge. They crawled out of the subterranean world beneath the farm, and appeared by ones and by twos in the yard.

426

They scrambled and slithered their way down through the walls of the house, making so much noise that for an awful moment it seemed to Tess that the house was falling down around her. They surfaced from the drains in lengthening columns until suddenly the yard was flooding with rats, all blinking in the bright daylight and making their way towards the source of the urgent message.

Orla and Colm pointed and squealed in excitement, but they seemed unafraid and didn't stop dancing. Their views on rats, however, were clearly not shared by their parents. There was a blood-curdling shriek from the hall below as Aunt Deirdre realised what was happening, and a moment later, Uncle Maurice was striding across the yard, waving his arms around and making loud shooing noises. He swept Orla up under one arm and Colm under the other and carried them over to the oil tank, where Brian was already set up, enjoying a grandstand view of the action. Colm wriggled and kicked so hard that he lost one of his precious wellingtons, but once he was parked up on the tank beside his brother and sister, he soon forgot about it.

For now Kevin had begun to move off; still playing his strident and unmusical trills, still repeating his urgent warnings in Rat, but adding now a bit of more encouraging information.

'New homes, happy rats. Green woods, rats rolling in hazelnuts, fat and healthy.'

In the shed where they were locked, Bran and Sceolan howled and scratched and rattled the door. From his perch on the apple tree the white cat watched intently as the rats flowed along the ground behind Kevin like the train of a royal robe. Now that they were fully awake they were more organised,

427

though still extremely perplexed. Kevin stopped for a moment to get his bearings, trying to remember Tess's description of the crag from their conversation on the telephone. As soon as he saw it he recognised it, and took the most direct route towards it; straight over the wall and into the first of the meadows. The rats surged over behind him like a single, slithering creature, and then they were gone, leaving the yard empty except for Colm's fallen boot.

The three children had jumped down from the tank and were heading off in pursuit when Uncle Maurice intercepted them at the wall.

'It's dangerous,' he said. 'Them rats could get nasty.'

So they clambered back up on to the tank and watched as the boy from nowhere receded towards the grey hills, dragging a strange brown carpet behind him. Not until he had disappeared beyond the furthest wall of the farm did they come down, and look around, and find to their amazement that life was exactly as it had been before he came.

Tess was in the kitchen garden, helping her aunt with some weeding when Kevin came back to collect his bike and his gear. He waved across and held out his arms in a questioning shrug.

She communicated with him in Rat so that no one else would know what she said. 'Morning, huh?'

'Morning, yup, yup,' Kevin returned. 'Tent in the trees, near the road, near the hump-backed bridge. Us two drinking tea together.'

Aunt Deirdre was looking at Tess in a quizzical manner.

'That boy's back,' said Tess.

'So I see,' said her aunt.

428

They both looked across at him again and, without her aunt seeing, Tess winked.

'Maybe it was something he had on him in the way of a smell or some such,' said Uncle Maurice over dinner that evening. Since Kevin's visit he had been in great humour, and if he remembered the incident with the wild goats, he did not mention it.

'I think it was that whistle,' said Aunt Deirdre. 'You know the way there are some notes only dogs can hear. Maybe it's the same with rats.'

'Could be, I suppose,' said Uncle Maurice. 'Where is he from, would you say? Do you think he's a traveller?'

Aunt Deirdre had no opinion and the conversation ended. Tess looked around at her cousins. Beside her, Colm was putting his dinner away with no fuss or mess, taking the business of eating extremely seriously, as usual. Opposite, Brian was engaged in his daily ritual of hide-the-vegetables; a wasted effort, since soon his mother would notice and begin the daily ritual of eat-the-vegetables. Beside him Orla, the special child, the sickly one, could get away with eating or not eating, whatever she chose. What she was doing with her food, however, was of no interest to Tess. Orla's face was lit up with an inner light; she wore an expression of almost saintly bliss. Tess looked away before her cousin could catch her eye. She understood Orla's feelings but they made her uncomfortable nonetheless. For Orla, without doubt, saw Kevin's removal of the rats as a demonstration of magic; further proof that there was truth in fairy tales. And Tess had no way of letting her know the plain and simple truth.

CHAPTER EIGHT

That night, Tess took on rat form again and slid down through the walls of the house as she had done before. But unlike the previous night, the house was empty and silent. In the sitting-room a crumpled crisp packet smelt of heaven to her rat nose, but no one was there trying to get inside it. A few peanuts, dropped during the midnight movie, lay on the carpet beside the couch, untouched.

The kitchen was the same; empty and quiet. A new bar of soap sat beside the washing-up liquid on the draining board. Beneath the table half a dozen small cubes of cheese lay scattered on the floor, arousing a ferocious hunger in Tess's rat body and a strong sense of suspicion in her mind. There was something just a bit too neat about those blocks, as though they had been dropped there on purpose. What better test, after all, if her aunt and uncle wanted to find out whether or not there were any rats still around? So

Tess denied her hunger and backed off, slipping underneath the sink and down through the floor into the drains. A moment later she was outside and testing the night air with her nose and her ears and her whiskers.

There was no sign of the cat, and the dogs were safely locked away. Tess scuttled along the wall of the house, then crossed the moonlit yard to the buildings. In the feed-shed, the smell of the dairy nuts threatened to unhinge her. It was almost more than she could do to deny herself, and she might have Switched to avoid the temptation if she hadn't encountered something unexpected. In the corner of the shed, close to the feed-bins, a single rat was snuffling around short-sightedly. Tess recognised him immediately as the old, one-toothed lad she had seen in the sitting-room the night before, having trouble with the fruit gums. Clearly he had missed Kevin's call; maybe because he was old and image-blind, maybe because his sleep was just too deep.

When he caught sight of Tess, the old rat jumped, then ran forward delightedly to greet her.

'Every place empty, huh?' he said. 'House empty, yard empty, heaps of food and no one eating it.'

'Yup, yup,' said Tess. 'Rats gone, rats in new home in the woods.'

The old gentleman twitched his whiskers and sniffed the air.

'Rats gone, huh? Us two all alone, huh?'

Tess's heart lurched. She didn't know how to answer. For it wouldn't be the two of them staying behind but just him, abandoned and bewildered, completely alone for what remained of his life. It was too sad to think about, so instead Tess got busy, collecting the broken nuts that the broom had missed

431

that morning and heaping them in a dark corner where her old friend could eat in peace. It was almost more than her rat mind could bear, to gather food and not permit herself to eat it, but it was vitally important that the old gent didn't go chewing at bags or leaving any other sign that he had been there. She had to pull out all the stops.

When at last she had gathered all she could, she left her friend chewing away in quiet contentment, and slipped out under the door into the yard. Back in the house she became human again and, still in the grip of rat hunger, did a thorough job of raiding the fridge.

Tess dreamt the dream again; the one in which Kevin was a rat. She woke in terror and sat up in bed. It was already light and the birds were singing their loudest and most delighted songs, which they only did on bright, clear days. Tess sat up and looked out of the window, trying to shake off the fear which still gripped her heart. Everything out there was normal and safe. And she had a plan of some sort; some reason to get up.

When she remembered, enthusiasm rushed in and washed away the sense of dread. She had arranged to meet Kevin. Wasting no time, she slipped out of bed and gathered her clothes. It seemed that Orla really was asleep. But as Tess looked down at her in the bed, she saw something that brought the fear straight back. On top of the covers and wedged against the wall was a book which, presumably, Orla had been reading the night before. The title was *The Old Gods: Story or History?* Beneath the title was a picture of a man, or something like a man, with antlers on his head. Tess turned away, but curiosity compelled her to turn back. The picture was just like the shadowy form that she had seen drifting through the woods the first time she had been there. She had assumed that she was imagining things, but if so, it was clear that she was not the only person who had imagined the same image. Why? Was it possible that such a being really did exist? With a shudder Tess tore her eyes away from it and crept out of the room.

She chose the kestrel again to find Kevin. The last time, she had been in a rush to see what Bran and Sceolan were up to, but now she could afford to explore the sensations of flight and the nature of the bird. Kevin had told her that another Switcher he had known had chosen a hawk as her permanent form when she reached fifteen. As she climbed into the heights Tess could easily understand why. The hawk was strong and clear-sighted. Tess always found the basic nature of animals and birds much simpler and less muddled than the complicated business of being human, but the hawk, above all others, had a purity of essence that was thrilling. The bird knew neither doubt nor hesitation; neither empathy nor remorse. Its eyes were designed for daylight but its heart belonged to the moon. Tess relished its sharp simplicity of being, and the knowledge that she might never experience it again made the sensations all the keener.

She could see the ground beneath her in the minutest detail. It wasn't at all like using binoculars; her sight didn't magnify the ground and make it seem nearer than it was. She just saw. She saw blades of grass, distant and tiny, bending beneath the weight of a stag beetle. She saw a bird tugging a worm from beneath a stone. She saw a matchbox toy, lost by some child many years ago and rusted now, barely visible among the grasses that had grown up over it.

Missing nothing, she climbed higher, widening her field of vision, scanning the landscape. She flew east and west, hovering occasionally to stabilise her vision, covering two or three square miles before the smell of smoke reached her and narrowed the search area. Eventually she found what she was looking for. Alerted by movement, she banked and overflew a stand of ash trees beside the narrow little bridge that Kevin had mentioned. Through the trees she could see the stretched dome of the tent and the resting spokes of the bicycle wheels. Delighted with herself, she dropped out of the sky, dodging through the branches at breakneck speed and coming to a hovering halt in the air, right in front of Kevin's nose.

Kevin jumped and took a step backwards, then realised who it was. He grinned and made a lunge at the bird, but she dodged out of his way and then Switched, judging the transition so perfectly that her feet met the ground as lightly as a feather.

'I keep forgetting you can do that,' said Kevin. 'Not fair.'

'Not for much longer, though,' said Tess.

Kevin nodded. 'Any plans?' he asked.

'No,' said Tess. 'It's driving me mad. What would you be if you had the decision ahead of you again?'

Kevin thought about it for a moment or two, then said, 'A rat. I always felt . . . I don't know . . . cheated, somehow. Because of being forced into a decision when it was time for me to choose. I'm sure that if I'd had a chance to think I would have decided on a rat.'

His words gave Tess an uncomfortable reminder

of her dream, but she said nothing and Kevin went on, 'Maybe it doesn't make that much difference, in the end. I mean, the best thing was being able to Switch. Nothing could be as good as that, really, could it?'

Tess sighed. 'It's like having everything, isn't it?' she said. 'I can't stand the idea of losing it.'

Kevin had a neat little campfire going in front of his tent, carefully confined inside a ring of stones. On top of it a billy of water was coming to the boil.

'Tea?' he asked.

Tess sat down on a stone. As though it saw her, the smoke changed direction and drifted into her face. She waved her hands at it and waited. Sure enough, it soon returned to its previous course.

'Anyway,' said Kevin, dropping a fistful of tea leaves into the billy, 'what happened? How come you didn't warn them that I was coming?'

Tess groaned and related the story of Uncle Maurice and the wild goats. As she told it Kevin nodded, understanding and approving in a way that no one else ever did or could. Their friendship warmed her heart as it so often had in the past. As time went on it became more valuable, not less, no matter how different their lives appeared to be.

In the silence that followed the end of Tess's account, Kevin rooted around in his rucksack and found another cup. Tess watched him. He was still as tough and as scruffy as the town rats which had been his main companions during his Switcher days. He would never fit into normal human society, not in a million years. In a sudden, uninvited leap of imagination, Tess saw him as an old tramp, a bag man rummaging around on the edges of society; a human rat, unloved and unwanted. She had seen

435

people like that, adrift on the city streets. They existed without the anchors that kept most people stable: family or education or job. Tess wondered whether their minds drifted in the same way, untethered, unfocussed, unaware of time.

'Maybe it's best to leave it that way,' said Kevin.

Tess came back to reality with a jolt. 'What?'

'No need to tell them now that you know me, is there?'

'No,' said Tess. 'In fact it would be a bit awkward, since I didn't say anything yesterday.'

Kevin used a grimy T-shirt to protect his fingers from the heat of the billy as he poured the tea into two battered enamel mugs.

'Trouble is, though,' Tess went on, 'I won't be able to invite you to my birthday party.'

'Are you having one?'

Tess shrugged. Kevin spooned milk powder into the cups. 'We can have one,' he said. 'Just you and me. A midnight one.'

'That would be good,' said Tess. 'That would make everything easier.'

'It's a date, then,' said Kevin, then blushed. 'I don't mean that kind of a date. I mean . . .'

Tess laughed, but she could feel herself colouring as well. For a moment each of them struggled separately, trying to think of something normal to say. Tess got there first.

'What do the rats think of the woods?' she asked.

Kevin burst out laughing. 'They were very funny,' he said. 'They were like a coach-load of middle-aged tourists who have been brought to the wrong hotel.' He lapsed into fluent Rat as he continued. 'Feedshed, huh, huh? Soap? Cupboards?'

Tess laughed.

436

'Usguys wet and cold,' Kevin went on. 'Usguys breaking our teeth on hazelnuts!'

If anyone had been watching through the trees they would have thought the two friends were quite mad, sitting in silence and laughing at nothing at all. But they understood each other perfectly.

'Blackberries sour! Yeuch! Hard work hunting, hard work making new nests!'

Tess could visualise them; fat pampered house rats, amazed at the lives their forerunners led, returning with the utmost reluctance to their wild roots.

'Will they stay, do you think?' she asked, returning to human speech.

Kevin nodded confidently. 'For a few generations at least. I painted a ferocious picture of Pestokill. They'll be telling their children and grandchildren about it. Like the bogeyman.'

Tess finished her tea but declined the breakfast that Kevin offered, not because the bread was squashed and the butter was full of grit but because she felt it would be better politics to make an appearance at the house.

'See you later,' she said.

Kevin was trying to cut the bread with a blunt knife, but he looked up when, a minute later, Tess was still standing there, as if undecided.

'You OK?' he asked.

Tess nodded. 'I was just wondering,' she said.

'Wondering what?'

'Did you see anything in the woods? Anything strange?'

'Not exactly. But there was a funny feeling about the place. I didn't really want to go in. Just left the rats at the edge like you suggested. Why?'

Tess shook her head. 'Just wondered.'

437

'Did you?' Kevin asked.

'I'm not sure,' she said. 'It was probably just my imagination. Maybe we could go there together some time?'

'All right by me,' said Kevin.

'It's a date, then,' said Tess.

Then, before Kevin could question her more closely, she Switched into a hawk again and sprang away into the sky.

CHAPTER NINE

Uncle Maurice was in much better humour that morning. He was so cheerful, in fact, that Tess was suspicious. Something had to be wrong.

She helped him, all the same, as he finished the milking.

'You're up early,' he said. 'Do you always get up so early? At home, I mean?'

'Not usually,' said Tess, pulling open the sliding door of the milking parlour to let the last of the cows go out. 'Specially not at weekends. It's different here, somehow.'

'It is,' said Uncle Maurice. 'The light is different. It comes earlier in the country than it does in the town.'

It didn't, but Tess knew what he meant. There was a clarity about the dawn and an urgency in it. Maybe it was the racket that the birds made, or the fact that no buildings or exhaust fumes obscured the sun.

Maybe it was none of those things, but Tess's own urgency; her knowledge that time was running out.

Her uncle's voice disturbed her thoughts. 'What do you make of that boy, then?'

'Which boy?'

'The lad that took the rats away. Did you see that?'

'I did. It was amazing, wasn't it?'

'Amazing is right,' said Uncle Maurice. 'Would you say he could do it again? In another place, like?'

'I don't see why not,' said Tess.

'No. I don't either.' He took the pipe out of the creamery tank and connected the milking system up to the tap to be cleaned out. He was whistling as he worked, uncharacteristically happy. There was definitely something wrong.

After breakfast, Tess and Brian shared the washing-up. Orla sat in the corner of the kitchen wheezing, and reading the book with the deer-man on the cover.

'Did you ever read this, Tess?' she asked.

Tess shook her head. 'We did a lot of that stuff in primary school,' she said. 'I've forgotten most of it now.'

'You should read it,' said Orla. 'It's all about the *Tuatha de Danaan*.'

The mention of the name of the old gods of Ireland sent one of those electric feelings up Tess's spine, but before she could analyse it she was distracted by an excited yell from Colm outside. Brian ran to the front door and, when he didn't come back, Tess and Orla followed.

The source of Colm's excitement was Kevin, who was just arriving at the yard gate on his bicycle. Colm was there before him and had climbed up to the top bar when Uncle Maurice caught up and gathered him into his arms. It seemed that everyone was converging on Kevin.

'Come in, come in,' said Uncle Maurice, setting Colm down and opening the gate. Again his cheerful mood set alarm bells ringing in Tess's mind.

'Come in till we get a cup of tea,' he went on, leading the way into the house. Everyone followed except for the ever dutiful Brian, who was left with the job of closing the heavy gate.

Aunt Deirdre had come in from the garden and the kettle was already on. Kevin sat down at the table or, more accurately, he slumped. Tess was so accustomed to seeing him that she hadn't noticed the changes in his body, but all of a sudden they had become obvious. He was like a bag of bones, big bones, all loosely connected and not very well coordinated. His feet were enormous and his hands were long, with knuckles everywhere. He seemed acutely embarrassed by this strange body but it would, Tess realised, soon begin to make more sense. The hollows would flesh out and the shambling slackness would turn to smooth strength. Kevin was growing out of being a boy and would soon be a man.

The dawning truth was a shock to Tess. Kevin shifted uncomfortably and she realised that, while the rest of the family had been bustling about getting comfortable, she had been staring at him. She turned away quickly and helped her aunt to get out cups and biscuits. Uncle Maurice was settling himself into a chair opposite Kevin. As Tess poured milk into a jug and set it down on the table he began to speak.

'Have you done much of it, then? This rat clearance?'

Kevin tapped his fingers on the table and watched them. 'Not so much, really,' he said.

'You wouldn't be well known, then? Around the place?'

'No. I wouldn't be, I suppose.'

Tess set out the cups. She didn't like the way the conversation was going. Uncle Maurice nodded, absorbing what Kevin had said. In the brief silence, Colm climbed on to a chair beside Kevin and reached across the table for the best biscuit; the pink wafer.

'Colm!' said his mother, in a warning tone.

But if Colm heard her, he made no response. He continued with what he was doing and, to everyone's surprise, handed the special biscuit to Kevin. His face was as pink as the biscuit, glowing with shy charm. When Kevin shook his head his face clouded over with disappointment.

'He wants you to have it,' said Brian. 'He'll be disappointed if you don't.'

Kevin took the biscuit and ate it. Uncle Maurice began again.

'Where do you live, then?'

'Dublin,' said Kevin.

'On holiday down here, are you?'

'Sort of,' said Kevin. Tess made a point of not looking at him, but from the corner of her eye she could see that he was acutely embarrassed by the continued attention of the children. Colm was standing on the chair and gazing into his face with undisguised adoration. At a slightly more respectful distance, Orla and Brian were also staring with admiring expressions. It was clear that, as far as the younger members of the family were concerned, they were entertaining royalty. But Uncle Maurice was not of the same opinion.

'Are your mother and father on holiday with you?' he asked.

It was one question too many. Kevin stood up. 'If you don't mind,' he said, 'I'll take my money and get on my way.'

'Ah, now,' said Uncle Maurice, standing up as well. 'No need to be hasty. I didn't mean to pry. Sure, what does it matter, anyway?'

Aunt Deirdre spoke for the first time. 'Have your tea, now. 'Tis made and all.'

She poured it out and Kevin sat down again, reluctantly. Colm handed him another biscuit, a jam one. The silence while he ate it threatened to be a long one, and Tess broke it before it became too awkward.

'You have great weather, anyway. For your holiday.'

'I have,' said Kevin.

'He has, he has,' said Uncle Maurice and Aunt Deirdre together.

The silence fell again and Uncle Maurice finally got round to saying what was on his mind. 'No,' he began. 'It's only . . . Just . . . I thought you could make a great business out of that rat-catching game.'

'I could, I suppose,' said Kevin.

'If you had the right backing, that is. The right kind of manager.'

Tess turned away to hide the expression of disgust on her face. So that was what he was up to.

'I'm not sure,' Kevin began, but Uncle Maurice had launched his campaign and could no longer stem his excitement.

'No, c'mere, listen,' he said. 'I could get the world of business for you, the world of it. There are loads of farmers and houses in towns and all, and they have the same problem. Sure, a cure for rats is worth a fortune. A fortune!'

Tess looked around the room. Kevin was dumbstruck and she could only imagine what was going through his mind. From the expression on Aunt Deirdre's face it was clear that she hadn't been let in on the plan and was as surprised as everyone else. Once more Kevin opened his mouth to say something, but Uncle Maurice was still not finished.

'Think of it, lad,' he said. 'If you can do a farm and buildings this size, what's to stop you doing a whole village or even a small town? Can you imagine it? We could get TV people there and radio. We could set up interviews and all . . .'

Kevin stood up, his tea untouched.

'Thanks for your concern,' he said. 'It's a great idea but I'm afraid I have no interest in it.'

Uncle Maurice shut his mouth and the brightness left his features with frightening speed. Anxiety, almost visible, crept over the other members of his family.

'So if you'll just pay me what we agreed,' Kevin went on, 'I won't take up any more of your time.'

There was a sinister pause, then Uncle Maurice said, 'What was it we agreed, exactly?'

'One hundred pounds,' said Kevin.

'One hundred pounds,' Uncle Maurice repeated. 'If you got rid of all the rats.'

'That's right,' said Kevin.

There was menace in Uncle Maurice's voice as he replied. 'But you didn't, did you?'

Silence dropped again. The faces of the children showed shocked disappointment, but Kevin was not going to be fobbed off without a fight. 'What makes you say that?' he asked.

'Just this,' said Uncle Maurice. He stood up and went over to a plastic bag which lay inside the back door. 'Something the dogs caught this morning.' He reached into the bag and pulled out the carcass of a rat. A jolt of pain caught Tess off guard.

'That . . .' she began, but stopped herself while she still could. What she had started to say was that she recognised the carcass. It was the old rat, the one who had been left behind.

The others were still looking at her expectantly, even Kevin.

'That's what?' said Uncle Maurice.

In the nick of time it came to her. 'That's been dead for a couple of days,' she said. 'I saw it round behind the milking parlour yesterday.'

Kevin shut his eyes in relief and took a deep breath.

'Oh, is that right?' said Uncle Maurice. 'Well, you'd know, I suppose.'

Tess said nothing and the only sound was the high-pitched drone of Orla's constricted breath. Uncle Maurice followed up his advantage.

'I mean,' he said, 'you'd know the difference, wouldn't you, Miss Cleverclogs, between this dead rat and any other dead rat.'

He looked around triumphantly, as though expecting applause. But he hadn't won, yet.

'I think I would,' said Tess. 'I think that rat has only one top tooth at the front.'

Uncle Maurice's mouth dropped open in astonishment. But Brian was already at his side and staring into the slack mouth of the dead rat. Rapidly, Uncle Maurice dropped it back into the plastic bag, but he wasn't quick enough.

'Yep,' said Brian. 'She's right. Only one front tooth. How did you know that, Tess?'

Colm had understood little of the preceding conversation, but no nuance of mood or atmosphere ever escaped him. He knew now that his hero had been

445

vindicated and he was delighted. An affectionate soul at the best of times, he flung his arms around Kevin's neck and hugged him tight.

But it was not a wise move, given the circumstances, and not only because of the embarrassment it caused Kevin. Uncle Maurice was a tyrant, without doubt, but he loved his children with a fierce passion. To see Colm's affection so freely given to his adversary was more than he could stand.

'Get out,' he said, his voice low, his face dangerously dark.

Kevin gently disengaged himself from Colm's embrace. As she watched, Tess saw the best of Kevin's rat nature emerge; his courage and, above all, his sense of justice.

'I'll leave when I've been paid,' he said.

'You'll leave right now,' said Uncle Maurice. 'Right this minute. And if I see you around here again I'll call the police.'

'The police? On what charge?'

'Loitering. Harassment. Whatever I like. Do you think they'll believe you for one minute? That you played on a tin whistle and the rats followed you out of my yard? They'll lock you up, more like it.'

Kevin stared at him in silent anger and Tess saw that he was defeated. Everyone knew that he was right, but that against Uncle Maurice's word he hadn't a leg to stand on. For a long moment, time seemed frozen in the room. Then Kevin strode to the door and was gone.

'Good riddance,' said Uncle Maurice, throwing the dead rat in its plastic bag out after him. But everyone knew that the matter was not closed, and the silence which still hung in the room was full of gloom and foreboding.

446

CHAPTER TEN

If Tess thought that the bottom had fallen out of her world, she was wrong. The worst was still to come. The dust had barely settled behind Kevin's bicycle on the drive when a Mercedes car pulled up and two men in expensive suits got out.

Uncle Maurice threw the door open wide and went out to meet them, then preceded them into the kitchen where Aunt Deirdre, yet again, put on the kettle.

'Deirdre, this is Mr Keating from Keating Development.'

'Pleased to meet you,' said Mr Keating. 'But don't make any tea for us.' He gestured to the other man and turned back to Uncle Maurice as he spoke.

'This is Peter Mahon, the surveyor I was telling you about. We've come to walk the boundaries of that land, if it suits you.'

Tess had no interest in what was happening and

447

was about to slip out when the reaction of her cousins changed her mind.

'Can we come, Daddy?' said Orla.

'Please?' said Brian.

'Sure, we're only walking around the land,' said Uncle Maurice.

'But we love the crag,' said Orla. 'We won't get in your way. Honestly.'

'The crag?' said Tess.

But no one heard her. Uncle Maurice had given his permission, and the children were cheering and racing off to get their boots. Tess followed them into the hall.

'Did you say the crag?' she asked.

Orla nodded.

'You mean the land up there?' Tess pointed in the direction of the mountain, though all that could be seen was the wall of the kitchen.

'Yes,' said Brian. 'We're going to play around up there while they walk the boundaries.'

'But,' said Tess. 'Wait a minute. You mean that's the land that your dad was talking about?'

Orla nodded, a little sadly. 'Want to come?' she asked.

Tess didn't answer the question. She was still finding it difficult to believe what she was hearing. 'You're telling me your dad owns that wild land up there under the mountain. And he's selling it?'

Brian nodded. 'There's no point in trying to make him change his mind,' he said. 'He hates the place. He's been trying to sell it since he inherited the farm. He says he'll take us all on holiday with the money.'

Tess thought back to her experiences of the place. Despite her fear of it, the thought of those wild and beautiful woods being bulldozed and turned into a holiday village filled her with horror.

'But all the wild creatures who live there . . .' she began, then stopped, remembering the rats and the promises that Kevin had made to them about their new home. Her cousins were staring at her, waiting for her to finish. When she said no more, Brian said, 'Come with us, Tess. Please.'

Tess climbed into the back of the pick-up with the others, and they set out along the much longer road route to the crag. Behind them the developer and the surveyor followed in their smart, black car. From the mood of her cousins, Tess couldn't be sure whether it was a tragic occasion or a joyful one. It seemed to be both; their excitement at going to the crag counterbalancing their sorrow at having to part with it. Orla was still wheezing slightly but her cheeks, for a change, had a bit of colour. Little Colm spent the whole journey jumping around. Occasionally his red wellies missed their aim on the metal floor and landed on someone's toe, but no amount of complaining could persuade him to sit down.

Tess craned her neck and looked out through the front windscreen, hoping to catch a glimpse of Kevin, but there was no sign of him. She tried to imagine how he must be feeling; how full of anger and bitterness, and she wished that she had decided to go and look for him instead of coming on this family outing. Apart from the irritation of her cousins' manic mood, she was wasting precious Switching time. Like a dark cloak her worries began to close in again and she concentrated on the road ahead.

They were just turning down the stony track that led from the back road to the land around the crag.

Behind them the developer followed a bit more slowly, mindful of his suspension. On either side of the track tall hedges of hazel grew up, obscuring the view of the surrounding wilderness and creating a closed-in, tunnel-like effect. The bumpy ride meant that Colm's balance went haywire, but he still couldn't be persuaded to sit still and he ended up pitching wildly from one lap to the next. By the time they finally came to a halt, Tess was suffering from a combination of cabin fever, claustrophobia and bruising. She couldn't wait to get out.

But after the noisy ride, the atmosphere of the crag was uncannily silent. It was a silence that seemed to demand respect, and there was no one in the party who was not sensitive enough to become quiet in response. It was almost as though someone or something was present in their midst, and it made Tess uncomfortable. She looked around at the other members of the party. Her cousins looked thrilled, their eyes bright with excitement. The businessmen looked bewildered, as though they had expected something entirely different. But it was Uncle Maurice's reaction that made a shiver run down Tess's spine. He was standing beside the pick-up, still holding on to the handle of the door as though he wanted to be ready to get back into it in a hurry. The apprehension on his face was almost painful until he noticed Tess looking at him and, with a visible effort, he disguised it.

What was he doing? Did he know about the strange things in the woods as well? If he did, how could he allow his children to come there, and how could he sell the place?

'Right so,' he said, briskly. 'Where do you want to start?'

While the surveyor sorted out his maps and got his bearings, Orla led her brothers off across the rocks.

'Not too far, now, you hear?' said their father.

'OK,' said Orla. 'Come on, Tess.'

Reluctantly, Tess followed.

The place where the track ended and the cars were parked was to the far left of the crag. The mountain rose away less steeply there and the woods were just beginning like the point of a triangle. Orla led the way across the rocks, keeping the crag and the deepening woods to her left. Tess was relieved about that. Although her cousins clearly knew the place better than she did, she couldn't help feeling responsible for them since she was the eldest.

They hadn't gone far when Tess spotted the raven. It was circling above the adults, as though it was checking out what they were doing there, and as she watched, it changed tack and drifted above her, turning its head to look down with its sharp black eye. She looked away only to find, to her amazement, that all three of her cousins were waving cheerfully at the menacing bird.

'What are you doing?' she asked. 'Are you mad?'

But Brian winked, and Orla put her finger to her lips and said, 'Shh.'

To their right, Uncle Maurice and the businessmen were following the boundary wall, which led them away from the children at a wide angle. Still Orla continued along the bare rocks beside the woods. By the time she came to a stop, her father and his companions were three hundred yards away across open country.

Orla changed direction and walked towards the woods. Tess and the others followed. At the ragged tree-line they stopped and looked into the green shadows. Tess felt the familiar ambivalence; the magical attraction overshadowed by fear. Bird wings fluttered loudly among the branches. Orla turned to her and smiled delightedly. If she felt even the slightest anxiety she did not show it, and nor did her brothers. Once again, Tess found herself wondering if her experiences of the place owed more to an over-active imagination than to reality.

Colm led the way in among the trees and Orla and Brian followed. Tess was about to take her first step when she saw, or thought she saw, a vague figure standing in the shadows.

'Wait!' she hissed. The others stopped. She could just make out, far away within the dappled green interior, a figure just that bit too tall to be human. His face was turned towards the newcomers, but he seemed to be made not of flesh but of shadow and light. Tess strained her eyes, trying to get a better view. Was it a trick of the leaf-filtered sunlight, or was there a pair of antlers growing from the figure's head? As she watched he lifted a translucent hand and beckoned.

A cry pressed at Tess's throat but she held it back.

'There! Do you see?' she said to the others. But to her horror they were already moving, running with surprising agility over the mossy rocks and among the trees, straight towards the terrifying figure.

'Stop!' she shouted. 'Wait! Don't you see him?'

Briefly, Orla halted and turned back. 'Of course we do!' she called. 'Come on!'

Above their heads a brilliant light suddenly shone out from the level of the deer-man's eyes, blinding Tess so that she lost her bearings and had to hold on to a tree. The sensation was so disorientating that she wondered whether it was really happening or whether she was suffering from some sort of seizure; a migraine perhaps, or an epileptic fit. By the time her vision cleared, all she could see were branches and occasional flashes of bright, dazzling sunlight between them. There was no figure among the trees. There were no children, either. The woods appeared to be empty.

'Orla?' she called. 'Orla? Brian?'

There was no answer. Abruptly Tess's nerve failed. She turned and, despite the rough going, ran. Uncle Maurice saw her coming and met her halfway across the intervening space. Panting hard, he grabbed her arm so tight that it hurt.

'What is it? What happened?' he said.

'They're gone. They disappeared,' said Tess.

'What do you mean, disappeared?' said her uncle. 'Where?'

'Under the trees,' said Tess. 'I got dazzled. I . . .'

She stopped, aware that her uncle's attention had shifted. He was looking towards the woods, and Tess followed the direction of his gaze. To her amazement and relief, Kevin was standing on the limestone slabs at the edge of the trees. It made sense of everything. The strange figure in the shadows must have been him all along, and the antlers just a trick of the light.

Tess was about to call out to him when she remembered that she wasn't supposed to know him. Then she noticed that there was something odd about the way he was behaving. He was waving over at them, a strange little grin on his face, as though he was sneering. As they watched, the businessmen caught up with them, so there were four witnesses to what happened next. In a gesture whose meaning was unmistakable, Kevin snubbed his nose at them and vanished among the trees.

CHAPTER ELEVEN

They searched for hours. Tess stayed close to Uncle Maurice, whom she felt safe with despite his foul temper. The businessmen made up a second party to scour the woods. Backwards and forwards they went, lengthwise and crosswise and every possible way in between, until the place became as familiar to Tess as her own back garden. But there was nothing to be seen or heard. No children, no wolfhounds, nothing. Even the wild creatures and the birds stayed silent, so that it seemed that there could be nowhere on earth more tranquil or more innocent.

By the time they gave up, Uncle Maurice was hoarse from shouting and from describing what he would do to Kevin if he got his hands on him. Tess's heart was in her boots as she dragged after him and into the pick-up to drive home.

*

When they broke the news to Aunt Deirdre she lowered herself into a chair.

'They can't be far away,' she said. 'Sure, where could they be?'

'I don't know,' said Uncle Maurice. 'But the four of us have already been searching for them for hours. There's no sight nor sound of them.' He said nothing for a moment, then burst out with startling vehemence, 'Oh, God, I hate those woods!'

Tess's mind was working overtime. She looked at her watch, astonished to find that it was late afternoon. What on earth did Kevin hope to achieve with that kind of stunt? And where could they all be hiding?

Aunt Deirdre looked up, her face suddenly white with terror. 'He has kidnapped them,' she said. 'As sure as I'm sitting here, that's what has happened. The same way as in the story.'

They all knew which story she was talking about, and the realisation sent a creepy shiver down Tess's spine. Surely Kevin wouldn't do something like that. Or would he? He was going through so many changes these days. What was to say that his mind wasn't changing as rapidly as his body? Maybe he wasn't who she thought he was? Maybe money mattered too much to him, just as it did to Uncle Maurice.

'We have to call the police,' said Aunt Deirdre. 'Who knows what that terrible boy will do to them?'

Tess's spirits were so low that she found she didn't care. Maybe her aunt was right. If Kevin was going to pull stupid stunts like that, then perhaps he deserved what was coming to him. It had already occurred to her that he might take to crime. Maybe it was inevitable with someone like that? Everything Tess trusted was letting her down, and there seemed to be nothing left to believe in. But to her surprise her uncle shook his head.

'No, Deirdre,' he said. 'This isn't police business.'

'What do you mean?' she asked.

'I can't explain,' he said. 'It's to do with those woods. There's something I never told you.'

Tess was watching her uncle as he spoke but now she turned to look at her aunt. The colour was draining from her face and a kind of desperation came over her.

'But we must call the police,' she said. 'We have to get the children back!'

Again Uncle Maurice shook his head. 'It's . . .' he began, then faltered. Then he tried a different tack. 'Declan . . .' Again he couldn't, or wouldn't say what was on his mind, but the effect of the name on Aunt Deirdre was dramatic. As though she had been slapped, she jumped to her feet, her hands gripping the tea-towel that was draped over her shoulder, her knuckles tight and bloodless.

'You're mad,' she said. 'I'm calling the police.'

But Uncle Maurice, despite his obvious distress, was not beyond resorting to his usual method of getting his own way. In a sudden, red-faced rage he stood up and struck the table a massive blow with his fist.

'I won't be disobeyed in my own house,' he roared. 'If I say we don't get the police then we don't get the police! Understand?'

Aunt Deirdre looked away, but the gesture of submission wasn't enough for her husband.

'Understand?' he repeated.

Aunt Deirdre nodded, and tears of helplessness began to trickle down her nose. Tess wished she was invisible. She felt like an intruder, eavesdropping not just on a family row but on the demolition of a human spirit. She hated them both at that moment; her uncle for his cruelty, her aunt for her passive acquiescence in her own destruction. She wondered how her cousins survived the atmosphere, and was shocked back into the present when she remembered where they were, or rather, where they weren't.

Uncle Maurice was already going out again.

'Keating and his friend are leaving,' he said. 'They've already done a lot more tramping around in the woods than they bargained for.' He was outside the door and pulling it closed behind them when he paused and turned back. His tone was soft and apologetic as he said, 'I'll find them, Deirdre. Don't you worry now. I'll find them.'

As soon as he was gone, Tess realised that she had made no offer to help. There seemed no point. But her uncle's mention of Declan had given her an idea.

'I'll make you a nice cup of tea,' she said to her aunt, who stood leaning against the table as if in shock.

'You're a good girl, Tess,' she answered, straightening up and moving over to the window.

'Where does Uncle Declan live?' said Tess.

Her aunt turned slowly to face her. 'What do you know about Declan?' she asked.

'Nothing,' said Tess. 'It's just that Orla told me this morning that she'd bring me to meet him, and then Unc . . .'

But she didn't get to finish her sentence. 'That stupid girl,' said Aunt Deirdre, her voice carrying an unusual note of anger. 'She spends half her life with her head in a book and the other half with it in the clouds.'

457

Tess nodded, expecting more, but it seemed that her aunt had no more to say. She decided to press the matter.

'But maybe that's where they've gone?' she said. 'If he lives around there somewhere, maybe they met up with him?'

'Whisht, child,' said Aunt Deirdre. 'That's enough of that talk. Orla was wrong to be misleading you like that.'

'Why? What do you mean, misleading?'

Aunt Deirdre realised that she couldn't evade the question any longer. She sighed deeply. 'Your uncle Maurice had a brother,' she said. 'A twin brother. That's who Declan is. But the children haven't gone to see him, I promise you that.'

'Why?' said Tess.

'Because,' said Aunt Deirdre, 'he doesn't exist. Your uncle needs his head examining, and so does Orla. Maurice's brother Declan has been dead for twenty years.'

Tess went upstairs and stood at the window of Orla's room. As she looked across at the mountain, there was a horrible, empty feeling beneath her ribcage, and it had nothing to do with hunger.

Tomorrow was her birthday. Tonight she would have to decide on the form that she would take on for the rest of her life. But the world didn't seem to make sense any more. She couldn't get a proper grip on what was happening; still less on what was going to happen. It was like trying to put a jigsaw puzzle together; it ought to have been simple, but the pieces kept changing their shape whenever she looked at them. She felt sorry for herself, that all these things should get in the way of the momentous decision that was facing her. But no sooner did she feel the self-pity beginning to get a grip than she became disgusted with it. She could waste what remained to her of her powers or she could use them. At that moment, it was the only choice that she had to make. Other bridges would have to be crossed when she got to them, but for the moment she could only take one step at a time. And once she realised that, the next step became clear. There was only one way to make a proper search of the area. And there was only one person who could do it.

CHAPTER TWELVE

Tess dropped down from the window and caught herself on jackdaw wings to fly clear of the house unnoticed. The bright little bird was fun to be, full of cocky courage; both wild and people-wise, the way the rats were. As she flew, Tess considered the jackdaw as a possible future. It would allow her to stay close to human life and to observe it from the chimneys and ruins which jackdaws chose for their nesting sites.

There were other possibilities among the bird world, as well. Swallows, perhaps, or swifts, both species forever on the wing, making great journeys across the world, following the sun. Their grace and speed, and the perfection of their aeronautic design had always appealed to Tess's aesthetic sense. She Switched now, choosing the swift for its greater size and speed, and its tendency to fly higher.

Soon she was above the woods, darting and

wheeling, peering down through the trees. There was movement down there all right, but there was nothing unusual about any of it. There were bluetits and chaffinches flitting between the branches, and rats scuttling over the mossy floor. Tess needed to get closer. A moment later she was gliding on sparrow-hawk wings to break her fall. If the swift represented nature's finest long-distance design, the sparrowhawk was her prototype for the low-flying jet plane. Barely clearing the highest branches, she skimmed above the trees, missing nothing that moved beneath them. The birds clucked and rattled and scolded, warning each other of her presence, but her hard hawk-heart despised them. Let them natter away all they liked. She had more important things on her mind.

She was close to the face of the rock when she spotted Uncle Maurice. Rising, tilting her wings at right angles to the ground, she wheeled across the sheer surface and swept in for a better look. What she saw as she overflew him for a second time puzzled her and she decided to gear down and get closer. As a wood-pigeon she dropped down among the branches and made a clattery, feather-ruffling landing, making a mental note to remove that par-ticular bird from her 'possibles' list. At least there was no harm done. The other woodland birds were well accustomed to clumsy pigeon landings, and if Uncle Maurice noticed at all, he gave no sign.

Tess cocked her head and looked down with one eye. Her uncle was standing at the foot of the crag, so close that he could have reached out and touched the bare rock where it rose from a jumble of large boulders, fallen from above. Now that she was close, she could hear that he was speaking but, as always when she was in animal form, Tess could not under-

461

stand the words. She could, however, often get a sense of the mood of the speaker, and it seemed to her now that Uncle Maurice was pleading, or begging, or even praying.

But why at the rock-face? She Switched again, to a robin this time. It was the only bird that would, under normal circumstances, get as close to a human being as she now wanted to be. As she dropped down to the ground, she recognised where she was. It was where the wolfhound had appeared when she had been driven into the woods by Bran and Sceolan. She had passed it several times already that day, during her searches with Uncle Maurice, and each time he had hesitated, and called extra loud and extra long. It had given Tess the creeps then and it gave her the creeps now. She puffed out her feathers and ruffled them all, then hugged them tight around herself again.

She was just about to hop closer, on to a nearby branch, when Uncle Maurice suddenly thumped the rock with his fist. It must have hurt, but he did it again anyway, and then again. The pleading tone in his voice had changed to one of anger. He kicked the rock with one foot, then the other, shouting at it, working himself into a frenzy of flailing boots and fists like a child having a tantrum.

The power of his anger was too much for the sensitive little bird. Tess hopped up through the branches and reverted to the sparrowhawk shape again to complete her aerial search of the woods.

It didn't take long. Nothing worth seeing could escape the keen eyes of the hawk. On the assumption that if Kevin and the children were not in the woods then they must have left them, Tess flew high again and began to survey the surrounding countryside in slowly widening circles.

Still there was no sign. A pair of tourists were climbing up the other side of the mountain. A few more were on bicycles pedalling slowly along a meandering back lane. The usual sparse traffic of muddy cars and tractors crawled along the narrow roads.

Tess flew higher and widened the area of search. She flew over a farmer and her dog checking cattle, and a bird-watcher who watched Tess through binoculars, tempting her to give him a display of aerobatics that he would never forget. She flew over a boy on a bicycle, heading away from the area. There was something familiar about him, and she wheeled about and flew back. She lost height to get a closer look and then, unable to believe her eyes, she dropped on to a telegraph pole and watched as the boy on the bike approached. There was no doubt about it, now. It was Kevin.

Tess dropped down behind the thick hedge and Switched back to her human self.

'Kevin!'

He nearly fell off the bike with surprise, then came to a wobbly halt.

'Here!' Tess called, trying to find a break in the hazel wide enough to climb through.

'Oh, Switch, for cripe's sake,' said Kevin. 'There's no one about.'

She did, just for a moment, slipping easily through in the shape of a stoat before emerging on to the road as a human again.

'Where are you going?' she asked. 'Where are the others?'

'What others?' asked Kevin.

Tess was surprised at the anger her reply revealed. 'You know perfectly well who I'm talking about!'

But Kevin was angry, too. 'I'm sick of you, Tess!' he shouted back. 'First you promise to set up a scheme for me and then you back out and drop me in it on my own. Then, when it backfires in my face, you don't even come and look for me! You just leave me to try and cope with it and carry on as though nothing had happened!'

'Oh, right,' said Tess, discovering that she was shouting as well. 'So you kidnap my cousins to get your own back!'

'I what?'

For a moment, Tess believed that Kevin's astonishment was genuine. Then she remembered what she had seen; his expression as he snubbed his nose at them the last time she saw him.

'It's a good act, Kevin,' she said. 'But it doesn't cut any ice with me. I saw you, remember? I was there when you went off with them into the woods.'

Kevin shook his head in bewilderment. 'I don't know which one of us is cracked, but I haven't got a clue what you're talking about. I haven't been anywhere near the woods since I left the rats there.'

'But I saw you!'

'No, Tess. You didn't. You couldn't have done. It must have been someone else.'

Tess shook her head. 'Where were you, then,' she said, 'if you weren't at the woods?'

'This is ridiculous,' said Kevin. 'Getting the third degree from you, of all people! But if you must know, I was back at my camp site.'

'All this time?'

'Yes, all this time. I was wondering if you were ever going to turn up!' His face coloured with embarrassment, but he went on. 'I was angry and lonely, Tess. I couldn't believe that you didn't come and see if I was all right.'

Tess sat down on a rock. Her spirit kept doing somersaults, then landing flat on its face. She wanted to believe what Kevin was saying; his friendship meant so much to her. And yet she had seen him with her own eyes. He had to be lying.

Kevin sat down beside her. 'What did you see, Tess?' he asked. 'You'd better tell me what's happening.'

Tess struggled with the idea that he was playing some awful trick on her, then gave in to trust. Feeling slightly foolish, she went through the events of the day from beginning to end. Kevin listened carefully, looking down at the ground between his feet. When she had brought him up to the present, he shook his head in bewilderment.

'I don't know what's going on,' he said. 'I can't even begin to explain it. But I can tell you one thing for certain. Whoever it was that you saw in the woods today, it wasn't me.'

'Who was it, then?' said Tess.

Kevin shrugged. 'I don't know. Your guess is as good as mine. Maybe someone who looks very like me. Maybe . . .' He stopped.

'Maybe what?'

'I don't know. But do you remember asking me once if I had noticed anything strange about those woods?'

Tess nodded and he went on, 'Well, what if there is something we haven't thought of yet? We get complacent so easily, even people like us who have seen so much. Especially us, perhaps. We think we've seen all there is to see, or been all there is to be. But maybe we haven't. Maybe there are things even we haven't imagined.'

Tess nodded, aware of the tingle of truth in her veins. She knew that he was right. There was something in those woods that she didn't understand. What was more, she didn't want to understand it. It made her much too afraid. It was easier to turn away, to keep close to Uncle Maurice, to pretend it wasn't happening. And when Kevin came even nearer to defining what it was, his words brought increasing fear along with them.

'Whatever is in those woods,' he said, 'made me think of the krools. Not because it's bad, necessarily. It might be. I don't know. But it reminded me of them because it's old. Older than we are, Tess. Older than civilisation, even.'

Tess nodded, remembering the shadows, the strange figure, the ghostly atmosphere.

'Whatever it is we're dealing with,' Kevin went on, 'it's ancient.'

CHAPTER THIRTEEN

Tess took to the skies again to have a look around. She flew back towards the farm and spotted Uncle Maurice walking away from the woods and back across the meadows, his eyes downcast. The dogs were at his heels, equally dejected.

While Tess patrolled above, Kevin cycled back along the narrow, meandering roads and down the stony track which led to the crag. At the edge of the woods he hid his bicycle among thick stalks of hazel and, satisfied that they hadn't been spotted, Tess dropped down and joined him in human form.

Together they stood looking in among the trees. Evening was approaching and shadows were beginning to creep out from beneath the rocks and bushes. The raven flew over, looking down at them, making Tess feel exposed and vulnerable. She stepped forward and Kevin followed.

Among the branches a bird fluttered and a leaf fell.

Everything else was silent. Even though she felt much safer with Kevin beside her, Tess found that she was holding her breath. Despite the fresh, vibrant greens of the mosses and leaves, the woods were eerie. Like a stone circle or an earthwork, they had the atmosphere of a place which belonged to another age, a place where the living were somehow as insubstantial as the dead.

The two friends stayed close together as they made their way through the trees, keeping roughly parallel to the crag, calling occasionally as they went. Gradually the birds became accustomed to their presence and began to sing again, making the woods seem less forbidding. When they reached the opposite end and came out of the trees and on to the limestone pavement, Kevin sat down and shook his head.

'It doesn't make sense,' he said.

'I know,' said Tess.

'No. I mean, it doesn't make sense to search like this.'

'Why?' asked Tess.

'Because humans are the worst thing to be. You should do it, Tess. As a dog or a hawk or something.'

But Tess shook her head. 'I've already covered the place from the air. And I'm not going in there on foot. Not on my own, whatever form I'm in.' She told him about the wolfhound she had met, but found that she couldn't bring herself to mention the antlered figure, even to him. 'And in any case,' she finished, 'Uncle Maurice has just been here with Bran and Sceolan. Surely they would have found the kids if anyone could.'

Kevin sighed. 'I suppose there's no alternative, then,' he said, standing up and moving towards the woods again. 'But there doesn't seem to be much point, really, does there? I mean, if they were in there, surely they would have been found by now?'

Tess had to agree. 'But what can we do? We can't just give up on them.'

They had just entered the woods again when the sudden scuttle of a startled rat made them both stop. For a long moment Kevin stared at the spot where the worm-like tail had disappeared, and then he said, 'I can't believe we're being so stupid. Why are we wasting our time searching for the kids when there's bound to be someone here who saw where they went.'

'Of course!' said Tess. 'The rats!'

Kevin nodded. 'But I'd better leave it to you to talk to them this time. I don't think I'm in their good books.'

They moved on towards the centre of the woods, where they would have the best chance of gathering all the rats. Then, while Kevin settled himself among the trees, Tess walked a short distance away and Switched. To a human the woods appeared quiet and empty, but to a rat they were anything but. The surroundings were alive with rustlings and squabblings and a profusion of irritable images as the farm rats continued their unwilling resettlement. For a few moments the altered perceptions were disorientating, but it didn't last long. By now Tess's rat form was nearly as familiar as her human one and, since her rat mind was scarcely concerned at all with the worries that beset her as a human, Tess found it oddly comforting. She had a sudden insight into the way Kevin felt and his reasons for wishing that he had remained in rat form, but before she could dwell on it, he flashed her a reminder of her business.

'Tail Short Seven Toes having a snooze, huh?' In

469

his thought projection he used the name that had been given to her by the Dublin rats more than a year ago. To have a name she needed some kind of distinguishing mark, and one of the city rats had obliged her by biting off the end of her tail. Kevin sent another image; of Tess in rat form sitting in the lotus position, eyes closed.

'Tail Short Seven Toes meditating, huh?'

In return, Tess sent an image of Kevin in a huge glass of lemonade, floating around among berg-sized ice-cubes. 'Boy chill out, huh?'

But she got the message. She listened until she could hear nothing that sounded threatening, then sent out a gentle Rat invitation.

'Usguys gathering, huh? Usguys telling stories huh, huh?'

Rats are basically sensuous creatures; they love to eat and sleep and bring up their young as safely as possible. But Tess had learnt that they also love stories and often told them as a way of transmitting information about their surroundings and the world beyond. Tess had spent hour after hour telling her Switching stories to the rats at home in Dublin, and had become known as something of a star performer. But on this occasion she was eager to listen, not to tell.

The rats finished what they were doing before making their way along the network of subtle little pathways which criss-crossed the woods. They came in dribs and drabs and in no particular hurry, so the meeting had a casual air about it. Tess waited patiently, greeting the rats as they arrived, exchanging scents and names. There was an extremely awkward moment when the group of kitchen adolescents arrived, but their mother was far too busy instructing

470

them on the rules of introduction to bother about an old argument with Tess. By the time she had disciplined them into orderly and respectful behaviour, the numbers had swelled surprisingly. Beyond the gathering a few stragglers were still arriving, but Tess decided there was no need to wait any longer. As soon as the introductions were over, she began the story-telling procedure herself by giving the gathered rats the image of the old one-toothed rat, hanging dead by his tail from Uncle Maurice's hand. A wave of sorrow passed through the assembly and there was a brief, respectful silence. Then the other rats began to tell their stories.

Tess had to work hard to hide her amusement. With minor variations, the accounts of the last two days were the same. The rats had been happy at the farm but they had believed the Big Foot who knew their language and they had followed him with fear and trembling to the woods. Everything was exaggerated, from the surprise at being woken to the promises of an idyllic haven. Tess was particularly amused by their image of Kevin, which was about as unflattering as it was possible to be. She glanced across to where he sat, in beast-learnt silence among the trees. He winked back, clearly glad that the rats didn't know he was there. They were very angry with him. No sooner had they arrived in the promised land than they had been invaded by dogs and a great many Big Feet tramping everywhere.

A human being is huge to a rat; earth-shakingly heavy and genuinely frightening. But in their telling of the day's events, the rats were outrageously magnifying the size and numbers of the searchers. Uncle Maurice and the businessmen crashed back and forth, their feet colossal and clumsy, crushing rocks

471

and making craters in the ground. Even her own trainers appeared as killing machines, and the care she always took when walking in the countryside was distorted by the rats into purposeful malevolence. The dogs were monstrous bloodhounds with noses that vacuumed up whole litters of baby rats and blew away the carefully constructed nests of the beleaguered settlers. The images piled upon each other, exaggeration upon exaggeration, giving the impression that there was barely a square foot of the woods that had not been occupied all day by massive, tramping feet. Tess listened patiently, showing her appreciation by joining the occasional chorus of 'yup, yup,' and waiting for the excitement to run its course. When everyone had calmed down a bit, it was possible that she might get some more accurate information.

But suddenly an absurd image entered the babble. The pictures of huge, stomping boots were being repeated again and again, almost like a drumbeat or a chant. But thrown in among the big feet, like the tinkling of a little bell, was a tiny pair of red ones.

Tess focused as hard as she could, waiting for the stray image to return and hoping to identify the rat that had produced it. Sure enough it came again, bright and ridiculous among the almost military drabness. The picture was coming from somewhere on the left-hand side of the crowd, and the third time it was sent, Tess zoned in.

The rat who had seen the red wellies was fully grown but very small compared to the rest of the fat, meal-fed rats. There was something odd about her as well; she was sitting on her haunches and nodding fervently, like some religious zealot of the rodent world. With a faint shock, Tess realised that she had seen her before, and at the same time she remembered where. She had met her in the hall-way on her first visit to the rat world beneath the farm, and she had flashed her that strange, poetic welcome. She had forgotten it at the time because of the argument in the kitchen, but now that she thought about it she began to wonder whether the rat who had sent it was the full shilling. If not, the sighting of the red wellies might prove to be unreliable.

The story of the Big Feet was still continuing. While she waited for it to come to an end, Tess glanced over at Kevin again. But this time he was not looking towards her but away, at something deeper in the woods. For a reason that she didn't understand, the sight gave Tess the creeps.

She turned back to the gathering and joined the chorus of 'yup, yups' that greeted the end of the story. The protocol of such occasions required that she, as the visitor, now tell another one, but as politely as she could she declined the honour and, in the general melee that followed, she made her way over to the strange, dissenting rat.

As Tess approached she nodded again, so deeply that it was more like a bow.

'Cat Friend,' she said, her images fresh and clear.

'Tail Short Seven Toes,' Tess replied and, wasting no time on ceremony, continued, 'Little red wellies, huh? Huh?'

Cat Friend was delighted to cooperate. 'Yup, yup,' she said, and flashed again the image of Colm's red boots.

'More feet, huh?' said Tess, offering various feet-images but purposefully avoiding any that might prompt Cat Friend into an untruthful answer. If she

473

was a little uncertain about her facts, she might now be tricked into giving herself away.

But Tess needn't have worried. Cat Friend's next image was clear beyond any shadow of doubt. There were four pairs of feet; three small and one big. Apart from the red wellies there were Orla's boots, and Brian's and, to Tess's surprise, a pair of very familiar trainers.

'Huh? Huh?' she said, needing to see them again, needing to be sure.

Cat Friend repeated obligingly. There was no doubt about it. The trainers were Kevin's.

Tess sat up on her haunches and turned to look at him, but the spot where he had been was empty. She craned her neck, then jumped up on to a rock for a better view. Between the trees she caught a glimpse of him, moving swiftly away, almost out of sight already. Unwilling to frighten the rats she raced after him on foot for a few yards before Switching into a pigeon and dodging among the trees in wild pursuit.

But it was already too late. There was no sign of him. It was impossible, but it was true. She had seen him only a moment ago, but now he was nowhere. She flew until she met the crag, then flew back, quartering the area in one direction and then the other. She flew until her own panic exhausted her pigeon wings, and then she came to a quivering halt on a dead branch lodged between two trees. It couldn't have happened. He had to be there.

She dropped down to the ground and Switched back to human form, her limbs still trembling from fear and fatigue. The rats were gone, vanished back beneath the rocks and roots and leaves. Once again, Tess was alone in the woods.

'Kevin?' she called.

There was no answer.

'Kevin! I know you're there!'

In the pause that followed, a faint breeze sighed among the branches. It seemed to carry words.

'Come on, Tess. Come with me.'

Fear grasped her like a claw and, without knowing where or from what, she began to run. As though it had somehow succeeded in its aim, the voice came again, whispering through the trees.

But this time, it was laughing.

CHAPTER FOURTEEN

Tess's fear and disappointment made her reckless. In the form of a jackdaw she tore back to her open window and, without even bothering to check that the coast was clear, she flung herself inside. Before she hit the bed she Switched, and along with her human form came all its attendant miseries. Maybe Kevin was right. Maybe a rat was the best thing to be.

And maybe he wasn't right. Maybe he had always been the scurrilous, criminal-minded truant that she had believed him to be when she first met him, all that time ago during the freak winter. Perhaps she was wrong to have ever trusted him, or to have rescued him when, in phoenix form, he was trapped in the zoo. She wanted so badly to believe that he was innocent; that he had nothing to do with the kidnap of the children; above all that he hadn't lied to her. But all the evidence suggested otherwise.

Emotionally she was numb, too exhausted by the ups and downs of the day to feel anything any more. But her body still had needs. Much as she dreaded an encounter with her distressed aunt, Tess knew that she would have to get something to eat. The ordinariness of it was comforting, but as she crossed to the door of the bedroom her eye fell on the book that Orla had been reading, lying open on its face, the deer-man gazing up from the cover. Whatever it was that she was mixed up in, it wasn't over yet.

As she had expected, her aunt was in the kitchen, sitting at the table as though she hadn't moved all day.

'Where on earth have you been, child?' she said.

'Nowhere. Why?'

'You were gone. I didn't hear you come in. How did you come in without me hearing you?'

'You were dozing, probably,' said Uncle Maurice. He was standing by the back door, leaning against the wall so quietly that Tess hadn't noticed he was there. His face was grey and deeply lined, as though he had aged ten years in the last few hours.

'At least we have one of them,' said Aunt Deirdre. 'God forbid that we should lose my sister's child as well as our own.'

She was glaring at Uncle Maurice as she spoke, and then, as though Tess's presence had made her brave, she burst out, 'Please, Maurice. Please let's get the police in on this.'

Tess had been edging towards the bread-bin, but the anguish in her aunt's voice brought her to a standstill.

'Tell him, Tess,' she went on. 'Make him see sense. What's past is past, we know nothing of that. But

477

what is happening here is a kidnap, isn't it? Surely you can see that? We need to call the police!'

Tess looked from her aunt to her uncle and back again. She had no idea what the reference to the past was about, but it was clear that Deirdre and Maurice understood each other perfectly.

'I've told you a hundred times, Deirdre,' said Uncle Maurice. 'The police can do no good here. They'd only be wasting their time, just like before.'

'Before?' said Tess. 'What do you mean, "before"?'

Aunt Deirdre shook her head, and there was a horrified expression on her face. 'You're mad, Maurice,' she said. 'I never thought the day would come when I'd hear myself say it. I always denied it, always. Even when others said it I refused to listen. But I believe them now, all right.'

A glimmer of fear crossed Aunt Deirdre's features as she spoke, but for once it was unfounded. Uncle Maurice had no anger left in him.

'They'll be home,' he said. 'Wait till you see.' And before she could answer, he stepped out through the door and walked away across the yard.

Aunt Deirdre stared at the place where he had been.

'What did you mean?' Tess asked. 'About the past.'

'Hush, child,' said Aunt Deirdre. 'Don't be worrying. Get yourself a bite to eat, there. You must be starved.'

Tess didn't need to be asked twice, but nor was she so easily put off track.

'Do other people really say that Uncle Maurice is mad?' she asked.

'That's enough about that, now,' said her aunt.

478

Tess pressed on. 'But why? Why would they say he was mad?'

Aunt Deirdre sighed deeply and then, as though her resistance had finally given way, the words began to pour out of her.

'I wouldn't have told you, child, but I can't see the harm in it now, to tell the truth. There was an awful tragedy here, you see. Awful.'

The hairs on Tess's neck stood up, but she buttered bread calmly, willing her aunt to continue. She did.

'Your uncle had a twin brother. Declan was his name, and it's said that the two of them were so close that you rarely saw daylight between them. But Declan died, as I told you earlier.'

'How?' said Tess.

'That's the mystery,' said Aunt Deirdre. 'No one knows. He disappeared in the early hours of one morning and no trace was ever found of him.'

'They didn't find his body?'

'No. Nothing.'

'Then how do they know he died?'

'There was no other explanation,' said Aunt Deirdre. 'A boy can't just vanish into thin air, now, can he?'

Tess nodded in agreement.

'Where?' she said. 'Where did he disappear?'

'No one knows, for sure. All we know is that Maurice believed that he was in those woods, and for weeks afterwards he had to be carried out of them at night, otherwise he would never have left them at all. Calling his brother's name, he was. Convinced that Declan was in there and would come out.'

Aunt Deirdre stood up and moved around in an agitated way, putting on the kettle and emptying the teapot into the sink.

'There were even some who said . . .' she stopped and stared at Tess vacantly, and it was as though her anxiety had brought her to the brink of madness as well.

'What did they say?' Tess asked, but Aunt Deirdre shook her head and turned to look out of the window, in the direction of the mountain. It was clear that she had said as much as she was going to.

But it didn't make sense. Why had Orla said that she would take Tess to meet Uncle Declan? How could she meet someone who was dead? And where did Kevin fit into the picture?

Tess found cheese in the fridge and made sandwiches, then took them up to her room. Far from making things clearer, her aunt's words had only made the mystery deeper and more frightening. It was almost as though history was repeating itself, with Uncle Maurice's own children vanishing in the same way that his brother had. But if that was the case, why would he be so reluctant to call in the police? And who was it that whispered to her in the woods?

She sat on the bed and ate the sandwiches without enthusiasm. Afterwards, tired and dispirited, she threw herself on to the bed. Every mystery had a simple explanation, she knew that, and she was fed up of being thwarted in everything she tried to do. Miserably, she rolled on to her side and curled up like a baby.

She thought of the land again, the fresh, green beauty of the woods and the greed of the people who wanted to destroy it in order to line their own pockets. She didn't want to be an adult in a society like that, where no one cared about anything except money. She envisioned the world as a grey, barren place, where nothing lived except human beings and nothing grew except the food they ate. Like a plague on the earth; like locusts they destroyed everything before them, like locusts they could see no further than their own, immediate greed.

She wouldn't join them. Better to be an animal, even a greedy one like a pig or a rat. At least they didn't pretend to care. People were worse. People were hypocrites. A few tears ran down her nose and dripped on to the pillow.

Thoughts of Lizzie returned. If only she could see the old woman. She was sure that Lizzie would have the answer. She always did. But Lizzie lived two hundred miles away, and Tess couldn't think of any way of getting to her in time.

Her mind ran back over their last conversation. What was it that Lizzie had said? Something about ancestors.

Ancestors?

Despite the seriousness of the situation, Tess laughed, struck by the image of old men in medieval attire roaming round in the landscape.

'Lizzie sends her regards,' she said to the empty room.

A sudden gust of wind rattled the window hard, and Tess flinched. There was something else that the old woman had said. What was it? Tess concentrated and, obligingly, the words came to her.

'Does we believe what we sees, or does we see what we believe?'

Across the fields, at the foot of the mountain, something was happening that she didn't understand. She stood up to go to the window, but her eye fell on Orla's book. *Story or History?* What did it mean? Idly, Tess reached out and picked it up, wondering

481

if there was anything in its pages that might give her a clue. But when she saw what was lying beneath it, she gave up all thoughts of reading.

It was Orla's inhaler.

Tess knew now that the chips were down. She could still cop out, of course; give her aunt the inhaler and let her worry about what was happening to Orla out there in the woods with the evening drawing in. She could stay here in her room with the light on and eat sandwiches and worry about her future. But if she did any of those things it would be an admission that her fear had defeated her. And suddenly she realised that she didn't need Lizzie to tell her what to do. The truth, plain and simple, was that if anyone had a chance of finding those children it was her. What could she possibly encounter, after all, worse than the bone-chilling krools or the terrible vampire that Martin had learnt to become?

When the sun rose the next morning her powers would be gone. The events of the day were moving too fast, robbing her of time and space to think, and it looked now as though she wasn't going to have time to make a considered choice about what to be. But perhaps it didn't matter. Perhaps it didn't help to have time to think. Up until now all the thinking in the world hadn't helped her to arrive at a decision.

She slipped the inhaler into her pocket and moved towards the window. For the moment, at least, none of it mattered. For the next few hours she still had her Switching powers. If she did not use them while she could, she might spend the rest of her life regretting it.

With a feeling of courage returning, of becoming herself again after a long absence, Tess flung open the window.

CHAPTER FIFTEEN

Tess had thought that her Uncle Maurice had set out for the crag, but as she flew out of her bedroom window, in jackdaw shape again, she spotted him beneath her, letting in the cows to be milked. She was relieved. It would give her a bit more freedom in the woods.

As she flew, she thought about what she needed to do, and by the time she reached the woods she had worked out what her first step would be. She dropped down through the trees near where she had last seen Kevin, then Switched into rat form. She had some information to gather and, as soon as she had adjusted and checked the environment for safety, she gave out a call in Rat. But this time she wasn't summoning a gathering. She was looking for Cat Friend.

It wasn't long before she arrived; puzzled but cooperative. Tess realised that she liked this strange little rat despite, or maybe because of, her idiosyncratic behaviour. And it seemed, by the affectionate way that Cat Friend touched noses, that she felt the same way. Tess felt a wash of sadness as the thought came to her that she would soon be leaving the animal world for ever. No sooner had the thought arrived, however, than another superseded it. Why should she think like that? She hadn't made her mind up. Perhaps she would stay a rat, be a rat forever, living and dying alongside Cat Friend and the others. Why not?

But there was other business to take care of first. Cat Friend had told her that she had seen Kevin and the children in the woods earlier that day. Now Tess wanted to know if she had seen where they had gone.

'Yup, yup,' said Cat Friend, nodding like a car toy again; full of certainty. 'Cat Friend watching Small Big Feet. Cat Friend following.'

Tess was delighted. 'Wise Cat Friend,' she said. 'Cat Friend following into the woods, huh? Out of the woods, huh? Huh?'

But the image that Cat Friend returned in answer shook Tess's confidence in her severely. It showed the people involved as clearly as ever; Kevin leading and the other three following closely behind. But where they went was quite impossible. According to Cat Friend, they walked right through the solid face of the crag and disappeared.

It didn't seem to surprise her at all that four humans should do such a thing. But it didn't fit into Tess's interpretation of reality.

'Nananana!' she said. 'Small Big Feet bumping into the rock, falling over backwards. Small Big Feet walking into the crag and hurting themselves.'

Cat Friend was offended by Tess's attitude and puffed out her coat and turned her face away. Tess tried to repair the damage, explaining about doors and how they worked, but Cat Friend was adamant. She had been there. She had seen what happened. Over and over again she repeated the image of what she had seen. The four people had walked up to the rock-face and vanished into it.

Tess didn't know what to do. If there had been any other leads at all she might have forgotten about Cat Friend and her rambling mind. Since there weren't, she did the only thing that presented itself to her. She asked Cat Friend to show her the place where it had happened.

The other rat came out of her sulk instantly and skipped on ahead energetically. Occasionally she hung back and waited for Tess to catch up, touching her nose delightedly before bounding on across the rocks again. As she followed, Tess found herself wondering if the whole world hadn't gone mad around her, or whether it was she herself who was mad. It wasn't until they came near to their destination that she realised there had to be some truth in what Cat Friend was saying. Because it was the place that, somehow, she had been led to every time she had gone into those woods. It was the place where she had seen the strange wolfhound, and where Kevin had been when she last saw him yesterday. There was no doubt about it; there had to be a secret door of some kind. Cat Friend was probably right about that. It was just her way of seeing it and explaining it that was odd.

She stood back now and watched as Tess scuttled along the base of the rock, standing on her hind legs from time to time and stretching up with her front paws, trying to find some clue to where the entrance might be. There was nothing, though, and when she

485

had exhausted all the possibilities that her rat mind could conceive of, she realised that she needed to be human again.

There is no way to apologise in Rat, but Tess was truly sorry for what she did next. Because when Cat Friend saw Tail Short Seven Toes disappear and a rather large Small Big Foot appear out of nowhere, she got the fright of her life. In a sudden, furry flash she was gone, out of sight beneath the nearest rock. Tess hoped that she wasn't too badly shocked, and that she would see her again.

But there were other, more urgent matters on her mind. She walked back and forth along the base of the crag and then, seeing no obvious signs of a door of any kind, prepared herself for a long, meticulous search. Yard by yard and inch by inch she examined the face of the rock, prising at every crack and fault, poking into every overhang and shadow. When she had covered the whole area and a good distance either side she went back again with a stone, knocking the rock at intervals and listening for hollow resonances. But no matter how hard she tried or how careful she was, she could find no sign of an entrance of any kind. Eventually, tired and despondent, she hurled her sounding stone far out into the trees and sank to the ground.

It was beginning to get dark. Already the moon was rising and trying to peer in among the trees. Whatever chance she had of finding her cousins seemed to be fading fast. Every fibre of Tess's being screamed against the sheer frustration of it. First she believed that there was a door, that there had to be to explain the mysterious appearances and disappearances in the area. Then she was equally certain that there wasn't a door, not now or ever. And as she

486

swung wildly between these two conflicting certainties, she became aware that she was being watched. Not far away, on a moss-coated boulder that was just about level with Tess's eyes, a brown rat was sitting.

'Cat Friend?' she called.

'Yup, yup,' said Cat Friend, scrambling down from her perch and approaching along the ground until she was close to Tess's outstretched leg. Tess shook her head in surprise. In all the years that she had been using her powers to Switch she had never known an animal to make a connection between her human form and her animal ones. Not even Algernon, her pet white rat, had ever realised that the brown cousin that regularly visited him in the evenings was actually her. But there was no doubt now that Cat Friend understood.

'Tail Short Seven Toes, huh? Huh?' she asked, giving the clear image of Tess's rat form and then an image of her Switching to human form which was so accurate it made Tess tingle all over.

'Yup, yup,' said Tess. 'Cat Friend watching, huh? Cat Friend not afraid?'

The little rat shook her coat then tightened it so that she looked her sleek, proud best.

'Cat Friend watching,' she said. And then, in a series of images so clear that they had to be truth, she showed Tess that she was not the first Switcher she had come across. To Tess's growing amazement, her new friend revealed that the white cat in the farmyard, the one whose friendship had given her the name, was itself a Switcher. The images followed, one upon the other; the white cat becoming a stoat, a hare, a raven. Nor were the descriptions anywhere near an end when Cat Friend, quite abruptly, sent an urgent image of rats fleeing from danger, then turned on her heel and vanished among a cluster of nearby tree-roots.

Instinctively, Tess leapt to her feet and turned to see what it was that had frightened her little friend. Not more than a few feet away, leaning against the sheer face of the crag, was Kevin.

He smiled. 'Hi, Tess,' he said.

'How . . . But how did you get there?' Tess replied.

'Easy,' he said. 'I just crept up on you.'

'I don't think so,' said Tess, realising that her frustration was rapidly turning into anger. 'Or at least, you might have crept up on me, but you would never have been able to creep up on her.'

She pointed at the roots of the tree where Cat Friend had disappeared. Kevin laughed.

'Good thinking,' he said.

'So where did you appear from?' Tess asked. 'And what have you done with my cousins?'

'I haven't done anything with your cousins,' said Kevin. 'It's not my fault if they followed me, is it?'

'Followed you where?'

'In there, of course.' He pointed to the bare rock. 'Where else?'

'Show me, then,' said Tess. 'I'm fed up of searching and getting nowhere. If there's a door, where is it?'

'I can't show you what you're not able to see,' said Kevin. 'But perhaps if you follow me I can lead you in.'

With that he Switched into a barn owl and, with a brief swish of heavy wings, he flew up through the trees.

Tess stared after the bird, ghostly pale against the night sky. Despite the evidence of her eyes, she was unable to believe what she had just seen. All the laws of her world, every last one of them, seemed to have been turned on their heads. Kevin could not Switch. He had passed fifteen and, as all Switchers must, he had lost the ability. And yet she could not doubt that she had just seen it happen.

Already the owl was out of sight above the trees. Tess found that she was rooted to the spot, and couldn't follow. But Kevin wasn't about to leave without her and soon returned, Switching back to human form again.

'But you can't, Kevin!' said Tess. 'It's impossible!'

'Come with me, Tess,' he said. The words and the way he said them rang a bell in her mind, but before she could remember why he spoke again.

'Come on. Let me show you what's possible and what isn't. Let me show you what you could be, Tess. Before it's too late.'

And with that he was an owl again, lifting towards the skies. This time, Tess followed.

It was exhilarating to be up there, with eyes that pierced the darkness and wings as silent as the watching moon. Beneath them as they flew, the woodland creatures clung to their shadows and waited for their pale enemies to pass over. Tess followed compliantly as the owl that had been Kevin spiralled higher and higher. The lights of the house became visible, and so did the dejected figure of Uncle Maurice, crossing the fields yet again on his way to search for the children.

Higher still the two birds rose, until they were above the level of the crag and looking down on to its plateau-like summit, where the moonlight threw shadows from heaps and jumbles and circles of stone which were almost as ancient as the mountain itself. Beyond that the grey, fluid shapes of the Burren range stretched away to the edges of vision.

Tess was so entranced by the surroundings that she missed the exact moment when the other owl began to drop down out of the skies again. She followed at a distance, and he waited for her, swooping up again, then falling past her, almost drawing her into his wake. This time she kept up, reminded of another time, long ago, when she had followed Kevin in an electrifying dive into a building in Dublin. He had been a different kind of owl on that occasion and both of them had been different people. It seemed like an eternity had passed since then.

Faster and faster they fell until the thick canopy of the trees was racing up to meet them. Without hesitating, the other owl plunged straight through the leaves and, holding her breath, Tess followed. What came next happened in the blink of an eye, but there was somehow time for a thousand thoughts to flash through Tess's mind.

They entered the woods close to the crag, and the instant that Kevin was beneath the trees he levelled up and flew at breakneck speed straight towards the rock. A shock-wave passed through Tess's body, and at the same time she began to flap madly, trying to slow down and change direction at the same time. It seemed that Kevin was certain to be killed, but he wasn't. If Tess hadn't seen it with her own eyes, she would never have believed it.

Without slowing, without changing direction, he continued to fly straight towards the rock-face. But just when the bone-crunching collision seemed inevitable, he vanished. There was no doubt at all about what had happened. The owl that was Kevin hadn't Switched, nor had it become invisible. It had simply flown straight through the solid face of the rock.

CHAPTER SIXTEEN

Despite her best efforts, Tess couldn't reduce speed fast enough. Her left wing glanced against the rock and she tumbled down the last few feet of its face like a fluttering Catherine wheel. At the bottom she picked herself up and shook her feathers, then Switched into her human frame.

Her left arm was sore and she knew by the feel of her hips and shoulders that she would have a few bruises tomorrow to show for that fall. But on what kind of body she still couldn't imagine. Tomorrow was a blank in her mental map.

And today was a disaster. She slumped to the ground and sat with her back against the rock, ignoring the damp which was beginning to soak from the mossy ground into her jeans. She found that she was no longer afraid, but she was angry. Angry at Kevin for playing tricks on her. Angry at Lizzie for talking in riddles. Angry at herself for failing to gain entrance to the rock. Even as the thought came to her, she understood why it was that she had failed. There had been an instant, she remembered, immediately after the other owl's disappearance, when she could have followed it. In that instant she had known that the key to the door in the rock was not a thing that she could find or touch, nor was it a puzzle that she could work out with her mind. The only things that could get her through were faith and courage; the ability to let go and allow herself to be governed by another reality; one that she did not understand. In that brief moment she had known all that, and she had chickened out. That was why she was still there, all alone on the outside; the one who had failed. The one left behind.

Lizzie's words returned to her again. What did she mean by believing what we see or seeing what we believe? She was certain that the words had some bearing on her situation, but she didn't know exactly how. Tess stood up and looked at the rock, but she knew in her heart that it was already too late. She had missed the moment of truth and she couldn't recreate it. She could hear her uncle's arrival at the edge of the woods; the snap of a broken branch, a whispered call.

Tess no longer knew what to believe. Somehow she had entered another world, where things weren't as they seemed, and where the rules she had come to have faith in didn't seem to apply. She wanted to believe in it. She just didn't know how.

But someone else did. The touch on her ankle was so soft that she thought a moth had brushed her and she leant down to scratch the itch. But it wasn't a moth.

'Tail Short Seven Toes sad, huh? Huh?'

Cat Friend was standing on her hind legs, clutching on to Tess's jeans with her front paw.

Tess couldn't help smiling despite her dejected mood. 'Yup, yup,' she said. 'Tail Short Seven Toes trying to get into the rock. Left all alone and sad.'

'Cat Friend helping,' said the little rat. 'Cat Friend leading Tail Short Seven Toes into the rock.'

The images were perfectly clear and Tess's spirits soared. She knew that it could work. There was no doubt at all about Cat Friend's belief and Tess felt sure that it could bolster her own sufficiently to cross the subtle barrier. But they would have to be quick. From among the trees came the sound of a grunt and a mild curse as Uncle Maurice lost his footing. He was almost there.

Tess Switched into rat form and, although Cat Friend jumped at the abruptness of the change, she didn't falter. A moment later they were scurrying towards the rock. At Cat Friend's suggestion, Tess took hold of her tail and closed her eyes. And as they began to move forward, she called on all the courage that she had ever had.

It seemed to take forever to get there. Tess waited for a resistance of some kind, or a shift in the atmosphere like the one that she experienced every time she Switched. But it didn't happen, and after a while Tess began to think that Cat Friend must be making a fool of her. But when she opened her eyes she was amazed to find that she was inside the hill and, judging by the distance they had covered, had been for some time.

She let go of Cat Friend's tail and stopped to look around. They were in a long, dimly-lit hall like a broad tunnel, lined with rough stones from the base of the walls to the crude arch high above their heads.

To a rat the place was enormous, but Tess guessed that the roof would not have been much higher than a man's head. She wondered vaguely who would have built such a place, but more perplexing was that still there was no sign of Kevin or the children.

Cat Friend seemed equally perplexed, and the two rats conferred briefly before moving on across the stony floor. At the end of the hall a stone wall blocked their way, but on the left, low down, was a hole in the wall. Although it was huge for a rat, it was small for a human. A child might have crawled through, but an adult would have had to lie down on their belly to squeeze in. Since there was no other way forward, the rats went in, all their senses straining for any signs of danger.

Before they had gone more than a few feet along this smaller tunnel, they heard sounds of life ahead, and their way was lit by a strange, golden light. A moment later they emerged into a second hall. It was roughly the same size and shape as the one they had just come through, but there all similarity ended.

For this hall was, without doubt, a fairy *sidhe*. The mysterious light that they had encountered flooded the enclosed space, but there were no lamps nor was there any opening to the outside. Tess and Cat Friend crouched at the end of the small tunnel, trying to get their bearings in the extraordinary surroundings.

The first thing Tess noticed was Orla and Brian, who were standing nearby and were involved in what appeared to be a rather cruel game. They had a small, black kitten, and they were tossing it between them as though it was a ball. Beyond them was a table, covered with the most scrumptious food that Tess had ever seen and, further on still, she could see

Kevin sitting on a pile of silken cushions, looking sulky.

Tess touched noses with Cat Friend and was about to move forward when she felt a large hand grasp her tail and lift her from the ground. Quicker than thought, she twisted in the air, in an attempt to bite the aggressor, but before her teeth reached their target the hand jerked away and she found herself being flung through the air in a wide arc.

Before she began to descend she Switched into a bat and flew on up towards the ceiling, where she gripped a rough edge of stone with her paws and waited to get her bearings. Beneath her the game had abruptly ended and Orla was clutching the kitten, which clung to her jumper with tiny claws. Beyond them Kevin was on his feet, and they were all staring towards a boy who stood beside the crawl-hole.

He, in turn, was gazing up at her. He appeared to be a teenager, around her own age. His eyes were grey and he had fair hair, but beyond that it was hard to describe him in terms of the human race. He was dressed in clothes that glimmered and moved like molten silver and gold, and his skin shone with the same, golden light that suffused the *sidhe* so that it was difficult to say whether he reflected the light or created it. But despite his extraordinary appearance, there was something about his face that was familiar to Tess. She was still racking her brains, trying to work out what it was, when he began to speak.

To her bat-brain the sound was meaningless; a booming resonance bouncing around the confined space. Intrigued, she dropped from the ceiling and fluttered to the floor beside the table, where she Switched into human form.

'Yay! Here's Tess!' Orla shouted.

'Yahoo!' yelled Brian. 'What took you so long, eh?'

Orla tossed the little black kitten towards her. As she caught it, it transformed itself into Colm, red wellies and all. Tess was so surprised by the sudden change in weight that she dropped him, but he changed into a huge, brightly-coloured butterfly as he fell, and went fluttering off around the hall.

Tess laughed, delightedly. It was like a dream come true, being among friends, all Switchers, with no one to keep secrets from. And when she perused the loaded table, she knew that she was really in heaven. All her favourite foods were there; macaroni cheese and sausages and heaps of chips with vinegar and tomato ketchup, and trifles and cream buns and too many things to take in. She reached for a chip and was about to put it in her mouth when Kevin roared from the other end of the hall.

'No, Tess! Don't eat it!'

She turned and stared at him, dumbstruck. He ran over.

'Don't eat it, Tess,' he said again. 'Don't eat anything, you hear? Nothing at all.'

From the opposite end of the hall, the strange boy advanced, speaking as he came.

'Don't listen to him, Tess. He has some very strange ideas. I can't imagine where he got them from.'

The boy was so handsome and had such an ethereal quality that Tess found it hard to disbelieve him.

'Take some, go on. Help yourself.'

But Kevin was determined. 'No, Tess. Please listen. You know it yourself, if only you'll stop and think.'

'Think about what?' asked Tess, her irritation

496

growing. She was remembering Kevin's deceitfulness earlier, and was not inclined to give him the benefit of the doubt. But her dilemma was shelved for the time being by a new turn of events.

Brian stepped forward and, as proud as punch, stood between Tess and the radiant boy.

'In any case,' he said, 'we are forgetting ourselves. I think we all know who you are, Tess. But I don't think you have met our Uncle Declan.'

CHAPTER SEVENTEEN

Tess took several steps backwards, not because there was anything threatening about Declan's manner, but because she was afraid that if she took the offered hand it might not feel like flesh. Kevin moved over to her, protectively she thought, but it didn't stop the blood draining from her face, and for a moment or two she was light-headed and faint.

Declan smiled at her reaction.

'What's wrong?' he said. 'You look as if you've seen a ghost.'

'And haven't I?' said Tess.

He laughed. 'I can understand why you should think that,' he said.

The butterfly came flitting over and landed on Tess's shoulder. This time she was ready for the change, and she hefted Colm down on to her hip as he Switched.

'Go home, Tess?' he asked.

'Of course we will, Colm. I'll bring you home soon.'

But Kevin shook his head. 'You can't, Tess,' he said. 'He won't let them.'

'How can he stop them?' she said. 'Will somebody please explain to me what's going on?'

Colm wriggled to the ground and headed towards the table.

'Don't eat anything, now,' said Orla.

'Wanna sausage,' said Colm, reaching for one.

'Why can't he have one?' asked Tess.

'Because he'll have to stay here for ever if he eats anything,' said Brian.

'He's right,' said Kevin. 'Don't you remember the rules?'

'What rules? The rules of what?'

'Of places like this,' said Kevin. 'About not eating the food, no matter how delicious it looks.'

Orla had succeeded in prising the sausage out of Colm's hand, and was standing between him and the table, warding off the well-aimed blows that he was raining upon her.

'But that's ridiculous,' said Tess. 'That's just stuff out of fairy stories.'

Her words met with silence, and as she looked around the hall, she discovered that every eye in the place was turned to her, as though she was an idiot; the last one to get some glaringly obvious joke.

'It's ridiculous!' she said. 'You can't be for real.'

Still everyone stared, until she went on. 'This is the twentieth century, for cripe's sake! You're not trying to tell me there's such a thing as fairies!'

The silence that met her words was her answer. She shook her head incredulously.

'Where are they, then? These fairies?'

All the others turned their eyes towards Declan.

'But he's not a fairy!' said Tess. 'Fairies are little people who flit around in the woods and play tricks on . . .' She stopped, remembering some of her recent experiences. ' . . . and they're small,' she finished, lamely.

Declan laughed; a clear, birdlike sound that echoed throughout the long chamber.

'They're small except for the big ones,' he said.

'And they're big except for the green ones,' said Orla.

'And they're green except for the pink ones,' said Brian. 'And they all have wings except for the ones without them!'

The hall rang with laughter, and Tess would have felt left out; like a new girl at school all over again, if it hadn't been for Kevin. He wasn't laughing, and he took another protective step towards her.

But she hadn't forgotten his deceit. 'I don't know how you can be so stuck on the rules anyway,' she said, glaring at him. 'Since you seem to be able to break them when it suits you.'

'What rules?' said Kevin. 'What rule did I break?'

'Only the one that says you can't Switch any more after you're fifteen!'

Kevin shook his head in bewilderment. Colm came back and slipped a sweaty hand into hers.

'Go home, now?' he asked.

'Soon, Colm. Soon.'

She turned back to the others, and as she did so the blood left her brain again and she had to lean against the wall for support.

For there were two Kevins, identical in all respects.

The one beside her, the real Kevin, went pale and turned away. The other one laughed, and, just for an instant, the shadow that he cast upon the wall behind him grew about three feet taller and sprouted antlers. Tess took a step back, but before she could take any more drastic action the looming figure shrank and the second Kevin became Declan again.

For a long moment, everyone was too stunned to speak. But eventually Kevin found his voice. 'So that explains it,' he said. 'That's how you saw me in the woods. Except that it wasn't me at all. It was him.'

'But which one was him?' said Tess.

'The one who took the kids,' said Kevin. 'The other one was me. The one on the bicycle.'

'So how did you get in here?' Tess asked.

'Declan invited me in,' he said.

Declan nodded. 'People can't see the door because of an illusion; fairy glamour, it's called. But we can take it off if we choose to. If there's someone we want to let in.'

Tess felt hurt. 'Why didn't you take it off for me, then?' she asked.

To her disgust, Declan roared with laughter. 'I wanted to see if you could find your own way in,' he said. 'And besides, it was fun watching you wearing your brains out trying to understand what was going on.'

He laughed again and Tess decided to ignore him. She turned back to Kevin. 'Why didn't you come out, then?' she asked. 'Since you seem to be especially privileged around here.'

'Would you have, Tess?' said Kevin, looking towards the three children. 'Would you have left them here with him?'

Tess's heart seemed complete again. Whatever else might happen, she was reassured. This was the Kevin she knew and trusted.

If little Colm understood the conversation, he showed no interest in it. He tugged at Tess's hand and, when she didn't respond, he let go of it.

'Go home now!' he whined, and set off for the hole at the entrance to the hall.

He was small enough to crawl through easily. At least, in his own shape, he was. But as he dropped towards his hands and knees to go through, he turned into a pig. A large pig. Far too large to go through the hole.

Declan snickered, and despite herself Tess laughed as well.

'Why doesn't he try something smaller?' she said.

'Because it isn't him that's doing it,' said Kevin. 'It's Declan.'

Declan smiled and gave a mock bow. 'A simple enchantment,' he said.

'But how?' said Tess. 'I don't understand.' She turned to Declan. 'Who are you, anyway?'

'You know who I am,' said Declan. He nodded towards her cousins. 'I'm Maurice's brother; their uncle.'

'But you can't be. You're too young.'

Declan shook his head. 'I just look young,' he said. 'I'm what you could be, and your cousins. And what he could have been if he'd had the sense, poor soul.'

'Don't "poor soul" me!' said Kevin. 'I don't need your pity!'

'Maybe not,' said Declan. 'But I bet you'd change places with me if you could. Don't you think so, Tess?'

Tess suspected he might be right, but in deference to Kevin's feelings she said nothing.

'I did what you all wish you could do,' Declan went

502

on. 'I didn't give up the gift when I turned fifteen. I kept it.'

'But you can't!' said Tess. 'You have to . . .'

Declan interrupted her. 'You have to blah blah blah,' he said. 'You have to nothing. We discovered something, your uncle and I.'

'Uncle Maurice?'

'Who else? Shall I show you, Tess? Shall I show you what Maurice and I discovered in these woods?'

Tess hesitated, remembering the weird things she had seen and the fear she had experienced. What was happening here still frightened her.

'I'm not going anywhere,' she said. 'Not until I understand what's going on here. Will someone please explain?'

As soon as Colm stopped trying to get out of the crawl-hole he was relieved of his pig shape. To keep him occupied, Brian Switched into C3PO, and in immediate response, Colm turned into R2D2. Tess was satisfied as another mystery was explained, but she couldn't help wishing that she had thought of it herself, and tried it. The two metal men went to the far end of the hall, where Brian responded to his brother's bleeps and whirs in soft, patient tones.

Meanwhile, the others flopped around on the silken cushions and listened as Declan told his story.

'Maurice was the first to discover that we could change ourselves into other things,' he began.

'You mean Uncle Maurice was a Switcher, too?' said Tess.

'Is that what you call us?' said Declan. 'Switchers?'

Tess nodded, still trying to absorb the unlikely information.

503

'It isn't the word I would have used,' said Declan, 'but I suppose it doesn't matter. He was the first of us to discover it, and for a long time I was afraid, and wouldn't join him when he came out here to play with the Good People.'

'The Good People,' said Tess. 'You mentioned them before, Orla, didn't you?'

'Fairies,' said Orla. 'It's what people called them in the old days.'

'That's right,' said Declan. 'And back then there were still people who believed in their existence. In our existence, I should say. My mother was one of the last of them, I suppose. No one believes in us now.'

'Of course they don't,' said Tess. 'I mean, fairies! How could anyone believe in them?'

Declan plumped up a few more cushions and stretched himself out comfortably, propping his chin on his elbow. 'I think,' he said, 'that we'll have to start at the beginning. In ancient times. Do you want to explain it, Orla?'

Orla nodded and took up the story. 'I'm sure that there's nothing you don't know already,' she said. 'But maybe you forgot. Everyone does.'

'I didn't,' said Kevin.

Tess kicked him playfully. 'Smarty-pants,' she said. 'You didn't even go to school!'

'That's why I remember it,' said Kevin. 'I read it because I wanted to and not because I had to.'

'All right, all right,' said Tess. 'Go on, Orla, will you?'

She did. 'Do you remember all that legendary stuff about the *Fir Bolgs* who were the first inhabitants of Ireland, and then the *Tuatha de Danaan* came along,

504

Danu's people, from across the seas, from *Tír na nÓg*?'

'The Land of Eternal Youth,' said Tess.

'That's right. There are lots of stories about those people,' Orla went on. 'The books are full of them. They were a race of magicians and they could change their shape and work magic spells.'

'Oh, yes,' said Tess. 'Like the Children of Lir.'

'But do you remember what happened to them? To Danu's people?'

'I do,' said Kevin. 'There was a great battle when the Milesians came to Ireland. The Tuatha lost. They were allowed to stay in Ireland on one condition.'

Tess's skin crawled. 'I remember that bit,' she said. 'The condition was that they stay below the ground.'

There was a pause as she allowed the new implications of the old story to sink home.

'So they did,' said Declan. 'Most of the time, at least. But sometimes at night they came out and danced in the ruins of their old homes, and the rings came to be known as fairy forts.'

'And sometimes people caught glimpses of them by day as well,' said Orla. 'In wild places, like this one, where people rarely come.'

'The country people saw them often enough to know that they still existed,' said Declan. 'Even the Church failed to wipe out belief in them, though the priests tried hard enough. But a strange thing happened over the generations.'

'What happened?' asked Tess.

'We diminished in size,' said Declan.

'How?'

Declan readjusted himself again. 'It wasn't exactly that we got smaller,' he said. 'It was that people believed that we did. It's a feature of fairy glamour

505

that we exist as people perceive us to exist. So if people expected to see "Big People", then that's what they saw. And as we became known as "Little People", then people saw us as little.'

'Anything to oblige,' said Kevin.

'Maybe,' said Declan. 'But in any event, as people's belief in us diminished, so did we.'

'But why do you keep saying "we"?' asked Tess.

'Because all of us here have *Danaan* blood in our veins. That's why we have the powers that we have.' He glanced at Kevin. 'Or had, as the case may be. For myself, I chose to keep them.'

'You were going to explain that,' said Tess. 'This is where we started from.'

'I'm getting there,' said Declan. 'When our fifteenth birthday came around, I decided to stay as I was. One of the *Tuatha de Danaan.*'

'A fairy,' said Kevin.

'If you like,' said Declan.

'And Daddy didn't,' said Orla.

'He promised he would,' said Declan, and a tone of bitterness entered his voice. 'But when it came to it he lost his nerve. He didn't believe strongly enough.'

It was like getting to the end of a jigsaw. Everything was coming together, now.

'That's why he kept visiting the woods after you disappeared,' said Tess. 'Of course everyone thought he was mad. He couldn't tell anyone the truth.'

'And that's why he wants to sell the land,' said Brian, who had run out of patience with the *Star Wars* game and come over to join them. 'And why he's so angry all the time. It still hurts him to know that Declan is here.'

Declan nodded. 'He feels that I abandoned him,' he said. 'But it was him who chickened out.'

There was a great depth of sadness in his tone as he spoke, and Tess realised that the same sense of loss was in Uncle Maurice as well, beneath the anger that arose so readily. She remembered hearing about twins; about how close they could be, and she was aware that there was something unresolved in the story.

'And now you're getting your own back, is that it?' she asked.

Declan's face revealed the bitterness he felt. 'He wants to sell the land, don't you understand? He wants to destroy my home; the only thing I have.'

'And what would happen if he did?' asked Kevin. 'Where would you go?'

'Where the rest of us go who have been displaced by what you call "development",' said Declan. 'Away from your world forever. Back to *Tír na nÓg*.'

At last Tess felt that she understood. Uncle Maurice, perpetually tormented by loss and guilt, intended to get rid of the problem once and for all, in the only way he could.

'He thought he could be free of me,' said Declan. 'But I have outwitted him.' He turned to Kevin and laughed, a sound made sinister by the words that followed. 'It was your pied piper antics that gave me the idea,' he said. 'He'll never, ever sell the place now.'

CHAPTER EIGHTEEN

While they were talking, Colm had resumed his efforts to get out of the crawl-hole. Each time he failed he retreated and tried a different shape: a beetle, a snake, a mouse. But as soon as he got anywhere near the entrance he turned back into the porker and got stymied again.

While she watched him, Tess reflected on what she had learnt. It seemed that Lizzie was right yet again, and that it was ancestors and not ghosts that haunted the woods and wild places of the land. It made sense, too. There were plenty of stories about affairs and marriages between members of the fairy host and humans. Why shouldn't a bit of the old, wild blood have survived to enable children to use the ancient, magical power?

Colm retreated once again, and the puzzled expression on his face would have made Tess laugh if the situation hadn't been so serious.

508

'You can't do this,' she said. 'You can't hold the children here for ever.'

'Who says I can't?' said Declan. 'Besides, I don't have to. As soon as they get hungry enough they'll join me at my table. Then they will belong to this world, and they'll never return to that other one, out there.'

'But that's not right, Declan,' said Kevin. 'You know it's not right. People have always been tempted by the fairy world, but there was never anything in the stories about coercion. You can't force anyone to stay here if they don't want to.'

'Why not?' said Declan. 'This is my *sidhe*. In here I am the king. I can do as I please.'

Tess feared that he was right, and that none of them would ever know freedom again. But she couldn't give up.

'Why should you keep us here, though?' she said. 'Why should you want to? Your brother is out there now. He's sure to agree to any kind of deal you want, if you offer him his children in return.'

'I made a deal with him before,' said Declan, bitterly. 'He broke his word then and I don't have any reason to believe that he won't do it again. Why should I trust him?'

'Because that's what all this is about, really,' said Kevin. 'I've just realised it. This isn't the first battle of the war, is it? It's the last one. This feud has been going on between you two since you were both fifteen.'

Declan looked away and Tess knew that Kevin was right.

'He has always denied my existence,' said Declan. 'Even though he knows the truth he refuses to believe it.'

'Then talk to him,' said Tess. 'You have to give him a chance to negotiate.'

'Why?'

'Because . . .' The answer wouldn't come to Tess. She dried up. But Kevin surprised her.

'Because he's your brother,' he said. 'He's your brother and for twenty years you have lived without him, and missed him. And because he misses you every bit as much. That's why he wants to sell the land, to forget about you, not to have you haunting him every day of his life.'

'Haunting him?' said Declan. 'What do you mean, "haunting him"?'

'I've seen you,' said Tess. 'We all have. Sitting at his windows in the shape of a cat, flying over as a raven.'

'How else do you pester him, Declan?' asked Kevin. 'As a wild goat, perhaps? As a hare?'

Declan opened his mouth to speak, but what came out was more like a howl.

'He betrayed me! My whole world. He left me here alone and took over the farm. He might as well have murdered me!'

'No!' Orla had been listening quietly, but she couldn't contain herself any longer. 'Daddy wouldn't do that. He loves you, Uncle Declan, he told us that. It's why he gets so angry all the time. He's only half alive without you!'

And for all his power, for all his wealth beneath the hill, it was suddenly clear that Declan felt the same.

Tess agreed to go with Declan to be an observer in his talks with Maurice while Kevin and the others stayed behind in the *sidhe*. Declan went ahead and

510

dived into the low tunnel as a hare. Tess followed. But as soon as they emerged into the second hallway, Declan stopped. He was staring at the exit which, Tess could see, was wide open. On the other side of it, Uncle Maurice was standing in the moonlight, head in hands.

Tess froze, but Declan Switched back into his boy-like form. After a moment, Tess joined him.

'It's hard to believe that he can't see us,' she whispered.

'Could you see into the rock, from out there?' said Declan.

'No. But I can see out, now.'

'It's different from this side. It doesn't matter what we do; he can't see in.'

To demonstrate his point, Declan skipped along the hall and did an energetic jig just feet from where his brother was standing. Tess watched, breathlessly. Declan was a strong and graceful dancer, as skilled as anyone she had seen in any of the Irish dancing shows that had recently become so popular. He grinned at her and winked, then turned and made insulting gestures at his brother.

But Uncle Maurice might as well have been blind for all the notice he took.

'Why?' asked Tess. 'Why can't he see or hear us?'

'Glamour,' said Declan. 'There aren't so many *sidhes* like this left now, but once they were all over Ireland. We hid them; not with any actual thing, but with illusion. The door exists only in his mind, as it existed in yours before you succeeded in breaching it.'

'But if he was a Switcher himself, why doesn't he know that?'

511

'Because he doesn't believe any more. He has denied the past as well as the present.'

As Tess watched, Uncle Maurice struck at the invisible barrier, first with one fist and then the other. From her perspective, it looked as though he was hitting unbreakable glass.

'Are all the doors the same?' she asked.

'They work on the same principle, yes. But some are grassy hill-sides and some are in the ground. Wherever they are, they work in the same way; by deceiving the mind of the onlooker.'

At that moment, Uncle Maurice sighed loudly and turned away from the door. Without pausing for an instant, Declan transformed himself into a barn owl and, with a shrill shriek of alarm, went bursting out of the opening.

More quietly, Tess followed. As she swept up through the trees and joined Declan circling above them, she could see her uncle on the ground below, shaking his fist after them. She was glad that he couldn't see little Colm's predicament inside the hill. Angry as he was now, that would have made him mad with fury.

Still in owl-form, Declan circled above the trees and Tess followed while Uncle Maurice watched on helplessly. Not until he got tired of craning his neck and sat down despondently on a mossy rock, did Declan alight. For a while he sat in a tree, looking down, while Tess waited on a nearby branch. Then, as though he had finally plucked up courage, he dropped on to the ground below and Switched. Choosing her spot carefully, Tess glided down from the trees and Switched behind a broad trunk, from where she could look on unseen by either of the others.

In the moonlit clearing, Declan's clothes had a quite different appearance. Without colour their sheen was silvery-grey, so similar to the surrounding light that it was not easy to see him at all. Except that, when he moved in a certain way, a gleam of bluish light would suddenly shine out for an instant, then vanish again, reminding Tess of the mysterious flickerings that she had seen from her bedroom window.

It was some time before Uncle Maurice became aware of his brother's presence. When he did, his jaw dropped. Seeing them together, Tess realised why it was that Declan had seemed familiar to her when she had first set eyes upon him. The family resemblance was quite remarkable; the two boys must have been stunningly similar when they were the same age.

When they were the same age. How could they have once been the same age and be the same age no longer? Tess was trying to get her mind around the paradox when Uncle Maurice spoke.

'It really was you, then, all along?' he said. 'The raven and the cat and the brown hare. I was never sure.'

'It was me,' said Declan.

'Sometimes I thought there was nothing there at all,' said Maurice. 'Nothing except a figment of my imagination.'

He fell silent, but crossed the clearing slowly until he was close to his brother. There was no difference in their height, but one was a boy and the other a man. For a long time neither of them spoke, and Tess felt embarrassed, a stranger eavesdropping on a highly emotional reunion. Then Uncle Maurice spoke again.

'I still can't believe that it's true,' he said. 'I'm so

513

used to mistrusting my own senses. Everything was so confused at the time when you . . . when you disappeared. If I tried to explain what had happened, people thought I was mad.'

'People believe what it suits them to believe,' said Declan. 'Sometimes when tourists come wandering around I go and stand right in front of them and they don't see me at all.'

'That's what I'm afraid of,' said Maurice. 'Sometimes I think that you must have died, and that I created the whole story in my imagination to save me from having to face the truth.'

Declan thought for a moment. 'I've forgotten,' he said. 'I have forgotten how it feels to have a mind that needs to discover truth, instead of one that creates it.'

Maurice nodded. 'I've forgotten the other kind,' he said. 'Or at least, I stopped believing in it.'

'Why did it matter to you, then?' said Declan. 'Why did you feel the need to sell off the land and get rid of me?'

Uncle Maurice shook his head, and Tess realised that there was something he was withholding.

'Why, Mossy?' Declan pressed him. 'Why couldn't you just let it be?'

'I could have, possibly. If you had let me. But you wouldn't, would you? You had to keep haunting me. You were always on my mind, Dec. I haven't known a moment's peace since you . . .'

'Since I what, Maurice? What is your version of the truth? Since I disappeared? Since I went through with it? Or since you chickened out on our agreement?'

'Is that what you think?' said Maurice. 'All these years, you thought that I didn't have the courage?'

514

He shook his head. 'It wasn't like that. It was just the opposite.'

'Oh, yes?'

'Yes. Until that moment it had all been a game, like all the other "what if" sorts of game. But when you made the change, when I saw you become one of *them*, then it wasn't a game any longer. It was for real. And then I knew that I couldn't do it. Because one of us had to stay with our mother and father, Dec. If we had both vanished for ever it would have killed them.'

Behind the trunk of the tree, Tess could understand all too well how Uncle Maurice must have felt. Her parents had always been a concern of hers, whenever she thought about her future life.

'So you took the decision, there and then, is that it?' said Declan. 'Without asking for my opinion?'

'I hesitated,' said Maurice. 'I hesitated and then it was too late. The moment had gone and the sun rose. I had missed my chance.'

'You hesitated and I was lost,' said Declan.

'But you're not lost, Decco. Don't you see? At that moment, at the moment when the sun rose, I became fifteen. A fifteen year old boy, destined to become a man and a father, and then grow old and die. But you . . . You, Dec . . .'

Maurice's words tailed off as emotion choked him.

Declan looked long and hard at his brother, and something seemed to give; some hardness in him seemed to melt away and allow space for understanding to enter.

With a massive effort, Maurice succeeded in gaining control of his emotions. 'It never occurred to me before now that you should feel aggrieved,' he said. 'As far as I was concerned, I was the one who had been left behind. Stuck in a black and white world, while you're out there in the colourful one.' He paused, and then, before his sorrow could silence him again, he continued, 'For ever, Dec. For ever.'

For a long moment, the two brothers stared at each other, and then, quite suddenly, the resentment that had stood like plate armour between them for twenty years dropped away.

'I'm sorry,' said Declan. 'I never thought of those things. I never saw it like that.'

'You're not as sorry as I am,' said Maurice.

The two brothers contemplated each other for a few moments, then Maurice said, 'Are you solid? Can I touch you?'

Declan stepped forward and held out his hand. Maurice took it, held it, then pulled his brother close and hugged him tight. When he released him and stepped back, Tess could see a new light in her uncle's eyes, as though years of bitterness had dissolved away, revealing him as he had been; youthful and hopeful and kind.

'I'll let the children go, Mossy,' said Declan. 'Will you keep the land?'

'You have my word on it,' said Maurice. 'As long as I live, I'll never sell it, nor touch it in any way at all.'

'If I trust you on that, will you trust me?' said Declan. 'Will you let the children visit me?'

Uncle Maurice laughed, a new kind of laugh that Tess had never heard him make before, light and exuberant.

'I will of course,' he said. 'And I'll come myself as well. Picnics with the fairies. You can be sure of it!'

516

The two brothers embraced again, then broke apart and shook hands. Then Declan took two steps backwards and melted away in the moonlight.

CHAPTER NINETEEN

Tess scanned the surroundings, trying to get a fix on where Declan had gone. But apart from a fresh breeze that was swishing around in the treetops, there seemed to be nothing moving. Uncle Maurice sat himself down to wait for the children and, after another minute or two, Tess returned to the *sidhe*.

Now that her mind had dispelled the illusion that hid the door in the rock, Tess had no difficulty passing through. Inside, she found that the easiest way to negotiate the dim hall was as a bat, and she was still in that form when she whisked through the crawl-hole. The moment she entered the second hall her hearing and her sonar perception were both assaulted by chaos.

She needed eyes. As quickly as she could she Switched into human form and tried to make sense of what she was seeing. In the middle of the hall an enormous bear was throwing its weight around in what seemed like a terrible rage. Beside it, C3PO was trying to calm it in a terribly British sort of voice, while a jackdaw fluttered around its face in a way that was clearly intended to distract it. A few feet away, Kevin was in the process of overturning the table, and the piles of food were crashing to the floor.

'Help, Tess,' he shouted. 'He's gone berserk!'

At last she realised what was happening. Little Colm had finally had enough of being thwarted. His hunger and frustration had become bear-sized, and so had he. It was a frightening situation, but Tess didn't realise just how dangerous it was until she saw what was in the bear's paws. He had succeeded in reaching the table before Kevin overturned it, and he was clutching a bear-sized fistful of sausages. The only thing preventing him from getting them into his bear-sized mouth was the persistent irritation of the jackdaw, which was in grave danger of being swiped by a flailing paw.

There wasn't a second to lose. Tess allowed her instinct to guide her as she Switched, and was surprised to find herself in the shape of a wolfhound. She was already springing forward as she took on the form, and an instant later her jaws clamped tightly around the bear's forearm. But she had under-estimated Colm's power. With a bellow of rage, he swung the arm in a great arc, crashing her into Kevin and knocking him over before sending her hurtling through the air to the other end of the hall. It all seemed to happen infinitely slowly. Even as she was hitting the wall and struggling to her feet she was watching what was happening in the fray. The bear knocked the flapping jackdaw aside. His paw, with sausages sticking out like fingers, approached his mouth. And then, when it seemed impossible for anything to stop the terrible progress of fate, the bear turned into a tree.

For a moment, Tess thought that the collision with the wall had jellified her brain. From the expression on Kevin's face as he scrambled to his feet, he was having similar thoughts. But beyond him, just inside the crawl-hole, Declan's smug expression revealed the solution.

'How did you do that?' asked Tess, testing out her bruised limbs as she walked towards him.

'I'll show you,' he replied. 'As soon as I have sent this lot home.'

Orla and Brian had returned to their own forms, and if they were surprised by what had happened, they didn't show it. But Kevin was shaking his head in disbelief.

'I see what you mean,' he said. 'About the rules changing.'

Declan was picking sausages out from among the branches of the tree and eating them. 'He'll have to be careful, this one,' he said. 'He doesn't know his own strength.'

'He just gets hungry,' said Orla. 'He's good at home and at playschool. He understands.'

Declan nodded and, as soon as all the sausages were safely out of the way, he turned Colm back into a small and tearful human being.

'Don't worry now,' he told him. 'Your daddy's outside. You're going home.'

Colm did a red-booted dance of delight at the news, and Brian hefted him up on to his hip and hugged him. But Orla's face fell.

'Is he cross?' she said.

Until that moment Tess had completely forgotten about Orla's asthma. It was only now that she realised there hadn't been the slightest hint of a wheeze in her cousin's breath the whole time they had been inside the hill.

Declan was shaking his golden head. 'He's not cross at all,' he said. 'In fact, I wouldn't be surprised if he wasn't half so cross now as he used to be.'

Colm wriggled to be put down and headed for the crawl-hole. But at the point where he had become accustomed to turning into a pig he stopped and looked over at Declan.

'Go home, now?' he said.

Declan nodded. 'Go home, now,' he said.

And Colm was a red fox, scooting out through the small space as though a pack of hounds was on his tail.

'Me too,' said Brian, and was gone. But Orla hesitated.

'Will you be back soon, Tess?' she asked.

'I . . . I don't know,' said Tess. The question had brought back the terrible question of choice, and Tess knew that the ordeal of that night was very far from being over.

'I know it's your birthday,' said Orla. 'Maybe you'll come back and visit us anyway. Whatever you decide?'

Tess was surprised to discover a new respect for her young cousin. Maybe it was the illness that had caused it; the continual struggle for breath and for life, but the girl seemed wise beyond her years.

'I will, of course,' said Tess. 'Even if . . .'

Orla nodded. 'Even if,' she said. And then she was gone.

'How did you do that?' Kevin asked Declan.

Declan shrugged. 'Desperate circumstances call for desperate measures. Like a sausage?'

'Thanks.' Kevin took it and was about to put it into his mouth when Tess realised what he was doing.

'Watch what you're doing,' she yelled.

Kevin dropped the sausage, an expression of horror on his face. 'You tried to trick me,' he said.

Declan shrugged. 'Why shouldn't I? That's what I am, it's what I do.'

Tess expected to feel as horrified as Kevin, but part of her was beginning to be enchanted by Declan. His abilities seemed limitless; his power excited her. Not only that, but in comparison with Kevin's awkward, gawky frame, Declan was graceful and handsome.

'You said you'd show me,' she said. 'How to Switch other people.'

'I will,' said Declan. 'I'll show you more than that as well, if you come with me.'

'Where?'

Declan nodded towards the crawl-hole. 'Out there. To where the night is waiting for us.'

'Careful, Tess,' said Kevin.

'You could come with us, too,' said Declan. 'If you eat fairy food you become fairy, Kevin. You could be what you once were; experience your old powers again, keep them forever.'

Tess could tell that Kevin was interested. 'Why not, Kevin?' she said.

He shook his head. 'There has to be a catch,' he said. 'I'm not sure that I want to stay here forever.'

'You could be a rat again,' said Tess.

'A rat?' said Declan. 'Is that what you like best? A rat?'

Kevin looked sulky and didn't answer.

'I could sort that out for you if you wanted,' said Declan. 'Turn you into one for good. Would you like that?'

Kevin shrugged, but Tess knew that he was tempted.

'You don't have to decide right now,' said Declan. 'Have a think about it while we're gone.'

And before either Kevin or Tess could answer, Declan had become a hare again and vanished out of the crawl-hole.

'Don't go, Tess. What if he tricks you?'

'He won't,' said Tess. 'I'll be OK.'

Kevin nodded wistfully. 'You're your own boss,' he said. 'But promise me one thing?'

'What's that?' asked Tess.

'Promise me that you'll come back before dawn. Before you make your final decision.'

Tess nodded, sobered by the reminder of the short time remaining to her.

'I promise,' she said.

From the skies high above the woods, Tess and Declan could see Uncle Maurice and the others walking across the fields towards home. The grass was covered with dew and the three who were walking left straggly trails behind them as though they were in no hurry. The fourth one, little Colm, was already fast asleep, secure in his father's arms.

Beside her in the high air, Tess could sense Declan's sadness, despite the disdainful look in his eagle's eye. Somehow she knew that it wasn't only his brother he missed, but the other things as well; the life he would never lead as a farmer, the children he was unlikely to have. As though he sensed her intuition intruding upon him, he banked on the wind and drifted down to a nearby field, where cattle lay sleeping in the grass.

'Go on,' said Declan, when they had taken on human shapes again. 'Turn them into pigs first. It's good practice.'

'But how?' said Tess.

'Why ask me?' said Declan. 'How do you Switch?'

Tess knew what he meant. Although Tess could Switch as quick as thinking, there was no way she could have explained to someone how she did it. It was one of those things like wiggling your ears; you could do it or you couldn't. And when she thought about it like that, she realised that she did know how to change the shapes of other things as well; she had just never realised that she could.

The cows didn't know what hit them. One moment they were happily sleeping and the next, one after another, they were all turned into pigs. Tess laughed delightedly, and then the pigs were sheep, bleating anxiously and gathering themselves into a defensive group. But Tess wasn't finished yet. In fact, she was just beginning to get the hang of it. It was the same process as Switching; the combined use of will and imagination, and she was already regretting all the lost opportunities.

The sheep became goats, and then half of them became kangaroos. Then, while they were still staring at each other in astonishment, some of them became hyenas and began stalking the others.

'Careful,' Declan warned. 'We don't want to cause any damage.'

He was right. Things were beginning to get out of control as goats and kangaroos began to panic and spring out over the walls and away. Before they got too far, Tess Switched them all back into cows again, which is how the farmer would find them the next morning; scattered around in different fields with no evidence to show how they had got there.

'I can't believe I never discovered this before!' said Tess, turning a rock into a tractor and a field full of round bales into an igloo village. 'I could have had a great time! I can just see it, too. All those times my dad drove me mad reading the paper, I could have turned him into a sloth or a slug or a tortoise or something. And my mum, droning on. A queen bee!'

Declan came along behind, returning Tess's transformations to their original selves.

'There's a girl at school always copying what everyone else says,' Tess went on. 'I'd love to turn her into a parrot.' As she spoke, Tess changed a hawthorn bush into a Japanese pagoda and a steel gate into a large patchwork quilt. 'And there's a boy who's really horrible to his poor little dog. I'd turn him into a toad and let the dog eat him!'

With Tess Switching everything in sight and Declan changing everything back again, they made their way across the fields until they had come to the road, a half mile or so from the farmhouse.

'Haven't you had enough, yet?' Declan asked. 'There's other things I want to show you before daybreak.'

'Daybreak,' said Tess. 'Oh, my God. I keep forgetting.'

'There's still plenty of time,' said Declan. 'But I want you to meet the others.'

'The others?'

'Of course. You don't think we're the only ones, do you?'

525

As a last trick, Tess turned a thoroughbred brood mare into a donkey and, just for the hell of it, Declan left it as it was. Then the two friends made owls of themselves again and lifted into the darkness.

CHAPTER TWENTY

Declan rode an upcurrent towards the top of the crag, where he landed and Switched to his golden, fairy form. Tess followed and became human. Side by side they sat for a while and watched the moon slipping down towards the horizon, then Declan turned to Tess and said, 'Want to try the weather?'

Without waiting for a reply, he stood up and held out his arms like a conductor in front of an orchestra. Tess stayed where she was. She thought it was a joke. Even when the first clouds began to appear from beneath the setting moon and creep across its face, she put it down to coincidence. But a moment later she had to reconsider.

Like a speeded-up film the white clouds advanced, obscuring the moon and rapidly covering the sky. The night became darker, and Tess dimly remembered something about the darkest hour being just before the dawn. But it didn't stay dark for long. First, a

527

few faint pulses of light began to bounce around among the clouds.. Gradually they grew stronger and more brilliant until suddenly a streak of lightning leapt from the clouds and struck the ground nearby. There was a cracking sound that could only have been made by a rock splitting.

'Woah, woah,' Tess shouted. 'Steady on, now!'

But her words were swallowed by a mind-numbing boom of thunder right above her head. She ducked instinctively and turned to suggest to Declan that they get out of there. It was clear, however, that he had no intention of moving.

The expression on his face was ecstatic, as though the chaos that he was creating in the skies around was divine music. He turned to her and smiled a brilliant smile. Again a bolt of lightning struck nearby, and then another and another, but Tess no longer feared that they would harm her. There was a smell of burning vegetation, but when she looked down towards the woods at the foot of the crag below them there was no sign of fire.

It seemed indeed that the lightning storm was confined to the top of the mountain. Tess wondered whether anyone was awake at that hour and watching. It must have been a spectacular sight. And no more extraordinary, she mused, than a lot of unexplained things that happened in human life.

The rain began, bucketing down out of the firework skies. Declan whooped and turned his face up to the downpour. And when she stopped resisting, Tess began to enjoy it as well. So heavy was the deluge that in no time at all the top of the mountain was awash with run-off, and small streams began to develop and join together to make larger ones, which raced for the edge of the crag and launched themselves over.

Suddenly, remembering Lizzie's words, Tess knew that wild blood did indeed run in her veins. With careless delight, she Switched into a salmon and flipped and flopped herself into the nearest stream. The water lifted her and rushed her towards the edge until, with heart-stopping speed, it catapulted her out over the edge of the crag.

She turned in the air; head over tail in empty space. As she fell she knew the delirium of recklessness, of trust in her own power, of the thrill of the moment. Below her the trees were emerging out of the darkness. Any moment now and she would smash into their branches, become fish-cakes, a surprise delicacy for the rats. In the nick of time she spread eagle wings and soared away, every feather vibrating in the rain-filled air. Out and away she swung, while above her the downpour ended and the clouds quietened and rolled away and dispersed, like a flock of sheep released from a pen.

The moon reappeared, sinking behind the horizon. For a few minutes Tess drifted, enjoying the sense of freedom and grace that the massive wings gave her. Then she flapped lazily upwards until she reached Declan's side again.

Back in human form, Tess was so wet that tiny streams dribbled from her hair and from her cuffs, but the excitement still ran so high that she didn't care at all.

'What next?' she asked.

'You have to learn to ride,' said Declan.

'Horses?' Tess was reminded of the unfortunate brood mare and hoped that her owner liked donkeys. He would probably think that a neighbour, or someone who bore him a grudge, had changed the animals over for the mischief of it. The more she thought about it the more Tess realised that life was full of inexplicable happenings. And in their insistence on concocting 'logical' explanations, people tried to force their world into the confines of a set of laws that made it seem much smaller and less interesting than it really was.

Even when it clearly didn't fit. For now a wind was rising in the west. But this wind was not caused by changing pressures in the earth's atmosphere. This wind was Declan's, and it was summoned by a combination of will and imagination which, the old people knew, was called magic.

Declan's wind was warm and brisk. Tess wrung out her hair and her sleeves and spread out her arms to dry. But there was no time for that. Under Declan's silent command the wind began to twist and turn and, like some restless animal, it brushed against Tess and knocked her off balance. She sat on a rock and watched as Declan sent it whipping across farmland, swirling through the trees below, and howling above and between the surrounding hills. Then he brought it back where it waited at his feet with a strange quivering that made Tess's eardrums vibrate.

'You want to try?' he asked.

'OK.' Tess stood up again and took hold of an imaginary pair of reins. But it was not as simple as it had looked when Declan did it. At her first command the wind lunged away so powerfully that Tess was almost dragged over the edge of the cliff and Declan had to come to her rescue. More delicately, she tried again until, gradually, the wind began to respond to her wishes. She circled it first, like a horse on a lunge rein, round and round the flat mountain-top. Then, when she was confident with that, she sent it blustering off to the sea, so that it returned damp and salty and sounding of gulls. And then, just as she was beginning to feel confident, Declan said, 'Are you ready to ride it?'

Before Tess could reply, he rushed forward and disappeared over the edge of the crag. Tess's heart stopped, but he was only gone for a moment. When he reappeared he was astride the invisible wind, tossing backwards and forwards on its restless force as he waited for her.

'Come on, Tess!' he called.

Throughout her life, there had always been steps Tess was afraid to take. She realised now as she looked out over the immense drop below that there would never come a time, no matter what she decided to be, when there would not be another step that required courage, and then another. But there would never be another night like tonight, when there was so much to learn in so little time.

The knowledge that she could save herself by Switching gave her courage. She called up her wind and, at the same time, launched herself out over the edge.

And fell. Down, down towards the trees below. In a panic she grabbed at imaginary reins and yanked hard. Instantly, her descent began to slow.

'Up!' she yelled.

And up she went, rising with swift and certain power until she passed Declan on a level with the crag.

'East!' he shouted.

Tess banked as though she was riding a motor bike, and beneath her the wind responded. Left and right she leant. Left and right the wind turned. Declan was lost in the night ahead, but suddenly his clothes gave off a blue, moonlight gleam, and Tess sped off in pursuit. As she caught up, the two breezes buffeted around each other and gave their passengers a bumpy ride, but after a while they settled. Side by side, Tess and Declan raced through the night sky.

Not since she and Kevin had been dragons had Tess experienced such a sense of exhilaration. Beneath them the country was laid out like a map, but not a map of towns and roads and rivers. What they were seeing was a fairy map, made up of ley-lines and *sidhes* and the strongly radiating focal points of magical power.

'Scenic route,' said Declan, indicating the glowing shapes of Tara and New Grange far below. They veered north and, in a surprisingly short time, over-flew the prehistoric site of Eamhain Macha.

'Where are we going?' asked Tess.

'The gathering,' said Declan. 'I just thought you'd like a little look around on the way.'

'What gathering?' asked Tess.

Declan didn't reply but turned towards the west again, and soon they were dropping down to an area where it seemed that dozens of lines of energy came together and caused a warm, inviting radiance.

'It's Ben Bulben,' said Tess, as the unmistakable profile of the Sligo mountain revealed itself in the moonlight.

Long before they landed on its broad back, Tess could see the fairy hordes gathered there.

'Many of the *sidhes* have been desecrated,' said Declan. 'But there are still a great many undiscovered. This has always been a favourite place of our people.'

532

Tess hung back, intimidated by the numbers that were gathered below.

'Come on,' said Declan. 'You won't feel a bit shy when you get there. Believe me!'

CHAPTER TWENTY-ONE

And he was right. Any shyness that Tess might have experienced evaporated as soon as she arrived. That night, on Ben Bulben, Tess moved among the people of Danu who come from the Land of Eternal Youth. She danced as she had never danced before, even in her imagination. For the first time in her life, she was home.

Crowds of them were there, the eternally young, all glowing with the soft, vibrant energy that was a property of *Tír na nÓg*. They welcomed her with ceremonial gifts; a torque of heavy gold that fitted around her neck; a ring of the same material, broad and bright. The women were beautiful and the men were handsome, but none was more handsome that night than Declan, and it was with him that Tess chose to dance.

On top of Ben Bulben and under it the party went on, and if people can never reveal or remember their visits to fairyland it is because the people and the places are not of this world and cannot be described in its terms. Lizzie's words, remembered there, were not in the slightest bit puzzling, and Tess passed on her regards to the people of *Tír na nÓg*. For these people were, she realised, her ancestors. These were the immortal ones who still lived on beneath the green fields of Ireland and would live on there as long as there were wild and unpopulated places for them to inhabit. They were older even than the ancient mountain beneath their feet, and would remain long after it had been swallowed by the sea.

On top of Ben Bulben and under it, Tess discovered what it meant to have wild blood running through her veins, and she celebrated it with reckless delight. She danced without stopping and Declan danced with her until, like a discord, a different light began to appear in the sky.

Tess stopped and, reluctantly, Declan did too. Around them the dancers whirled on and away, and vanished into the night as though they had never been.

'Dawn,' said Tess.

'Not yet,' said Declan. 'But it's coming.'

'We must go back. Quickly!'

'But why? Now that you know what you are, you need never go back there again.'

'But I have to,' said Tess. 'I promised Kevin that I would.'

Declan opened his mouth to protest but, with an authority that surprised her, Tess summoned a wind and commanded it to carry her back to the *sidhe* in the crag.

Kevin was waiting outside the door in the rock. As Tess made her dramatic arrival, he jumped to his feet.

'Thank God,' he said. 'I thought you weren't going to make it.'

'Don't worry,' said Declan, who had swept in behind her in the trees. 'There isn't any hurry.'

'I think there is,' said Kevin. 'I think that any moment now the sun is going to rise.'

'So what if it does?' said Declan. 'Tess has made her decision, haven't you, Tess?'

There was a rustling and a whispering among the trees. Although she couldn't see them, Tess knew that there were others there with them, waiting to welcome her into their company. She nodded, realising that Declan was right. She had made her decision. Now that she had found her heritage, how could she renounce it?

But Kevin was adamant. 'No, Tess. No. Think again.'

'But why?' said Tess. 'You could join us if you wanted to. You can't imagine how it feels.'

'Maybe not,' said Kevin. 'But I've been doing a lot of thinking.'

'Don't think,' said Declan. 'It's a terrible weakness that people have. I thought you were set on being a rat, anyway?'

As he said the words, he pointed at Kevin and Switched him. There he was, the rat with two toes missing, so familiar to Tess from the days when she had first known him. She experienced a sense of *déja vu*, then remembered her dream and the strong sense of foreboding that had accompanied it. Something was very wrong.

Kevin spoke to her in rat. 'Girl changing rat back

536

into boy. Very fast! Rat turning into boy! Rat turning into boy!'

In the background another rat voice added itself to the demand and Tess realised that Cat Friend was there, watching everything that was going on.

Tess remembered her lessons with Declan and Switched Kevin back, delighted to show off her new powers. How could she possibly give them up, now that she was discovering the full extent of them?

'Changed your mind?' said Declan, as Kevin became human again.

'Yes,' said Kevin. 'I have. I want to be human, Tess, and I think you should, too.'

'Why?' said Tess. 'Give me one good reason.'

Kevin glanced towards the east, and worry was carved into his features.

'I will,' he said. 'Just hear me out, will you?'

Declan looked disdainful, but Tess nodded and Kevin went on.

'I could live a happy life as a rat. I know I could. And you could live forever as you are; young and beautiful, a magical being. But neither of us would have influence, you see?'

'Influence?' said Declan, and as he spoke a wind rose and began to bluster around in the trees above their heads. 'What would you know about influence?'

'I'm not even sure what you are, Tess,' Kevin went on. 'Are you? Remember what Declan was saying about adapting to people's perceptions? What if that's all you are? Just a figment of someone else's imagination?'

Declan's face darkened, and he took Tess's arm as though to draw her away. But she shook her head and turned back to Kevin.

'Go on,' she said.

'I don't know,' he said, rushing his words now in a desperate race against the irresistible turning of the planet. 'I don't know what you are or what he is. But I do know that if you become like him, if that's the choice you make, then you won't belong to this world any longer.'

His words unsettled Tess. The wind in the trees got rougher, more insistent. Declan gripped her arm again.

'Don't listen to him,' he said.

But Kevin was not going to be put off. 'This world, Tess. This world that we both love so much.' He tore a clump of moss from a rock and held its earthy scent to her nose. 'I came to an understanding tonight,' he went on. 'About what it meant to be a Switcher. I realised that it doesn't matter whether or not I can change my shape; not any more. What matters is that being a Switcher taught me ... taught you as well, Tess ... how to adapt. How to change to meet whatever situation arises, even though we might look the same from outside.'

Tess nodded. What Kevin was saying was something that she knew and believed, even though she had never succeeded in putting words on it.

'I can see my future at last,' he was saying. 'It came to me tonight as I was waiting here. I'm going to get off the streets, Tess, get some education if I need to, do whatever it takes to get into a position where I can make a difference. These woods are safe, now, they will stay as they are. But all over the world there are wild places being destroyed. I'm going to be there, Tess. I'm going to campaign, try to stop it happening, stand in front of the bulldozers if I have to.'

A few drops of rain began to fall, but despite them

538

the first blackbird sang a tentative phrase from a nearby branch.

'All those creatures, Tess! We know them better than anyone. Who will fight their corner if we don't, eh?'

A light touch, light as a moth, tickled Tess's ankle. Cat Friend was there again, reaching up, her whiskers twitching. The simple gesture of trust brought a charge of emotion into Tess's bones.

'We can be their ambassadors, Tess; their voice in the world. It will help the fairy people, too, if we can save the wild places!'

Declan was tugging at her again. 'Don't listen to that nonsense,' he said. 'Stay with me, Tess, and ride the wild winds at night. Look at the gold you have on you. Look at your wealth. You'll never have such power in any other life.'

The rain fell harder. A second bird began to sing and there were two small voices in the darkness. As the first ray of the rising sun found a way past the clouds and crept in among the leaves another bird voice joined them, and then another. Kevin held out his hand.

And Tess took it.

Then all hell broke loose around them as Declan unleashed the full fury of the storm. Instinctively, Tess ducked down and shrank against the flat wall of the crag. Kevin joined her, shielding his head with his arms as lightning blasted the heart out of a huge boulder just feet away.

'It's OK,' said Tess, clutching at his jacket. 'It's OK.'

Again the lightning struck, and again. High above them it hit the exposed crag once, twice, three times.

An ominous rumble began, deep inside the mountain.

Rain drenched their hair and ran down their faces. Kevin got to his feet and dragged Tess up.

'Run, Tess,' he yelled. 'The whole lot is about to come down on top of us!'

Even as he spoke there came a deafening crack from above, as though the cliff itself had split in two.

'Come on, Tess! Run!'

But Tess held her ground. She shook her head. 'No.'

'Are you mad?' Kevin was shouting now, his voice barely audible above the creaking and groaning of splintering rock and the splashing of monsoon-like rain.

'No!' Tess shouted back. 'I'm not mad. But I know that Declan won't hurt us!'

'What do you think he's doing, then?' Kevin yelled.

There was terror in his voice. To their right they heard the crash of fracturing trees as the first huge boulder hurtled down on the woods from the crag above.

But still Tess held her ground. 'He won't hurt us,' she repeated. 'None of them will.'

Another massive chunk of rock crashed into the trees. Lightning struck repeatedly nearby, making the world smell of sulphur.

'But they're trying to kill us!' said Kevin.

Tess shook her head, absurdly calm amid the raging chaos. 'They won't kill us,' she said. 'They won't hurt us at all. They're the Good People, Kevin. The Good People.'

And as though the forces of nature themselves had heard her words, the wind dropped and the storm died away and the rain continued for just long enough to extinguish the lightning-fires, then it stopped, too.

Tess and Kevin sat on the wet moss at the foot of the crag, absorbing their experiences and waiting for daylight. Gradually the birds regained their confidence and resumed their singing, and from a nook in the rock beside them, Cat Friend peeped out.

'Lightning finished, huh, huh?' she said.

'Yup, yup.'

Tess bent down to talk to her, and as she did so, something in her jeans' pocket dug into her stomach. She pulled it out. It was Orla's inhaler.

'White Cat at home in the rock, huh?' said Cat Friend.

'Yup,' said Tess. 'White Cat, raven, hare, all back inside the rock.'

Cat Friend slipped away and disappeared, and Tess felt a stab of regret, knowing that she was unlikely to see her again, or Declan either, at least in his handsomest form.

'What's that?' said Kevin, noticing the inhaler.

'It's Orla's,' said Tess. 'For her asthma. I'd better get it back to her, in case she's looking for it.'

She stood up and Kevin joined her. 'You should, I suppose,' he said. 'Although I've got a funny feeling that she won't be needing it any more.'

He slipped an arm around her shoulders and together they began to make their way through the trees. But after a few yards, Tess stopped.

'Did you hear footsteps?'

Kevin listened hard. 'I don't think so.'

Tess looked back. 'It's like a dream,' she said. 'As though it never happened at all. If you saw the rock now, would you believe that you could walk straight into it?'

Kevin shrugged. 'I think I'd have doubts, to be honest.'

He turned back to her, and as he did so he fixed his eyes on her throat and shook his head in astonishment.

'But it happened all right,' he said. 'There's your proof.'

Tess remembered the torque and reached up to take it off. In her hand was nothing but a few twists of rusty old wire, and around her finger, where the gold ring had been, was a plastic washer from a tap.

Kevin started to laugh. 'There's your gold, Tess,' he said. 'There's your glamour.'

Despite herself, Tess laughed too. At the same moment they both stopped, each of them certain that they heard another voice laughing along with them.

But no matter how hard they listened, all they could hear was silence.

ABOUT THE AUTHOR

Kate Thompson is one of the most exciting
new authors to emerge for some time, a born
storyteller with a deft and subtle touch. She
has trained race horses in England and the USA,
studied law in London and travelled extensively
in India, working and learning.
She has worked a small holding in County Clare
for ten years and now lives in County Galway.

Kate Thompson has twice won the Irish
Children's Book of the Year, Bisto Award:
in 2002 for *The Beguilers* and in 2003
for *The Alchemist's Apprentice*.

The Missing Link

KATE THOMPSON

The Missing Link charts the journey of Christie as he travels with his step-brother Danny on a quest to find Danny's mysterious mother in Fourth World. In this tremendous novel of genetic mystery and adventure, Christie is about to discover some unexpected and amazing truths. For Fourth World holds many secrets, some of terrifying significance ...

'A thoroughly satisfying and thought-provoking read' *Guardian*

RED FOX

0 09 926629 6

KATE THOMPSON

Only Human

In this thrilling sequel to *The Missing Link*,
Christie and Danny undertake another dangerous
journey, which brings them into contact with
their genetic origins in the most unexpected
ways; Danny encounters the merpeople under
the sea, while Christie comes into possession of
the mysterious yeti stone in Tibet.

'The strands of the plot are cleverly linked in a
story full of appeal' *TES*

'. . . hugely enjoyable' *Books for Keeps*

RED FOX
0 09 943224 2

Origins

KATE THOMPSON

Dreadful events are about to strike Fourth World ...

In the secret community where, through genetic
experiments, animals can talk and children carry animal
genes, an unimaginable alien presence makes its
appearance. Vividly described by Christie in his diary,
this creature raises terrifying questions. Is it a threat
to all civilized life? Can it be destroyed or contained ...?

Alternating with the diary is the extraordinary story of
Nessa and Farral. Will their dangerous journey heal the rift
that exists between their two communities?

In the final exciting novel of the *Missing Link* trilogy,
Kate Thompson, twice winner of the Irish Children's Book
of the Year, Bisto Award, raises startling and relevant
questions for the twenty-first century.

'Intelligent, blackly amusing and ingeniously put together,
this part novel, part fable is a masterful piece of writing'
Nicholas Tucker

'... a tremendous plotline ... a great series' *The Times*

RED FOX
0 09 940906 2

THE
BEGUILERS

KATE THOMPSON

Winner of the Bisto Book of the Year Award 2002

Every night they came drifting through the sky above the
village streets, issuing their mournful cries, terrorising the
population. It wasn't safe to go out after dark. Everyone
was aware of the power of the beguilers.

No one knew what they were. No one had ever caught one.
But every generation produced a beguiler-hunter: a tragic
soul considered by the rest of the village to be insane.

Rilka isn't mad. But the desire to catch a beguiler is about to
change her life and the lives of those around her for ever.

'. . . powerful and very readable' *Children's Books in Ireland*

'Kate Thompson writes with marvellous and magical ease'
TES

RED FOX
0 09 941149 0

tHE ALCHEMIST'S APPRENTICE

KATE THOMPSON

Winner of the Bisto Book of the Year Award 2003

Jack is on the run. Alone in the world with nowhere
to turn, he finds a strange object floating on the rising
tide of the Thames. In trying to assess the value of the
relic, Jack meets Barnstable, an alchemist who only adds
to the boy's perplexity by his enigmatic ways.
Dramatic events escalate and Jack's fortunes change
beyond all expectation. But the mystery surrounding
the alchemist won't go away. Has he really discovered
the secret of making gold?

In this gripping novel, Kate Thompson, master storyteller,
describes the extraordinary adventures of a boy trying to
understand what really matters in the world.

'A rewarding read' *Joanne Owen, book buyer for Borders*

RED FOX
0 09 943948 4

Annan Water

KATE THOMPSON

Against a fascinating background of horse-dealing and
show-jumping, Kate Thompson explores a theme about
which she feels deeply and of which she has proved
herself a master – that of a young person on the brink of
adulthood trying to find independence and meaning in life.

Michael first sees Annie on the river bank at the end of
the green lane when he is exercising the horses. Is she
destined to bring warmth and colour into his life and
allow him some respite from the pressures of school
and home? Or will she, as she herself believes, bring him
bad luck? And what of the dark, mysterious river that runs
between their homes? It has its own story to tell – but
does this story relate to their love for each other?

THE BODLEY HEAD

0 370 32822 1